The Forbidden City

The Forbidden City

Book Two of Rogue Elegance

K A Dowling

ISBN-13: 9780692943564
ISBN-10: 0692943560
Library of Congress Control Number: 2017913587
Kelly Dowling, Sharon, MA

For my mom, who has always liked what I've written,
even when it wasn't very good.

Property of S. Mathew

Chancey

The Great Forest

Royal Port

Beasts Here

Eagle

Westernles

Cira

Harvest Cycle 1511
Summer
Day one

The Rebellion is an old, creaking beast—a fortress of groaning wood, holding stalwart against the buffeting waves. She is a beast, and I am in her belly. My stomach is sick. My bones are rattling in this endless chill.

But it is good to be free. It is good to be free of her ghost. Every secret, shaded corner of Chancey mocked me with the breath on her lips, the shadow of death upon her porcelain face.

The task that has been entrusted to me weighs heavily upon my heart. The golden key is an anchor in my pocket, keeping me awake—aware. My spirit is a battlefield, and I—I am hungry for a ceasefire; my soul yearns for tranquility.

I will find it here, on this journey west.

Or I will die trying.

Eliot Roberts

Curse of King Lionus Wolham
The footsteps of the ancients lead to find
The blood-wealth of the blessed Saynti's kind
Yet if ye seek what lies beyond the blood red stone
A treasure beyond measure that is not your own,
You'll find those ancient footsteps are erased,
For dead men's footsteps in the sand cannot be traced.

Harvest Cycle 1525

Summer

CHAPTER 1

The Westerlies

IN A ROWDY, run-down tavern somewhere along the eastern coast of the Westerlies, Captain Alexander Mathew slumps facedown upon the bar. He doesn't care that his last precious coppers have been lost in a bad hand of cards. He doesn't care that he should have stopped drinking three pints of rum ago. He doesn't even care that his right cheek, thick with several days' worth of scruff, is now resting in a puddle of ale.

"It's hopeless," he mumbles.

"What's hopeless?" asks a rather unexpected voice. Unexpected because, on the one hand, he had been talking to himself. On the other hand, the voice belonged to a woman who could not have—*should not* have—been anywhere near dry land.

A sideways face appears in his field of view. For a moment, Alexander studies the pointed nose and the long, narrow lips without immediately recognizing the woman to whom the features belong. Tousled black ringlets escape from the leather binding that holds them, springing errantly around an angular jaw and tangling in the golden hoops that hang from the woman's ears. Two catlike green eyes blink at him in a semblance of concern.

Right, he remembers. The Rogue. The gypsy. The stowaway. The thorn in his backside. The damned nuisance that he had picked up back on Chancey months ago, after blindly agreeing to help rescue her from the clutches of Rowland Stoward's golden thugs.

The woman he *specifically* instructed to stay on the ship.

He tries and fails to summon up the energy to be furious. His anger fizzled out several drinks, several coppers, and several broken glasses ago.

1

"What's hopeless?" Emerala the Rogue repeats. He stares up at her blankly; beginning to realize that it is not her face that is sideways, but rather, him.

"Life," he slurs.

"Life," she echoes, one thick black eyebrow arching dubiously.

"My life, to be specific."

Emerala frowns. "How terribly morose."

"You don't seem that sorry for me," Alexander observes.

"I'm not. I'm bored. You left me on the ship. Again."

"And you've ignored my orders," Alexander points out. "Again."

Emerala drops down onto the stool next to him, studying the gloomy surroundings of the tavern as she tries and fails to straighten out the fabric of her ruffled taupe gown. Leaning backwards, she snatches a pint out of the unfurling grasp of an unconscious drunkard to her left, sniffling at the contents before taking a sip. A look of disgust passes across her pointed, olive features and she replaces the pint on the bar.

"Is this part of your all-important mission?" she asks, studying the peeling molding on the ceiling through narrowed eyes. "Getting drunk off of cheap rum and losing all your money in cards?"

"You saw that, did you?"

Emerala glowers at him and says nothing. He sighs.

"I'm following a lead." He pauses and adds, "Or, I was. It was a dead end. They've all been dead ends."

"What exactly are you looking for?"

"Not what," Alexander says, sitting up and pawing at his dripping face with his sleeve. "*Who.*"

Emerala rolls her eyes, procuring a handkerchief from beneath her tightly laced corset and leaning forward to dab the sticking ale off of his cheek. He sits slumped upon his stool and allows her to dry his face, his stomach beginning to feel more than a little bit ill.

"Who are you looking for, then?" she asks, her breath tickling his nose.

"If you must know, I'm looking for a mapmaker."

Emerala pauses, drawing back upon her stool to get a better look at his face. "You need a map made?" she asks. "Don't you already have one in your quarters that you've been studying day and night?"

"That map is written in a dead language. I can't make heads or tails of it. Look," he starts, an aura beginning to swim at the edge of his vision. "My head is killing me. I just want—"

"So you need to find a mapmaker to translate the map for you? That doesn't seem that hard." Emerala hops off the stool. "But we're not going to find one in the middle of the night, and we're most certainly not going to find one in the bottom of a pint glass. So let's find a place to sober you up, and we'll go tomorrow."

"Slow down," Alexander says, grabbing her wrist and drawing her back to him. He pulls at her harder than he'd meant to, and she collides into his chest, nearly knocking him off the stool. "Ouch. It's not that easy. I don't need any old mapmaker. I need Charles Argot."

Emerala frowns up at him as she draws back, prying her wrist free of his grasp. "I haven't the faintest idea who Charles Argot is."

Alexander groans. He tries to remember when Emerala arrived at the bar, or how he ended up in this conversation. Everything before this moment seems like a disjointed collection of lights and sound. "Nor did I. Not until recently. Any pirate worth their salt has heard of him, as the Hawk keeps reminding me."

"And he can decipher your map?"

Alexander frowns up at her, pressing one throbbing eye closed. "You're asking a lot of questions, and I've really resigned myself to spending the rest of my night ruminating in my failures. Preferably alone."

"Maybe I'd be less invasive if you hadn't left me alone on the ship all day while you gambled away your belongings," Emerala suggests.

"I told you, I was following a lead."

Emerala flicks at an invisible speck of dust on her forearm, looking bored. "Yes, so you've said. Seems like you've been making impressive work of your search."

Alexander grimaces. "You're mocking me."

3

"Drunks are always easy to mock."

"It isn't nice."

They are interrupted, then, by a phlegmy *hem-hem*. Alexander follows Emerala's eyes as she turns toward the newcomer to the conversation. A few feet away from them teeters a rotund man with a ring of unkempt, greying hair around his temples. His sagging cheeks and overlarge nose are ruddy with drink. He hiccoughs loudly, brandishing a small slip of parchment in Alexander's direction.

"I was told to give this to you," he says, and hiccoughs again.

"What is it?" Alexander demands.

"Don't know," says the stranger, pawing at his scraggly, grey beard as Emerala takes the parchment from him. Alexander leans forward, plucking the paper out from between her fingers before she can so much as protest.

"Who gave it to you?"

"Don't know."

"You don't know much, do you?" Emerala asks, crossing her arms across her chest. The man hiccoughs in response, teetering dangerously where he stands.

"He's drunk, Emerala," Alexander says distractedly. He feels himself sobering quickly as he fumbles with the folded bit of parchment.

"So are you."

Alexander glances up at the stranger, now scratching the top of his head as he glances around at his surroundings with no clear sign of recognition in his glassy eyes.

"I'm not nearly *that* bad," he argues.

"Maybe not in terms of intoxication," Emerala assents, wrinkling her nose. "But certainly in odor."

Across from them, the stranger seems to have resigned himself to his current circumstance. "Well," he says cheerfully. "Good day to you."

"It's the middle of the night," Emerala counters, taking a step back as the man's eyes roll back into his head and he plummets to the floor.

"That'll hurt in the morning," Alexander remarks, his attention returning to the parchment in his grasp. Five words march across the page in cramped, crooked penmanship. The letters are transcribed in blood, the macabre ink still wet. Alexander's heart rises to his throat, all traces of inebriation falling away from him as adrenaline creeps into its place.

Traitors are sent to Caros.

"What does it say?" Emerala demands, snatching the parchment out from his hand. He allows her to take it, reaching across his stool for his hat, still resting in a sticking puddle of ale. Emerala's green eyes scour the parchment, not comprehending.

"What does this mean?"

"It means my lead wasn't as dead as I'd thought it was," Alexander says, grinning. He heads off across the bar, his headache abating. Emerala trails in his wake, her unruly, black curls bouncing with each step she takes.

"Where are you going?"

For once, her ceaseless onslaught of questions fails to irritate him. Excitement swells in his chest—anticipation crowds his thoughts. Month after month spent searching fruitlessly for the infamous old mapmaker and now he finally has a solid lead.

"I need to gather the rest of the crew. We leave for Caros at first light," he says, and rams his cap back on his head.

CHAPTER 2

Chancey

THE MAN RACES down the winding path as fast as his feet can carry him, stumbling as he loses his footing upon the sticking mud underfoot. His untamed hair blows back from his face. His skin pulls taut across the lines of his skull, causing him to appear skeletal beneath the lingering fingers of night that spill across the earth.

"HALT," James Byron cries, not for the first time. His voice rings out across the dew-laden grass. Several birds take flight from a nearby tree. The branches spring upward in their wake, their fluttering green leaves shaking loose the grip of night as the rising sun breaks across their unfurling veins.

Up ahead, the man runs faster. James stifles a sigh, his brows furrowing low over his eyes. He picks up his pace, following behind the man as he makes his way through a sparse copse of tangled trees. The mud beneath James's boots is heavy and damp, scarred with the shallow, indistinguishable grooves left by both hooves and wagons. The sleeping world before him is cloaked in muted grey. Only a minute tinge of gold smolders faintly upon the eastern horizon, dying the purple sky overhead an uncertain shade of blue.

There's no good reason for James to be awake at such a colorless hour—no good reason for him to be miles from the city walls, chasing down a stranger as he ducks in and out of the shadows of the trees.

No reason at all, and yet here he is all the same. He has been unable to sleep. His nights as of late have been frequented by unrest—his sleep interspersed with lurid, fleeting fragments of dreams. His subconscious, like the whip of some relentless master, is determined to drive him into remaining constantly awake.

He takes a deep breath, filling his lungs with air.

"HALT," he cries again. "HALT IN THE NAME OF HIS MAJESTY, THE KING!"

His words barrel into the running man. The figure stumbles and slows upon the path up ahead. He turns on his heels, cupping his hands to his mouth.

"BUGGER THE KING!"

James inhales deeply through his nose, scowling as the air leaks out from between his lips. He wishes, not for the first time—and certainly not for the last time—that he had stayed in bed. He can feel the heat of the rising, summer sun tickling the back of his neck.

A thought occurs to him, suddenly, as he idles alone upon the disfigured path, staring at the stumbling figure up ahead.

How can two months have gone by, and nothing?

He starts off down the path at a brisk jog, squinting up at the steadily widening expanse of gold that leaks across the sky like spilt ink. Two months have passed since the Cairan people disappeared—two months have passed since the streets went silent—and still the unsatisfied king demands that his Golden Guards search the city.

Rowland Stoward is desperate, they all know, to find Emerala the Rogue—to have her once again within his grasp. And yet she, like the others, has disappeared into the wind. James did not sign up for a life of picking drunkards off the street and settling disputes between rivaling blacksmiths, and yet those are the tasks with which his shifts have been filled as of late.

Still, the mystery remains.

How can an entire race of people disappear without a trace?

The question that plagued James for the past few months blazes through his mind, searing the backs of his eyes with the burning desire for some sort of answer—any answer.

The Chancians did not take the sudden absences quietly. Gossip sprung up in taverns and bakeries immediately following the strange disappearance. The dwindling months of spring were laden with false whispers about the Cairan whereabouts. The paltry gossip followed James like a hound all throughout the planting season. He could not escape them, not even in his own mind—not even as the rainy spring gave way to the sticking heat of summer.

He happened to overhear two women discussing the possibility that the Cairans had merely managed to blend successfully into the crowds of commoners around them. James immediately dismissed the rumor as nothing but the trivial gossip of bored housewives. There were far too many gypsies—and each of them well known among their neighbors—to have dissolved so completely and seamlessly into Chancian society.

And yet for weeks James peered into the faces of everyone he passed on the street in the vain hope of finding some spark of recognition. He was looking for her, he knew—was looking for the blue eyed woman he had kissed beneath the paltry moonlight on that fateful night—and yet to admit that to himself would have been an entirely different type of treason.

No. He pulls himself back to the present, batting away the thoughts of the Cairan woman. The trees around him are ablaze with golden sunlight. Heat creeps into his skin, burning his forearms through the heavy cotton of his uniform. James has always been the man with the answers. He does not enjoy puzzles, and, to be sure, he is not enjoying this one.

His eyes narrow as he again draws to a stop. He is closing the space between himself and the racing man—drawing nearer as the emaciated figure continues to stumble across the earth. They are approaching the western cliffs of Chancey at an alarming speed.

It's high tide; James can hear the muted roar of the waves below as they pummel against the sheer face of the cliffs. A jolt of adrenaline surges through his body as he realizes what the man is about to do. He draws his pistol from the holster at his waist.

"Halt," he cries. His voice sounds alien as it cuts through the muted symphony of the sunrise. He points his pistol up into the air and fires. The figure before him jumps in fright, slumping to his knees and pressing the palms of his hands against his matted hair.

"Thank you," James mutters under his breath, closing the gap between he and the stranger at a brisk walk. He grabs the man by the collar of his tunic, drawing him upright and setting him on his feet. Circling around the reeking figure, he takes in his tattered countenance—studies the hollows beneath his wild, blues eyes.

It's the eyes that stop him—those deep blue eyes, the telltale sign of pure, gypsy blood. Something in James's stomach knots. He feels momentarily robbed of air, as though someone punched him in the gut. The whispering instinct that led him to follow the man screams at him to grab the man, to move him from the edge of the cliffs. Yet he finds himself suddenly unable to move.

"I know you," the stranger slurs as soon as James has slowed to a stop. "I knew you," he amends.

"I don't recognize you," James replies.

"No. You wouldn't. I stayed well out of trouble in those days, I did."

"You disappeared. All of you. Where did you go?"

The Cairan appears unfazed by the presence of one of the most formidable guardians before him. He looks away from James, singing to himself as he peers thoughtfully out over the sea.

"And sweet sirens that sing sick love songs to me…"

"Where have you come from, just now?" James demands of the man.

"…love, the lyrics of sirens are setting me free…"

"Did you hear me?" James asks, raising his voice. "I asked you a question."

The Cairan is deaf to his commands. He stumbles forward, licking his lips. His watery eyes are transfixed upon the wild ocean.

James reaches out and grips the man by the shoulders. He shakes him, forcing the Cairan's attention back to his face. A mildewed odor penetrates the clinging undershirt below his tunic. "The other Cairans, where are they?"

The man chuckles dryly, and his eyes regain some of their lucidity. "You think I'd tell you? Tell you, so you can go tattle to your prat of a king?" He wrenches himself forcefully out of James's grip.

"Her voice, it falls down like the rain from the gods, dear the sacred queen Saynti is pushing me on." The man pauses at the edge of the cliff, his bare

toes hanging precariously over the jagged rock. The song on his lips trails off into silence as he peers over his shoulder at James.

"Which is better, do you suppose? To dive or to jump straight down?"

"Excuse me?"

The Cairan shrugs. "I guess it doesn't matter, much. The end result is the same, either way." He looks back out to sea. "The waves are wild today. Hungry."

James swallows thickly, the wind tugging at his golden cloak.

"I'm going to need you to step back from the cliff," he orders, already knowing his words will be futile. The Cairan teeters unsteadily, and for a moment James is sure that the wind will nudge this skeleton of a man over the edge. He remains with his feet planted upon the ground, laughing into the salty spray.

"It will feel like freedom," he says, and he leaps.

James chokes back a shout. Heart pounding against his chest, he stares at the place where the Cairan just stood. He strains his ears to hear a splash that he knows will never reach him. The waves are far too loud against the eroding rock wall. He saw it coming—knew the man was half mad—and yet he did next to nothing to prevent him from jumping.

He remains where he stands, feeling the sharp exhale of the wind against the back of his neck.

Where did he come from? And where are the rest of them?

His mind is a battlefield of thoughts. He is not a man who likes puzzles, and yet he has just been handed another piece.

CHAPTER 3

The Forbidden City

"WHO'S THERE?"

The shout resonates through the stale dusk of the cavern. Darianna the Rose freezes where she stands, cringing as she listens to the slowing clatter of the rock upon which she carelessly stumbled. Before her, positioned within the pale stream of light that spills onto the serrated and crumbling entrance of the Forbidden City, are two Listeners— members of the Cairan king's elite crew of spies. They stare with detachment into the darkness.

Unseen from her position in the shadows, Darianna glares back at them.

"Saynti, it's too dark," one Listener grumbles. He falls back against the rock upon which he was leaning prior to the mysterious disruption. "It wouldn't hurt Topan to put just a torch or two out here."

The other man scoffs. "Right, and within the hour we'll have the entire Chancian navy at our door."

"The entrance isn't even facing the mainland. One of the ships would have to be far offshore to even catch a glimpse of the flickering torchlight. It's hardly probable that we would even be found."

"Hardly probable isn't impossible, is it, friend?"

Darianna rolls her eyes, tuning out the argument of the two Listeners in the entryway. She glances behind her. She stands at the very top of the steps that lead deeper into the cavern the Cairans have come to call home, staring down at the paltry flicker of a torch far below in the shadows of the cavern. From the top step, scarcely a light can be seen from within the Forbidden City. The entryway is cleverly designed so that any stray passerby will not be able to see the opening unless they know exactly where to look. It's an optical illusion—the work of brilliant architects and years of purposeful labor.

The set up works only as long as the entryway is kept in complete darkness. Any flicker of light might be seen from a passing ship.

And they can't have that. Not with Rowland Stoward's hateful heart on the Chancian throne. So they are kept in constant darkness, shrouded in shadow and left to waste away beneath the earth.

We're living like rats.

Darianna frowns as the thought scurries through her mind. It's not the first time she found herself making the comparison, but each time she does it becomes harder to stomach. She wonders how she looks, cowering in the dark corner; her back against the cool, jagged rock surface, her auburn hair spilling over angry blue eyes. She meant no harm by coming out as far as she did, and yet she knows she'll be heavily reprimanded should she be discovered by the Listeners.

This isn't the first time she tried to get as close as she could to the entrance—far from it. In fact, she was able to get closer before without being noticed. All she wants is to be able to creep just close enough to the entrance to see outside. Just a glimpse—that's all she needs. For a few price-less moments, she wants to be able to gaze out upon the moonlit glass of the ocean. She wants to be able to swallow the fresh air—to feel her throat sting with salt.

The Cairan king, however, made it clear to the Cairans that no one was allowed up the main staircase. He didn't want to risk anyone being seen or heard. The only ones permitted to be at the entrance were those precious few Listeners. As if that wasn't bad enough, her mother had per-sonally threatened to box her ears should she be caught within a mile of the opening.

The Listeners that perch in the moonlight ahead have forgotten all about disruption. Their amiable argument drifts off into bored silence. Darianna exhales, disappointed.

She'll just have to try again tomorrow night.

Its not like she has anything better to do.

Careful not to trip over any more loose stones, she tip-toes around the dark corner of the cavern. Her hands travel lightly across the now familiar grooves of the wall, guiding her through the near pitch black of the clammy expanse. She knows when she reaches the very top of the steep steps that lead down into the main living areas of the Forbidden City. She can see the bright flicker of a torch before her. Warm light emanates from underneath a low hanging ceiling that slopes parallel with the stairs. It's a clever illusion. Without the torch, a passerby would never know that he stands next to a man made staircase—the steps carved painstakingly into the ancient stone.

Darianna drops herself down onto the second step, relieved when her feet hit a flat surface. Pushing away the defeat that crowds her stomach, she hurries down the curving staircase. With each step she takes, the area around her grows lighter. Finally, she can make out the torch sitting in its black sconce. It throws deep orange light onto the rock walls around it. Behind the torch is a solid stone wall. A dead end.

Or, at least, it looks like a dead end.

Darianna knows better.

She steps forward, moving beyond the glow of the torchlight. Swallowed by darkness, she shuts her eyes and holds her hands out in front of her. Robbed of her eyesight, she is forced to rely on her sense of touch. She moves deeper into the dark, heading towards the stone wall with her arm outstretched, her palm flat. When she feels her hand touch stone, she opens her eyes. She stands in a gulley of staggered rock, her palm pressed up against the wall. To her left is a narrow, dark opening. From beyond this she can just hear the sounds of voices and music. She slides through the opening with ease, coming out into a grand and bustling room.

Torches line the walls every few feet, casting a cozy light about the expanse. The walls around her rise up towards the darkness and curve out of sight. The ceiling, far out of reach of the dancing flames, is cast in piercing black shadow. The floor of the room is lined with table after table, each one carved out of crude stone. Milling about the expanse are dozens of familiar faces. Darianna watches as a group of younger children dance merrily to the twang of a guitar. To her right a few women mingle quietly, their heads bent close together in conversation. Before her, at the nearest table, sits a group of men deeply involved in a game of cards.

Darianna ambles through the crowd, glad for her uncanny ability to go unnoticed. Scooping a half-full pitcher of ale off of a table, she takes a sip and continues on her way. She keeps an ear peeled as she meanders among the Cairans, listening for any news from Chancey—from the world they left behind. Hearing nothing, she stifles a yawn and takes another sip.

The carafe is wrenched out of her grasp before the foamy, amber liquid can so much as graze her lips.

"Should I start with the stealing, or do you want to talk about your secret trips to the city entrance?"

Darianna wipes a line of foam from her upper lip with the back of her hand.

"They're not very secret if you know about them," she gripes, glowering up at the towering figure of her father. He stands framed by the glow of the candlelight, his fingers twisted in his thick, auburn beard. His eyes narrow as he tries and fails to hide his amusement, throwing back the remnants of her stolen drink.

"If you're going to skulk about the cavern, you might be more cautious. Your mother is out for your blood today. She heard about yesterday's incident with Rayland the Bull's boy."

"He deserved it," Darianna snaps, the words flying away from her before she can help herself.

Her father chuckles, his face crinkling. "He deserved the black eye, perhaps, but not the swift kick you delivered between the knees."

"You told me not to let myself get pushed around," Darianna accuses.

"I also told you never to kick a man when he's down," her father reminds her, setting the now empty mug onto a deserted table. "Look, why don't you head back to the quarters for the afternoon? I think you've had enough excitement for the day, don't you?"

Darianna's gaze slips towards the sheer rock wall to her left. Deep grooves, almost like a ladder, are carved into the wall. Some rise higher on the face of the stone than others, but each set of steps stop just before a gaping, irregular hole. Beyond the openings, each hole is hollowed out into a deep pocket. She shares one of these holes with her mother and father.

Holes. That's all they are. Pockets of nothing, just empty space carved into silent stone.

"That fox den we're staying in isn't our quarters," Darianna snaps, her mood souring. "Our home is above Ma'am Rosa's Tea House, remember?"

She pictures the building of faded, red brick—pictures their apartment on the fourth floor, nestled atop several flights of creaking, carpeted stairs. The apartment was spacious enough for three, and at sunset the thickly paned windows allowed for deep orange light to sweep across the floorboards. There is none of that here. The hollow room they've been forced to call home is cluttered with creaking cots and a singular trunk to hold all of their belongings. The ceiling, if you can call it that, is far too low to allow for comfortable movement.

"This is the way things have to be, Dari," her father reminds her. "At least for now."

"That's what everyone keeps telling me," Darianna mutters darkly.

"And you see why, don't you? It's too dangerous out there. We're safer in here, hidden away in our fox dens, as you so eloquently described them."

"Until when?" Darianna demands. "Until we're dead?"

Her father laughs, but the smile leaves his eyes untouched. "Not until we're dead, Dari. Don't be so dire. The theatrics are quite unbecoming in a girl your age."

"Until the usurper is dead, then?"

Her father's silence is answer enough. His eyes dart around the room as he swallows thickly, tugging his beard.

"You've asked enough questions for the day, Darianna," he says. "I'd suggest you run along and keep out of sight of your mother."

"But—"

He cuts her off. "Unless, of course, you'd prefer to spend the afternoon kneading dough in the kitchens."

"I'm gone," she retorts, turning and ducking into the crowd before her father can say another word. His laugh trails her through the cavern as she is swallowed once again in stinging smoke and idle gossip. She glances once more at the rows and rows of inverted stone ladders, her gaze lingering on the unlit opening where she lives with her mother and father. Her mother strung ivory lace curtains in the opening, the strands of lace strung with glittering beads. It was an attempt to make the place seem more homey—to give them more privacy.

It failed on both accounts.

"We're living *just* like rats," Darianna mutters beneath her breath. She concludes that she can't possibly spend the day in her hole—not here where she can't see the sun or feel the breeze or even stretch out her legs. Reaching the outer wall at the outskirts of the crowd, she drops unceremoniously to the hard stone. She crosses her legs beneath her pale, peach gown and prepares to devote the remainder of her afternoon to sulking.

A sharp cry causes her to lurch back to her feet. She glances left and right for the source of the sound, pushing her mop of auburn hair out of her eyes. Before her, the occupants of the cavern go about their business, either not having heard the cry, or doing their best to ignore it. Darianna glowers at all of them in turn, her attention at last settling on two men heading quickly towards one of the twisting corridors that outline the outer labyrinth of the stone city. Between the men, her arms gripped tightly by either escort, is a woman. Her dark brown hair is pulled back from her face in a careless bun. Her face is pale and unpainted, her blue eyes glossy behind discolored lids.

Her interest piqued, Darianna follows the trio across the cavern, taking care to remain unseen. She is good at that—being invisible—her mother's simmering temper is always at risk of boiling over and singeing Darianna's skin. She tiptoes on the stone, her pale gown dragging across the ground without so much as a whisper.

Stopping just short of the corridor, Darianna leans against the cool stone wall and sets to absently twirling a strand of hair around a finger. Her blue eyes flutter to the ground as she strains to hear the snippets of conversation that drift towards her out of the darkness.

"I can't," she hears the woman snap. "I won't."

A second voice, male and weighted with exhaustion, chimes in. "You have to try and keep calm, Nerani. Throwing these tantrums won't help anything."

"Tantrums?" the woman called Nerani repeats. The pitch of her voice escalates dangerously. "Tantrums?"

"Poor choice of words, I should think," the second male reproves. His voice is familiar to Darianna. She recognizes with a start that it belongs to none other than the elusive Cairan king.

"How can you be so indifferent?" Nerani demands.

Someone—the first man, perhaps—sputters wordlessly for a moment before finding his voice. "Indifferent?" he echoes. "Indifferent? You think I don't care? You think this doesn't affect me as much as it affects you?"

"You—" Nerani begins, but the man cuts her off.

"She was my sister, Nerani." His voice is hoarse. "My *sister*. How dare you—"

"Roberts." The Cairan King, again, his tone a clear warning.

"How can you stand it, Rob?" asks Nerani.

"Stand what?"

"This. Being here, being safe, when she's out there and needs our help."

Darianna leans forward, taking her chances in order to catch a glimpse of the trio. It is dark in the corridor beyond. She can see the shadowed outline of a woman's gown—can see the woman standing behind the protective stance of the Cairan king. She can't see the third figure—the man called Roberts—and she doesn't dare to move any closer to the opening in order to try.

When Roberts speaks, his voice is heavy with defeat. "We've had this conversation, Nerani."

"Well, let's have it again," she snaps.

"How can I say it in a way that makes it easier to hear? She's dead." Roberts's voice cracks. "You *saw* her die. You can't keep convincing yourself she isn't."

"I didn't see anything," Nerani insists. "I ran away."

"She's gone, Nerani."

"If she was dead, why would the Golden Guard still be searching for her? I heard the Listeners telling you that they're still conducting city wide sweeps, even after all this time."

"Yes, Nerani, for *us*. They're looking for all of us. They don't waste resources searching for the dead."

"She's not dead!" Nerani nearly screams. "He said he would stop executing the Cairans when she was in his custody. He wouldn't keep looking if he knew she was dead, you have to believe me."

This time, it is the Cairan king's voice that fills the darkened expanse. "The usurper is a deceitful man. We can't believe any of his empty promises. I'm afraid Roberts is right, as terrible as the truth may be to hear."

Darianna doesn't get to hear Nerani's response before a firm hand whips her unceremoniously out of her hiding place.

"What do you think you're doing, dropping eaves on the Cairan king?" It is one of the Listeners from the entryway—the one who complained about the darkness. Behind Darianna, the three figures have fallen into silence. She can feel the blue eyes of the young woman boring into her skin.

Damn.

"I—" She stops short when she sees the expression on his face. His brows are knit together in consternation. She's astute enough to know that his dismay isn't meant for her. Something else is going on—something bigger than an eavesdropping girl. It's time to leave, and leave fast.

"Sorry," she mumbles, prying her shoulder from beneath his grasp and fleeing the scene. As she runs, she catches the beginning of the Listener's message, his words clipped with concern.

"We've lost another one to the sea, Topan. This time, the general saw."

CHAPTER 4

The Forbidden City

"How close was he?"

The door slams behind Roberts, sending a gust of air through the room. On the wall, the lit torches sputter, snapping their orange tendrils against the impenetrable stone.

"General Byron, you mean?" The willowy Listener that idles by the door watches Roberts through careful blue eyes. His bony fingers dance along the sleeve of his coat. The collar of his undershirt is low and Roberts can just see the pale line of skin where the summer sun has not quite been able to reach. The rest of him is dark and crisp, baked like bread left too long in the oven. "He didn't even come close to finding the wooded entrance. I'm not worried."

"You're not worried?" Roberts echoes, fighting to keep the derision from leaking into his voice.

"That's what I said."

"But that's how Regalad got out, isn't it?" Roberts asks.

Regalad the Hapless, until very recently, was quite alive. Very recently, that is, until he threw his body from a cliff—until he dashed himself to pieces on the rocky shores of Chancey. The thought makes Roberts feel like he's going to be sick. He turns abruptly on his heel, pacing the length of the room. Orange light twists and turns with his movements, casting his long shadow across the ceiling overhead.

"He escaped through the wooded entrance, which means General Byron must have been close enough to see him, and that's too close for me."

Across the room, Topan catches his gaze. His dark eyes—almost violet in this light—are admonishing. "Another poor choice of words, friend,"

19

he begins. "To say that Regalad escaped is to imply that I've entrapped the Cairans here, which I haven't."

"Haven't you?" Roberts retorts. Even as the words fly unguarded from his tongue, he knows he's being unfair. He hasn't been able to think straight. Not since Emerala's death.

Her murder. He can hardly bear to think the words, even to himself.

Two months are hardly enough time to allow such a deep wound to heal.

Across from him, Topan's eyes glitter like beetles in the dark.

"Careful," he warns. "I understand that tensions are high, but let's not begin throwing out false accusations. This city is a safe haven, and those who came here came of their own free will. I didn't force a single Cairan to come, surely you must know that."

Roberts does know. He knows all too well. There were Cairans who chose to stay, to blend in as best as they could, but they were few and far between. The vast majority had eagerly fled. Seeing two of their people so hastily subjected to a public slaughter was enough to send anyone running for the hills.

Roberts allows his attention to rove back to the Listener by the door.

"Did you at least manage to get close enough to hear their conversation?"

"Afraid not." The Listener scuffs a toe against the stone floor beneath his feet. "Couldn't give away my cover. I've got a nice plot of radishes growing in this summer heat, among other things, and we desperately need the food down here. Anyway, Regalad was scarcely sound of mind at that point—days in the tunnel will do that to you, we're finding. I don't think he could have given the general a lot of useful insight."

"On the contrary, he could have told him anything. A madman is more dangerous than any other. General Byron could be leading a platoon of Guardians to our back doors as we speak." Roberts's voice rises in volume as he throws an implicative glance towards Topan.

"And then what?" Topan asks, ever the picture of serenity. His voice is measured, patient. He takes a step closer to Roberts, his hands clasped in the small of his back. Behind him, his shadow contorts and rises, stretching out over his slender frame. "He couldn't have given the general a turn by turn map to follow back through the darkened catacombs of the Forbidden City, could he? Let me ask you, Roberts, how many of our people have gone missing in the two months since our arrival?"

Roberts clears his throat. "Seven, but I don't see what this has to do—"

Topan cuts him off with a curt wave of his hand. "And how many have the Listeners found wandering about the Givalen farmstead?"

"Three."

"That's four of my people, then, that have, most sadly, perished in the tunnels. The catacombs are dark and deep. The tunnels branch off like tangled roots, each one of them winding through pitch-black gloom and leading wanderers to a dark drop and a sudden stop. Only one path leads its follower out. Strangely enough, it is not the same one that leads the follower back in again. If the general were to find the wooded entrance—if he were to lead a platoon of men in to discover us—he would quickly be swallowed within the blackness inside."

"He would die, you mean?"

"I'm certain of it. And his men, too."

For a moment, the room is filled with pressing silence. The Forbidden City seems suddenly less like a fortress and more like a tomb. Roberts tries and fails to shake off the chill that has crept into his chest, taking hold of his bones like an unwanted houseguest.

"If it's that dangerous, why don't we close it off?" Roberts prompts. "It would keep our enemies from chancing upon us, and it would prevent people from going missing within it. If I'm not mistaken, the last victim of the catacombs was only a child."

"Indeed, she was. And indeed, it would," Topan agrees, his expression darkening.

"But you won't do it."

Topan doesn't provide an immediate answer. He instead turns his attention to the silent Listener by the door. "Selven, am I correct in remembering that you are fond of hunting?"

"I am," the Listener assents with a nod. "Like I said, we need food."

21

"Would you care to enlighten us as to how you would go about capturing your prey? Not killing it, mind you, I'm sure there are plenty of ways to skin a beast. I'm more interested in the process of capturing it."

Selven considers the question for a moment, and then shrugs. "I'd back it into a corner. Once it has nowhere to run, I'd move in for the kill."

"Precisely." A knowing smile inches its way across Topan's face as he looks back at Roberts.

"I won't be cornered, Roberts. If they breach our defenses and those golden bastards start streaming in through our front door, I won't leave my people with no escape."

For the first time, Roberts notes that the distorted shadow that dances at Topan's back looks less like that of a man and more like that of a wolf; idling on its haunches and waiting for the moment to pounce. He thinks of the wolves of the wood, those silent, grey predators—they are capable and dangerous, but even wolves are hunted by forces that are larger and more daunting than they.

He thinks of a wolf with wild, violet eyes, its haunches raised—snarling, backed against the wall.

And then he remembers the darkness. He remembers death. He thinks of Emerala and what it must be to die. He thinks of the parents of that little girl, and how they had called to her at the entrance to the catacombs, their disconsolate voices reverberating off of the pressing stone walls of the Forbidden City.

Wolves are capable, yes, but they are only beasts in the end. They cannot understand reason. Not like men.

"You'd blindly lead them into those tunnels, knowing that they'll most likely die?"

At that, Topan's smile widens. "Not blindly," he says. "The Mames know the way."

The Mames know the way.

Nerani lingers outside the door, breathless from anticipation. Her mind feels like a pot too full of water. Her thoughts boil and bubble, threatening to spill over the edge. She remembers the sound of Emerala's voice against the oncoming rain, can still hear her cousin telling her to run. She remembers glancing back over her shoulder—remembers seeing Emerala fall to her knees, those dark green eyes wild with fear.

In all of their youth together, Nerani had never seen so much as a flicker of fear pass across Emerala's face. Her cousin had always been fearless, even as a girl. Brave to the point of recklessness. And yet Nerani had seen the fear that day, plain as the nose on Emerala's pointed face. Her expression had become a mask of sheer terror, her dripping curls plastered against her olive skin.

The Guardians held her down beneath the blades of their swords, their golden cloaks gleaming ever brighter beneath the lightning that snaked its way across the violet sky.

You're in no position to negotiate, scum, Nerani heard one of them growl.

And then Emerala smiled.

Nerani had played that moment over and over in her mind—had dreamt about it night after tormented night. At first she thought she must have been mad, to think that her cousin had found some sort of deranged source of joy within the seconds before dying.

A gun went off and someone's scream rent the air, but by then Nerani had rounded the corner.

Emerala smiled at something Nerani could not see.

At someone.

She knew it. She knew she remembered correctly.

The fear had been there—the mask was visceral and real. And then it was gone. Wiped clear by the rain and replaced by that familiar, wicked grin.

Roberts wouldn't hear of it—he couldn't bear to be reminded.

Stop trying to find ways to bring her back to life, Nerani. She's gone. Damn it, she's gone and you can't just let it alone.

He's hurting. He thinks his only sister is dead—thinks that she's been murdered in cold blood. He's dealt with too much death, and it is chipping away at him—numbing him to loss.

But Nerani knows otherwise. Emerala is alive. She has to be.

The Mames know the way.

She'll prove that she's right. She'll find a way to bring Emerala back.

CHAPTER 5

Chancey

WHEN ROWLAND STOWARD ordered a great, stone labyrinth built in honor of his wife, he hadn't suspected that the cursed thing would come to haunt his dreams at night. He hadn't known that he'd spend his few precious hours of sleep tossing and turning, his subconscious hurtling down corridors of stifling grey and colliding into oppressive dead ends at every turn.

He hadn't known he'd be trapped by the memory of her ghost, unable to go back—unwilling to move forward.

Haunted.

He is a haunted man—a ghost of a once great king.

And Victoria?

Victoria is gone, always gone. Her memory dissolves like the rain of a summer afternoon. Her laughter rings out somewhere in the depths of the labyrinth, just out of reach—always out of reach. The nightmares are vivid. Real, all too real. As if he could touch her again, hold her again, if only he could reach her.

And then—then.

Rowland doesn't know if he'd embrace her or snap her neck.

His eyes snap open. He stares up at the translucent lace of his grandiose canopy and blinks away the remnants of nightmare that cling to him in beads of sweat. His body is twisted in the sheets. He coughs and the sound echoes back at him in the grey loneliness of his empty quarters. He sits up, dots of color swimming across his vision. For a moment, he wonders if he might pass out.

Anything to bring the dreams back.

The night terrors are his only chance of seeing Victoria—of facing her penultimate betrayal.

He clears his throat and reaches over to his nightstand. His swollen fingers grope blindly for the small golden bell that sits waiting to summon the help. The tinny clanging clatters mercilessly within his ears.

He sets the bell down, listening to the fading echo reverberating off of the walls. It grows silent in the room. Too silent. His perpetual frown deepens, casting deep grooves in his sleep filled eyes. Propping himself up against the multitude of golden pillows at his back, he folds his arms across his chest and waits.

The silence continues.

How much time passes, he cannot day. Moments, hours, days. Finally, he hears the slow creak of hinges. A small, wiry man creeps through a narrow slit in the door. Averting his gaze, he drops into an overzealous bow.

"I rang the bell," Rowland snaps.

"Yes, your Grace," the man says to the floor. Stray strands of his thinning hair fall down into his face.

"Did you hear the bell?"

"I did, you Grace."

"Why then, did you make me wait?"

"I came as quickly as I could. I was preparing your things for the day."

"Preparing my things?"

"Yes, your Grace."

"Why was that not done before I rose?"

The man's feet shuffle across the stone. "My apologizes, great king, but you awoke early today. The sun has not yet risen."

Rowland glances toward the tall window at the far end of the room. Outside, fingers of red bleed through a violet sky.

"So I see."

There is another spell of silence. Rowland glares down from his vast bed at the quivering man before him. He despises weakness. Fear is an ugly thing in a man. Real men—strong men do not feel fear.

Coward, he thinks.

Imbecile.

"I'm sick at the sight of you," he says at last. He does not attempt to conceal the revulsion in his words. "I want you gone. Find someone else to take your place for the day."

"Y-yes your Majesty." The man bows even lower before turning to rush out of the room.

"Stop!" Rowland commands. The man freezes. His back is to his king. His shoulders are hunched. "Where are you going?"

"Your Grace has ordered me out of his sight." The man's voice is scarcely loud enough to clear the breadth of the room.

"I haven't yet finished giving you your orders." Rowland sighs; feeling for all the world as though the burden of dealing with such incompetent fools day after day is a cross he is to be forced to bear until the day he dies.

"What would you have me do?"

"Fetch General Byron. Send him to me."

"Right away, your Grace."

Silence.

"Get out."

And with that, the man flees from the room.

Rowland watches him go, allowing his eyes to flutter closed only once the heavy door slams shut behind him. He is weary. His head has begun to throb. He wonders if perhaps he might be inclined to remain in bed the whole day. He will need to send for someone to bring him breakfast soon. As it is, he can already feel his stomach grumbling beneath the folds of his silken nightdress.

Just as he leans over to reach for the bell, he hears the door opening once again. His eyes travel up from his outstretched fingertips to see General Bryon entering the room.

"Ah, at least someone around here is quick."

The general cracks a small, comfortable smile. He drops into a respectful bow.

"I've sent for some trays of food to be sent up from the kitchens, your Highness. You must be hungry."

"Why, James, you are even better than those bungling menservants I have on hand! If you weren't such a great leader to my Guardians, I would have you moved to my personal staff."

General Byron's stiff smile does not falter as he proffers a small chuckle. He remains as still as stone before the king.

"I suppose you are wondering why I called you here," Rowland says.

"I am, your Majesty."

"It's that gypsy wench. The witch keeps creeping into my thoughts." He shudders, shaking out his fingers as though attempting to rid himself of something unclean.

Before him, General Byron is silent.

"Is there any news?"

"I'm afraid we've heard nothing about Emerala the Rogue, your Grace."

There is something strange about the way General Byron speaks. The Guardian's words seem stilted—his manner stiff. Rowland peers at him closely for a moment before continuing.

"I don't like that this murderess is wandering about my streets, uninhibited."

"With all due respect, your Grace, we don't know for certain that she is. We haven't found a single Cairan since the day of the execution, let alone the Rogue."

Rowland shudders again. "Don't remind me. I don't like to think of it. Evil stuff, that witchcraft."

"Witchcraft?" General Bryon echoes. His face remains blank.

"Do you really think the entire Cairan clan could have conducted a mass exodus right under my nose without me noticing? It's inconceivable. Not without witchcraft, anyway. Dark and powerful magics, the likes of which have been forbidden around these parts since long before you or I were born."

"You think that Emerala the Rogue used witchcraft to escape as well, then?"

"Think? I know it!" Rowland brings one balled up fist down hard on the downy surface of his mattress. "Think about it, James. You're a man of war. Three members of my elite service of Guardians were holding down one, unarmed young woman. How could she have escaped them? Not on her own, I'll concede as much. Not being held at the edge of three sharpened blades."

He pauses a moment to let this sink in. General Byron nods slowly, waiting for him to continue. His lips are pressed together in a tight line.

"They were found dead, my men. Good men they were too, with families at home. I don't think I need to remind you, James, *how* they were found—their throats slashed with their own swords, copper coins over their eyes. She's playing with us, the witch. She takes delight in killing."

A pause. "Of course, your Majesty."

"I want her found. I want her to pay for her crimes."

"And we're searching for her daily, my liege," General Byron reminds him.

"Have you combed the great forest?"

"We have."

"And the Givalen farmstead, what about there?"

General Byron shifts his weight upon his feet, his gaze unblinking. "Everywhere you have asked us to, your Grace, we have searched and searched again."

"She is concealing herself from you with dark magic, James. I can feel its presence in my skin. It itches at me. I only thank the gods that my Victoria went to the Great After before such evil times came upon us."

"Gods rest her soul, your Grace."

Grey light is beginning to creep in through the windows. Rowland blinks in the muted haze and feels his stomach grumble. An unusual prickle of discomfort has begun to itch within him at the mention of Victoria's name.

Why do I spite myself with her memory?

"Have you ever heard the story of the Forbidden City, James?"

At this, General Byron falters. "Once," he admits. "When I was a boy."

Rowland chuckles. "It is, indeed, a children's tale. It was told to me by my father, and his father before that. It's a parable of great wealth and old magics. I doubt they believed any word of it. Do you remember the tale?"

"Vaguely, your Majesty. I'm afraid my capacity for fable is not great. I was never interested in fairy tales as a boy."

"Ah, but this is no fairy tale. The story of the Forbidden City is quite true."

General Bryon clears his throat and says nothing.

"They are there, James—the Cairans. They have hidden themselves away within the walls of the fabled Forbidden City. We cannot find them, because we don't know where the city is hidden. But there they are, laughing at us—reveling in our confusion. And Emerala the Rogue is laughing with them."

Silence again. The general either does not know what to say, or he is unwilling to speak his mind. Either way, his continued silence only serves to irritate Rowland.

"If you've heard the story as a boy, then you will know that the stolen treasures of the false queen Saynti are buried deep within the city. I cannot stomach the thought of that vile wench Emerala the Rogue rolling about in gold that belongs to me. I want it, James, I want it returned to its rightful place."

"And the Cairans?" General Byron asks.

"It is no secret that I want them dead."

"All of them? Or are we talking only about the Rogue?"

Rowland feels a sneer tugging at his lips. "Better to do away with the entire nest than to try and flush out one, I think."

"What do you command?" asks General Byron. His face has compressed into a puzzle of stone.

"Find them. Flush them out like the rats they are and bring them here to die for their treason. The rewards will be great. The treasures of the Cairans are beyond measure."

"It will be done," General Byron says with a bow. He exits without being dismissed. Rowland watches him retreat. He feels a small shiver of pleasure run down his spine as he thinks of the vast fortunes hidden away just within his reach.

He thinks of Emerala the Rogue, adorned in jewels—*his jewels*—and imagines her head on a platter. The image of her haunting green eyes devoid of life gives him great satisfaction. He will kill the green-eyed ghost of his nightmares if it is the last thing he does.

He will cross this chasm. His smile deepens. He will finally finish the labyrinth.

Harvest Cycle 1511
Summer

I'm afraid I've lost track of the days. When the bottomless blue ocean stretches as far as the eye can see, it can become difficult to retain one's bearings. Even now, my grip on certainty seems to be slipping away. There is something bewitching about being lost upon the rolling waves. The topsail took a tear a fortnight past and the captain has been rushing to get it repaired. We were heading to a place called Eisle of Udire, but for now, we are adrift. Captain Samuel is wary of me, I can tell. He knows that the cross I bear is enough to drown us all.

There is a boy onboard—a stowaway with startling golden eyes. He prefers to keep silent, save for a rather haunting tune he whistles when the winds are low. He has taken to following me. Even now, I feel him watching my every move. He is like a bird of prey, calculating, ruffling his feathers, those yellow eyes glued to the key I now wear around my neck.

I will continue to practice caution. Out here, on the merciless ocean, I am my own savior. I am my own demise.

Eliot

CHAPTER 6

Caros

NOT FOR THE first time that day, Emerala the Rogue nearly steps directly upon the heels of Evander the Hawk's beaten leather boots. She draws back into the shade provided by a nearby copse of unfurling ferns, her heart pounding in her throat. Up ahead, in a narrow shaft of sunlight that spills down through the leafy canopy, the Hawk freezes, his golden eyes slitted against the glare. A dark groove appears at the top of his narrow nose, drawing his thick, black brows close together. The pirate studies the shadows, those piercing, golden eyes hovering for a moment too long on the thin veil of fingered ferns that separate him from Emerala. For the breadth of a heartbeat, Emerala is convinced she's been discovered. She stiffens, bracing herself for the inevitable lecture. She had, after all, been thoroughly warned against leaving the relative safety of the ship that morning, as Captain Mathew and the Hawk prepared to venture ashore without her.

She almost scoffs aloud at the memory. As if they expected her to actually listen to them.

As if she'd ever listened before.

Their brief stint on the mainland had done nothing but whet her appetite. They should have known she would be the more enticed by the prospect of some action. Any excitement at all would be a small reprieve from night after night of choking on stale smoke below deck, watching the crew count cards and get drunk on flat ale. The drunk messenger in the Westerlies had delivered the first promise of adventure in months, and she wasn't about to miss a moment of it.

Traitors are sent to Caros.

Caros's reputation preceded it. Emerala had grown up hearing dark stories of the infamous port Caros—the pirate graveyard. It was where men with black hearts and bloody hands were sent to be forgotten and eventually, to die. It was the kind of place where loyalty meant nothing and any sense of men's honor twisted into something tangled and dark, where outsiders were likely to be killed as quick as they could draw a breath. Of course, the very idea of it called to Emerala. The prospect of danger—the potential for an adventure—hummed in her bones.

This, she'd thought, staring angrily at the wherry as it carried the captain and the Hawk farther and farther away from the ship that morning. *This is what piracy is supposed to be.*

Now, by what little light falls through the veined undersides of the ferns, Emerala can just see a subtle twist of the Hawk's lips. He shoves his hands deep into his pockets as he turns to survey the tangled jungle before him. Another moment passes and then he continues on, his footsteps silenced by the thick undergrowth.

Emerala bites back the sigh of relief that rises to her lips, watching as the sunlight slips off of the pirate's back, leaving him ensconced, once again, in formless shadow. She takes a second to slump against the thick trunk of an ancient tree, exhaling the breath that sits stale in her lungs.

That, she thinks, *was too close.*

A lifetime of slinking around the back alleys of Chancey, expertly dodging King Rowland's Golden Guard, has made her a much better tail than that. Evander the Hawk might have been a thief by trade, but she was a thief by necessity. Orphaned and ostracized, she spent her childhood with her hands in the back pockets of merchants and ladies alike. She should not have come so close to being caught. Not once, and especially not twice.

The unfamiliar sounds and shapes of the jungle are throwing off her senses. All around her, the dank undergrowth breathes back at her as if it's alive—as if it has a heartbeat of its own. Something living—something big—pants at her from up in the trees. The feathery flap of wings grazes the top of her head, stirring her unkempt black curls.

Captain Mathew and the Hawk had split up the moment they reached the main village at the jungle's edge. A wooden post, the words *Exile's Alley* smeared across a bit of driftwood in what could only be blood, stood askew at the outskirts of the crowded huts. It was there that the two pirates said their goodbyes, their attention flitting across the shadowed corners—their hands at their swords. Emerala watched from her hiding place behind the skeletal remains of a beached shipwreck, her green eyes slitted against the glare of the morning sun off the sea. She watched as Captain Mathew disappeared down a narrow dirt road, heading into the heart of Exile's Alley. The Hawk made for the jungle, the towering trees still untouched by the morning sun. For the space of several heartbeats, Emerala stood cradled in the rotting curve of the ship's belly and weighed her options. If she were to follow Captain Mathew, she'd have a much harder time avoiding the unsavory occupants of the village.

The jungle was a far safer option. There, the shadows would be her ally. The unknown was far less dangerous than the men that lurked within the bounds of the township.

She sets off after the Hawk, sticking as close to him as she dares. Her gown, knotted at the hem to avoid tangling in the trees, whispers against her skin. Already, the sticking morning has left a thin sheen of sweat upon her brow. Her curls tighten impossibly, growing wild and wayward in the humidity. Up ahead, the Hawk pauses upon a rock, the grey surface carpeted with moss. She draws to a standstill, her eyes trained upon the slope of his shoulders, the shadow of a frown upon his face.

For a moment, she wonders if he's lost.

And then, it dawns upon her. He draws his pistol, his fingers dancing restlessly on the trigger. His golden eyes study the tangled web of flora before him, watching. Waiting.

He's expecting someone.

But who?

And why?

Her pulse quickens as she scans her surroundings, desperately hoping that whomever the Hawk is expecting doesn't stumble upon her first.

Somewhere deep in the jungle comes the crunching of undergrowth—the sound of a twig snapping beneath a boot. Someone is approaching. Still perched atop the mossy rock, the Hawk tenses. Even from where she stands, Emerala can see the tremor of his fingers.

He's afraid, she realizes. Whoever is coming—whoever he is expecting—terrifies him. Emerala's toes curl in the rich soil underfoot as a new kind of energy takes hold of her. Anticipation, perhaps, or excitement. In all her time onboard the Rebellion, not once has she seen the arrogant pirate show so much as an ounce of fear.

"Finally," she whispers. Maybe now she'll get to take part in a bit of fun.

She thought she was setting sail onboard the Rebellion for a new life of adventure. She hadn't expected to leave the oppressive protection of her older brother only to stumble into the care of two domineering pirates. Sorry excuses for brigands, the both of them. They treated her as if she were made of glass, forbidding her from leaving their sight onboard the ship, and leaving her behind whenever they docked.

But not today, she thinks, her lips curling into a smile.

Across the expanse, the Hawk begins to whistle. The shrill melody reverberates through the tangled jungle. A low laugh echoes out in reply. And then, from within the jungle, comes a voice:

"I haven't heard that old shanty in years."

The whistling cuts short. Off in the trees, a mockingbird trills a phantom echo of the song. "Aye, I wouldn't think you had." The Hawk's voice is cold. "Only traitors go to Caros, and Captain Samuel didn't hire traitors."

"Didn't he? He hired you." The shape of a man, bowed and bent with age, materializes among the narrow trees. The newcomer's features are obscured by the mist that rises up off of the earth in clinging clouds of grey.

"I'm no traitor," the Hawk disagrees.

"You're about to be, from the looks of it."

The Hawk's grip tightens upon his pistol, but he angles the gun down towards the ground. Emerala stands as still as stone, hardly daring to breathe, and watches the tremor of the Hawk's fingers against his trousers.

"I'm no traitor," the Hawk repeats.

"Not to Old Sam, maybe," the man agrees. "But you serve a new captain now, don't you?"

"I serve myself."

A laugh, then, high and cold. "You always did. Why are you here, boy? I take it you didn't come all this way to say hello to an old friend."

"You know why I'm here," the Hawk says.

A pause. "I suppose I do. You'll do it quickly?"

"As quickly as I can."

Another pause, followed by a sigh. "Don't leave your damn coppers on my eyes, boy. It's tawdry."

Emerala leans forward to get a better view, desperate to see more of the man in the jungle. Her mind is brimming with questions, each piling atop of the other faster than she can possibly process. Who is the man in the shadows? Certainly not Charles Argot. They came here for his help, not to kill him. How did this man know to meet the Hawk here, far beyond the prying eyes of Exile's Alley? Does Captain Mathew know they're here? Did he send the Hawk this way, or is he acting alone?

She inches slowly forward, her green eyes pinned to the stranger in the shadows. Between them, the Hawk steps down from his vantage point upon the rock and begins to make his way through the grasping ferns. His unshaven face, usually rosy with drink, has adopted a sickly pallor beneath the trickling sun. His golden gaze looks everywhere but at the stranger in the trees.

So focused is Emerala on the scene unfolding before her that she fails to hear the footfalls upon the earth at her back. A fist grasps at her curls and she is wrenched backwards. Her scalp screams in pain as she bites back a shriek, slamming into the chest of her captor.

"Did ye know," hisses a man's voice in her ear. "That beasts of prey grow eyes on the sides of their heads in order to see predators coming up from behind?"

"Good thing I'm not prey," Emerala snaps, and swings her leg backwards in a well-aimed kick. Her captor groans, stumbling back a step and relinquishing his hold upon her curls. Emerala twists out of his reach, nearly losing her footing on the uneven earth. Up ahead, the Hawk is nowhere to be seen. She has lost him within the trees, lost him behind the veil of mist that curls around her waist like a wraith. Behind her, her assailant lets out a string of curses before barking out a hoarse laugh.

"Plucky little thing, en't ye?"

Emerala twists around on her heels, drawing her dagger out of her corset and shoving the sleek blade into the sunbaked face of a middle-aged man, his right eye gone white with blindness. A raised, red scar runs across the length of his gleaming, bald scalp and down across his cheek. He grins, flashing several golden teeth.

"I'll kill you," she spits. Her heart flutters wildly within her chest.

"If that were true, ye would have done it already, little fawn." His one good eye flickers away from her face, glancing toward the rock where the Hawk had perched only moments ago. "Was that your lover over there? Strange, then, that ye wouldn't call for him to help ye."

Emerala scowls and says nothing, still holding her dagger between them. The sunlight catches on the edge of the blade, dancing precariously along the knife's edge.

"Or," the man says, and chuckles. "Perhaps he wouldn't have come. An unrequited love, is it? Ye were making quite the show of lurking after him."

"What do you want with me?" Emerala snaps.

"With ye?" the man asks, his eyes widening in a show of surprise. "Nothing at all, little fawn. You're a lovely lass, but I'm afraid I'm a ruined man. Ye could open up my chest and you'd find no beating heart left in its cage."

He presses the tip of his tongue against an incisor and surveys her through his one good eye. "Your captain on the other hand—now he's got something of which I am in desperate need."

Emerala fights to keep the dread out of her voice. "And what's that?"

The man's smile widens impossibly, the folds of his skin nearly swallowing his eyes. "A ship."

"A ship?" Emerala echoes.

"Aye. His ship. The infamous *Rebellion*. Saw it drop anchor in the harbor just before sunrise."

Emerala's mind races as she desperately grasps for a plan—any plan—any bargaining chip she can possibly use. "He'll never let you board the ship alive if you kill me," she says, the words tumbling from her lips far too quickly to sound confident.

"Kill ye?" A laugh. "Great After, no. I'm not going to kill ye."

"Then what do you want with me?" Emerala repeats.

The man leans in close, his good eye twinkling in the sun. From his waist, he draws a long, thin cutlass, the curved blade still crusted with blood. He smiles at Emerala. "I want ye to run. There's nothing that draws a pirate in quite like a damsel in distress. Like a shark to blood, his kind."

Emerala's nose wrinkles in spite of her budding terror. "I'm *not* a damsel in distress."

"Nay?" The man charges without warning, slamming her hard into the trunk of a tree, his cutlass at her throat. Emerala gasps, losing her wind at the impact, her vision going momentarily fuzzy. When her eyes refocus, the man's face is inches from her own. "Ye look like one to me."

He shoves her aside, grinning wickedly. "I'll give ye a head start, little fawn. Run. Run as fast as ye can."

CHAPTER 7

Caros

THE AIR IS sweltering. Storm clouds swallowed the sky hours ago, but Captain Alexander Mathew can still feel the heat of the sun on his skin. He wipes a bead of sweat from his forehead and leans back against the heavy mortar wall behind him. How long has he been waiting? He can't remember. He sighs, shifting his weight from one foot to the other. His toes are hot inside his worn leather boots. Cramped.

His hand reaches inside his coat almost involuntarily. His fingers brush against the torn edges of the rolled up map in his pocket. It has developed like a tick, this constant need to reassure himself that the map is indeed still with him—still a tangible entity of which he is in possession.

The trampled dirt path before him is void of any passersby. No doubt the inhabitants of Exile's Alley have found a tavern to hole up in to ride out the oncoming storm. Even murderers and traitors are at the mercy of the sea and all she can throw at them. Thunder and lightening can tame the wildest of men, Alexander has discovered. Overhead, the violet clouds are edged with flashes of silver. Thunder rolls in off of the sea, carried ashore by the whipping wind.

Alexander presses his cap to his head and lets out a low whistle. The tune is ripped from his lips by the stinging gale of the oncoming storm.

"Cap'n."

Evander the Hawk's voice barely reaches him over the distant bellow of thunder. The pirate's familiar lanky figure ambles towards him from beyond the line of tangled trees. His golden eyes are sharp and unreadable. His lips twist into a grimace as he takes in the darkening sky. He draws to a stop a few feet away from Alexander, thrusting his hands deep into the pockets of his pants.

"So?" Alexander lets the word hang heavy between them, tasting the aversion on his tongue.

"So?"

"Did you find him?"

His question is met with silence. The Hawk tilts his chin up towards the sky, one eye shut against the storm as he surveys the skeletal clouds that blow in from the west.

"Storm's coming."

"Did you find Charles Argot?"

Two golden eyes find his in the settling dark. The Hawk sighs audibly, his chest deflating. "Aye, I found him."

"Where is he, then?"

"Dead."

The full weight of the word collides with Alexander like a hammer to an anvil. He quickly feels the hope within his gut extinguish.

"No. That's—that's impossible." His eyes flicker back and forth, surveying the churning sea. Charles Argot was his only hope. He spent months on a wild goose chase, and for what? His search led him halfway across the world for a corpse.

"How did he die, did any of the men say?"

"He was alone when I found him." Evander pulls his cap from his head, letting his wild black hair fall across his eyes. "His body was rank with rot and half devoured by beasts. I'm not surprised. He was traitor, aye, but not a hardened criminal. Mapmakers aren't in good company among murderers and thieves."

Alexander swears under his breath. "He must have been dead for days. We've come all this way for nothing."

He kicks at the ground and feels immediately foolish. Hope isn't lost. Yes, Charles Argot is dead. Ultimately, this is of little consequence to him. He doesn't need to lose his faith in the entire mission over a stiff.

The mission.

What, in the end, is the point of his entire quest?

Why does he continue to torment himself—torment his crew—to no foreseeable end? He's spent the better part of two years dragging his crew from one end of the earth to another without being able to so much as explain to them what it is he seeks with such ceaseless resolve.

It's getting to be madness.

Obsession is the more fitting word.

And yet, Alexander can't bring himself to let it go. He desperately needs to find someone who can decipher the map for him, and he's running out of possibilities. All of his other options were hunted down to no avail. He glances up at the Hawk, who stands silently surveying the rolling thunder-clouds on the horizon.

"You pushed me into this blind pursuit," Alexander says, unable to keep the hostility from creeping into his voice.

The Hawk shoots him a sideways glance. "What pursuit?"

"Argot. You were the first to tell me about him. I'm beginning to think you're purposely wasting my time."

"Aye? And how, pray tell, would that benefit me?"

"I haven't quite figured it out yet."

The Hawk wets his lower lip, shoving his hands deep into the pockets of his moth bitten jacket. "I'm going to have to disagree with you then, Cap'n. It was Tomas Naples, Argot's devoted little protégé that insisted we'd have luck were we to track the bloody mapmaker down. You were the one that talked the poor boy's ear off in the Westerlies, if you'll recall."

"But you were like a little bird on my shoulder, whispering encouragement."

"Well sink me, it was our best lead, mate. I didn't know he'd be dead."

A heavy silence falls between them. Alexander's chest rises and falls beneath the sticking fabric of his undershirt. He can feel defeat weighing him down like an anchor. A bead of sweat drips from the rim of his hat and snakes slowly down the bridge of his nose. He licks his lip, tasting salt.

"Where to next, then?"

"How should I know? You're Cap'n, not me." The Hawk's voice imbues barely concealed dislike. Alexander knows he covets his position. It should have been his. And yet Samuel Mathew overruled the code for a reason. He remembers the name his father whispered as he straddled the precarious line between life and death. His mind going, he had grasped Alexander's sleeve and uttered what Alexander had then supposed to be gibberish.

Ha'Suri knows the way.

His fingers twitch again at his sides. He thinks of the indecipherable map. He thinks of his father's equally indecipherable words. He thinks of the unbearable heat pressing against his skin and of the fact that the thunderclouds are rolling in fast, bringing with them the merciless wrath of a stormy sea.

"Who is Ha'Suri?"

He first asked the Hawk the very same question as they played a tense game of cards back in Chancey. He has since brought the name up at every possible turn, determined to wear the pirate down by whatever means necessary.

Now, the Hawk smiles. "Getting a bit desperate, aren't you, Cap?"

"How do you mean?"

"We keep covering the same ground."

"We wouldn't if you'd just work with me."

"I've told you everything I know."

"That," Alexander says, "is a lie."

The Hawk is about to answer before he is cut off by a familiar sounding yelp. Alexander's blood runs cold.

Emerala.

"Bloody Below, she'll never learn," the Hawk curses as the two men whip about simultaneously. They stare into the wild jungle, their fingers dancing at the hilts of their daggers. Up ahead, two figures emerge from the tangled jungle.

Emerala the Rogue stares helplessly across the beach, her curls spiraling down into her green eyes as she struggles against the silver dagger pressing against her throat. Behind her, holding her arm firm against her back, is a man Alexander has never seen before. He's an exile of Caros—a pirate, perhaps, or a murderer from the West. A deep red scar runs down the left side of his face, starting at the top of his shaved head and ending over his raised cheekbone. His jaw is thick with stubble and his exposed arms are lined with the curling black ink of several tattoos. The wiry definition of his muscles indicates years of hard labor.

"Found this little fawn wandering the jungle," he shouts. A low rumble of thunder punctuates his words. "Reckoned she belonged to ye. Pretty lasses like this one don't last long on Caros."

"Once again," calls Alexander, "I told you to stay on the ship."

"This doesn't feel like the right time for this conversation," Emerala snarls back at him, freezing as the blade presses harder against her skin.

"I disagree," he says. "It feels like the perfect time."

He pries his pistol from the leather holster at his hip, clutching the weapon steadily within his hand. Next to him, the Hawk has gone as still as stone, his golden eyes murderous.

"I'll kill you," he snarls, his fingers bunching into fists. "I'll put a bullet right through your skull, I swear—"

"Relax, boy," the stranger calls, shouting to be heard over the roiling waves. "I en't looking for trouble."

Alexander shoots the Hawk a sideways glance, unsettled by the abrupt change in the typically nonchalant pirate's attitude. "What *are* you looking for, then?" he asks, returning his attention to the stranger.

"Who says I'm looking for anything? Just returning the lass safely to her captors."

"That's friendly of you," Alexander mutters dryly, at the same time that Emerala snaps, "They're not my captors."

The stranger ignores both of them. "If you'll excuse my dropping eaves, I heard ye talking about the wind woman of the north before I interrupted."

Alexander scowls, not understanding. "The wind woman of the north?"

"Ha'Suri. Surely ye know the story of the four winds of the sea."

"I'm afraid I missed that one," Alexander retorts.

"What your trigger-happy friend here was about to tell ye, I'm sure, is that Ha'Suri resides in the Eisle of Udire."

"Sounds like a folk tale to me," Alexander says, but something in the stranger's voice makes him hesitate. In his pocket he can feel the weight of the map, like an anchor. He thinks again of his father's dying words.

"It's quite real, I can promise ye. Men en't like to believe in things that predate civilization. Makes them feel real uneasy. But spirits as old as the winds don't need men to believe in them in order to exist."

Alexander stares unblinkingly at the scarred man and says nothing. His thoughts have churned themselves into froth, weightless and useless—the words dissolving as soon as they touch his tongue.

The stranger continues. "Are ye lookin' for her? If so, I can bring ye there."

"If what you're telling me is true," Alexander begins, "If it's more than just the mad ravings of a man left too long in exile—"

"I tell ye true," says the stranger, cutting him off before he can finish his sentence.

"Yes, well, I know the way to the Eisle of Udire. We've no need of your aid."

The stranger lets out a laugh as dry as crinkling paper. "Aye, maybe not. But ye need the girl, don't ye?"

He presses the dagger harder against Emerala's neck. One ruby red droplet of blood runs down her taut olive skin. Her thin lips contort in pain. Alexander opens his mouth to protest but Evander the Hawk beats him to it.

"Give her to me," the Hawk says. His demeanor has changed entirely, turning from murderous to desperate in a matter of seconds. He lurches forward, brows furrowed low over pained, golden eyes. "Whatever you want, damn it, just give her over."

The stranger's smile stretches wider, two sharp incisors appearing at the corners of his lips. The friendliness melts away, and he looks suddenly wicked in the light of the settling storm. Overhead, lightning snakes across a violent sky. Alexander's insides tighten into a knot, threatening to upend the meager contents of his stomach.

He could do it. He could leverage her life for the truth. If she's so damn important, the Hawk will never let her die. Maybe then, with her life hanging by a thread, the Hawk will finally be honest for once in his rotten life. Maybe, then, Alexander will finally get the truth. He squints up at the sky and feels pinpricks of rain upon his skin. Beneath the line of trees, Emerala has been silenced by the blade against her skin, her blood pooling in the hollow of her throat. His fingers shake at his sides.

He's never been any good at cards. He loses every hand he plays.

Those green eyes, storming like the sea, glower at him across the darkening sand. He's not so sure he's willing to up the ante—not anymore. He returns his attention to the grinning face that hovers over Emerala's shoulder.

"You want safe passage off the island." It isn't a question.

"Ye read my mind. Caros en't exactly my idea of a happy retirement."

Alexander's lip twitches. "The trouble," he says, "is that I'm not currently hiring new crew for my ship."

"That's too bad," the stranger muses. "I'd make a fine pirate." His dagger dances against Emerala's skin, eliciting a whimper.

"This isn't a negotiation, Cap," snarls the Hawk. "When I told you we needed her, I meant we needed her *alive*, not dead."

"We?" Alexander asks, his gaze glued to the dagger. "Or you?"

Next to him, the Hawk is silent.

"You're taking an awful long time to make up your minds," the stranger observes. "Maybe I was wrong. Maybe the lass en't as important to ye as I thought."

He twists Emerala's arm hard in her back, forcing her down onto her knees in the sand. She lands with a grunt, grimacing as he tangles his fist in her mane of curls and wrenches back her skull. Her throat stretches, bare and exposed, beneath the gleaming blade of his dagger. Rivulets of rain run down her skin, pooling with the water and staining the white lace of her blouse.

"Last words?" asks the stranger.

"Drop Below," Emerala hisses through gritted teeth.

"How ladylike of ye."

"All right, that's enough," Alexander calls, shouting now to be heard over the ceaseless thunder. Fingers of lightning streak across the sky. "Leave her be, we'll let you on board."

The stranger considers this, his one good eye flickering back and forth between Alexander and the Hawk. At Emerala's throat, the blade relaxes, falling away from her skin.

"Tricks, is it?"

"No tricks—we need the girl alive," Alexander shouts. "You want off the island? You've got it. You've had your fun. Give her here."

"I don't think that's smart," the stranger calls, wrenching Emerala to her feet and shoving her several steps forward across the sand. He studies the sky for a moment, his blind eye scanning the clouds without seeing them, his good eye narrowed against the rain. "No, I think I'll keep her here with me until we're safely on the ship."

He shoves Emerala between the two pirates, pressing her forward with a twist of her arm. She bites her lip, her gaze boring into Alexander as she passes him. He expects to find fear written on her face but finds only the slow, simmering heat of rage. In spite of her anger, he feels a sudden, unwanted desire to reach for her—to pull her away from the scarred stranger.

He hates himself for feeling the way he does.

A stronger man would have let her die.

A better pirate would have bartered for information. The man who has nothing to lose is the strongest of all—that's something his mother used to say.

He isn't strong, not now. Not in this moment. *Perhaps*, he thinks, *not ever.*

He turns and follows in the stranger's footsteps, watching as the Hawk falls into step beside him. The lanky pirate's fingers shake with barely suppressed rage.

"If he spills another drop of her blood, I'll slit his throat."

At that, the stranger before them laughs. He spins around lithely upon his heels, grinning like a madman in the rain.

"It occurs to me that I didn't introduce myself properly," he says, his eyes flashing silver as lightning cracks across the sky. "The name's Lachlan. Lachlan the Lethal. Ye might recognize the name, it tends to carry some weight on this side of the world."

Next to Alexander, the Hawk groans. "The mass murderer from the Westerlies," he says, flashing him a cold smile. "Great."

"*Retired* mass murderer," Lachlan the Lethal corrects. "I'd like to make that clear. I reckon that once this blows over, we can all be friends."

"Not bloody likely," the Hawk growls as Lachlan the Lethal continues to drag Emerala back towards the looming silhouette of the *Rebellion*.

"Don't do anything stupid," Alexander mutters, keeping his eyes trained upon the two figures up ahead.

"Stupid?" the Hawk repeats. "That moment passed the second you let the bastard live."

"Careful, Hawk," Alexander admonishes. "Let's not forget who's in charge here."

"Never." The word drips with poison.

"Let's just get back to the ship," Alexander urges. "We can deal with this properly once he's removed the dagger from Emerala's neck."

He watches her struggle quietly within the arms of Lachlan the Lethal. Lightning illuminates the beachfront, casting her silhouette in a halo of silver.

As a street rat in the alleys of Senada, he often fought like a boy with nothing to lose. It was the only way to put food in his belly—it was the only way to survive.

In Emerala the Rogue's time onboard the *Rebellion*, she has proven herself to be invasive, disobedient, and stubborn in every sense of the word. And yet she has wormed her way into his thoughts, has inked herself into his skin. He no longer feels like a man with nothing to lose.

The admission bothers him—unsettles him. It feels unnatural, this anger that takes root in his gut, this fury that writhes in him like a flame. And deeper still, this sickly coil of jealousy that tightens, tightens, tightens with every glance at the Hawk, his golden eyes slitted against the rain, his fingers balled into fists.

Up ahead, the Lethal whispers something into Emerala's ear.

"Pig," Alexander hears her snap.

His fury ignites, coursing through his bones. Lachlan the Lethal will be welcome onboard his ship. For now.

They will set sail immediately for the Eisle of Udire.

And that's as far as the murderer will go.

King U'Rel and his band of hunters will take care of him there, on the arctic shores of the north.

Harvest Cycle 1511

It has been raining for weeks on end. I have never seen rain such as this, not in all of my days on Chancey. It pounds relentlessly at the deck of the ship, beating the wooden vessel and its drenched crew into weary submission.

Charles Argot has been working tirelessly at constructing the map. He writes in a dead language, charting the course in symbols and lines that only he can understand. Captain Samuel swears he is the best man for the job, and yet something about his manner irks me. Even now he watches me far too closely, studying my every move as if he thinks he can read me. No one can read me. I am an enigma, even to myself. My mind is uncharted territory.

The golden-eyed boy—the Hawk, as I have come to know him—does not like Argot either. He says he doesn't trust a map that only one man can read. I feel similarly, although I will not voice my concerns. My orders were clear, and if I am to follow them I must not leave a trail. There is too much at risk to make a mistake now.

We are only days away from the Eisle of Udire. In the brief breaks in the rain, I can see the grey strip of land growing larger on the horizon. I am looking forward to being warm and dry, even if only for a short while.

Eliot

CHAPTER 8

Chancey

THE CLINK OF utensils being scrubbed in the scullery acts as a menacing substitute for the metallic whistling of the guillotine. At the very least, it seems that way to Blaine the Eager. He clears his throat and averts his eyes as a scullery boy shoves past him, holding aloft a pot that reeks of day old meat.

Never in his lifetime did he think that fate would lead him here, to Rowland Stoward's royal kitchens. Never in his lifetime, and yet here he is, keeping his head down and his ears open—praying to whatever gods may be that tomorrow won't be his last, won't be the day he is discovered for what he truly is.

Tainted blood.

A gypsy.

He's really only half of a Cairan. His standing as a half-blood is what got him into this mess in the first place. His familial connection to the purist bloodlines of Chancey is the only thing that made the Cairan king look his way, he's certain of it. He would have been all too happy to stay out of trouble—to keep his nose in his drink and his hand in the coffer.

But fate, and Topan, had other plans for him.

His grandfather's name was Harold Blaine. He supposes he has the old man to blame for his current circumstance. He'd been a chef in Rowland Stoward's kitchens long before Blaine was even born. When Blaine was a child, he knew his paternal grandfather only as a subject in his mother's stories. They weren't permitted to visit him in the palace, nor did he visit them. He was family in name only, his legacy the one thing that kept him bound to them as tensions grew in the city. Back in those days of youthful ignorance, Blaine—content to spend his days running barefoot through the puddles in abandoned street corners—was blissfully unaware of the cultural strife that was brewing in Chancey. He didn't know that his muddled bloodlines would one day make him a target of hate.

It wasn't until the executions began—wasn't until his mother spent her weary nights crying herself to sleep—that Blaine began to realize that things were coming unraveled all around him. His mother and father would argue late into the night—would shout at one another over the flickering candlelight when they thought Blaine was asleep.

They're killing us, and you don't even care, his mother would cry.

I care, he'd hear his father snap. *Damn it, I care what happens to you—to my son.*

Then why won't you contact your father? He can help us. He has connections.

Because, Lariana, his father would say, exasperated. *Because he'll be strung up as a traitor, and then they'll come for us. It isn't safe. Best to stay away. Forget about it.*

Blaine went through his adolescence hating the old man, hoping he'd die. After all, he had turned his back on family, hadn't he? He would stand among the crowd at the executions, watching friends and neighbors pleading for their souls as the drums rolled out a slow march, and think of his grandfather preparing an extravagant celebratory meal in the kitchens.

Eventually, he stopped thinking of his grandfather at all.

It wasn't until one night nearly two decades later that he even heard the name. By then, his parents had been dead for years, the memory of his Chancian connections all but faded into oblivion. He had been quietly enjoying a cigar on the stoop outside his dilapidated apartment when a figure dropped down onto the step beside him.

Who's that? he demanded coolly, blowing out a smoke ring. He watched as it drifted aimlessly up into the air, the weightless grey tendrils breaking apart and fading into the darkness.

Roberts the Valiant, the newcomer said. His tone was hushed, hurried. *I come with a message.*

Is that right? From who?

Nobody.

Blaine immediately recognized the alias for the elusive Cairan king.

Pull the other one, he said, and took a deep drag from his pipe.

I mean it.

Of course you do. And I'm the archduke of the Stoward court.

Will you really turn me away? the Valiant asked. *In times like these, I don't think you can afford to.*

At that, Blaine relented. He exhaled, emptying his lungs of air. *Fine. What kind of message can No One have for a simple man like me?*

The Valiant either didn't pick up on his scarcely concealed cynicism, or he'd merely chosen to ignore it, because he pressed on.

Are you Blaine the Eager, grandson of Harold Blaine?

At this, Blaine coughed, choking on smoke. It had been a long time since he heard the name.

Yes. His voice grew cautious, quiet. His lungs burned. *But I haven't met the man, nor spoken to him in my lifetime. He could be long dead, for all I know.*

He's alive. He lives in the castle, in one of the dormitories off of the kitchens. He tends to the garden when he can, but otherwise he's grown too old to be of much use to anyone.

What use is this information to me? Blaine inquired after a spell of thoughtful silence.

No One is gathering a group of men together to look out for the well-being of our people. It's no secret that the status of the Cairans has been greatly devalued in the past few decades—so much so that it has become dangerous to continue identifying with our culture. We're being killed off one by one. No One wants to fight back. We need eyes and ears to infiltrate the city.

Blaine's mind worked quickly to put the pieces together. He was a smart man—quick as a whip, his mother used to say—he knew what it was the Valiant wanted from him. *You want me for my connections, then?* he asked. *What makes you think that my grandfather would even be willing to give me a job in the kitchens? What makes you think he isn't in league with those upper class elitists?*

The Valiant smiled, and his unusual green eyes glinted wickedly in the moonlight. *It's true. He may very well be on the wrong side of this fight. I have no way of knowing that. I never said this job wouldn't be dangerous.*

That's how Blaine arrived here, one of Topan's Listeners, working in Rowland Stoward's royal kitchens. Every day is a gamble—a roll of the dice. He never knows when he might be accused of being a Cairan. Accused, as though to be born a Cairan is to knowingly commit come unspeakable, carnal sin.

It happens to others almost weekly. He's nearly sick every time he's forced to line up against the wall of the kitchen and watch as the Guardians drag away another protesting scullery boy. Rowland Stoward is growing paranoid. Paranoid and impatient. Everyone knows that he's targeting innocents, but who would dare speak out against the king? The fear of retribution is far too great.

In the sweltering kitchens, every man is his own friend. They entrust one another with basic tasks and nothing more. Each knows that if the opportunity arises he will sooner sell out one of the other men than be placed under arrest. Blaine keeps to himself, working diligently at whatever task he is given. As he works he's careful to keep his ears open and listen information that might be important.

He jumps, rocketing himself out of the way of an oncoming cook. The rushing man, clad in a flour stained apron, fights to balance a large pot of some bubbling liquid or another. A bit has spilled out the side and now lies steaming upon the ground between the two men.

"A hand, Will?" The cook uses the common name Blaine chose to go by when he first came to his grandfather. A hint of impatience lines the words of the disgruntled cook, and Blaine makes haste. A surefire way to attract unwanted attention, he's learned, is by moving too slowly. He grips the other end of the large pot, helping the portly cook to balance it out.

"We already assembled breakfast for His Majesty, surely he can't be eating again so soon," Blaine ventures. Conversation is a good thing, even idle talk. If there is anything the men and women of the Stoward court love more than themselves, it's gossip. No information is useless. Not in times as dangerous as these.

"Bloody soldiers have a hankering for black pudding," the cook grumbles.

Blaine wrinkles his nose at what he now knows to be congealed pig's blood gurgling within the steaming pot. "We don't serve the soldiers."

"Today we do. His *royal Majesty*," the cook says, emphasizing the king's title with a grunt as he hoists the pot up higher, "is in a good mood this morning. He's given the orders to prepare whatever the soldiers want."

"Ah." Blaine doesn't dare to ask what has put the king in a good mood. Asking too many questions looks suspicious. Anyhow, he'll find out everything he needs to know eventually. People love to talk, if you let them.

The cook continues, "It's damn near going to kill me, too. I've too much to do today. He's dining with Lord Anderson and his wife tonight and he's ordered boar's head. Boar's head! And not even a full day's notice. The huntsmen will be hard pressed to find a fat boar in this heat, I'll tell you that. I'll be serving up last night's roast pig and His Majesty will be serving up my head."

They turn sideways and push through the heavy swinging door that leads to the Guardians' kitchen. Boisterous singing reaches his ears as soon as he steps across the threshold. He recognizes the song immediately—a bawdy commoner's ballad about a drunken lord who falls into bed with a beautiful Cairan woman.

Funny, he thinks darkly, *that they should scorn our culture but desire our women.*

He helps the cook to place the pot down on the nearest table. Several of the Guardians—their formidable golden cloaks removed—push and shove on their way over to the table. The others remain crowded around the four Guardians that continue to sing the finale of the song.

"I fell for a lady, oh-a-lee-oh-a-lie,
"A lady with blue in her eyes."

Blaine resists the urge to roll his own eyes, uncommonly dark for a Cairan man—and luckily so. As the laughter and applause subsides, he catches the fragment of a muted conversation somewhere behind him. His breath snags in his throat and he strains his ears to listen.

"He's mad, that's what the officers are saying."

"That's treason."

"Is it treason if it's true?"

"General Byron would have your head if he heard you talking that way about the king. Most of these men here would."

"It was General Byron who first commented on the absurdity of the king's order."

"Is that the word he used? Absurd? I find that hard to believe."

"Well, no, but Thompson was privy to the conversation and he said Byron had a rather short fuse over the whole affair."

"I've never even heard of a Forbidden City."

There it is again, the phrase that first caught Blaine's attention and brought his stomach into his throat. The Forbidden City.

A Guardian is hooting next to Blaine, the volume of his laughter rising well above the two soldiers at his back. He attempts to take a step backwards without drawing any attention to himself. The voices come back into focus, their annoyance evident.

"Where do we even begin looking?"

"I wouldn't know, would I?"

"We've combed the whole island time and time again."

"Don't you think I know that? I suppose General Byron will brief us on our new duties tonight. Provence says he's called a meeting in the barracks. Even off duty Guardians are meant to attend."

"How do we look for something that doesn't exist?"

How indeed? Blaine turns and heads towards the door. The cook has already disappeared—probably to try and find a way to dress up one of the palace pigs as a convincing boar. Blaine has lingered far too long in the company of soldiers. It will draw unwanted attention if he idles any longer.

This is terrible news. The beauty of the Forbidden City—the magic of it, really—is that no one thinks to look for something that doesn't exist.

If Rowland Stoward knows—if General Byron has caught the scent—it means the stakes just became a little bit higher.

Lost in thought, Blaine backs through the swinging door and collides directly into the portly frame of the chef.

"There's to be a reward, you know," he says.

Blaine turns around to meet his gaze head on. He does his best to look confused.

"I saw you dropping eaves on those two Guardians in there. They should be more careful, speaking so boldly in mixed company. His Majesty does not take lightly to treason."

Blaine swallows. "You mentioned a reward?"

"The officers broke fast in one of the dining halls earlier this morning, and Margaret Wilmer heard them discussing the fabled wealth of the false queen."

Blaine hasn't the slightest idea who Margaret Wilmer is. He assumes she is another gossip hungry member of the royal staff.

"The reward will go to the person who can discover the whereabouts of this hideaway. His Majesty is desperate to find the city." The cook lowers his voice, leaning in as though he's about to share something dangerous. "It's a bit strange, I think. I would have thought Rowland would be happy enough just knowing that they're no longer corrupting the streets of Chancey."

"He wants them all killed for their insolence," Blaine says, for a moment forgetting to keep his anger from infiltrating his voice.

The cook harrumphs loudly. "With good reason." He flashes Blaine a cold look, as if daring him to challenge his assertion—daring him to disagree. When Blaine only nods, the cook turns and heads wordlessly away. Blaine watches him go, fighting the urge to leap upon the man and pummel him for his ignorance.

But what good will that do?

What good will anything do?

Blaine takes a steadying breath and processes his newfound information.

Rowland Stoward knows that the Cairans are seeking refuge in the Forbidden City.

That is a very, very bad thing.

Blaine takes momentary reassurance in the thought that he doesn't know where the city is. Roberts the Valiant thought it best not to tell him. Should he be discovered—should he be the next staffer to be dragged away in paranoid suspicion—they won't be able to beat the location out of him. He'll go to his grave unable to sell out his people.

His stomach churns. He scans the kitchen, taking in all of the busy work that bustles about him. He needs to get back to work soon or his inactivity will become noticeable to his companions.

With grim silence, he sets to kneading a lumpy bit of dough, processing the news and waiting for an opportune moment to sneak away and inform the Listeners.

CHAPTER 9

Chancey

SERANAI THE FAIR is having a particularly bad day.

It's not the fact that she was awoken far too early that morning by the unwelcome sound of lewd romance in the room overhead. It's not—surprisingly—that while dressing herself behind a flimsy three-paned room divider she found a rather prominent tear in the hem of her newly acquired red brocade gown. It's certainly not that she proceeded to spill hot porridge on the lap of the very same gown when being jostled by one of the over-exuberant harlots in the dining hall.

She is having a bad day, but not for those reasons. Instead, it's the fact that—for a purpose that she cannot quite fathom—General James Byron is quickly approaching Mamere Lenora's notorious little whorehouse in broad daylight. She saw him the moment he rounded the corner—how could she not? James Byron is a man that commands attention.

She stares at him in agitation, watching the sun spill off of his gold-clad shoulders. His gait is confident; his stride is even. His firm jawline is locked as his impassive brown eyes scan the crowd of women that linger on the stoop, fanning themselves in the blistering summer heat and tittering excitedly at the approach of such a handsome officer.

Seranai fights the urge to roll her eyes, drawing back against the peeling outer wall of the house and attempting to remain invisible. She is not the only one concerned with his approach. Mamere Lenora must have spotted him from one of the soiled windows upstairs. She can hear the uneven patter of feet on the creaking steps—can hear the breathless grunts as the matron of the Chancian harlots attempts to catch her breath.

"Out of the way, out of the way," she snaps, and Seranai can see her hands shoving through the throng of women in agitation. "Get inside, all of you. He's not something to be ogled at. There's no business for you here."

James draws to a standstill a few feet away from the stoop. That familiar smile—the charming smirk used only when dealing with people of lesser fortitude than he—suddenly plants itself upon his face. Seranai snatches an elaborately decorated fan from the bustle of the girl before her, snapping her wrist so that it drops before her face. It smells strongly of old perfume—that spicy odor of cologne gone sour. She fights the sudden urge to sneeze.

"You too, dear," Mamere Lenora mutters with sudden urgency. "No need to be out here in this heat. Get on inside."

"It's quite all right, Mamere," James says warmly, and something in his voice makes Seranai's breath catch in her throat. "It's the woman right there that I'm looking for."

Seranai allows her grey eyes to slide over to where he stands and sees that he is looking at her. Directly at her. Sighing, she snaps the fan shut. The game is up. She wonders how long he has known that this is where she was setting up camp—among the filthy fringes of the city—among the women with no morals.

Next to her, Mamere Lenora grows tense. When she speaks, her voice is fraught with trepidation. "With all due respect, General, there's no reason you need to talk to any of my girls, this one included."

"Of course not," he assents, "but this woman isn't one of yours. Let's not insult my intelligence by continuing to pretend that she is. We both know she's a Cairan."

Mamere Lenora inhales so deeply that for a moment it seems as though she has sucked all of the air off of the stoop. The heat that bakes the stones underfoot singes the inside of Seranai's nose.

"I'm not harboring any gypsies," Mamere asserts. "I knew her father. He was a local butcher—a Chancian man through and through."

Seranai cringes inwardly at the mention of her father. Her lips draw into a thin line. Her tongue feels as though she has tasted something acrid. She wipes her palms against her red brocade gown, the itching memory of blood on her hands bringing a chill down her spine—sickly sweet against the sweltering summer air.

"And her mother was a Cairan," James is saying. "Half-blood or not, a gypsy is a gypsy."

Mamere idles on the step, caught between the darkness of her foyer and the spilling summer sun on the step. "Please," she says at last, her husky voice dropping into a whisper. "Please, I can't afford to be charged with sheltering gypsies. I'll lose the business."

"And that would be a shame, wouldn't it?" James asks, his tone deprecating. "I won't say a word, I only wish for a brief audience with our Cairan friend."

"Of course." Mamere's voice cracks as she speaks. Her heavily painted lids flutter over eyes filled with dread.

"Alone."

"Take as much time as you need," Mamere says, ushering him up the steps. She reminds Seranai of a feathered hen ripe for plucking, fretting to and fro and bobbing stupidly upon the creaking steps. For a brief second, an image of the woman roasting on a spit creeps through her thoughts.

"Come—come, use the front hall where you won't be seen."

James draws besides Seranai on the porch, his cloak brushing her arm. She fights the urge to recoil even as somewhere within her, a flicker of memory compels her to lean into his frame—to melt away against him.

She scowls, slapping the fan hard against the palm of her hand. Mamere jumps at the sound, sputtering nervously as James lays a palm upon her back. He leads her inside, hardly bothering to glance in Seranai's direction.

"Thank you, Lenora," he says, bowing his head towards her in a show of cordiality. "And I trust I can count on your confidentiality in this matter. I'd like my visit to remain unknown."

"Of course," Mamere promises. "Chancey's best kept secrets live in this very house."

Seranai follows silently behind them, reentering the stuffy front hall of the brothel. Hovering on the threshold, she glowers at the broad, golden shoulders of her former lover—stares daggers at the shadow of the boy that once loved her as only a young man could love. He lingers in the fusty hallway, his cloak sweeping the threadbare carpet underfoot, and runs one finger through the film of dust atop a wooden table.

"In here," Mamere gestures, pointing a heavily ringed finger at an open door closest to them. James flashes her a gracious smile and dips out of sight into the room. Seranai sighs and follows suit. What else is there to do?

As soon as the door closes behind them, the words come tumbling from her lips.

"I'm not selling myself."

A brief glimmer of mirth passes across his features. "I don't particularly care either way."

He means it. The blunt delivery pummels into her, nearly bowling her over. She rebukes herself silently. She shouldn't be so affected by his indifference anymore—not after all this time.

"I'm only wasting my time in this hovel because it provides a good cover," she explains.

"Not that good," he disagrees. "I've known you were here for quite a while."

The admission comes as a surprise. All this time she thought that her continued safety meant that she had managed to remain undiscovered.

"And yet you never thought to have me arrested?"

"Clearly not."

She can't resist the urge to pry. No point in being subtle about it. "But why? I've seen your men overturn every rock in this city searching for any trace of Cairans."

"You've never identified with your people, Seranai, and they've never identified with you. Quite frankly, I would have been surprised had you disappeared with them." He looks around at the room—his eyes scanning the faded carpet, the yellowed wallpaper—and smirks. "A whorehouse is much better suited to you, I think."

It is meant as an insult, and it works. Cheeks burning, she resists the urge to slap him across the face.

"You came here for a reason," she snaps. "Get on with it and leave."

The look he fixes her with is chilling. "Most people wouldn't dare to give orders to an officer of the Golden Guard."

"You forget that I knew you before they raised you up on a pedestal, James," she says, spitting out his name like poison.

He ignores her comment. "Where did they go? The Cairans?"

"The Dark Below, with any luck."

He scowls. "I asked a serious question."

"And I gave a serious answer."

"You've no idea where they went?" James asks, looking doubtful. His posture is stiff, his movements stilted. He looks out of place in this faded old room, a stark spot of polished gold against rusted brass and moth-bitten fabric.

"Oh I do," Seranai disagrees. "But I don't see why I should share anything with you."

"Perhaps because I have the power to have you killed."

Seranai dithers upon the rug before him, trying to gauge his sincerity. It wouldn't be worth it to call his bluff—not when she has come so far in her plan. Not when she worked so hard to rid herself of Emerala the Rogue—to set herself in the perfect position to run into Roberts the Valiant.

James doesn't wait for her to calculate a response before asking, "What is the Forbidden City?"

The question startles her, but she recovers quickly. She cannot afford to lose face. Not here. Not now. Not ever.

"It's a children's story," she says, twisting a finger within a silvery lock of hair.

"Is there any truth to it?"

"Of course not. I took you for a more practical man, James."

He proffers a small shrug, glancing up at the low ceiling overhead. "The king has ordered us to search for it."

She laughs wryly. "You'd be wasting your time."

His attention drops back down towards her face. "Would we?"

"Yes," she says, but her laughter dies in her throat as she notes the conviction in his gaze.

"I don't think so," he disagrees. "I saw the way you caught yourself when I asked. You believe in it, even if I don't. Tell me the truth. Is that where the Cairans have gone?"

She runs a slender finger down her forearm, frowning. *Think fast.* He can torture the answer out of her if he so choses, especially now that he knows she has an answer to give. Somewhere outside, a rooster screams. A carriage rattles down the street, the wheels catching in the pocketed grooves between the cobblestones. A thought occurs to her, then, and she smiles.

"Do you know that old Lord Chadwin is one of our most frequent visitors? No, it's true," she says, her smile widening at the disbelief that crosses James's face. "In fact, he'll be coming by for a spot of afternoon pleasure in just a short while. He comes every third day, just after lunch and right before tea."

James chews at the inside of his cheek, his eyes darting all around the paltry room before coming back to land upon her. "I'm not sure how this information relates to the Forbidden City."

"It has nothing to do with that old fairy tale," she admits. "But if you'd like your visit here to remain a secret, you'd be wise to take the back door in the next minute or so. He arrives with an arsenal of your very own Guardians, each one highly paid to hold their tongues."

Before her, General Byron is silent.

"I'm not sure they'd do the same for you," she comments. Lowering her voice to a whisper, she adds, "There are a lot of men who'd give anything to see you fall."

"Did you learn that secret here as well?" he asks, his gaze dark.

She lets a quiet laugh leak out between parted lips. "I'm sure you'd like to know."

He exhales deeply through his nose. "Goodbye, Seranai."

The sound of her name on his tongue is as unwelcome as it is familiar. She frowns, feeling that nostalgic sense of heartbreak creeping in and settling in her bones. She remains frozen to the carpet as he moves past her to leave the room. His golden cloak brushes against the outturned palm of her hand. It is cool despite the pressing heat, and she resists the urge to grab it within her fists and hold tight.

She hears the door squeal open, and he is gone. His muffled footsteps fade into silence on the musty carpet outside. Somewhere in the distance she hears the overlapping patter of hooves on cobblestones. A loose wheel squeaks. *Lord Chadwin.*

So James Byron knows about the Forbidden City. Even worse, perhaps, Rowland Stoward knows about the Forbidden City. If they find it first, Seranai is certain she'll never see a lick of the fortune she so craves. If they find it, everything she's worked for will have failed.

She thinks of the Hawk, and remembers the bloody rain that dripped down his face after he slaughtered the three Guardians in the square. Emerala the Rogue was unconscious in his arms. His chest, skin glistening in the downpour, heaved with exertion. And yet it was not the exertion of having committed a necessary evil, but from the labor of elation. He *liked* killing. He craved it. His golden eyes had gleamed with ecstasy across the dark expanse.

I've done my part, he'd said. *Now it's your turn.*

What do I do? she asked, lingering in the shadow of a narrow alleyway. The three corpses in the street unnerved her.

Nothing. Forget Roberts. He's not important. Wait for me. I'll be back by summer's end.

So far, she has obeyed his orders. And yet—even Evander the Hawk cannot stop her from watching. She has remained hidden in the shadows, studying the Cairan—watching as Roberts the Valiant rose to the ranks of the Cairan king's right hand man. He is frequently out in the streets of Chancey—stealing food and water and bits of news.

Meanwhile, the Hawk remains at large, lost at sea without so much as a word. Seranai is not the kind of woman who likes to be kept waiting, and she is getting quite bored of sitting around in the company of harlots.

Her goal has always been singular in nature—claw her way into the upper elite. She is a victim of circumstance, a Cairan half-blood by birth, left to always hover in the middle, never belonging anywhere. All she has ever wanted is a place in Chancian society. What love has failed to procure for her, she is determined to achieve through manipulation.

Whatever means necessary, she thinks.

Her plan is simple. Or, it should have been simple before Emerala the Rogue complicated matters. Now that the wretched girl is gone for good, the plan is simple again. The Cairan king has access to Saynti's Treasure, buried away within the depths of the Forbidden City. Roberts the Valiant has access to the Cairan king. Seranai, therefore, needs access to Roberts the Valiant. To the Dark Below with the Hawk and his instructions.

She knows him, Roberts. She knows his comings and goings. She's seen him angry. She's seen him afraid. She's seen his weakness and his strength. Seranai knows how to make a man fall in love with her, and Roberts will be no different.

Evander the Hawk told her to wait, but she is done waiting.

It's not safe to stay put at Mamere Lenora's. Not anymore.

James knows she's here, and he knows she has the answers he seeks. It won't be long before he returns to the brothel. The time is coming to make herself scarce. The Hawk wishes to gain entrance to the Forbidden City upon his return to Chancey, so she'll be sure she's already there when he arrives.

From now on, she'll do things her way.

CHAPTER 10

The Forbidden City

"What you want is impossible."

Orianna the Raven's voice is too loud for Nerani's comfort. She shushes her with a stunted wave of her hand, glancing around nervously at the supply room full of bustling women.

If, of course, one could call it a room. It is more reminiscent of a hollowed out hole in the middle of deep, impenetrable rock. The Forbidden City is meant to keep their enemies out, but right now all Nerani can focus on is how effective it is at holding her hostage.

"It's not impossible," she disagrees.

Before her, Orianna sighs. She puts down the freshly washed linen she has been folding, placing it gently atop the growing pile of mismatched cloth by her knees. The ebony skin of her hands is dry and cracked from repeated exposure to soapy water. Her black hair falls before tired blue eyes and she pushes it away with a flick of her finger.

"I can't do what you're asking."

Nerani's sullen frown is replaced by the first hint of an eager smile. "So, you're not willing to do it, but it's not impossible."

Orianna slumps forward, sighing wearily. "I didn't say that."

"It was implied."

Nerani understands why Orianna is hesitant. She understands the significance of what she is asking her friend to do. Orianna was the only young woman of their name-year chosen to train for the exclusive right to call herself a Mame. It is an honor and a privilege to be accepted into such a rank among Cairans. If she's to be caught carrying out Nerani's wishes, she will most certainly pay the price.

But Nerani needs her. She can't find her way through the endless, black tunnels of the Forbidden City without her.

The Mames know the way.

That was what she'd heard Topan say, clear as day.

The Mames know the way.

She wouldn't dare to ask one of the Mames for their help. If they knew what she wanted—if they knew what she was planning—they would put an end to it at once. No one is permitted in or out of the city, save for the precious few Listeners granted prior approval from Topan.

If any of the women were to feel sorry enough for her to give her aid, they would simply give her a riddle and send her on her way.

Nerani has no time for riddles.

Orianna reaches her hands across the space between them and places her palms over Nerani's balled up fists. Her coarse hands are warm, and Nerani becomes suddenly aware of how thin and cold she has become. Her fingers are locked into perpetual talons, the bony knuckles pulling against stretched, white skin.

"Nerani," Orianna begins, and her voice is soft. Her dark blue eyes swim with grief. "I know it's hard. It's hard on me, too. After all these weeks, its still so difficult to believe that Emerala is gone."

Nerani fights the urge to pull her hands out from beneath Orianna's grasp. "Did Roberts tell you that?"

Orianna's frown deepens. "No, he didn't have to. I was there with you."

"Then you know that she's alive. You saw the same thing that I saw."

Orianna shakes her head. Her eyes flutter closed. "What we saw were three armed Guardians standing over her body in the pouring rain." Her eyes open again and there are tears sitting in her lower lids. "What we saw, Nerani, was her slaughter."

Slaughter.

The word is cold. Callous. It cuts the heart like a knife. Nerani feels sick at the sound of it, even as it slides off of Orianna's tongue and slices the air between them. Slaughter; as though Emerala was nothing more than a palace swine, gutted and served for dinner with a seasonal garnish.

Was. She catches herself using the past tense and her throat tightens. *Is.*

"She's alive," she says, her voice cracking under the weight of repetition. "I feel it in my gut. If you don't believe the evidence, at least believe that."

Orianna is silent, her forehead lined with worry. "Nerani, stop this," she says after a moment. "You can be in pain. You can be in denial, but you can't go looking for ghosts. You won't survive the catacombs—no one does. Can you imagine what that would do to Rob? To me? We can't bear another loss."

"I would survive in the catacombs if you would consent to help me."

At that, Orianna groans. "I don't know *how* to get through the catacombs. Even if I wanted to help you, I couldn't."

"But the Mames know," Nerani points out.

"They do," comes the grudging agreement.

"You can find out."

Silence again.

"Please," Nerani adds. "I'm going to attempt to navigate the catacombs with or without your help."

"That's absolutely mad."

"I know."

"You'll die within hours."

"I know."

The thought of traversing through the pitch dark of the tunnels alone terrifies her. Beneath Orianna's hands, she feels her own start to tremble.

"Emerala would have done the same for me," she adds.

One corner of Orianna's lips twitches upward. "Emerala was like a dog with a bone when she had her mind set on something, too."

Is, Nerani thinks again, although she refrains from saying anything out loud. *Emerala is like a dog with a bone.*

"Okay," Orianna relents, rising from where she sits. The folds of her violet gown fall away from her like water as she paces a short length away from Nerani.

"Okay?" Nerani echoes, scarcely daring to hope.

Orianna groans, running her hands through her glossy, black hair. She turns and marches back toward Nerani, leaning across her to snatch at the basket of linens from Nerani's lap. As she draws in close, she whispers, "They use a light."

"A light?" Nerani repeats.

Orianna nods, shushing her.

"I don't understand."

"It's a candle or a lantern of some sort," Orianna explains, setting the basket down at her feet. "I'm not sure. I don't know how it works, but it does."

"Any sort of light would illuminate a dark tunnel," Nerani says, doubt lacing her words. "That won't help me to decide whether to go left or right when the time comes."

"Yes, but this light only illuminates the correct path."

"How?" Nerani asks. Orianna's demeanor changes suddenly, a smile dancing on her lips. Nerani follows suit, her pulse racing, as a slender woman with curly brown hair stoops down to pick up the basket containing Orianna's hastily folded linens.

"Thank you," Orianna says. The woman nods and continues on her way, shooting them a fleeting backwards glance as she turns down a narrow, stone corridor and out of sight. Orianna waits for her to be fully out of earshot before turning her attention back to Nerani. "Look, I don't know *how* it works, I only know that it's some sort of light source."

"Magic?" Nerani asks, feeling ridiculous even as the word leaves her lips.

Orianna suppresses a small laugh. "Don't be mad. I'm sure there's an explanation."

"Can you find out?" Nerani probes. When Orianna hesitates she adds, "I know I'm asking a lot of you."

"You are." Orianna crosses to a low table, upon which several candles have nearly sputtered out. Molten beads of wax harden into the wooden grain, mottling the surface of the table with clumps of white. Orianna runs her fingers over the candles, sending the flames dancing upon their wicks.

"I'm not making any promises," she says at last, addressing the shadowed wall before her. Nerani feels a bead of excitement building within her chest, but she swallows it down, forcing herself to remain steady—calm. She can feel Orianna's reluctance from here, even if she can't see the woman's face.

"I know."

One candle extinguishes beneath Orianna's fingers. Only a shivering, blue nucleus is left on the blacked wick. A portion of the low, stone room is cast into darkness. Sighing, Orianna turns back to face Nerani. Her ebony features take on a golden hue against the light of the remaining flames. She looks lovely in the darkness. Lovely and sad.

"You really think that she's alive?"

"I know she is," Nerani replies, without missing a beat. "You have to believe me—she's out there somewhere."

For a long time, they stand in silence. Orianna chews her lower lip, her blue eyes glimmering like sapphires as she studies the empty space above Nerani's head.

"Okay," she says at last, exhaling deeply. Her chest deflates beneath her white, ruffled blouse. "I don't know that I'll be able to help you, but I'll try."

"I understand."

"Listen, give me a few days to sniff around Mame Minera's quarters and see what I can uncover. I'll come find you once I know more."

"Thank you," Nerani says, rising from her chair. The stone is cold against the soles of her feet.

"Don't thank me yet," Orianna cautions. "The Mames guard their secrets very carefully. I may fail."

"But it's a start," Nerani whispers. Her fingers dance nervously against the sky blue fabric of her cotton gown—a color she chose intentionally in her continuing strike against the traditional black worn by family members in mourning.

I will not mourn the dead, she thinks, *when there are no dead to mourn.*

Across the room, Orianna has extinguished all but one of the candles. Only a small oval of orange light washes across the jagged stone.

"We should probably go," Orianna says. "We've finished the linens. If Mame Minera finds us spending time in here with no task, she'll put us to work somewhere else, and I'm quite through with chores for the day."

73

"Agreed," Nerani says. As the final candle extinguishes, she finds herself smiling into the dark. The bead of excitement grows in her chest—a sense of anticipation buzzes in her veins. She heads for the beckoning glow of light in the tunnel beyond, eager to head back to the quarters she shares with Roberts and begin preparations for her journey.

"Nerani, wait." Orianna's voice stops her cold. She pauses in the mouth of the corridor, glancing back over her shoulder at the shaded silhouette of her friend in the darkness.

"Promise me you won't do anything dangerous until we figure out the light source."

"I won't."

In the silence that follows, the stone room whispers back at her.

I won't. I won't. I won't.

Finally, Orianna says, "You're a lot more like Emerala than you think, you know."

"Maybe," Nerani whispers, and smiles. She turns to go without another word, feeling lighter than she has in a long time. Orianna may doubt her abilities to find out the answers they need, but Nerani knows she'll turn over every leaf until she's found the way through the tunnels. Orianna the Raven is nothing if not tenacious. Once her mind has been made up, she'll stop at nothing to get her way.

Nerani is aware of how much she is asking of Orianna—she's aware of the weight her actions will carry if Orianna should be caught. The payoff is worth the risk. Emerala needs them. She's out there, alive and abandoned, and Nerani is the only one who believes it.

She'll wait for Orianna to discover the means of traversing the tunnels, and then she'll prove everyone wrong.

Harvest Cycle 1511

Sometimes, against the driving rains at sea, I begin to think myself a man unraveling.

Eliot

CHAPTER 11

The Rebellion

EVANDER THE HAWK finds Emerala the Rogue skulking about below deck, her wild curls pulled back from her temples in an even wilder bun, her green eyes storming.

She stands in a puddle of colorless light that falls in through the gunport overhead, her face a mosaic of emotion. Her customary green gown has been traded in for a pair of black trousers and leather boots. Her white blouse remains cinched to her narrow waist by a whalebone corset, her collarbone left bare where the ruffled, white lace doesn't quite reach. He shifts his focus away from her olive skin, looking instead at the large, silver cage that swings to and fro before her. Behind the rounded bars, seven silver parrots preen and flutter noisily, their black beady eyes following Emerala's every move.

The seven parrots of the Rebellion—one for each pirate lord of the Western Seas.

The seven screaming demons that live in the belly of the ship.

Evander would snap all seven feathered necks if it wasn't considered a high crime to do so. The damned birds hadn't let a single human anywhere near them since the death of Captain Samuel. They'd been vicious and wild, like to bite down on anyone fool enough to stick their fingers close to the bars of the cage.

The moment Emerala the Rogue entered the hold of the ship the birds were smitten by her. Evander would have called it spell work, had he not been a wiser man—had he not known exactly why the creatures were drawn to her, why they hung onto every single word she said.

Had he not known the value of even a single drop of her blood.

"Pretty, pretty girl," the largest parrot squawks, nuzzling his face against the bars by her hand. "Pretty Emerala."

Evander draws parallel to the Rogue in the pale oval of light, leaning against a creaking wooden beam. "You've taught the foul thing your name, I see," he observes.

The Rogue jumps at the sound of his voice, startled by his presence in the hazy grey of the expanse.

"No," she disagrees. "He started calling me that on his own."

Evander flashes her a look of disbelief, flicking his cap up out of his eyes as he does so. Several black strands of hair fall across his forehead. The Rogue returns the stare, her green eyes unabashed.

"He did," she insists. She shoves one finger through the cage to smooth down the feathers on its cocked head. The parrot squawks happily, ruffling its wings. "He's smart."

Evander clicks his tongue against the roof of his mouth, crossing his arms over his chest. "It's an animal, Rogue. The only thing it cares about is the next time it's going to be fed."

As if the bird knows he's talking about it, the vile thing cocks its silver head in Evander's direction and surveys him through black, marble eyes. It lets out a hoarse scream, beating its wings against its sides.

"He doesn't like you," the Rogue admonishes. "You should be a little nicer."

"Ah, did he tell you that?"

"Yes," she mutters darkly, frowning into the cage.

The parrot screams again, craning its neck towards the bars of the cage. "Ha'Suri! Ha'Suri knows the way!"

Evander's blood runs cold.

"Did you teach it that, too?"

"No. I've never heard him say that until now."

She reaches through the bars, shushing the flustered bird with one waggling finger. With her free hand, she presses an unruly curl back behind her ear.

"Why are you here?" she asks, still staring into the cage.

"I was looking for you. Here you are."

Those green eyes slide his way, flecks of gold cupping her pupil like a halo. She studies him in silence for a long time.

"Well, I'm furious with you. So you can go away."

"Me?" he asks, affronted.

"Yes, you."

"What have I done?"

"You, Captain Mathew—all of you rotten pirates. Time after time you leave me stranded on the ship, acting like I'm some fragile doll of porcelain, and then the one time I finally come ashore—"

She trails off, huffing angrily. "He almost let me die. I saw it on his face—he thought about calling the murderer's bluff."

"He didn't let you die," Evander counters, though he had seen it too. Alexander was planning to play on Evander's desperation in order to finally squeeze some answers out of him—some honesty. It was a stupid plan. Stupid and dangerous. Evander is grateful that Alexander thought better of his harebrained scheme to call a notorious murderer's bluff.

Grateful, because he knows he would have told the captain anything he wanted to hear in order to keep Emerala the Rogue alive.

Before him, the Rogue is sulking into the cage, her lips tight.

"But he *thought* about it," she says.

"Aye, well, that's what piracy is about."

"Betraying your crewmates? Letting renowned serial killers onboard your ship?"

Evander flashes her a grin. "Just a day in the life, love."

The Rogue turns away from him, her attention returning to the cage of fluttering parrots.

Evander wets his lower lip, sighing. "I wouldn't have let him touch you."

No response. The Rogue's unblinking gaze remains trained upon the caged birds. Even so, Evander notices a slight stiffening of her joints—a knit forming between her brows. Above the drooping fabric of her ruffled blouse, her shoulder tense.

He clears his throat.

"Anyhow, I didn't come here to talk about that. I came here with orders."

"Orders?" The Rogue bites back a scoff, still refusing to look his way. "From Captain Mathew?"

"No," he says. "From me."

This gets her attention.

"I want you to stay away from Lachlan the Lethal, do you hear?"

She chews the inside of her cheek, her gaze flitting across his face as if she can read upon his features every unspoken word—as if she can see straight through his constant façade. She shifts her weight to one leg, her right hip jutting to the side in a telltale posture of defiance.

"Why would I go near someone who tried to kill me?" The question is innocent enough, but he knows better. She is cut from the same cloth as him—is driven by the same passions. Some deep-seated predisposition towards insolence is rooted within her. The parrot screams again, this time more agitated than before.

"Murderer!" it screams. Evander shoots a dark glance in the bird's direction, fighting the urge to reach within the cage and snap its neck.

"You have a tendency to put yourself in exactly the wrong place at precisely the wrong time," he explains. "I don't expect a run-in with the Lethal to be any different. He's a dangerous man."

"So are you," the Rogue retorts.

Evander bites back a less than savory retort. "Maybe so, but my goal is to keep you alive. He would snap your neck for the fun of it and enjoy himself while watching you die."

Again, the Rogue's fleeting attention wanders back to the cage. She leans toward the bars, her wild curls obscuring her face from view as she murmurs softly to the largest parrot. Elated, the feathered beast leans into her caress, its pupils pinning in and out with each stroke.

His temper flaring, Evander reaches out and grabs her wrist, jerking her attention away from the cage. They are suddenly nose-to-nose in the belly of the ship, dusky light running across their features like water.

"I need to know that you hear me," he growls.

Anger flashes in the Rogue's eyes as she wrenches her arm free of his grasp.

"I heard you."

"And you'll listen to me?"

The Rogue purses her lips, her own temper bubbling at the surface. "Last I checked, you're not the one in charge," she says at last, her words laced with defiance.

He takes her chin between his thumb and forefinger, forcing her gaze to meet his.

"He will kill you," he says, his voice gruffer than he'd meant it to be. "Don't be stupid, Rogue. You know he will. He's already tried once. I can't lose you. You're too important."

He sees confusion cut through her anger—sees a thousand questions rise to her parted lips. Her breath tickles his skin. Her eyes search his golden gaze for answers. Finding none, she draws away from him, retreating into the feeble protection of the shadows.

"You keep your dirty hands off of me," she snarls. She does a brisk about-face, storming away from him as fast as her feet will carry her.

Evander watches her go, cursing into the emptiness as soon as she's out of earshot.

"Keep your dirty hands off!" screams the parrot.

"Oh, shut it," snaps Evander, whipping his cap off of his head and batting it in the bird's direction. The bird remains at the bars of the cage, its pupils narrowed to pinpricks of black. It hisses at Evander, sidestepping across its perch.

"Daughter of Roberts," the bird says. "Pretty, pretty girl."

The name *Roberts* sends a chill down Evander's spine. He stands frozen in the trickle of pale light, studying the bird. The parrot glowers back, its tongue protruding from its gaping, black beak.

It doesn't matter whether or not Emerala the Rogue chooses to respect his wishes or to ignore them. She's much too important of an asset for him to risk any harm to come her way. He'll have to watch her closely—at least until they arrive in the Eisle.

Feeling irritable, he shoots one last murderous look at the parrot before heading back to his bunk. He enters through the low hanging door of the sailors' quarters, grateful that the rest of the crew will be in the gallery preparing for dinner.

He is caught off guard, therefore, when he sees a lone figure idling silently besides his cot. He draws to a standstill, his hand moving to his scabbard. Lachlan the Lethal waits in the shadows, brandishing a worn leather journal bound by a bit of twine. He shoots a toothy grin at Evander as he draws to a stop before him.

"Interesting choice of literature, boy."

"That's my property," Evander seethes.

"Is it?" the Lethal muses. "Your name is Eliot Roberts?"

Evander is silent in the shadows, his already bad mood souring still further.

"That's the name inside this journal," the Lethal continues. "It's really quite an interesting name, isn't it? Been cropping up a lot, lately. I've heard it before, ye know? From our good friend Charles Argot, shortly before ye slit his throat."

Evander freezes where he stands, his feet turning leaden in his boots. His golden eyes narrow dangerously, his pulse racing.

"I don't know what you're talking about."

The Lethal clucks his tongue. "I thought you'd be a better liar than that, boy."

When Evander doesn't reply, he continues, the ghost of a smile swimming on his lips. "Ye don't think I knew? Ye don't think I was watching your every move? It's very scarce that a ship of the *Rebellion's* fortitude docks within a mile of our shores. I wasn't about to pass up an opportunity to hitch a ride."

Evander remains silent, waiting—his eyes glued to the journal that Lachlan the Lethal clutches within his grasp. His pulse pounds in his ears, drowning out the creak of the ship—the rush of the sea. He feels suddenly dizzy.

"What I can't seem to figure out," the murderer continues, "is *why* ye killed him. He could have been a help to ye, as I'm sure ye know. He was a great scholar. A skilled mapmaker."

Evander bites down on his tongue, pressing his lips into a tight line. At his sides, his fingers ball into fists. From the galley below comes the faint ring of a dinner bell—two erratic clangs that set his heart to pumping faster.

"What do you want from me?" he asks.

The Lethal exhales through gritted teeth, his breath seeping out in a slow rush of air. "What makes ye think I want anything?"

"Everyone wants something."

The Lethal shrugs. "Perhaps I was just admiring your handiwork, one murderer to another. I like the use of the coins over the eyes. Religious, maybe? Or perhaps just a superstitious fear of the ghosts of the dead gazing upon ye."

"What do you want?" Evander demands again, drawing closer.

"Strange, isn't it?" the Lethal asks, one finger running down the spine of the journal. "To have the tables turned on ye. I can tell you're a man that's used to having the upper hand."

Evander bites back the sudden snarl that rises in his throat, suppressing the urge to put a bullet between the murderer's eyes. He takes a steadying breath, battling back his temper. A tepid smile creeps across his face, his golden eyes still shining with frustration.

"Just tell me what you want," he says. "We'll trade. A favor for a favor, aye? One murderer to another."

"I want safe passage on this ship." The Lethal tosses the journal back onto Evander's cot. Evander watches it fall, his stomach twisting. He berates himself for not being more careful—for leaving it out in the open. He should have been smarter—should have been more guarded. He's been off of his game lately, distracted as he is by the map—distracted as he is by that wretched Rogue, parading about the ship as if she's untouchable—invincible.

"You already have safe passage," he reminds the murderer. "You made damn sure of that back on Caros."

"Do you take me for a fool?" the Lethal asks, crossing his arms over his chest. A wraithlike woman, her tattooed figure painstakingly inked into the flesh of his forearm, writhes upon his skin.

"I wouldn't dare," comes Evander's derisive response.

"I heard your plans to hand me over once we dock in the Eisle of Udire. I know what season it is there this time of year. I know what game they hunt. I en't about to be left behind."

"You want me to convince the Cap'n to let you stay onboard," Evander says. It isn't a question—he already knows the answer.

"I do," the Lethal affirms, grinning. "Otherwise, I'll be the first to let him know that it was ye who were the last man to see Charles Argot alive."

Harvest Cycle 1511

Charles Argot knows who I am, I'm certain of it. He knows where I've come from, and why I've left. He's dangerous, the mapmaker. He has too much power.

Does he know what I carry with me? Does he know its value?

And the map he on which he works so diligently—does he know what Samuel and I intend to do with it? Does he understand the kind of secrets we intend to bury?

I am afraid my paranoia has grown into a creeping, shivering beast

But I can take no chances. I am already responsible for too many mistakes—too much heartbreak. There can be no more accidents.

I don't trust Argot I am suspicious of his power.

If he wanted to, he could drown us all.

Eliot

CHAPTER 12

Chancey

PRINCE PETERSON, THE youngest son and only remaining heir to King Rowland Stoward, paces the checkered marble hall of his father's court. His violet doublet swishes audibly as he walks, the whispering sound of fabric on fabric making his skin crawl.

Stopping in his tracks, he glowers at the two Guardians who remain frozen before the grand double doors that lead into the throne room. Thick as they are, the heavy wooden doors with their elaborate brass handles are far from soundproof. On the other side he can just make out the soft twangs of a harp—can hear his father's boisterous laugh emanating out across the hollow expanse. He saw the jester being ushered through hours before, his face painted white and gold, his checkered outfit loose on his frame. The eerie echo of obedient courtiers mirrors the laughter of the king.

"Open the doors."

By now, he has repeated the phrase so many times that the words have lost all meaning to him. Certainly, they've lost all meaning to the two fools that stand guard. The two men blink absently at the space over his head, feigning deafness.

"Perhaps you haven't heard correctly," Peterson snaps. "I'd like to see my father."

"He's busy," the shorter of the two Guardians explains. He glances briefly at Peterson from over the bridge of his nose.

"Doing what?" demands Peterson, his words saturated with annoyance.

"Ruling the kingdom," says the second Guardian, the hint of a sneer inching across his pocked face. Peterson wrinkles his nose, disgusted by their continued insistence upon treating him like a second-class citizen.

"I was unaware that my father hired court fools to help him make government decisions."

Again, the two Guardians at the door pretend they haven't heard a word he's said. He sighs, pressing his heels down hard against the marble floors. One shoe squeaks against the polish.

"Can you at least let him know I'm here?"

"He isn't pleased with interruptions," the shorter Guardian says, taking care to address the empty-eyed bust that sits on a pedestal just over Peterson's shoulder.

"He's not pleased with me whether I interrupt him or not," Peterson says coolly. "I would like to see him all the same." He flashes his sweetest smile—the crooked, un-princely grin that works wonders on all the household maids. Before him, the Guardians remain immune to his charm. The smile falls away, replaced by a grimace.

"As your prince, I order to you open the doors."

Behind him, Peterson hears a familiar voice echo through the cavernous, marble corridor. "Anything you need, you can get from your nurse, your Highness. That's why you have the woman in the first place."

"General Byron," the shorter Guardian says, straightening his posture and nodding his head in a curt acknowledgement of his superior. The other Guardian follows suit, his polished heels snapping together.

"I hardly need a nurse, James," Peterson says, irritated. "I'm nearly fourteen."

He turns to face the general, letting a sullen frown fall across his features. James Byron grins at him, his clean-shaven face unusually bronzed from the sun. His golden cloak, tossed casually over to one side, nearly drapes down to the floor in the spotless hallway

"Fourteen, huh?" James prods him lightly in the chest. "When Frederick and I were fourteen, we were far more interested in chasing after the handmaids than in attending to your father in court."

"You know as well as I that it was never handmaids my brother was interested in," Peterson says dryly.

James narrows his eyes, laughing off the implication of Peterson's words. "You know what I mean, Peter," he says.

"It sounds like you're saying I should be a hopeless flirt like my brother." Peterson observes. "That's hardly proper advice for a soldier to give a prince."

"I'm saying there's better things for you to be doing with your time than standing around arguing with these two fools."

Peterson ignores him. "You'll also remember that by fourteen, Frederick was already sitting my father's council."

"Yes, I do remember. I also remember he hated every moment of it."

"It's my birthright to be in that room with him. I'm nearly an adult."

James pauses, studying Peterson closely for a long moment. "Living through fourteen harvest cycles does not make one an adult. Your father is a busy man. He hired an entire arsenal of staff to attend to your every need."

"An arsenal of staff cannot substitute for a father," Peterson snaps.

For a moment, James's eyes flash dangerously in the well-lit corridor. "Careful how you speak to me, Peter," he warns, his brown eyes still regarding him with compassion. "We're not children anymore. There's certain protocol to be followed. I may be your friend, but I'm still a high-ranking officer in your father's court. Show me the respect I'm due."

"You show me the respect *I'm* due," Peterson nearly snarls. "I don't care how high my father raises you, James, I'm his son, not you. You're still only a soldier, and I'm a prince. Your prince."

James says nothing, his jaw locking—his gaze hardening to stone.

"Does that sound familiar to you?" Peterson asks, hitting him where it hurts. "I know you and my brother had the same fight before he—"

"Died?" James cuts in, flashing a fleeting glance towards the two listening Guardians at the door. The soldiers continue to study the empty space overhead.

"If that's what you want to believe," Peterson mutters.

The sudden sound of bellowing reaches them through the heavy wooden doors. Even muted by the barrier between them, the voice is unmistakably the king's.

"Get him out of my sight," he hollers in agitation. "Immediately!"

Peterson fights the urge to roll his eyes. It's only ever a matter of time before his father loses his temper at those unfortunate enough to be in his company. The doors are wrenched open by the two Guardians that stand guard inside the throne room. The jester falls out into the hall in horror, his checkered paint running down his face in rivulets of golden sweat. The two Guardians who had previously been engaged in unwitting conversation with Peterson jump eagerly at the chance to escort the painted man out of the vicinity.

Peterson seizes his sudden opportunity. In a flash, he races inside the throne room as the heavy wooden doors fall shut behind him. The expanse before him collapses into hushed silence. Even the harp is still, the slender harpist placing his trembling palms on the taut string to steady their vibrating. The herald that stands erect by the door ogles Peterson in astonishment.

Across the room, Rowland Stoward clears his throat. He is gazing intently at his nail beds, his chest still heaving as he attempts to collect himself.

The herald lifts his golden trumpet and allows for four short, brassy blasts.

"Your royal Majesty, your son has arrived."

Silence presses upon the room. Peterson can feel all eyes of the court upon him. All eyes, that is, except for the eyes of his father.

"My son?" Rowland muses, peering now into an oversized ruby that sits in a twisted gold setting upon his middle finger. "Prince Frederick is dead."

The herald oscillates nervously, his gaze twitching back and forth between the young prince and the king. "Y-your other son, your Majesty. The young Prince Peterson."

Silence again. Rowland's eyes slowly rise to meet Peterson's. The throne room seems to stretch on for miles. Peterson has never been closer to his father than he is now. He has never been farther.

"Get the boy out," Rowland says. His voice is unnaturally quiet. "Get him out of my sight."

The wooden doors are again pulled open, slower this time. Peterson listens to the squeal of hinges, blood prickling in his cheeks. His vision blurs. He backs slowly out of the room, dropping into an awkward semblance of a bow as he does so.

The doors are slammed in his face and he stands frozen, his nose pressed against the lines of grain in the wood. At his back he hears James exude a low sigh.

"Peter—"

"Your Highness," Peterson corrects, wincing as his voice cracks.

James clears his throat. "Apologies. Shall we return to your wing, Your Highness?"

Peterson glances over his shoulder and sees that James is observing him with sympathy in his eyes—as though he's little more than a kicked puppy. As though he isn't the sole heir to the Chancian throne. The thought only serves to anger him. He swallows his rising temper, trying desperately to hold on to what little dignity he has left.

"No, thank you. I'd prefer to be alone, if you don't mind."

"Of course." James drops into a low bow before walking away, his cloak sweeping across the floor in ripples of golden fabric.

Peterson fights the urge to flee from the checkered hall, averting his gaze from the relics of war that line the walls—artifacts of courage, testimonies of honor. He's done nothing courageous. He's never been honorable. He's never even been given a chance to be princely—to be royalty. To live.

He doesn't belong here. He isn't wanted. He was always an observant child, and this sentiment had never been concealed from him. Rowland Stoward, his only remaining family member, spent the majority of his youth making certain that the young prince knew exactly where he stood.

Why? he wonders, feeling tears prickling behind his eyelids. *Why does he despise me?*

He kicks at an invisible speck upon the perfectly polished floor, cursing his elder brother for leaving him here alone. Everyone would be happier if Frederick hadn't turned down the possibility of inheriting the throne. His father would be elated to coronate his eldest son and Peterson would have been all too content to receive a lordship—to live out his days in a beach-front estate on the eastern shores of Chancey.

Prince Frederick is dead.

His father's words echo in his mind, taunting him, vexing him.

It is a lie, and everyone knows it. Everyone knows, but no one dares to acknowledge the falsehood. They allow Rowland to live within his delusions—to mourn the son he wanted rather than search for the son he had—the son he still has, somewhere out on the Western seas.

Liar, he wants to scream. *Frederick isn't dead. He left us. He left you. And I was fool enough to stay behind.*

His father's sanity is waning. He's falling into deep denial, and the men and women of his court are too scared to do anything about it. And James—fearless James, his brother's oldest and greatest childhood friend—is the worst of them all.

Peterson pauses in the rounded opening that leads to his private wing of the palace. For several moments, he lingers in the shadows, allowing bitter tears to engulf him. A shard of dusty golden radiance falls into the hall through a quatrefoil that sits halfway up the wall. He moves into the light, turning to face his reflection in an elongated mirror that sits along the length of the wall. He stares at his face—at his mother's face—and curses his father for not being able to look at him—for hating him so.

He doesn't hate you Peter, Frederick used to say, ruffling his wild black curls, so different from the starched auburn hair of the rest of his family. *You just remind him of mother, and it's difficult to be reminded of her. If only you knew how much he'd loved her, you would understand.*

Peterson doesn't understand. He will never understand. He is sick and tired of being the outcast in his own home—of being ignored by the people that are one day going to be his.

His temper flares hot within him and before he knows it, he is balling his fingers into a fist at his side—is thrusting his knuckles into the reflecting glass before his face. Pain, sharp and relentless, shoots through his arm as bright, red blood courses down his knuckles and stains the sleeve of his doublet. Beneath his fist, the mirror has shattered into fragments, the cracks fissuring outward with the audible sound of splintering glass. In every shard, an echo of his his stark green eyes, as vivid as emeralds, stares back at him in resentment.

CHAPTER 13

The Forbidden City

NERANI WAKES TO find Roberts staring at her from the other side of their stone hovel. He perches upon his cot, his hands running absently over a magnificent looking broadsword. The flawless blade catches in the light as his palm moves deftly from the central ridge to the point and back again. The crossguard has been handmade into a complex golden basket, with a glittering emerald sitting in the middle of the oval pommel. It is a handsome weapon—like nothing Roberts has ever owned.

"Good morning," he says mildly when he notices her looking back at him.

"Is it?"

"It is. The sun just rose out over the ocean a few moments ago."

"Oh." Her eyes drift closed. She struggles to hold onto the remnants of her dream, but they have already begun to slip away. Her heart is pounding just a little faster than normal. She had been lost among the pressing stone of a darkened alleyway, cocooned in a thick, golden cloak—a stranger's lips upon her own. The dream had ended in fire—as her dreams always did. She tries to call back greater detail, but the harder she focuses, the more the memory slips into obscurity.

At last she relents, letting the final, fleeting memory dissipate into some forgotten area of her subconscious. She is aware of Roberts's eyes upon her as he tries and fails to be patient. He has something to tell her—something big. She can practically feel the energy rolling off of him. She's always been able to read her cousin like a book—always been able to know exactly what he was thinking and feeling. His presence before her is louder than words as he waits for her to initiate conversation.

She sighs. "Where did you get the sword?"

"It was a gift." His voice is thick with implication. Nerani opens her eyes and rolls to her side, propping up her head with one hand and allowing her disheveled brown hair to pool around her elbow.

"Quite a generous gift," she observes. "It's beautiful. Who gave it to you?"

"Topan."

"That's very kind of him. What's the occasion?"

Roberts clears his throat. "It's tradition for a Cairan man to bestow a gift upon a Cairan woman's father before asking for her hand in marriage."

Nerani sits up straight upon her cot, all traces of sleep falling away from her. She stares at Roberts, her mouth a perfect "o" of horror—unable to bring any coherent words to the tip of her tongue.

Looking sheepish, Roberts continues. "Or," he says, not fully meeting her gaze, "if there's no father present, he would bestow the gift upon the woman's guardian."

"You're not my guardian," Nerani says.

"I'm the only remaining male in your family," he contests, and she hears what it is he really wanted to say. *I'm your only remaining family.*

Anger, warm and familiar, floods her veins. She stares hotly at her older cousin, a challenge written in her pinched lips, her wrinkled brow.

"Ani—" Roberts begins, using the name he called her as a child. He pauses, falling silent. One stray hand tugs at his mop of wild black curls.

"I'm not ready to marry."

At that, Roberts seems to regain his footing. "Ready or not, most young women your age are already betrothed. A few of them have even wedded and bedded their husbands."

She frowns at the term—*wedding and bedding*—and feels her stomach turn. She knows he's right. She knows that, were her parents alive, they would have already found a match for her. It would have been their responsibility to arrange for her a husband, as was custom. With them deceased the responsibility invariably falls to Roberts. It's tradition.

And yet it doesn't feel right.

"I hardly know Topan," she argues, her voice weak. She squeezes her eyes shut and tries to call his face into her memory. Instead, the face that swims into focus is the one from her dreams—square jawed and clean-shaven, with deep brown eyes as guarded as stone. Her eyes open and she blinks several times, her cheeks flushing crimson.

"Your mother had only just met your father when she was promised to him," Roberts reminds her. "And she was a full year younger than you are now."

"I know that."

If she's to be honest, she has long noticed the Cairan king vying for her affections. In fact, until now she has done her level best to ignore the subtle advances he made. It's not that she doesn't think him an attractive man. On the contrary—Topan is quite handsome, with his dark, angular features and his tall build. His blue eyes—so dark that they are almost violet—are often a topic of conversation in the circles of women that congregate in the main cavern. And yet some shard of her subconscious holds her back from accepting his courtship. Some small piece tucked neatly away within her reminds he is not the one—will never be the one.

"And you do know Topan," Roberts is arguing, "He's made quite the effort to spend as much time within your company as he can. Why do you think you've been asked to accompany me to all of those meetings with the Listeners?"

She fixes him with a galvanizing glare. "I thought it was because you needed my expert opinion."

Roberts laughs at that, his expression lightening. "Think about it, Nerani. If you're to be married anyway, you might as well be married to royalty. He's a good man and he'll treat you well. I'd say he even loves you, given the way I've seen him jump to his feet every time you enter the room."

The word *love* singes her like a brand. She sits up straighter upon the bed, her stomach twisting into a knot. Roberts notices her sudden shift in mood and leans forward, ready to defend his choice of words. Nerani is saved from whatever else he might say by the sound of Orianna's voice drifting through the rounded opening.

"Planning to lop someone's head off later today, are we, Rob?"

Embarrassment passes across Roberts's face as he places the sword down onto the cot. "If you're not careful with that tongue of yours, it could be you," he shoots back at her, emerald eyes blazing.

"What's the occasion for such a dramatic choice of weaponry?"

"Topan thinks he's going to marry me," Nerani says blandly.

Orianna's eyes widen into perfect circles. "Well," she says, "can't say I didn't see that coming."

"You're not surprised?"

"Absolutely not," Orianna insists, flipping her raven locks over her shoulder. "The man drools over you like a dog lusting after a bone. It was only a matter of time before he made some sort of grand gesture."

"That's crass," Nerani says, her voice meek. Her cheeks burn.

"Maybe," Orianna agrees. "That doesn't make it untrue."

"Are you here to provide unhelpful commentary, or is there a reason for your visit?" Roberts asks.

"Don't be so wretched, Rob," Orianna retorts. "You're entirely pleased to see me here."

"Is that so?"

"It is. You need me."

"How do you figure?" Roberts asks, pressing a palm into his knee.

"Nerani is set to be wed, and you're still hopelessly alone. I'm the closest chance you have of ever finding a wife."

Roberts flashes her a wicked grin. "I thought Mames aren't permitted to marry."

"They're not," Orianna says, her eyes widening as if she's only just remembered. "I suppose that means you're out of luck. Looks like it's to be the life of a spinster for you."

Their coquettish exchange does not go unnoticed by Nerani. Her frown deepens and she feels suddenly lonelier than she has in months.

"Why are you really here?" she asks Orianna, desperately hoping her friend has come equipped with an excuse—any excuse—to end this conversation. Orianna's sapphire gaze glitters as she flashes Nerani an implicative glance.

She's discovered something, Nerani realizes, her heart beginning to race.

"I'm here to steal you away," Orianna lies. At Roberts's questioning stare she adds, "We're short-staffed in the kitchens today and I've been instructed to rustle up some extra hands."

Nerani jumps instantly to her feet, snatching a crumpled cream cotton petticoat off of the edge of her cot. Shooting Orianna a look of gratitude, she slips into her gown.

"We'll continue this conversation later," Roberts insists in a tone that belies any opposition. He lays back upon his cot, placing his hands lazily behind his head. Nerani waves him off with an idle hand as she laces her corset.

"I'm going to give him my blessing, Nerani," Roberts calls to her as she slides out the door and down the carved rungs in the stone wall. She ignores him, pressing all thoughts of Topan out of her mind as best as she can.

The kitchens are overcrowded when they arrive, the air already hot and sticking from the steam that rises off of bubbling cauldrons of stew. Orianna leads Nerani to a low, stone table, ushering her towards a rising glob of dough that sits atop a dusting of flour.

"Knead," she orders.

"I thought you wanted to talk to me about the tunnels," Nerani protests.

Orianna shushes her, casting a furtive glance around the room. No one is listening to them. No one pays them any attention at all. Orianna pulls on a pinafore, tossing a spare apron towards Nerani. The white square of fabric is already coated with a fair amount of flour, and Nerani finds herself enshrouded in a chalky cloud of powder. Suppressing the urge to sneeze, she ties the apron around her waist and follows Orianna to the table. They knead in a silence for a long time, their heads bowed over their work.

"I suppose you don't want to talk about Topan," Orianna says at last.

Nerani shoots her a sidelong glance. "I want to hear what you've found out about the tunnel exits. I know you've discovered something—it's written all over your face."

A furtive smile sweeps across Orianna's lips. "Am I that easy to read?"

"Like a book," Nerani says. "Now talk."

"First, you should probably add more flour to your dough."

"What?" Nerani looks down at the table before her. Wet, untreated flour adheres to her knuckles. "Oh."

Grabbing some colorless powder from the deep stone basin to her left, she tosses it on the dough. Returning to kneading, she scours the room around them for any potential eavesdroppers. Everyone is wholly devoted to their individual tasks. No one shoots so much as a fleeting glance in their direction. Emboldened, Nerani redirects her attention to Orianna.

"So? Did you find out how they do it?"

Orianna's pause is thick with reluctance. "I did."

"Tell me."

Orianna sighs, her deep blue eyes scanning the room.

"It's some sort of incense. If my sources are correct, when you light a candle and hold the incense within the flame, the burning smoke will show you the correct path to take."

Nerani stares at Orianna for a long time without speaking, surveying her friend's face for any sign of insincerity. She stares back at her, unblinking, her blue eyes earnest. A streak of flour is smeared across her right cheek—stark against her skin.

"You're sure of this?" Nerani asks at last.

"I am," Orianna says.

"It sounds like spell work."

"It does," Orianna admits. "I find that the unexplained often sounds mystical to those who don't know any better."

Nerani considers this, grabbing more flour from the basin. "If it isn't mystical in nature, then how do you suppose it works?"

Orianna gives a small shrug, her shoulders rising and falling beneath her ruffled cotton blouse. "I've no idea, but I'm sure the Mames do."

"Right." The idea of trusting her life to a tool she doesn't understand frightens Nerani. If she becomes lost within the endless, winding tunnels— if she can't find her way forward or back—

She doesn't even want to think about how long it will take her to die there, alone in the perpetual dark.

"How did you manage to figure it out?"

Orianna smiles. "You forget I've spent the majority of my life stealing trinkets in the marketplace. Emerala isn't the only pickpocket with a good sleight of hand."

Nerani raises one eyebrow, leaning back from her beaten lump of dough.

"You stole the incense."

"I did."

"Orianna, if you're caught—"

She trails off, unable to finish her thought. If Orianna is caught having stolen from the Mames, she'll be stripped of her standing and forbidden from continuing her studies. As high as an honor as it is to become a Mame, to be disbarred from the title is the ultimate disgrace. Nerani realizes the weight of Orianna's actions—realizes the part she has played in arriving to this point. Her cheeks flush and she feels suddenly weak in the knees. Still, she cannot bring herself to apologize.

She did what needed to be done.

Next to her, Orianna has stopped kneading her dough. She turns to face Nerani, her dark blue eyes brimming with an intensity Nerani has seldom seen in her childhood friend.

"Do you really believe that Emerala is still alive?"

"Yes," Nerani says, not missing a beat. "I do."

Orianna scrutinizes her carefully, her lips twisting into a reluctant smile.

"Then it's worth it. Whatever happens next—it'll be worth it to have her back with us where she belongs."

Nerani smiles at that, reaching out to place one powdered palm over Orianna's. At her touch, Orianna freezes, her muscles going suddenly rigid. Her eyes roll back into her head, her lids drooping closed. Gasping, Nerani moves to pull her hand away, but Orianna's free hand slaps across her knuckles, holding her in place.

"What do you believe in?" she whispers. Her voice sounds ageless—distant—as if it has echoed from a thousand miles, a thousand years, away.

"Orianna?" Nerani leans forward, her voice nearly inaudible. She scans the room around them, desperately hoping no one is watching—no one is paying attention.

"Two golden men stand in a red sea," Orianna says, her voice melodic. "Two golden men drown in the tide. A traitor. A lover. A woman. Two hearts on the sand. One is shattered. The other is still."

"Orianna," Nerani urges. "What are you—"

Orianna's eyes pop open, fixing Nerani with a blind stare. A shudder runs down Nerani's spine. She tries to remove her hand, but Orianna's grip is like that of stone.

"Run, Nerani. Run as fast as you can. Before the red tide rises."

"Orianna, you're frightening me."

This time, when Orianna speaks, her voice is barely audible. Nerani has to lean in to hear it. She says it like a chant—her voice rising and falling in the cadence of a man marching to war.

"Gold blood bleeds red."

She drops Nerani's hand, blinking furiously. Wringing her palms together in her lap, she takes a shaking breath. Nerani says nothing. There is nothing to say. She sits frozen before her friend, thrust suddenly back in time to her naming ceremony, when the same four words had been uttered to her by Mame Galyria.

Gold blood bleeds red.

After all this time—after all these years—

Nerani had spent the better part of a decade convincing herself that the words were the ravings of an old, batty woman. She had all but dismissed the mantra as utter nonsense.

And now?

Now?

"What was that?" she demands of Orianna.

Orianna holds her shaking hands out in front of her face, staring at them as though she's never seen them before in her life.

"Your future," she says at last.

"My—" Nerani stammers, trailing off into bewildered silence. "I didn't know that you were training in the art of Seeing."

Orianna ignores her, prying her attention away from her hands and fixing Nerani with an accusatory look.

"I saw the general," Orianna says. "And you, wrapped in his golden cloak."

"I—" Nerani starts and stops, unsure of what to say. "Oh."

"He's a dangerous man, Nerani."

"I know that."

"I'm not certain that you do."

There is a long moment of silence between them. The clinking of cutlery against stone makes Nerani wince. The palms of her hands are slick with sweat and she rubs them compulsively against the powdered apron on her waist. It is Orianna who breaks the silence, reaching out and grabbing hold of Nerani's wrist. She jumps at her touch, but nothing happens. Orianna's vision remains clear and focused, her attention as sharp as a knife.

"When you're out there, if you see him, you need to stay as far away from him as you can."

The intensity of her gaze is unnerving. "What did you see?" Nerani asks, unable to help herself.

"Death," Orianna replies. "I saw only death and pain. Promise me you'll stay away from him, no matter what might happen."

Nerani clears her throat, prying her hand away from Orianna's grasp. "I promise," she says. She means it, although her voice has suddenly gone as cold as her insides. "Are you alright?"

Orianna nods, her breath rattling slightly as she inhales.

"It's unsettling, the visions. This is only the second one I've ever had. You can't call on them, they come and go on their own."

"I'm sorry," Nerani says, for lack of anything else.

"Don't be. It's a great honor to study under the Mames. I'm learning so much through their guidance."

Again, Nerani is reminded of how much Orianna has at stake—of how big of a risk her friend has taken in order to help her.

"Thank you, Orianna. You've done so much for me—for Emerala. I know what a gamble you've taken today. Words cannot express how indebted I am to you."

"Just find Emerala," Orianna says. "Bring her home."

"I plan on it. I'll come by to gather the incense from you later on this evening."

She excuses herself from the table, brushing her flour stained hands together. Her mind spins like a top. The room around her feels suddenly small—impossibly small. She wants to be anywhere but here, baking in the stifling kitchens and confronted with ghosts of her past—omens from her future. In front of her, Orianna is watching her intently. A thin sheen of sweat beads her brow.

"You love him," Orianna says. "General Byron. The accusation is jarring. Strange. Nerani swallows back a bitter tasting laugh.

"I can assure you that I don't."

Orianna turns back to her half-kneaded dough, her eyes glazed with sadness. "But you will," she says quietly. "And it will drown you both."

CHAPTER 14

The Rebellion

SOMEWHERE FAR AND away across the endless churning sea, Emerala the Rogue is pretending to be asleep. She lies as still as stone, the back of her arm thrust emphatically across her face, slowing her breathing so that her chest rises and falls convincingly beneath her bodice. A book that she cannot understand sits both open and upside down upon her stomach.

They are drifting, the lookout told her that afternoon, only half a day's sail from the shores of the Eisle of Udire.

Across the room, Captain Mathew and the Hawk are bent close together over a low table, speaking in hushed tones to none other than Lachlan the Lethal. She fights the irritable outcry that rises within her throat, her annoyance spurred on by the conflicting feelings of morbid curiosity and resentment that the two men should already be so intimate with a stranger that had essentially tried to kill her not three days past.

She smacks her lips together and shifts her position, angling her ear closer towards the conversation.

"No, no, no," groans an exasperated voice. Captain Mathew. Or Alexander, as he has repeatedly insisted she call him. "This is all wrong, we have nothing to leverage them with. They'll kill us as soon as they see us if we amble empty handed up to the frost forts."

"Nothing to leverage them with, aye?" Lachlan the Lethal repeats, his voice thick with implication. Emerala shifts again and the book nearly falls from her lap to the floor. She twitches, fighting the impulse to snatch it from slipping any farther. She can feel someone's eyes upon her, and she forces a sleepy sigh.

"He's made that clear, mate," comes the Hawk's pointed voice. A tendril of smoke has wound its way over to where Emerala lies, and she wrinkles her nose to keep from sneezing.

"If ye got nothing, take something, that's how I see it."

"Steal from U'Rel and his men?" Alexander asks. "A pirate would hardly go unnoticed within their midst, and none of us are any good at pickpocketing."

"We prefer to take what we want by bold show of force," the Hawk adds, and Emerala can hear the wicked grin in his voice.

"Likely that's true," the Lethal's voice leaks out with another heave of stinging smoke. "But ye do have a gypsy lass what hails from the island of Chancey, aye? Surely she'd be of some use to ye in that effect."

Emerala tries to keep resolutely still as she feels three pairs of eyes turn to survey her. It's the Hawk who speaks first.

"I'm not putting the Rogue in that kind of danger."

"I hate to say it, but he might be onto something here," Alexander admits. "She could slip in and out and they'd never know she was there. They wouldn't even be looking for her."

A muffled curse of dissent.

The sound of someone slamming their fist down onto the table.

"You'd send her into the midst of U'Rel's men in the winter?" the Hawk asks, a snarl rippling in the back of his throat. "They'd rip her apart, teeth first, if they were hungry enough."

When Alexander speaks again, his voice is tense. "Don't you think I know that? It's my call to make, not yours, Hawk. She's not a coward, and she's not a fool. She's capable of this."

"And," the Lethal adds, "Seems to me that the lass is like to come ashore whether she's invited or not. Better to have her along where ye can keep an eye on her."

Emerala's heartbeat quickens beneath her chest. She fights to keep her breathing steady—to keep her left leg, which has recently developed a ghastly itch, from twitching. For a long time, the room is silent. The quiet is torturous. Endless. The itch in her leg tugs at her attention, begging to be scratched.

Emerala pries open one eye, desperate to see the room. From her sideways vantage point, all she can make out is three pair of leather boots against a crooked, wooden floor. Flickering, golden light pulls through her eyelashes, contorting across her narrow field of vision.

"Lethal," Alexander barks, shattering the quiet.

"Aye?"

"Accompany me back to my quarters. I want to go over the tidal charts to see where the best place to drop anchor may be."

"Aye, Cap'n."

She hears the sound of two chairs scraping across the floor. Footfalls stomp across the creaking wooden floorboards, loud at first and then fading into silence—the echo swallowed by the distant rush of the sea.

"He's not your cap'n," the Hawk hisses, but the door has already swung shut behind them. Brief silence permeates the room. Somewhere beyond the walls, Emerala can hear the waves buffeting rhythmically against the side of the ship. It's a peaceful night, and there is little wind. For a moment, Emerala nearly drifts off into a legitimate sleep. The Hawk's voice breaks the quiet.

"You can stop pretending, Rogue, I know you're awake."

She is so startled by the direct address that her eyes flutter open. She fakes a yawn, stretching upward and blinking at the dimly lit expanse as though she has only just come to. Across the room, the Hawk leans back in his chair, his worn black boots resting upon the table. He grimaces at her, his piercing golden eyes skeptical.

"How much did you hear?" he inquires.

"Of what?" she asks, shutting her book and attempting to look as naïve as possible. A thousand questions bubble within her but she presses her lips together. He peers at her, unimpressed.

"I'll assume you heard all of it," he says wryly.

"Why does Alexander trust him?" she asks, the question spilling away from her before she can stop herself.

A smirk tugs at his lips. "Talking to me again, are you?"

She scowls at him. "I was never not talking to you."

"You've been avoiding me, then," he says.

She holds his gaze in hers, her unblinking green gaze unabashed. Rather than offering a response, she repeats her question. "Why is Alexander working with the Lethal? I thought you said he was too dangerous to be trusted."

The Hawk paws at the back of his neck, the skin around his eyes crinkling into a smile. "Welcome to the world of piracy, love. Dangerous men abound. The cap'n's trust goes to the man who he knows can keep him alive in a pinch. On the Eisle of Udire, that man just might be the Lethal."

"Why him?" Emerala asks.

The Hawk leans forward, his golden eyes glittering. "How many men have you met that have the power to cheat Death?"

Emerala frowns. "None," she mutters.

The Hawk nods, rubbing a palm across the dark scruff on his chin. "The Lethal can—he has."

His tongue drags across his upper teeth and he sucks in air as he studies her closely across the dancing shadows.

"Tell me something, Rogue, how fast can you run?"

CHAPTER 15

The Forbidden City

NERANI IS IDLING in the main cavern of the Forbidden City, her heart racing at the prospect of her impending plunge into darkness, when Topan finds her.

"Nerani," he says, his cheeks flushed. His violet eyes glimmer beneath his thick black lashes. "I've been looking for you. Going somewhere?"

Her skin prickles with unease at the question. For a moment, she frantically wonders if Orianna, changing her mind about keeping the excursion a secret, has spilled everything to the Cairan king. Topan, noticing her confusion, points to her wardrobe.

"It's only that its sweltering in here, and you're swathed head to toe in garment."

She laughs, relief creeping back into her bones. "Is it hot in here? I've been freezing all day," she lies.

In fact, she's drenched beneath the heavy layers of confining fabric. Contrary to her usual cotton chemise and skirt, she has chosen her most elaborate brocade gown, complete with a navy blue bustle and a striped petticoat. Concealed in the heavy blue swath of cloth about her corset is a bit of flint, two narrow candles, and several sticks of Orianna's stolen incense. Her fingers twitch at her sides as she resists the urge to cover her stomach, smiling dimly up at Topan.

He clears his throat, his violet eyes trained upon hers. "I thought I might invite you to dine with me tonight," he suggests. He attempts a smile but appears instead as though he has something stuck in his throat. "In my quarters," he adds, after an uncomfortable moment of silence has elapsed between them.

"Oh." Nerani hesitates before him, her toes pressing into the damp stone underfoot. She doesn't know what to say. What *can* she say? By the time dinner is prepared, she'll be long gone.

"Of course," she lies, and the taste of it is bitter on her tongue. "I'd love that."

Topan's expression brightens considerably at her acceptance, and she cringes inwardly. She imagines the look on his face later this evening when he realizes she was never planning to appear. The image nearly causes her to blurt out the truth right then and there.

Nerani hates lying. She has never been any good at it. Not like Emerala, who could twist any bit of ludicrous fantasy to sound exactly like the truth.

Can, she corrects herself silently. *She can.*

She bites her tongue and bares her teeth, wondering if she looks quite as mad as she feels. Topan lingers before her, waiting for her to speak. She scrambles for something—anything—to say to fill the silence that stretches between them.

"Will Roberts be attending the dinner as well?"

His smile wavers. "No, I thought we might dine alone this evening. Things have been so tense lately; it seemed as though you need a little bit of an escape from everything you've been through."

She doesn't know what it is he sees in her face that makes him reach out to her, but suddenly his slender fingers are grazing her cheek. The movement seems to have been involuntary—he stares at his fingers as though he doesn't quite know how they landed there without any conscious effort on his part. He blinks twice, his thick black lashes fluttering up and down, and fixes her with a look that is meant to be empathetic. "I know the loss has been very difficult to stomach. I understand Emerala was as close as a sister to you."

Nerani recoils, not from his touch but from his choice of words.

"I haven't lost her," she mutters, feeling her cheeks flush.

She is suddenly aware of the time that is slipping steadily away from her. She's eager to abscond from his company—eager to make her way towards the winding tunnels of the Forbidden City. Even from here she can feel the impenetrable darkness pressing against her back, beckoning to her with lifeless, black fingers.

"I have to be on my way," she says, her heart sinking deeper and deeper with each bit of the lie she weaves. "I was meant to meet Orianna for tea quite a while ago."

"Of course."

She notices that he appears lighter—happier—than she has seen him look since their arrival at the Forbidden City. If her heart could drop through her feet and collapse upon the floor, it would. She bites the inside of her cheek so hard that she tastes blood.

"When should I arrive for dinner?" Her voice cracks.

"I will send someone for you when our food is almost ready," he replies. Without warning, he leans forward and kisses her lightly upon the cheek. He pulls back, capturing her gaze within his own, and inclines his head respectfully. "Until then, Nerani."

His voice is low—his tone affectionate. She smiles back at him, glad he did not opt to take her hands, clammy with damning moisture, within his own. With her stomach twisting itself into unfortunate knots, she spins about and heads away as fast as her feet will carry her.

She finds herself lingering before the yawning entrance to the tunnels only moments later, her heart pounding beneath her ribcage. Even here, within the warm reach of the sputtering torches, she can feel the darkness preparing to swallow her whole. She stares at the opening for so long that spots begin to swarm before her eyes.

"Well," she remarks to no one in particular. "I'd best be on my way."

She steps into the opening and feels the immediate, cool rush of darkness upon her skin. Gooseflesh prickles across her forearms and she shakes herself in a futile attempt to quell her nerves.

In the thinning light that spills into the dark expanse she can just make out the gaping mouths of six winding tunnels. She gulps, tasting stale air. Her hands reach into the cloth tied about her waist, procuring one long white candle, a dark stick of incense, and a grey piece of splintering sediment given to her by Orianna. Flint.

She heads toward the nearest rock wall, her hands trembling as she reaches out with the grey stone to strike it upon the jagged surface before her. Orianna had repeatedly attempted to teach her how to strike the flint against the rock face in such a way that a spark would ignite and set fire to the wick of her candle. In spite of her multiple attempts, however, Nerani had only been able to get the flint to light the candle but once.

She tries to appeal to her muscle memory, flicking her wrist in a way that she imagines would cause red sparks to jump to life against the dark stone.

Nothing happens.

She curses under her breath. Her hands shake uselessly as she tightens her grip upon the flint and strikes again. She hears the barely perceptible sound of rupturing stone and a few red sparks fly off of the rock, catching upon the curling white wick of the candle. Nerani watches with bated breath as a frail bead of blue dances upon the braided cotton. And then the red tip of a flame leaps to life. She expels a sigh of relief, careful not to extinguish the small source of light.

Looking around at the still dark tunnels, she feels a surge of unease wash over her. The bead of light in her hand does next to nothing to illuminate the pitch black of the cavern. Instead, it seems to render the tunnels darker still, casting ominous shadows across the jagged limestone.

It is not the candle that matters, she reminds herself. *It's the smoke.*

Careful not to drop the flint, she replaces it within the cloth folds at her waist. She steps back from the rock wall, maneuvering herself so that she faces all six openings in the dark. The small bead of light from the candle burns her eyes, blinding her to the treacherous pathways. Beyond the warm orange glow she sees only blackness. Steadying herself, she places the stick of incense within the dancing light.

Here goes nothing, she thinks.

Almost immediately, she is overcome with a cloying odor reminiscent of the licorice candies Mamere Lenora used to give her when she was a child.

Dark smoke—cast in the most ominous shade of midnight violet she has ever seen—billows out from the stick and fills the expanse before her. She peers, blinking, into the darkness. Waiting.

And then—

She can barely hold back the gasp that rises to her throat as she sees a soft, white something begin to glow in one of the tunnels to her left. She moves towards it, careful to go slowly in order to preserve the tenuous flame. As she approaches, she is able to make out a cluster of fluorescent, white stones protruding from the rock wall just beyond the mouth of the tunnel. She surveys the remaining openings. They are as dark and as empty as they were moments before. She takes a cautious step into the tunnel, her heart racing. As the violet smoke twists down through the tunnel she can see the white glow of several more stones farther ahead.

Her heart in her throat, she follows the incandescent glow at her feet. Her nerves rage within her as she struggles to ignore the absolute darkness clawing at her skin. She focuses on the stones, keeping the incense thrust deep into the fat, blue belly of the flame.

She doesn't know how far she walks before she comes upon a dark cross-roads. Here, the path divides into three narrow tunnels. She pauses to chip away the dripping wax that has hardened itself to her scalded fist. The candle is growing lower and lower with each passing moment. Soon, she'll need to light the other that she has stowed away within her gown.

She hears—or thinks she hears—a quiet scuffling at her back. The hair on the back of her neck stands on end. She turns, cupping the dancing flame with one hand, and peers into the blackness. In the tunnel she has just departed, the white stones no longer glow. Seeing the cavernous darkness behind her instills within her a renewed sense of dread.

There's no going back.

Not anymore.

She thinks of Emerala—of her purpose here in these tunnels—and tries to be brave. Another scuffle in the dark—this time crisper, and more defined, like a footfall. Her blood runs cold.

"Hello?"

Her voice pitches upward into a vacuum of shadows.

Hello, hello, hello...

Her echo mocks her, bouncing off of the slanted walls and fading into oppressive silence. No one replies. Of course no one replies. She feels immediately foolish. It was probably nothing more than a rat.

Pushing the incense back into the flickering flame, she allows the smoke time to fill the expanse before continuing her journey. This time, it is the middle tunnel that contains the glowing stones. She makes her way towards the opening, her feet light upon the cool rock underfoot, and trips, her gown snagging on a stalagmite.

She sees the tepid flame of the candle snuff out only seconds before her skull connects with the stone floor below. She cries out, cringing against the sudden, suffocating darkness as blood trickles into her eyes. Ears ringing, she pushes herself to her knees. She reaches into the cloth to feel for the flint. Relief floods her as her fingers brush against her remaining supplies, still intact within the folds of her gown. She wipes the blood from her forehead with the back of her hand, trying in vain to clear her eyes of the sticking substance.

It is impossibly dark—endlessly dark. Her breath twists in her throat, hitching upon her terror.

"No," she whimpers. "Please, no."

The darkness whispers back at her, a mocking echo of her misfortune.

No, no, no...

Remembering what Topan explained to Roberts about the many deep pitfalls within the winding tunnels, Nerani drags herself gingerly across the cold floor. She clutches the flint protectively against her chest as she feels the ground below her with her free hand. She stops only once she feels herself collide into a solid rock surface. She grabs one of the remaining candles from within her gown, holding it up to the wall as she attempts to spark a new flame. The blood coursing from the gash in her forehead pulses with a heartbeat of its own behind her aching skull. Her fingers tremble and she nearly drops the flint.

"Please," she urges, her voice quivering. Stars dance before her eyes, swirling against the impossible dark. "Please."

Please, please, please...

She strikes the flint again and cries out in aggravation as nothing happens. She strikes again. And again.

Somewhere in the darkness, a warm glow dances into life. Nerani freezes, momentarily robbed of breath as she watches the flickering light chase away the skulking shadows. She presses both hands firmly against the wall in front of her, steeling herself as her vision swarms in and out of focus. In the dim orange light that now ripples across the expanse she can just make out the drying blood crusting the fingers on her right hand.

"Oh Saynti," cries a young girl's voice. "Are you alright?"

Her knees trembling, Nerani pulls herself to her feet. The pain in her head is bad, but not excruciating. She imagines the blood must make it look far worse than it is. She fights to control her breathing as she turns to face the stranger in the cavern.

The young girl that stands before her brandishes a large iron lantern, within which a fat candle twinkles merrily. Two deep blue eyes—nearly concealed by a mop of light brown tangles—glimmer like jewels from out of the dark. Nerani presses her fingers against the gash on her head, studying the girl.

"I know you."

Warmth creeps back into her skin as she moves within the lantern's reach. She recalls glimpsing the girl after she was caught eavesdropping on a particularly heated argument between her and Roberts. The girl had turned and run before they could get a word in, her eyes bright and unapologetic.

"Maybe." The girl's tone is laced with a challenge. She scuffs at the stone underfoot with a big toe.

"What are you doing out here in the tunnels?" Nerani inquires, horrified at the realization that the girl may have followed her. It's bad enough to know that Roberts and Topan will be fraught with worry searching for her, but she can't also be responsible for a missing child.

"I followed you," the girl explains, confirming Nerani's fears.

"Why?"

There's no trace of apology upon the girl's freckled face as she says, "I overheard you talking to your friend in the kitchens about leaving the

Forbidden City and I wanted to come. My mother works there, too—in the kitchens. I was hiding from her when you asked for help in getting out of the city."

"Why?" Nerani asks again, still astounded that anyone would willingly trek into the endless winding tunnels of the catacombs.

"My mother likes to put me to work. If I don't hide from her, I have to pummel dough all day until my knuckles bruise. It's absolutely dreadful."

Nerani is struck by how much the young girl reminds her of Emerala. In spite of the steady trickle of blood drying against the side of her face—in spite of the terror of looming journey in the dark—she smiles.

"And this was a better option?"

The girl shrugs again. "It's far more interesting than breathing in flour all day."

Nerani chews her lower lip, considering their options. Like it or not, the only way to go is forward.

"What's your name?"

"Darianna the Rose."

"I'm Nerani."

"I know."

"Right." Nerani dabs at her head, wiping away a fresh trickle of blood. "Darianna, I can't very well send you back alone, so I'll allow you to come with me, but you have to understand that this isn't an adventure. It isn't a game. There's danger out there in Chancey—real danger."

Darianna's eyes flash with barely concealed excitement. "I understand," she says.

"That was a warning, not a promise," Nerani chastises. *All too much like Emerala*, she thinks. "If we're not careful, if we make one wrong move, the Guardians will drag us before the king and we'll be executed."

"I understand," Darianna says again. She shifts her weight from one foot to the other, growing impatient. The reminder of Emerala again strikes Nerani. She feels something seize within her chest.

"We'd better continue," she says, shaking off the dregs of worry that creep through her. "I've only brought enough food for one, and we've still got quite a ways to go, I'd imagine."

Darianna nods, glowing with anticipation.

Naïve little girl, Nerani thinks, frowning down at her new companion as she takes the lantern and thrusts the incense into the flame within. They continue onward down the middle passageway, allowing the twisting trail of violet smoke to lead them along a glowing path of white.

Naïve as she may be, Nerani is secretly glad for the company in the endless dark. She glances over at Darianna the Rose as they walk, studying the girl from across the shadowed tunnel. She can't have seen more than twelve harvest cycles, if that. She's little more than a child.

Nerani will have to make absolute certain that no matter what the outcome of her journey; she brings Darianna the Rose safely back to the city.

She peers ahead into the darkness, watching in awe as more white stones begin to glow beneath the violet smoke. A path unfolds before them, lighting their way through the tunnels. In spite of her fall—in spite of her unexpected travel companion—she is filled with determination. Her heart brims with resolve.

I'm coming, Emerala.

Harvest Cycle 1511

Here, so close to the arctic north of the Eisle, the days and nights all blend together. In that darkness, I see her ghost. I see her pallid face, her folded hands—the stillness at her throat where a flutter of life used to be.

She haunts me.

I wonder if she haunts him too. I wonder if she leaves him sweating in his satin sheets, choking on his heartbeat. I wonder if he suffers the way I suffer.

I wonder. I hope for it.

Eliot

CHAPTER 16

Eisle of Udire

THE GATHERING SNOW beneath Emerala's feet is beginning to slow her down. She lunges forward, feeling the ridging on the bottom of her tightly laced boots crunch unevenly onto the downy white substance that coats the frozen dirt path.

She would have been better off without any shoes at all.

Her breath solidifies into icy grey vapor before her face, breaking over as she runs. She can hear the men behind her shouting out in their native language. Their coarse voices echo in her ears. They are gaining ground. She isn't as used to the terrain as they are. She can't run as fast.

Her heart pounds painfully beneath her chest. A cramp knots at her side. She peers forward through the snow and tries to gauge how much farther she has to go.

More shouts reach her, closer this time.

She clutches the tattered parcel she carries closer to her chest. She can see the turn off ahead in the darkness.

Almost there. Just a little further.

Swallowing the piercing winter's air, she wills herself to keep running.

She slows down as she reaches the turn, making sure to allow the men to see where she is going. She doesn't want them to lose sight of her in the snowstorm.

That, of course, would ruin the plan.

Curse the plan, she thinks. *And curse me for agreeing to it.*

She rounds the corner and is immediately shrouded in darkness. The snowfall has slowed considerably. The white downy substance is caught in the branches of the evergreen trees that sway over her head.

Before her, positioned between two trees and cutting off her path, is a tall pile of neatly stacked firewood. She runs towards it, her lungs burning.

How fast can you run?

She curses the Hawk for his subtlety.

At her back, her pursuers slow to a stop. They call out to her in their native language. She may not be able to understand their words, but she's quite capable of recognizing the triumph in their voices. They think they have her cornered. They think there's nowhere left to run. They approach her cautiously, their footfalls accompanied by the soft whisper of crinkling snow.

Steeling herself, she turns to face them.

"Ueu no hai'fe e'puel cutal, thief?" the man closest to her demands. His heavy fur coat causes him to appear frighteningly large in the darkness. Emerala takes a slow step backwards, doing her best to look fearful—hopeless.

Wait, she wills the men silently. She glances around at the trees, fighting to control her breathing. Where is Alexander? He should have been there by now—this should all be over.

One of the men draws a cutlass from his belt, bringing the curved blade to rest upon his free hand. As he saws the cutlass back and forth upon the air, he gazes towards Emerala with implication in his dark eyes. A wide grin splits his bearded face in half. Emerala stares back at him. In a moment of cruel realization, she understands that he is pantomiming sawing off her hands at the wrists. She swallows, hard, her impatience with Alexander replaced by the very real sensation of panic.

The stolen parcel in her arms suddenly feels too heavy within her grasp. Clutching it to her chest, she takes a small step backwards. The uneven surface of the stack of firewood pokes into her back. There is nowhere else to run. She glances left and right, trying to ignore the raucous laughter that now pervades the suffocating winter air. She can, she supposes, duck between the trees. The wood is so thick here—the branches of the trees dip down into the snow.

Maybe she'll lose them there.

More likely than not, she'll become caught in the forest, lost and unused to the cold as she is.

She won't get far—not with these men on her trail.

The men are nearly on top of her. The unarmed of the two takes hold of her with an iron grasp, dragging her away from the pile of wood. He towers over her, wrenching her upwards so that only the tips of her toes remain planted on the ground. The parcel drops out of her arms. Its glittering crimson contents spill across the earth. Emerala keeps her gaze pointed down, trying her best to ignore the man's rancid breath upon her face. The rubies at her feet are stark against the white snow.

Like blood, she thinks.

The man jerks her forward, pulling her arms to him. He flips her hands over and pushes back the sleeves of her grey jacket. She glances at the exposed flesh of her wrists, knowing what awaits her.

Any time now, Alexander, she urges silently. She fights to control the crippling panic that blossoms within her. Her wrists are pale in the ghostly moonlight that trickles down between the frost-laden needles of the trees. The rubies glitter red in the snow beneath her. Out of the corner of her eye, she sees the cutlass turn silver, the curved blade filling with moonlight as it rises to strike.

A strangled cry rises to her throat and she shuts her eyes, bracing herself for the impact.

It never comes.

Against the muted snowfall, she hears two sets of boots drop to the ground. Opening one eye, she sees the Hawk and the Lethal—weapons drawn—appearing like wraiths at the sides of the natives.

"Get your hands off of her," snarls the Hawk, his gaze murderous. He raises his dagger over the head of the man with the cutlass, bringing the hilt down hard across his skull. There is an audible crack and the man stumbles, his boots dragging through the snow. Leaning forward, the Hawk snatches the cutlass and flips the blade with practiced dexterity, holding the curve of it before the man's quivering throat.

"On your knees," he orders. He levels a kick at the back of the native's legs, bringing him down hard on the icy tundra. Next to them, the Lethal has already captured and bound his victim with rope, whistling a merry tune all the while. With his opponent secured, the Hawk turns his attention to Emerala.

"You're shaking," he observes. His golden eyes shine like coins in the moonlight. He pulls a pistol from the holster at his waist, pressing the barrel of the gun against his captive's temple.

"It's freezing," Emerala retorts.

"Don't let her fool ye, she's frightened as a hare," Lachlan the Lethal says, flashing her a wicked grin. His rusted dagger rests against the throat of his quarry. Emerala studies the shivering blade, remembering all too well the sensation of cold steel against her skin. Her scowl deepens and she averts her attention away from the murderer.

"Where's Alexander?"

"Here." The captain's voice emanates from out of the darkness behind them. Alexander appears beneath the shade of the trees, flanked on one side by the burly silhouette of Thom, his first mate.

"I see you decided to take your time," Emerala gripes.

Alexander's attention slides briefly toward the Hawk. "I was conducting an experiment."

Out of the corner of her eyes, Emerala sees the Hawk grow visibly tense, his golden eyes flashing against the dark. He says nothing, his brow furrowing as he stares daggers into the snow at his boots.

"What kind of experiment?" Emerala demands of Alexander. "Let's see how loudly the gypsy girl will scream while they saw off her hands?"

"They'd only have taken one," Alexander argues, spreading his arms in a sweeping shrug.

Emerala scoffs. "You're unbelievable."

"Tell me, Rogue, have you been injured in any way?" Alexander's eyes study her from head to toe and back again, as if he'll find the answer there. A small smile dances in the corners of his lips.

"Well, no," she admits. "But you could have warned me that they'd be armed."

"I could have. Would you still have agreed to the plan?"

"Are you mad? Of course not. They could have killed me!"

"How fortunate, then, that we arrived in the nick of time."

"I'm glad to see you find this so amusing," snaps Emerala, her irritation growing by the minute. Alexander studies her, picking beneath his nails with the blade of his dagger and ignoring the muffled protests of the men in the snow.

"You wanted to be a part of the forays ashore," he reminds her. "Didn't you?"

"I did, but—"

"This is what that looks like. Nobody said piracy would be glamorous."

"I'm not looking for glamour," Emerala argues. "I'm just looking to keep my limbs."

"Can't guarantee that, can we?" the Hawk asks, speaking for the first time in minutes. There is an acidity to his tone that suggests his words are not entirely meant for her. All the same, Emerala fixes him with her darkest glare.

"I don't recall asking you."

"Behave, children," the Lethal chides, kneeing his captive hard in the back in an effort to silence the foreign, angry mutterings that have begun spilling out from his lips like a prayer—or, perhaps more likely, a curse. Alexander crosses the gathering snow with ease, brushing the flakes off of his blood-red sleeve as he draws to a standstill beside Emerala. Thom trails closely in his wake, his round shoulders hunched, his eyes downcast.

"Gentlemen," Alexander calls, opening his arms to the two men kneeling before him. "Lovely of you to be so willing to meet with us."

"Si'fi," the Hawk's captive hisses. His thick brows are furrowed so deeply over his eyes that they almost disappear into his face.

"I think you know what it is I want."

He is met with silence.

"Not very conversational, are we?" Alexander drops into a squat, bringing himself eye level with the two men in the snow. "That's fine. You can listen. Allow me to make my demands perfectly clear. I want an audience with your king. An audience, mind you, not a feast."

"No pirates," the man growls. His accent is so heavy that it takes Emerala several seconds to process what he said.

"No pirates?" Alexander repeats. "I didn't think you could afford to be so selective this time of year. Although I suppose there's not much meat on our bones for your liking. You keep them nice and plump down by the farms, don't you?"

He rises to his feet, his hands clasped at his back. His dagger catches the moonlight, gleaming silver against the dark. For a moment, he surveys the men before him, his features twisted in contemplation.

"Thom," he barks, gesturing over his shoulder for the burly first mate to approach. Thom jumps as if he's been branded, scooting across the snow with a wild look in his eyes. His footprints leave shallow grooves in the powder. In front of him, Alexander gestures again, impatiently this time. "You speak the native tongue, correct?"

"Aye." Thom's voice is low against the pressing cold. Cautious.

"Will you apologize to our friends for our gypsy's sticky fingers?" An automatic protest rises to Emerala's throat, but she is quickly silenced by a deadly stare from the Hawk. Alexander continues. "And make it absolutely clear what will be expected of them if they hope to have their precious gems returned."

Thom turns to the men and begins to speak, but the dialect that spills forth from his mouth sounds more to Emerala like gargling than words. The men do not take their eyes off of Alexander as they listen to Thom.

When Thom at last falls silent, Alexander adds, "Explain to them in no uncertain terms that they're to bring me directly to their king, and only to their king. No one else is to know we're here."

Thom speaks again, his fingers twitching at his sides.

"Tell them that they'd be wise not to try any of their tricks."

Again, Thom translates. The man in the Lethal's grasp grins widely at Thom's final words.

"Hur ven?" he asks, and there is a trace of unmistakable defiance in his voice.

With frightening speed, the Lethal thrusts his wrist forward. The man at his feet lets out a guttural gasp. With a thud, his hulking mass drops down onto the ground. Emerala watches, mouth agape, as a deep scarlet stain leaches across the snow near his head. His empty eyes stare into the starry night sky.

"Was that necessary?" Alexander hisses through clenched teeth. The surviving man stares wordlessly at his dead companion, his breathing hitching in his throat.

"He was challenging us," the Lethal remarks.

"You speak their language now, do you?" Alexander asks, fighting to keep his reserve.

"Nay, but body language is universal." The Lethal nudges the corpse with his toe. "Ye should be thanking me. He en't going to try any tricks now."

"That's because he's dead," Emerala observes.

The Lethal flashes her a smile as he wipes his bloodied dagger upon his coat. "One will get us where we need to be just as well as two, aye?"

Alexander presses his lips together in a thin line but says nothing. He shifts his gaze back to the remaining man.

"Get him up on his feet," he orders the Hawk. "We're done wasting our time here. He *will* lead us to the fort."

With a silent nod of assent, the Hawk jerks the man up to his feet and pushes the pistol so hard into the back of his skull that he lets out a small grunt of pain. They head off into the snow, flanked closely by Thom. As the swirling snow engulfs their figures, Emerala sees the Hawk shoot one last look over his shoulder. His golden eyes catch hers, holding fast for a moment too long before he is swallowed by the dark, his silhouette turning first to black, then to grey, and then disappearing altogether.

Emerala idles in the crisp silence of the snow-covered landscape, her gaze trained upon the scattered jewels at her feet. She can feel Alexander's eyes upon her. After a moment she looks up, meeting his gaze.

"Why the theatrics?" she asks. "What are we doing here?"

"You'll find out soon enough," Alexander says, and shrugs. "Let's go, it's not a good idea to fall far behind on a night like this."

He reaches out to take Emerala's arm, but she draws back from him, her temper flaring.

"No," she snaps. "I was almost killed back there. Those men weren't just greedy drunkards—they were trained. They knew what they were doing. If you had waited a moment longer—"

"You survived, hands and fingers and all," Alexander interrupts. "There's no point in being angry."

"No point?" Emerala echoes, her voice growing shrill.

"Rogue." Alexander's tone is a wordless admonition. He reaches for her a second time. Again, she dances out of his grasp. His expression darkens beneath the shadow of his cap. "This isn't the time to be yourself. We need to move quickly."

"I'm not going another step," Emerala declares. "Not until you start telling me where that map leads—not until you tell me why you're willing to let me die for it."

Alexander stiffens, his gaze hardening as he gapes at Emerala through the falling snow.

"I saw it on your face," Emerala continues. "Twice now, you've considered the benefits of letting me be killed by a captor. I don't understand—in just a matter of days you went from treating me as if I were made of glass to tossing me aside the moment my life is on the line."

"That's not true," Alexander insists, reaching again for her arm. This time, his fingers close around the sleeve of her jacket, his grip tightening like a vise. "You haven't the first idea what's going on."

"Then tell me," Emerala pleads. "Let me in on one of your secrets, for once. I've been onboard the Rebellion long enough."

Her voice is drowned out by the resonant blast of a horn. The deep blast rattles her bones, sending her hair standing on end. Quick as lightning,

Alexander closes the gap between them. His lips graze her ear, his breath warming her skin. When he speaks, his voice is hoarse.

"Do you want to know why those men knew what they were doing?" he asks. "You're right—they were drunk, but they weren't drunkards. They're hunters."

Emerala pulls back, trying and failing to get a better look at his face in the darkness.

"Hunters?" she repeats, not following.

"When winter falls, the game migrates across the mountain pass. There is no food—not until spring. There are only the farms, and the cattle they keep there, well—" He trails off, staring into a gale of swirling snow. "There's only human meat."

Without another word, he turns and begins to march after their companions, his eyes scanning the dark line of trees. He drags Emerala unceremoniously through the snow, ignoring her cries of protest as she stumbles in his shallow wake.

As quick as it began, the horn falls silent. The feeble echo of its cry clings to the night like a specter. In the silence, a drumbeat begins. The slow beat sounds out a heavy march. Emerala freezes for a moment, nearly losing her footing in the snow.

Alexander doesn't slow. He doesn't look back. His grip upon her arm tightens as he pulls her deeper and deeper into the snowy wasteland, his cap pulled low and his eyes trained upon the dark horizon. In the distance, the steady drumbeat grows louder—closer.

"The men of the Eisle of Udire are cannibals, Emerala," he calls over his shoulder. "Their hunt is beginning now."

CHAPTER 17

Eisle of Udire

"TRY AND KEEP up, Rogue," the Hawk barks over his shoulder, not for the first time. Emerala scowls at his back, shoving her boot into the snowy footprints that trail behind the pirates like breadcrumbs.

"If there *are* hunters on our trail, it hardly matters how fast we travel," she says, sniffling against the cold. "We're leaving six sets of footprints in our wake."

At her side, Alexander scans the horizon. "Actually, we're safe just as we are. The hunters won't be anywhere near the Frost Forts."

"I take it that's where we're heading?" Emerala asks.

"Aye," the Hawk says. He shoves his captive in the back, forcing the burly man to stumble several steps forward in the snow. One finger jabs over the man's shoulder, gesturing across the dark. "Look."

Emerala follows the line of his finger, studying the swirling wall of white that howls across the landscape. For a long moment, she sees nothing but vague shadows and, beyond that, the black pitch of the mountain pass.

And then it appears—a yawning tower, as wide as it is tall, rising up from the snow like an ancient tree. The imposing fortress is stalwart against the storm; the grey stone and mortar as much a part of the frozen landscape as anything else. Several ribbons of light fall from sparse openings in the curved face, cutting across the untouched snowfall in swaths of gold. Emerala stands in the shadow of the tower, her mouth open as she studies the great, grey structure before her. The cold snaps at her cheeks like a whip.

"Move any slower, Rogue," calls the Hawk, "and you'll turn to ice."

Emerala breaks her gaze away from the tower to see that the rest of her group has moved several yards ahead of her, making their way quickly towards the base of the stronghold. She rushes to keep up with them, nearly tripping and falling into a particularly deep footprint—most likely Thom's.

Falling into step beside Alexander, she adjusts her cloak around her shoulders. "If they're not hunting us, then where are they headed?"

It isn't the captain who answers her, but the murderer.

"They're making their way to the valley, over to the east," Lachlan the Lethal says, falling into step to her left. "That's where they round up all of their cattle."

In spite of her well-laid plans to pretend as though the murderer doesn't exist, Emerala can't help but turn to him in surprise.

"Cattle?" she repeats, horrified. "But Alexander that that they were—"

"Cannibals, yes," Alexander interrupts. Then, "There's no need to frighten her, mate."

Emerala feels suddenly defensive. "I'm not frightened. Just curious."

At her left, the Lethal lets out a laugh like a bark. "Ye should be frightened, little fawn." He grins at her, his blind eye as white as the snow. His sallow, unshaven face is pale against the colorless night. As he leans in close, Emerala catches a whiff of stale liquor and tobacco. The smells cling to him like a second skin.

"When the long snow comes, the real game migrates over the mountain overpass. The natives here en't equipped to make that kind of journey, and so they turn to the villagers to the east. They hunt their own kinfolk and take them to the farms to fatten them up for the harvest. Years of doing that—of feasting on man—will do a body harm. Make a mind begin to unravel." He jabs one dirty finger against the side of his head. "It's beasts that live here, not men."

Emerala gives an involuntary shudder, her nose wrinkling in distaste. Discomfited by the proximity of the Lethal, she turns from him and focuses on the looming stone fortress. From where they stand in the snow, the commanding structure has nearly swallowed the night sky. It looms above them like a beast, the turrets looking to Emerala like great, stone teeth. A rounded doorway sits at the bottom of the keep, barred shut by thick, iron ingots.

In spite of herself, she turns back toward the Lethal. He is still studying her through his one good eye, a grin on the lower half of his face.

"What will they do to us?" she whispers, hoping that the howling wind is enough to mask her voice from the Hawk and Alexander. The last thing she needs is for them to think her frightened. Next to her, the Lethal lets out a laugh like sandpaper.

"If they decide to eat us, ye mean?"

She says nothing, her stomach churning at the very thought.

"They won't," he says. His eyes twinkle and he adds, "At least not right away—you're naught but skin and bones, hardly fat enough for a feast." He pinches her arm and she jumps, wrenching herself from his grasp.

"That's enough," Alexander commands, now several steps ahead. His shoulders are stiff against the cold as he draws to a standstill before the doors. "King U'rel may be a man-eater, but he isn't a savage."

"Are you sure of that?" the Hawk asks, eyeing the ominous slabs of pointed steel, like spears, that adorn the gate.

"We have his hunter and a few of his coveted rubies," Alexander replies. "He'll hear us out."

Thom grunts loudly at that, although whether in agreement or otherwise, Emerala cannot tell. She watches, her heart rate quickening, as Alexander raps loudly upon the door. For a moment, nothing happens.

And then, as if pulled by an invisible hand, the door opens with a low creak. The expanse beyond is as dark and as cold as the night air. Below the howling wind, a soft whispering seems to spill out across the snow. Alexander frowns at the doorway, gesturing silently for the Hawk to lead his captive inside. The Hawk obliges, shoving the native so forcefully that the man nearly loses his footing upon the slick stone underfoot. They disappear into the darkness, one after the other. Alexander stands at the door and waits, his ear cocked as he waits for a signal. The howling wind tugs at the tail of his jacket, threatening to tear his cap from his head.

A moment passes, and then there is a whistle—the pitch high and sharp. Alexander heads through the opening, gesturing for the remainder of the crew to follow. The room beyond the door brings no reprieve from the chill

126

of winter's air. Emerala stomps her boots on the grey flagstone underfoot, drawing her cloak tightly about her shoulders. Outside, the wind shrieks like a starving beast, buffeting into the great, stone fort as if a single gust might be enough to fell the entire structure.

The thought makes Emerala uneasy. She rubs her hands together, exhaling against her fists in a futile attempt to warm her fingers. Her breath hangs, grey and damp, before her lips.

"It's dark," she observes. Glancing around the cavernous room, she takes in the rows upon rows of high, narrow tables that span the length of the room. Her voice bounces off of the high ceiling, resonating across the shadows with an eerie echo. "And empty," she adds, feeling unusually grim.

"Where is everyone?" Alexander asks, his question aimed at no one in particular. He ambles up to the nearest table, running a forefinger across the surface. Bringing his thumb and forefinger together, he inspects his skin for dust. "It looks like its only just been abandoned."

"They've all gone to prepare dinner, I'd reckon," the Lethal mutters. Emerala notices as his grip upon his dagger tightens. "Meals are a communal effort here in the Eisle."

Something in his voice causes a shiver to run down the length of Emerala's spine. A smoky, cloying odor permeates the room. It churns her stomach. She tries not to think about what might be roasting in the kitchens. Tries, and fails.

A thud causes her to jump, her heart rising into her throat. Several hammers click into place on several pistols as the group turns their weapons toward the source of the sound.

"Err," mumbles Thom, standing astride an overturned chair. He gives a sheepish wave, averting his eyes. "Sorry."

The Hawk spits out a curse, lowering his gun. "Dark Below, are you trying to get us all killed?"

"En't trying t'do no such thing, mate," mumbles Thom, looking thoroughly apologetic.

"Aye, well, keep it together you clumsy bastard."

"That's enough," Alexander admonishes, flashing the Hawk a steely glare.

The groan of hinges brings their attention to the far side of the room. A door, all but invisible against the dark stone walls, is swinging slowly open. Flickering candlelight sweeps across the overlarge flagstone, bathing the crew in a square of gold.

"Captain Mathew of the *Rebellion*" croons a voice. "Please, come in."

The voice, husky and stilted, belongs to that of a woman. Emerala notices as Alexander and the Hawk exchange silent glances across the dark expanse.

"He goes first," Alexander orders, gesturing toward the prisoner.

"Aye, Cap'n," the Hawk says, shoving the burly man through the wide opening and into the well-lit room beyond the doorway. Alexander follows close upon his heels, holstering his gun.

"In ye go, then," barks the Lethal, giving Emerala a boost as he hurries her along through the doorway. Thom falls into step behind them, his fingers hovering upon the hilt of his sword.

The door swings shut as soon as they have gathered within the brightly lit room. Emerala jumps, glancing over her shoulder. No one is there. She swallows, feeling thoroughly uncomfortable with the whole affair. Next to her, Lachlan the Lethal stands at attention, his fingers steady and his features carved from stone. She takes inexplicable solace in his composure, and finds herself inching a step or two closer to him. The tobacco stink that clings to him like a shroud is a comforting change from the acrid smell of burnt flesh that seems to ooze out from between the stones. He hardly notices her approach, so focused is he upon the looming throne that sits at the far end of the low room. Emerala follows his gaze, her attention landing upon a slender woman clad in assorted furs. Her high cheekbones are taut as she surveys the crew from behind rich, honeyed irises. Her hair, knotted and thick, falls past her shoulders and down onto the floor of the room. Around her neck she wears a multi-tiered necklace of pearl white stones.

Teeth.

Human teeth.

Emerala gapes at the necklace, her stomach feeling more than a little ill. The woman rises from her throne and Emerala notes with a start that the chair upon which she has been seated is adorned with thousands upon thousands of blood red rubies. Even more startling, however, is that the chair itself, ivory and resplendent beneath the flickering sconces on the wall, is made entirely of bone.

"Captain Alexander Mathew," she croons, her broken accent alluring. Her ruby red lips unfurl into a smile. "Good of you to come. I have always had a fondness for Mathew men."

Alexander hesitates, his cheeks reddening ever so slightly. Emerala fights the urge to roll her eyes.

"You knew my father?" Alexander asks.

"Oh, yes," the woman murmurs, delighted. "I did."

"He's been here before?"

The smile on the woman's face fades ever so slightly. "You ask a lot of questions, Alexander Mathew. Strange, that you would be so, how you say, brazen, when my kin remains in your captivity."

One talon like finger, the tip filed to a point, unfurls as she gestures languidly toward the man who kneels upon the floor at the Hawk's feet.

"My turn to ask. Yours to answer, and answer true. What is the meaning of this?"

"We'd like an audience with the king," Alexander says.

"Is that so?" asks the woman, biting back a smile. "You may have it. Speak."

Alexander pauses, swallowing as he inclines his head respectfully. "If it's all the same to you, we came here to speak with King U'Rel."

The woman laughs, and the sound is like the resonating of bells. "He is here," she says, fingering the necklace of teeth that rests against her collarbone.

Alexander falters, stammering before saying, "I don't understand."

"Simple," the woman says, and shrugs. She steps down from the dais of rubies and bone, moving closer to the crew. She walks as if she's dancing through water, the deep burgundy folds of her gown rippling against an unseen current. "He's dead. I am king, now. King Ha'Rai."

Her honeyed eyes fall onto the man upon his knees.

"Tur'ret, ueu pa no Fi'ito come thetal?"

The man frowns, shaking his head. "Si'fi, ueu tur'ap Fi'ito ams e'te."

Ha'Rai's attention snaps back upwards. She studies Alexander through eyes that have gone cold. "Tur'ret tells me you killed my best hunter."

"My crew isn't always the most practiced in patience," Alexander says.

"Who killed him?"

The Lethal clears his throat, a barely concealed smile prying apart his lips. "That would be me, I'm afraid."

"Your name," Ha'Rai commands.

"Lachlan the Lethal, at your service." He pulls his cap from his head and dips his chin downward in a derisive bow. His bald scalp gleams red in the firelight.

Surprise flashes across the woman's lovely face, and her honeyed gaze slips back towards Alexander. "The assassin," she muses. "You harbor murderers on your ship?"

"Accidentally," Alexander says, shrugging as though it could not have been helped.

"Mhm," the woman breathes, pressing her blood red lips together as she draws up short just inches away from Alexander. One pointed fingernail traces a trembling circle on a brass button at his lapel. "If your father were here, he'd expect you to take more responsibility than that, Captain Mathew. You are the master of your ship, are you not?"

Beneath the shadows, Emerala sees the hint of a wince on Alexander's face. Before he can rustle up a retort, Ha'Rai is speaking again, her fingers dancing down the length of his jacket.

"It is a little boy's game you are playing, Captain—allowing yourself to be dragged along without knowing where it is you are going."

"I don't—"

She shushes him with a finger, pressing it lightly against Alexander's lips. It trembles against his skin, and Emerala notes that the tremor seems an odd contrast to the woman's practiced reserve. Against the firelight, Alexander's cheeks flush a duplicitous shade of crimson. Emerala finds herself repressing yet another eye roll as Ha'Rai turns her attention to the captive that kneels on the ground before the Hawk. When she speaks her native language, her words drip, sticking and sweet, from her lips. Her mastery of the language is a surprising contrast to the halting, butchered dialect produced by Thom.

She falls silent, listening carefully as the man on the floor offers up a reply, his consonants sharpened like spears. At the front of the room, Ha'Rai's expression turns first to surprise—then to anger—before passing once again into a placid, flawless countenance. She turns to Alexander, running the tips of her nails along a ring of bone that sits on her thumb, the bleached porcelain stark against her bronzed skin.

"You take my rubies?"

"Borrowed," Alexander corrects, appearing to have regained some of his decorum. "And we have every intention to return them to you." He gestures towards the Lethal. Flashing a grin to no one in particular, the murderer pulls open his tattered black jacket and pulls out the ripped parcel. He tosses it on the ground before his feet, allowing the glittering rubies to clatter across the flagstone.

"Safe and sound," he declares.

Ha'Rai stares at the jewels and says nothing. A crease forms between her finely plucked brows as she continues to play with the ring of bone.

"Untie Tur'ret," she orders. "Do it now."

The Hawk hesitates, his pistol still sitting at the back of the man's skull.

"You heard her," snaps Alexander. "Do it."

"Aye, Cap." The Hawk procures a small blade from within his sleeve. He saws deftly through the rope, his expression unreadable.

As soon as the binding hits the floor, Tur'ret scrambles to his feet. Wringing his wrists, he glowers at each of his captors in turn. His attention stops at the Lethal and his already sour expression darkens still further, his lips curling downward beneath his thick beard. He spits on the floor at the Lethal's feet.

"Enough," Ha'Rai barks. "Leave us."

For a moment, it looks as though Tur'ret has failed to hear her. He continues staring at the Lethal, his gaze murderous. And then he drops into a low bow, angling his attention toward Ha'Rai. Barking out a word in his native tongue, he turns and disappears through a small, dark opening to the right of the throne. The door slams in his wake, setting the firelight to dancing. Shadows flicker ominously across the curved stone walls. Emerala has the sudden and unwanted sensation of being in an oven, the heat turned too high. She swallows thickly, resisting the urge to fan at herself.

At the front of the room, Ha'Rai's attention is fixated, once again, upon Alexander.

"You come all this way to steal my rubies and kill my hunter. Such a fuss, all to see me." She leans down with startling grace, grasping a ruby between two trembling fingers. When she stands up again, her eyes pass briefly over Emerala. The ruby in her hand is as red as blood.

"You have my attention, so speak."

"I'm trying to translate a map," Alexander says.

Ha'Rai's eyes narrow dangerously. "You take the life of my best hunter for a bit of parchment? A costly price, no?"

"It's worth the price," Alexander assures her. "I can't make out a word of it."

"And you think I can?"

"Not you," Alexander says. "We're looking for Ha'Suri."

At that, Ha'Rai's bares her teeth in a full grin, her red lips nearly splitting her face in two. Somehow, Ha'Rai is even lovelier when caught in a laugh, and Emerala finds her dislike for the woman deepening.

"You have sailed far for nothing, I am afraid," Ha'Rai says. "Ha'Suri is pirate lore. The story of the four wind women is a tale that men tell to keep themselves warm at night."

"Are you certain of that?" Alexander asks.

"Ha'Suri is the wind woman of the north, no? I am king in the north. I tell you true—there is no Ha'Suri, not here and not over the mountain pass."

Alexander turns to the Lethal, fixing the murderer with a beseeching glare.

"You said—"

"Don't whine, boy," barks the Lethal. "It's horribly self-indulgent."

At the far side of the room, the Hawk leans back against a stone pillar, looking thoroughly pleased. "This probably isn't the best time, Cap, but I tried to tell you."

"You told me nothing," Alexander spits, rounding on the lanky pirate.

"I told you Ha'Suri was an old legend," the Hawk reminds him. "You didn't listen to me. And now, in a move that surprises no one, you've gone and made a fool of yourself all on your own."

Emerala turns away from the bickering pirates, glancing back toward Ha'Rai. The woman watches the pirates with amusement, running her trembling fingers across her necklace of teeth.

"Ha'Suri doesn't exist, and U'Rel is dead," Emerala observes. "That leaves you. Can you translate the map for us?"

Ha'Rai's honeyed eyes snap towards Emerala. "So the girl speaks. I was beginning to think you were a mute."

"Not a mute," Emerala says. "Just observant. You said you've met Samuel Mathew before. The map Alexander has in his possession is his father's map. Do you know it?"

Ha'Rai hesitates, her eyes glimmering as she studies Emerala. Behind the women, the pirates have fallen silent. Emerala can feel the Hawk's glare boring into her, but she ignores him, waiting for the woman crowned king to offer up a reply.

"You are asking dangerous questions, girl," Ha'Rai warns. "I am not sure if you will like the answers."

Emerala ignores her. "Do you know it?" she repeats.

"Impudence like yours is an ugliness," Ha'Rai says, fingering a ruby. The multifaceted gem glows in the firelight, sending refracted crimson light dancing across the stones. "You should be more respectful to royalty."

"You admire force," Emerala counters. "You'll answer my question honestly."

A small smile dances in one corner of Ha'Rai's lips. "Interesting. Why do you say that?"

"Because we stole from you—we killed one of your people in cold blood—and yet you haven't ordered us killed in return. You wanted to be king, so you assassinated the current king and claimed his throne. No one here calls you usurper. No one even calls you queen. You took what you wanted, and now all men bow to you. Whatever code you live by in the north, it's a code that respects strength."

This time, Ha'Rai's flashes her a wolfish grin, baring her sharp canines. "You are smarter than you look."

"Do you know the map?" Emerala repeats.

"I know it," Ha'Rai admits at last. At Emerala's back, she hears Alexander exhale quietly. The sound is one of relief, although whether he is relieved to have answers or relieved that Emerala's tongue hasn't gotten all of them sentenced to death, she can't be certain. Lachlan the Lethal lets out a low whistle, the sound barely masking his amusement. Only the Hawk is silent, still, his body tense and ready in the shadows.

At the front of the room, Ha'Rai is still studying Emerala with unabashed interest. "Samuel Mathew had it made here," she says at last. "Bound."

"What does that mean?" Alexander asks, drawing to Emerala's side.

"Samuel's map is dead speech," Ha'Rai explains. "It cannot be translated. Only unlocked."

Alexander runs his palm over his scruff, considering this. "Unlocked? So we need a cipher?"

"Not a cipher," Ha'Rai disagrees. "A key."

She returns her attention to Emerala. "You remind me of a man I knew, once. Same strange green eyes—same unapologetic vigor." Stepping closer to Emerala, she peers carefully into her face, scrutinizing every detail written upon her olive skin. Emerala fidgets beneath her stare, fighting the urge to break eye contact.

"Green eyes like yours are a singularity, did you know that? In all the old stories, green eyes symbolize royalty."

Emerala's reply is dagger-sharp. "I'm not royal."

"No?" Ha'Rai muses. "That's the very same thing the last green-eyed visitor told me." Her gaze travels away from Emerala and toward the far end of the room, where the Hawk stands against the pillar as if frozen, his features hardening to stone. "I remember him well. He traveled here with a child with sharp, golden eyes and a tongue for deceit. He was only a boy, but boys grow into men, do they not?"

The Hawk says nothing. His golden gaze smolders with displeasure.

"I was a girl, then, not a king. Curious, isn't it, how things tend to come full circle?"

Out of the corner of her eyes, Emerala sees Alexander turn to look at the Hawk, his temper burning quick and hot—the muscles in his jaw already working. Before he can speak, a gong resonates somewhere in the distance. The sound reverberates through the room, vibrating the flagstone underfoot and rattling Emerala to her core. Ha'Rai extends her arms as if in welcome.

"We dine," she cries.

Alexander scowls, approaching the dais. "What about the map?"

Ha'Rai closes the space between them, taking his face between her trembling palms. "First, we dine," she whispers, her lips dancing only inches away from his. "We will discuss more tonight. Already my hunters have led the rest of your crew inside. You do them an unkindness, Captain Alexander, to leave them aboard in this storm."

CHAPTER 18

The Great Forest

It took a full day for the rain to stop. Nerani sits up straight in the obscurity of the cool, stone tunnel, alarmed at the sudden silence that permeates the damp air all around her. She leans forward, allowing her hair to fall into her face as she peers out of the narrow opening. Several poplar trees march across her narrow field of vision like faceless, white soldiers. Sunlight falls through the leaves overhead, dappling the saturated leaves underfoot with patches of gold.

Her stomach growls loudly and she places one idle palm over her corset.

"Darianna," she whispers, nudging the sleeping young girl at her feet with her toes. "Dari, wake up, the rain has stopped."

The young girl grumbles incoherently, her pale brown hair tumbling into her eyes as she rolls over on her bed of leaves. Nerani watches the rise and fall of her shoulders, jabbing her big toe into the girl's back. Dari sighs, relenting, and sits up. Her dark blue eyes glare blearily at Nerani.

"I was having a good dream," she mutters.

"We need to keep moving." Nerani rises to her feet, ignoring the sensation of pins that tingles through her legs. She runs her hands down the thick fabric of her petticoat, fussing over a wrinkle within the folds of her gown. "The sun is out. It won't do to be caught right in the opening of the tunnels."

"It won't do to be caught at all, truly," Darianna retorts, pulling herself to her feet.

"Yes, well, all the more reason to make haste."

Nerani knew the risks of leaving the city. She knew how dangerous it would be—how high the chances were that she would get caught.

She knew, and yet she had still been willing to risk it. Alone.

She hadn't expected company—hadn't wanted it. And now, somehow, she has been saddled with a traveling companion still young enough to be considered a child.

Overnight, the stakes have grown considerably higher.

Nerani watches Darianna as the girl fastens an old russet shawl about her shoulders. Her cream colored gown is woven with simple cotton. The hem hangs just above her ankles, exposing her dirty feet. The plunging neckline of her white chemise is frayed—one ruffled sleeve hangs loosely off of her shoulder. She looks every bit a Cairan—every bit an outcast in Chancey.

Darianna's countenance is in stark contrast to Nerani, who took great pains to make sure she looked the part of a Chancian common woman.

Yes, the stakes have grown much, much higher.

Nerani shoots a sideways glance at Darianna as they step out of the tunnel and into the copse of poplar trees. "We'll need to do something about your clothes as soon as we get to the city."

"What's wrong with my clothes?" Darianna gropes around within the sleeve of her white chemise, at last procuring a red apple from within the folds of fabric. She bites down, spraying juice into the sunlight, and offers the fruit to Nerani.

"No, thank you," Nerani says, ignoring her growling stomach.

Darianna shrugs and takes a second bite, smiling easily into the sunshine. Her bare toes curl into the soil underfoot. Juice trickles down her chin. For a moment, Nerani finds herself resenting the girl's fearlessness— her sense of ease. She resists the unnatural urge to slap the smile off of her face. Darianna notices her staring, and she smile widens to a porcelain grin. She throws her arms out to the sides, turning into a graceful spin. Her cotton gown fans out about her. Nerani is reminded of a flower breaking through the frost—unfurling beneath the tickling sunlight. Darianna laughs aloud, spinning to a stop a few yards ahead. She runs a hand through her disheveled hair, her chest rising and falling; her cheeks flushed.

"It's good to be out here in the fresh air again, don't you think?"

Nerani inhales sharply, taking an unexpected sip of the crisp morning air—the scent of the world after a rainstorm. A wordless admonition dies in her throat, and she finds herself relaxing ever so slightly.

"It is," she agrees. "That doesn't mean we shouldn't be careful."

"Of course not." Darianna sashays to the nearest tree and takes hold, swinging herself around the trunk with ease. The leaves shudder on their branches, sending a few fluttering to the ground at her feet. Peering over her shoulder at Nerani, she adds, "I highly doubt any Guardians are going to be spending much time out here in the Great Forest."

"Maybe not," Nerani agrees. "But we can't be too cautious."

Her eyes scan the clustered trees all about them. Already, Darianna has already disappeared into the undergrowth, a quiet folk song trailing behind her as she moves effortlessly through the trees. Once again, Nerani finds herself reminded of Emerala. She swallows thickly, heading off after the young girl with her eyes open and her ears peeled.

After a time, she begins to relax. The tension seeps out of her body as a slight weight lifts from her shoulders. Overhead, the birds chitter amongst themselves in a cacophony of whistles and cries. The summer sun is warm against her skin and soon she begins to feel hot beneath her constricting layers of fabric. She pauses, fanning herself, and studies the idyllic woodland all about her. It is such a drastic change from the stale darkness of the Forbidden City that she feels suddenly giddy with relief. She inhales deeply, her eyes drifting closed.

It takes her several seconds to realize that the birds have stopped singing.

Her eyes pop open, her heartbeat already quickening. The total silence is unnerving. Unnatural. She was raised to be suspicious of the quiet— to question the stillness. The world, Mamere Lenora used to tell them, is always quietest before a storm. So too, she would add, are men just before they make a terrible decision.

The memory makes Nerani's skin crawl as she studies her surroundings, her ears ringing in the quiet. She stands in a small clearing, cast into shadow by a tall outcropping of stone upon which crumbling leaves and burnt auburn pine rot into compressed, pungent earth. Before her, thick shafts of golden sunlight carry in flecks of glimmering motes upon the air. She stares upward into the tangled branches. The birds stare back at her.

Where is Darianna?

Her silent question is answered almost instantly by the gauche sounds of the young girl sprinting through the underbrush. Several of the birds overhead take off with a shrill *chirrup* and a flutter of wings. As the girl enters the clearing—panting, sticks in her hair—Nerani immediately notices the look of panic upon her face.

"He saw me before I saw him," she gasps, her cheeks rosy from running. "I ran just as soon as I noticed him standing there, but it was too late."

Nerani's heart constricts within her chest. "Who? Who noticed you?"

A stick cracks somewhere out in the woods. Darianna swallows, closing the distance between them as though a fire has been lit beneath her.

"A Guardian."

Nerani falters. "Was he alone?"

"I think so." Darianna's blue eyes are wild with fear. "Maybe. I don't know."

"Was he alone or not?" Nerani asks, and her words fall away from her as quickly as a whip. "It's a simple question, Darianna."

"Yes. Yes, he was alone."

"And you know for certain that he saw you?"

Darianna nods. "I'm sure of it."

There is a fallen tree only a few feet away from them. The wide trunk, relenting at last under the strain of bearing its own weight, collapsed upon the earth with enough force that it gouged the soil with its body of heavy bark. It is hollow and weak now—a skeleton cloaked in musky green moss. It is a perfect hiding place.

"Get in," Nerani says, gesturing towards the opening. "Do not come out until I tell you."

"What about you?" Darianna asks, one leg already disappearing within the hollow.

"I'll be fine. Just stay in there and keep quiet."

She watches the opening in pithy silence as Darianna withdraws completely beneath the cover of moss. She pinches the inside of her wrist, fighting in vain to control the bundle of nerves that has coiled within her. If there is one Guardian in the woods, there will be others. It will not be long before the man informs his troops of the young woman alone in the woods and they begin to track her whereabouts.

She curses herself silently. She should have been more careful—should have paid closer attention. The presence of the Guardians this deep in the woods is a surprise, to be sure, but she should have been ready for anything.

There is the sudden sound of birds clamoring excitedly as a colony of thrushes take flight overhead. Hooves clatter against stone. Nerani can feel the shudder of it in the calloused skin of her heels. A large group of people is approaching—no doubt a platoon of Guardians hurrying at their companion's bequest. Several low shouts emanate from the forest, bouncing off of the thick trunks of the trees and setting her heart to pounding. From the sound of it, they are somewhere overhead, idling upon the stone outcropping that looms above the clearing like a dark cloud.

If they are to look over the edge of the outcropping, they will most certainly see her waiting there like a sitting duck. She will need to find a hiding place, and fast. Directly over her head she can hear the sound of hoofbeats settling to a stop against loose earth. There is a sharp whinny and she stifles a gasp as several clods of dirt break away from the roots and break apart against her forehead. She slides across the slick, rotting leaves underfoot as silently as she knows how, careful not to make a sound. Her back presses into the damp earth—her fingertips close around bulging roots.

Somewhere overhead, the remaining hoof beats have slowed to a stop. She hears a grunt and a whinny as someone slides from their saddle and onto the ground.

"See anything?"

Nerani silently urges Darianna to stay quiet and still within the trunk of the tree. She is starkly aware of her heart thudding too hard and too fast against her ribs. She does not move—she does not breathe. Dirt tickles the tip of her nose and she fights the sudden, terrifying urge to sneeze.

"No," calls another voice directly above them.

"Of course not," snaps a third voice.

"Are you sure you saw a girl, Thompson? Seems highly unlikely, alone in the woods like this."

"I saw her," insists the Guardian called Thompson. "I swear to you, she ran off in this direction."

"And how old did you say she was?"

"I didn't."

"You didn't."

"Well, I didn't get close enough, did I?" Thompson snaps, his tone defensive. "My orders were to report back to you *first* before taking any sort of action. I hardly got a good look before she went hopping off among the trees like a frightened hare."

"Of course you didn't," another Guardian groans. "Bloody waste of our time, this."

"Careful," chides the first man. His voice is low and dangerous, pitted with a nervous undercurrent. A horse whickers softly, pawing impatiently at the ground. Several more clouds of dirt burst across Nerani's shoulders.

"Careful of what, then?" demands the Guardian. "Who's around to hear me gripe? The birds? A fat, tasty boar, perhaps?"

The low rumble of laughter that spills away from the group is cut off abruptly, likely the result of a silencing glare from the superior officer.

"These woods are dark and deep," says the first Guardian. "You never know what may be lurking just beneath you."

Nerani's blood runs cold. Her lungs burn from the effort of holding her breath. Her vision swarms before her eyes, the greenery twinkling with speckles of white. Overhead, she hears a low scoff—the sound of a boot scuffing against the earth.

"Unless General Byron himself is lying in wait to catch me grumbling, I think I'll not fear any woodland eavesdroppers. Anyhow, we haven't found much among these cursed trees."

"Certainly haven't found the Forbidden City," adds another Guardian, dangerously close to her. Nerani exhales in surprise, her sprawling horror only mildly abating at the sound of a well-timed whinny from one of the fickle mares overhead.

How can they know about that? She scowls up at the dirt, her gaze fixating angrily on a wriggling earthworm that protrudes from the earth. *It's impossible.*

A whistle, sharp, sets her heart to racing.

"Alright, men—let's carry on, then." The voice sounds far away, the sound swallowed by the dense vegetation.

There is the shuffling sound of hooves scraping stone as the men and horses prepare to leave.

And then, "Bloody waste of our time, I say."

And then the last of them is gone, leading his horse away by foot. Nerani continues to glare at the fat, writhing worm, her gaze all but burning a hole through the earth.

It's just not possible. They don't know where we've gone. They can't.

The thoughts repeat on a useless loop within her head, rattling her nerves. The power of the Forbidden City—the protection—lies in its secrecy. With that secret gone, with the Guardians out searching for their hiding place—

Her thoughts trail off into silence. She does not dare to think what will happen if they are discovered.

"Well."

Nerani is startled out of her reverie by a voice that emanates from deep within the stump. Darianna the Rose pries herself out of the opening, her light brown hair laced with leaves.

"That was uncomfortable." She shakes her limbs, massaging her arms as though they fell asleep during her interlude within the tree.

"Would you rather have been caught?" Nerani snaps, her singing nerves getting the best of her temper. She presses her palm firmly against her cheek, surprised to find her skin hot to the touch.

Darianna glowers at her for a moment. "You seemed to do quite fine just where you were. There was no need to nearly break me in half. Halfway through, I found a toad lodged in my corset." She shudders at the memory, sticking out her tongue.

"You needed to stay hidden from them," Nerani says. "They're danger-ous men."

"I know that."

"I had no idea they would be combing the forest. They aren't supposed to know the Forbidden City exists."

"Looks like they do," Darianna observes, and the blunt ease of her observation acts as yet another sharp reminder of Emerala. Nerani frowns down at her, watching as the girl plucks pine needles from her hair. She is so young—so naïve. She should be quivering with fear at the prospect of running into the Golden Guard and yet here she stands, utterly unaffected by their near brush with Rowland Stoward's puppets.

Nerani had always admired Emerala's fearlessness—had aspired to be more like her. Here, in the dappled light of the forest, her heart still pound-ing, she stares at the young girl before her and wonders if fear is a good thing after all.

It has kept Nerani alive. That counts for something.

A bird screams overhead and she feels the sweeping shadow of wings brush across her face.

"We can't stay here," she announces. "We need to head into Chancey."

Darianna's plump lips drop into a frown. "I thought our plan was to stick to the forests for now."

"Plans change. We can't stay this close to the entrance, not with Guardians searching every corner of the woods. We need to get within the walls of the city. It'll be easier to blend in there, surrounded by people."

"Where will we stay?"

Nerani considers their options, turning over every possible venue in her mind. The apartment she shared with Roberts and Emerala will be too dangerous—the building was owned by a half-blooded Cairan and rented to tenants of largely Cairan origin. It will have been all but emptied by now, the residence crawling with soldiers. The cathedral, too, will only draw attention. That's where she met him—General Byron—it's the first place he'd expect her to return.

She doesn't want to think of him there, tall and menacing among the rows of candles, a fire burning in his coal dark eyes.

She doesn't want to think of him at all.

"Mamere Lenora's," she says at last. "We'll be safe there for a night or two while I search for news of Emerala."

"Isn't that a whorehouse?" Darianna asks. Her blue eyes widen into circles of fascination.

Nerani grimaces. "It is," she assents. "Which is precisely why it won't be crawling with Guardians. We can stay out of sight easily enough."

A small smile dances in the corner of Darianna's lips as she tries to hide her excitement. "I've never been to a brothel before."

"I'm sure you haven't," Nerani says tersely, taking hold of the girl's arm. Pulling her along through the thickening trees, she adds, "I don't plan to allow you to make a habit of it, either."

Darianna beams up into the mottled sunshine, her smile radiant, her cheeks pink. "This is already a wonderful adventure, don't you think?"

Nerani picks up her pace, tugging the girl's arm a little bit harder.

"Try and keep up," she orders, ignoring her. "We're going to get you back home as soon as we're able."

Together, they head off silently through the woods, keeping their eyes peeled and their footsteps silent. Overhead, the birds lurk in the thinning trees and ogle the meandering women as they head towards the forest's edge.

CHAPTER 19

Eisle of Udire

THE DINING HALL of the Frost Fort is only faintly illuminated. Tendrils of smoke swirl languidly above the heads of its patrons, casting the majority of the room in formless shadow.

Among the midst of dining natives and shivering silverware sits Emerala.

She is as still as stone, her stomach ill. Lodged between the hulking figure of Thom and the leaning form of the Hawk, she does her best to keep her eyes trained upon the splintering wooden tabletop before her. All around her are the silent, watchful members of *the Rebellion's* crew. A quick head-count upon arrival to their table revealed that all members were accounted for. Still, Emerala cannot shake the ominous feeling that churns within her. She shifts her weight on the elevated stool upon which she sits, her dangling feet cramped within their boots as they sway inches over the cold floor.

A plate of food sits before her, but she does not eat. She dare not touch the smoked meat that stares stagnantly up at her. Ha'Rai swore to them that it was the last of the wild bison left over from the spring hunts, but she doesn't believe the honey-eyed woman for a moment.

Not everyone at the table shares her reluctance.

At her side, Thom chows down upon the food with surprising ease; the sloppy sound of his smacking lips attracting the attention of many an uncomfortable member of the crew.

"We picked up Thom at one of the Eisle farms years back," the Hawk explains, perhaps noting the shade of green that tints Emerala's cheeks as she watches the first mate from the corner of her eyes. "Mate's eaten his fair share of human. Whether its beast or man isn't an issue for him."

Emerala swallows the lump that has formed in her throat. "I can see that."

"Here." The Hawk nudges her arm, pushing a bronze goblet across the table. The rounded base scrapes against the wooden surface. Emerala eyes the goblet suspiciously, doing nothing. "Drink up," he instructs. "It'll warm your bones."

Emerala lifts the goblet and sniffs at the rim of the glass, peering at the golden contents within. "Hmm," she murmurs, taking a slow sip. The warm dram slides down her throat, bringing heat back into her aching joints. She eyes the Hawk across the rim of the goblet, eyebrows raised.

"It's just a little ale, Rogue. You haven't eaten in hours. You need something in your stomach."

"Since when do you care?" she asks hotly.

His lip twitches ever so slightly. "You're the one furious with me, Rogue, not the other way around."

Emerala searches for a scathing comment and comes away with nothing, instead finishing the remnants of the goblet in a slow chug. The Hawk's golden eyes remain glued to her, his expression unreadable.

A chuckle from across the table draws her attention away from the lanky pirate. Lachlan the Lethal fidgets with the plate of meat before him, his one good eye flickering back and forth between Emerala and the Hawk.

"Seems to me like he cares an awful like, don't ye think?"

Emerala glowers back at him and says nothing, her cheeks feeling unnaturally warm. At the end of the table someone says something too quietly for her to hear, eliciting a laugh from several of the men. The Lethal studies her reaction, spinning his plate around and around on the wooden surface.

"It's curious, is all I'm saying."

"You're not to speak to her," the Hawk warns, voice low.

The Lethal doesn't miss a beat. "Last I checked, ye weren't captain. Anyhow, the lass hardly needs ye to protect her, try as ye might." His good eye bores into Emerala, the creases crinkling at the edges.

"I'm seldom wrong," he admits. "But I'm not too proud of a man to admit when I am. I sorely misjudged ye that day in the woods. You're no little fawn, you're a wolf."

"What do you mean by that?" Emerala asks.

"Only that I took ye for a creature to be preyed upon—a weak and easy kill. But the way ye handled yourself back there with Ha'Rai—I'd say ye were as capable as any man on this crew. Ye have my respect, for all it's worth."

"It's worth nothing," the Hawk reassures him. Emerala shoots him a scathing glare before returning her attention to the Lethal. The murderer grins at her, several of his golden teeth catching in the light.

"Everyone tells me that you're famous," she says. "I travel in the company of murderers and thieves. Good ones. Skilled ones. You make them all quake in their boots. Your respect means something." She flashes him a smile in return. "Thank you."

It was said to ruffle the Hawk's feathers, and it works. Next to her, the lanky pirate grows visibly tense, nearly snapping his fork in two. The Lethal lets out a laugh, his blind eye winking shut.

At the far end of the room, a gong sounds out. Emerala nearly jumps out of her skin. She watches as several scrawny and nervous looking young men rush to dole out second helpings of food. No one comes to their table. No one even looks their way. Emerala turns on her stool and scans the room, glancing toward the high table where Alexander is seated at the right hand of Ha'Rai.

"The guest of honor appears to be enjoying himself," the Lethal notes. Emerala watches as Ha'Rai leans into Alexander's shoulder and whispers something into his ear, her blood-red lips grazing his skin. He laughs, his cheeks dimpling, and Emerala finds herself inexplicably annoyed. She turns back towards the table, her cheeks flushing red, her skin feeling unnaturally feverish.

"They say her hands shake because she's eaten too much human meat," the Lethal explains. Emerala glances up at him, confused. "Did ye see the tremors of her fingers? They've all got it, the natives. Dead man's hand, they call it here. De'rea haba."

"De'rea haba," Thom echoes, looking up from his plate long enough to shake a palm in a theatrical imitation of Ha'Rai's tremors.

"Why does she call herself king?" Emerala asks. Next to her, the Hawk stabs his dagger into the piece of meat before him. Grabbing the handle, he pulls the weapon out of the meat and inspects the blade.

"The men of Udire wouldn't unite behind a queen," he explains.

Emerala glances over her shoulder, studying the radiant form of Ha'Rai seated at the front of the room. Her blood-red baubles glitter in the firelight. Her pointed nails trace a line down the seam of Alexander's jacket and he nearly spits out his drink, his skin turning a traitorous shade of crimson. Irate, Emerala turns her attention back to the table.

"Can't they see that she's clearly a woman?"

"Like ye noted back in the throne room," the Lethal explains, "the people of the Eisle admire force. The natives are like to fall in line behind whomever they fear the most."

Emerala considers this. "Do you fear her?"

Several members of the crew glance up at the question. Whether or not the famed murderer is afraid of anything is a subject of constant debate within the bowels of the ship. Across the table, the Lethal's dark eyes glitter like jewels. His smile widens at the corners as he regards her in silence, paying no attention to the eavesdropping crew on either side of him.

"Aye," he says at last. "Here, surrounded by deep stone walls and outnumbered by her bestial hunters, I do. Only a reckless man claims to be incapable of fear." He leans against the table, his voice lowering. "I am not a reckless man, lass."

"Seems to me you were reckless in the Westerlies last spring," the Hawk comments, prying his dagger out from the slab of meat only to thrust it in the pith once again. "Or perhaps you were looking to be caught and exiled to Caros. An early retirement, was it?"

If the table was not silent before, it is silent now. Emerala watches as one corner of Lachlan the Lethal's smile twitches.

"If ye think I was sent to Caros against my will, ye'd be incorrect," he says, his voice even. His eyes have dropped into dangerous slits.

"And we're expected to believe that you were there on holiday, mate?"

"I was there because I needed to be there."

"Aye? And what was it you were doing when we stumbled upon your sorry arse?"

"Looking out for an old friend. Unfortunately, he was killed."

The words are said deliberately. Slowly. The gaze that is fixed upon the Hawk is, Emerala thinks wryly, murderous. Next to her, the Hawk clenches his mouth shut, the lines around his jaw deepening. She can feel his arm stiffening as it brushes against hers, his fist closing tightly about the dagger in the meat.

"Hawk," she hisses, nudging him. His grip only tightens, the blade catching in the firelight. "Hawk, not here."

He breathes deeply, his nostrils flaring slightly as deep and obvious dislike creeps into his gaze.

"Evander," she says, using his given name for the first time. She places her fingers across his forearm, surprised to feel the tendons in his arm go lax at her touch. His golden eyes flicker to meet hers for an instant before dropping back towards his plate.

"Is there a problem here?"

Emerala spins upon her stool to see Alexander idling behind them. She wonders how long he has been standing there, listening. The table is teeming with tension. Behind them, the rest of the dining hall is rippling with a different type of movement than before. The dinner is drawing to an end.

"None at all," the Hawk assures him, his voice tight. He replaces his dagger into the hilt at his side. "Any news?"

The crew leans in almost unanimously, their eyes trained upon their captain, their reflexes tensed and ready to reach for their weapons.

"Ha'Rai claims to know how the map was bound. She has agreed to meet with me alone to decipher it." He lets the words hang upon the smoky air. The table before him is quiet. Emerala already knows the question that no one wants to ask.

What about the rest of us?

"Lachlan will stay here with me to translate the map," Alexander explains. A muffled protest from the Hawk draws all eyes to him. He fumes, his brows knitting over a turbulent gaze as he fights to remain composed.

"With all due respect, Cap'n, I think it should be me."

"Why?" Alexander asks.

"Because I—"

"Because you lied to me?" Alexander interrupts. "Because, once again, you've withheld critical information from me after repeatedly reassuring me you'd told me everything you know?"

"I never lied."

Alexander leans in close, his voice lowering dangerously. "I heard her, Hawk. You were here before, weren't you? You're the golden-eyed boy Ha'Rai was talking about."

The Hawk is silent, his lips disappearing in a thin line on his face as the muscles in his jaw work beneath his skin.

"That's what I thought." A humorless smirk pulls at Alexander's lips. "Unless you feel like telling me what it was you were doing here the last time, you're sitting this one out."

The Hawk exhales sharply, the sound just short of a scoff. "Fine," he snarls. "Entrust your life to a murderer."

"We've all got blood on our hands, Hawk," Alexander says. "At least he's honest about it." He turns his attention to the rest of the crew, bringing his row with the Hawk to an abrupt end. "Listen closely. When the cleanup begins, you'll need to get out and get out fast. Head back to the ship. Raise anchor and ride the tide in the cove. Wait for me there as long as you can."

The order is weighted—heavy with caution. Emerala feels suddenly uneasy. "What's going on?" she asks, searching the stony faces of the crew of answers.

It is Thom who speaks. "Food be rare this winter. The snows have claimed many at t'farms. Ha'Rai en't so inclined t'let us go easy."

Emerala swallows, feeling nauseous. Her skin grows hotter still, and her vision goes suddenly fuzzy. She glances down at the meat on her plate, feeling something sharp and acidic rising to her tongue. A hand, cool and firm, presses against the back of her neck. Alexander's mouth is next to her ear, his breath causing her curls to tickle her cheek.

"Stay with the Hawk. Do as he says."

"I can't come with you?" she mutters into her plate.

"No." His answer is immediate. Final. Across from her, Lachlan busies himself with examining the ceiling. Emerala frowns deeply at him, but holds her tongue.

Slowly, his eyes still upon the joisted ceiling, the Lethal rises from his stool. As he does so, Emerala catches a glimpse of his dagger sliding up the sleeve of his jacket. She watches as he and Alexander head across the crowded room, disappearing through the door that leads into Ha'Rai's room of bone and jewel.

As if on cue, a gong rings out. Its deep peal reverberates through the room, slicing through the noise like butter. Immediately, the occupants of the room rise and begin clearing the tables. For a moment, attention is turned away from the crew.

And then a man appears at the Hawk's back, his cheeks ruddy with drink, his features twisted into an expression of rage. Emerala glances up at him and recognizes him at once—he is the same man the Hawk disarmed and threatened in the snow, the same man that chased her through the storm only hours before, his curved cutlass reserved for her narrow wrists.

"Si'fi no et pa'al," he snarls, shoving the Hawk in the back with one balled up fist. "S'or el ni'id."

The Hawk remains as still as stone, glaring forward as if he's unaware of the man behind him. All around them, the crew is silent.

"S'or el ni'id," the man repeats, shoving the Hawk harder this time. Emerala glances down at the native's belt, unsurprised to see the curved blade of the cutlass nestled in its leather scabbard. She swallows, studying the Hawk's face for any sign of having heard the man. He continues to sit facing forward, his golden gaze burning.

"S'or el ni'id!" the man shouts. Spittle flies from his lips.

151

"He wants you t'get up and help with the cleanin'," Thom translates; worry creasing his face as he glances between the angry native and the unmoving figure of the Hawk.

The Hawk cracks his neck to the side, his expression unreadable. "Doesn't matter what he wants."

"Aye, and why's that?" Thom asks.

"Because he's already dead."

"Si'fi, et fi'al," snarls the native, grabbing a fistful of the Hawk's jacket in his hand. Quick as a flash, the Hawk spins on his stool and slashes the man's throat, his dagger dragging across his pallid skin with ease. The movement is effortless, practiced. Emerala stares in shock as the man drops to his knees, blood gushing from the gaping wound beneath his beard. Without batting an eye, the Hawk levels a kick at the man's chest, sending him falling hard against the ground. He gropes within his jacket with his free hand, procuring two copper coins from deep within a pocket. Tossing them upon the floor, he watches as they clatter against the flagstone. At his feet, the dying man's mouth opens and closes like a fish.

The Hawk turns toward the occupants of the table, his golden eyes cold.

"Well," he mutters. "I'd say we've overstayed our welcome."

As if his words are the kindling to a fire, everyone begins moving all at once. Emerala remains glued to the stone, watching the blood seeping through the grooves in the flagstone, her head spinning—her vision contorting. She feels like fainting. Odd, she has never been the type of woman to swoon at the sight of blood.

A hand, strong and steady, grips her arm. She looks up to see Thom's face inches away from her own.

"Let's go, Rogue," he says. "No time t'waste, aye?"

She sways where she stands, the meager contents of her stomach threatening to upend on the floor. Dizziness washes over her in waves. Thom's grip tightens, and she feels him wrench her several steps across the stone floor. Somewhere behind her, she hears the sound of running footsteps, the ringing of steel finding steel. The Hawk crows out a curse and a command, but his words sound foreign against the sudden ringing in her ears.

"Rogue!" the Hawk bellows. The proximity of his voice startles her, dragging her back to the present. She finds his golden eyes across the pandemonium. Blood spatters the side of his face, gluing his wild black hair to his skin.

"Run," he orders. "Now."

Harvest Cycle 1511
Eisle of Udire

The mountains here are endless—endless. The days are short and the nights unbearably long. Winter has sunk her claws deep within me and refuses to let go.

There is magic here. Old magic, trapped beneath the glacial ice. We can feel it, all of us. We can hear it crying out in the dark. If I was never a damned man before, I am certainly one now. Saints forgive me; I'm doing it to protect my children. What kind of man would I be if I didn't?

What kind of man will I be once I do?

What will be left of me when I've spilled my blood into that cup?

There is no going back, not anymore.

Eliot

CHAPTER 20

Chancey

SERANAI THE FAIR is halfway through her lukewarm cup of afternoon tea when the front door opens and Nerani the Elegant stumbles into the foyer. Strange, the sight of Emerala the Rogue's prim and proper cousin is out of place among the threadbare carpeting and moth bitten drapes of Mamere Lenora's brothel. Nerani stands framed in the doorway, statuesque and alarmed, her cheeks rosy from running and her traveling skirt bunched within her fists. Behind her trails a much younger girl—no more than a child—with a freckled nose and a lopsided grin. Two blue eyes as wide and as round as a barn owl peek out from beneath a mop of pale brown hair. She blinks twice, slowly, gaping at the harlots that mill about the tea room, their gossip rising and falling in waves.

At the far side of the room, Mamere Lenora rises from her divan with a strangled cry, her voice caught between joy and concern. Seranai's lips dip into a scowl and she sits back against her creaking chair, setting her cup down too hard against her lap.

"Mamere," Nerani cries, already weaving through the room. She throws herself into the matron's open embrace, her lovely blue eyes jeweled by tears. "Oh, Mamere, it's so good to see you."

Mamere Lenora draws the woman in closer, her own tears running freely.

"My dear, sweet girl," she murmurs. "You're all right."

Seranai studies the interaction, her mood souring impossibly. Mamere Lenora's demeanor, as a rule, is gruff and commanding. She is a woman who demands respect—who draws eyes solely by walking into a room. She is brassy, bossy, and boisterous. Never, in Seranai's several weeks at the

155

brothel, has she seen Mamere Lenora act so unprofessionally—so emotionally—toward anyone.

She nearly vomits into her teacup.

Next to her, Winifred Alastor clutches at her skirts, her fingers positively trembling. Seranai shoots her a sideways glance, taking note of the unmasked dislike inscribed upon the harlot's features.

"What's gotten into you?"

"Nothing," snaps Whinny.

"Right." Seranai lifts her teacup to her lips, forgetting that she has already drained the dregs of her cup. Only the loose leaves that stain the bottom reach her lips, the taste bitter on her tongue. She tries her level best to ignore the tearful reunion going on at the far side of the room. Nerani the Elegant doesn't know who she is. She has no idea of Seranai's affiliations with Emerala—has no idea that it was Seranai who paid the Hawk to take Emerala away.

And she'll never find out. Who could possibly tell her? There isn't a soul left on the island of Chancey who knows what transpired between Seranai and the golden-eyed pirate. Seranai is safe in that respect, at least.

"It irks me, you know," says Whinny. Seranai turns back toward the disgruntled harlot, her attention divided. She does her best to look interested.

"What's that?"

Across the room, Nerani is being ushered through the vestibule and into Mamere's personal dining space. It's a space reserved only for the matron's most honored guests, of which Seranai—although not a harlot—most certainly isn't. She has never so much as set foot in the room. The sight of Nerani stepping inside, the freckled brat at her heels like a dog, makes Seranai's insides boil. Beside her, Whinny is well into her tangent, her words going largely unheeded by Seranai.

"It's just that she goes everywhere with Roberts, doesn't she? She's the problem, that's what I think. She and his rotten sister. They're a distraction. They discourage him from anything what might be good for him. And you know, I've said she's just always been meddlesome. Always."

Whinny places her teacup onto the low table before her, glaring at the empty doorway to Mamere's dining room with a wounded expression on her face. Seranai scrutinizes the harlot closely, picking back through her tirade. Her thoughts catch on the name Roberts like a fish on a hook.

"We were childhood friends, you know."

Whinny is staring at Seranai through sad, doe eyes, her lids ringed with last night's charcoal paint.

"What?" Seranai asks, distracted. She wishes she could get close enough to Mamere Lenora's door to hear the conversation through the cracks.

"Nerani and I," Whinny says, her face wrinkling. "We played together as children. It weren't really her that was awful, you know. It was that meddling sister of his, Emerala."

The sound of Emerala's names tug at Seranai's insides, twisting her gut and pulling hard. She has a sudden vision, sharp and clear, of a bloated body sinking towards the ocean floor, pale skin and blue lips and wide, green eyes staring—unseeing—up toward the mottled surface of the water. Black curls fan out from a lifeless face. The thought is satisfying. For a moment.

And then it becomes horrifying.

Seranai blinks several times, clearing the image from her head. Her nails dig into the skin of her palms, nearly puncturing flesh. She refocuses her attention on Whinny.

"I didn't know you knew them—Roberts and his sister."

"Oh, I did," Whinny reassures her. "They were like family. Mamere raised them, you know. After their family was slaughtered. Terrible thing." She titters softly, three long fingers rising to cover her lips. The crumb of a tea biscuit clings to her lip stain. "You know," she says, leaning in close as if sharing a secret. "Roberts was always a little bit in love with me."

"I rather doubt that," Seranai says, but the doleful harlot is already lost in her own rewritten memories. "Excuse me," Seranai says, rising from her chair without waiting to hear if the woman has any more to say. An unrequited lover is useless to her. But Nerani the Elegant on the other hand—someone like her could be dangerous. Seranai moves through the room with ease, ignored by the lingering women that whisper amongst themselves, chatting and drinking and napping the day away. They dislike her, these women of the night. They dislike her fineries, her morals—however loose, however fleeting. They are women without. They are creatures in limbo, waiting to come alive when the sun dips down below the western sea.

She is idling here, hiding among them.

Perhaps Nerani the Elegant's arrival means the time for idling has come to an end.

She draws short just before the door to Mamere's dining quarters, her ear tilted toward the wood. The carpet underfoot, worn down by years of boots trudging up and down the hallway, muffles any footfalls. Through the thick wood, she can just make out the sound of a whispered conversation. She inches closer, her heartbeat quickening beneath her chest.

And then a voice close to the door catches her attention, the sound taking the shape of words. It is Nerani the Elegant, her tone tense—her words blunt.

"I need to find her, Mamere. Emerala is out here."

There is a sigh, followed by a deep silence. Parchment crinkles and Mamere's voice strikes up in the quiet. "These walls have ears my dear, and my, do they hear a great deal in the night. Men's lips are as like to become as loose as their breeches in the arms of the right woman. I haven't heard news of Emerala. Not even a whisper."

"She's alive," Nerani insists.

"I know you want to believe—"

Nerani cuts the matron off. "I don't want to believe, Mamere. I know. I didn't see her die. Nobody did. Surely you must be able to find out something for me."

Seranai draws back from the door, her breath hitching in her throat. Once again, the image of Emerala, bloated and sinking, flashes through her mind. Her olive gown fans out from her silhouette like a cotton ghost, the fabric rendered weightless by the sea. This time, the corpse blinks, a smile splitting her face like a wound. Seranai stumbles backward across the hall, clutching at her heart. Her palm stings and she glances down to see that her nails have indeed pierced through skin. Blood forms in crescent pools upon her flesh.

She cannot afford to have this kind of complication—not now. Not when the summer tide is ebbing and the leaves are beginning to drop.

Look for me when the leaves turn gold—that was what the Hawk told her. That was his promise to her. She cannot be discovered now. She won't be discovered now. Certainly not by a meddlesome gypsy such as Nerani the Elegant—prissy little wench.

Her mind churns, running through her options. She always has options. That's what a lifetime of clawing her way up the social ladder has taught her. There is always something to be done if you're willing to get your hands dirty. She thinks of Whinny, and of the way the harlot had withered at the sight of Nerani, the joy leeching out of her skin and giving way to naked distaste.

Seranai needs a scapegoat. She needs someone obvious, someone garish, someone with a preexisting grudge.

She needs someone stupid enough to do the deed that needs doing.

Glancing over her shoulder, Seranai searches the tearoom for the wretched harlot. She spots the wild head of curls seated at the gaming table, bent over a crumpled pair of cards. The woman fusses with her pierced earlobe, her painted eyes incapable of carrying out a bluff.

Yes.

A plan comes together, falling into place with sickly sweet satisfaction. Seranai heads back through the room, weaving through the women of the night with a newfound conviction in her step. She pulls an empty chair across the room, ignoring the stutter of the legs upon the floor. Dropping down into the seat at Whinny's side, she leans in close to the focused harlot.

"I've just heard a whisper in the house."

Whinny clutches her cards closer to her chest, trying and failing to conceal her hand from Seranai's eyes. A thin layer of dirt lines the bed of her nails. The cards are weak. She'll certainly lose the round. If it were Seranai, she would fold—would wait for something better to come along. But Whinny is not Seranai. Whinny lacks the gift of foresight—lacks the ability to sit back and wait.

"There's always whispers going about the house," she counters, pushing her coins toward the gathering pile at the center of the table.

"Always about you?"

Whinny puts her cards down at that, her flat nose twitching in consternation.

"I fold," she tells the woman across from her. Her opponent, a short, plump woman with a nest of gold ringlets on her head, sniffs loudly.

"It's too late to fold, you've already placed your bet."

Whinny smacks her cards down on the table. "Keep it," she snaps, rising from her chair and stalking out of the room. Seranai follows her, moving like water where Whinny had trampled across the floor, her footfalls a mere whisper against the carpet. She comes face to face with the harlot in the darkened hallway beyond the tea room.

"Out with it, then. Who's doing whisperings about me?"

Seranai makes a show of glancing left to right, scanning the empty hallway for any potential eavesdroppers. Whinny follows her gaze, her arms crossed tightly over her chest. One foot taps out an impatient rhythm on the floor. She is restless, paranoid. Seranai will make easy work of her.

"It's Nerani the Elegant," she lies. Her grey eyes are cool—unblinking. Whinny's arms uncross, her fingers falling limp at her sides, her palms upturned.

"How could you know that?" the harlot demands. "She's only just got here."

"I overheard her talking to Mamere through the door as I was heading back to my quarters."

Whinny's eyes widen into coins, the dark rings around her lids giving her the appearance of a striped rodent that digs through trash in the streets.

"You eavesdropped on Mamere?"

To Whinny, the act is an unspeakable crime. Mamere is all-powerful. Mamere is a woman not to be crossed. Mamere is a goddess in these crumbling halls—untouchable, impeccable. Seranai knows better. Mamere is a good businesswoman, nothing more. If you cut her open, she'd bleed the same as any other mortal being.

"Quiet," Seranai whispers, glancing around again. "I didn't mean to, of course. But I heard your name through the door and I just had to stop. And you're lucky I did."

"Why?" Whinny demands. "What did that rat have to say about me?"

"She's planning on outing you—saying you're a half-blood."

Whinny sputters indignantly, searching for coherence. "I'm nothing of the sort," she snaps. "I'm pure blood as they come. Me mum was a homemaker, and my father's old Chancey blood. We don't have a lick of Cairan in the family. Not a lick."

"You don't have to tell me," Seranai assures her, reaching out to brush the woman's arm. Whinny crumples into her touch, already coming unraveled at the lie. So gullible. So stupid.

"You know how it is out there," Seranai reminds her. "It's a witch hunt. Rowland Stoward doesn't want proof, he just wants bodies to burn."

"But why me?"

"I don't know," Seranai says, the lie slipping out as easy as air. "She told Mamere she's looking for her cousin."

"Emerala the Rogue," Whinny whispers. Loose strands of hair fan out from behind her ears, caught up in the static of the sun-spoilt hallway.

"Nerani thinks that the Guardians know what happened to her."

"Of course they know what happened to her," Whinny snaps. "They killed her, and rightly so, if you ask me. All that girl did was get herself caught up in one mishap after another. She was trouble—trouble for Roberts and trouble for everyone unlucky enough to know her."

Seranai fights to keep her gaze level—to keep a smile from spilling out across the lower half of her face. Easy. Easy. Too easy. The harlot is eating out of her hand, like a pig out of a trowel.

"Nerani doesn't seem to think she's dead."

"Is that what she said?" Whinny says, her voice high. "She's not very bright, if you ask me."

"She's bright enough to know that if she has someone to trade for information, she might be able to negotiate with the Guardians."

"I'm *not* Cairan."

"Do you think anyone will believe you? You—a lady of the night?"

Whinny swallows and says nothing. Seranai tightens her grip on her arm, her nails digging into the harlot's skin.

"You'd burn at the stake, Whinny, no questions asked. You know you would."

The high color leeches out of Whinny's face at that. She flies back from Seranai, the hollow at the base of her throat fluttering as she grasps for words that will not come.

"That brat," she cries. Her voice is shrill, and getting shriller. "That horrible, dreadful brat. I've been nothing but good to her all her life. I was her only friend in this hovel. Emerala the Rogue is dead. *Dead.* What could the Guardians possibly tell her that's worth my life?"

She sniffles loudly, an ugly sound, and wipes her nose on the lace of her fraying sleeve.

"Traitor," she mutters into the unraveling fabric. "Back stabbing gypsy."

"I can help you," Seranai says. Whinny shoots her a dark look, her eyes full of misgiving.

"Why? What do you care?"

"As it were, I don't particularly like Nerani the Elegant myself."

"No? Why not?"

Seranai pauses, wetting her lower lip. "I have my reasons. They're not important. We could work together, you and I."

"What would we do?"

"In war, kings often send their armies out into battle to meet the enemy head on, rather than sit and wait for death to arrive at their gates."

Whinny gapes at her, mouth ajar. Seranai notices she is missing a tooth. "I don't understand," the harlot admits, sniffling.

Of course you don't, Seranai thinks ruefully. She flashes Whinny her warmest smile.

"Nerani is a full-blooded Cairan. General Byron would just itch to have someone like her to interrogate. Rowland Stoward will string her up like cattle—make an example of her. We can sell her out before she has so much as a chance to talk."

Whinny's face scrunches, her features twisting as if someone has taken her nose and twisted it clockwise upon her face. The effect screws her plain face into something hideous. Seranai holds her breath, impatient, and waits for Whinny to mull through her options. It takes every ounce of her effort not to slap the harlot into speaking.

"It's a good plan," Whinny relents at last. Reaching up, she snatches at a stray curl and twists it round and round upon her finger. "Which one of us do you think should say something?"

Seranai bites back a groan.

"You, you silly dolt." Her tone has grown terse. Tired. She has never been one to suffer fools, and this fool in particular is grating on her nerves. "I can hardly tell them, being a Cairan myself."

"Right." Whinny scratches at her chin. "Right, of course. You know, Private Olmsted usually comes by in the afternoons when he's finished his shift. I might tell him."

"You might," Seranai agrees. She forces a smile, reaching out and squeezing the harlot's hand in her own. "Best to do it soon, don't you think? Before Nerani the Elegant can sell you up the river."

"I'll tell him tonight," Whinny says. "And then that backstabbing witch can burn."

Harvest Cycle 1511
Eisle of Udire

King U'Rel is a both gracious and affable host. We have been welcomed ashore with open arms; have been given the proper respect
due a pirate lord like Captain Samuel.

Even so, we have chosen to keep our quarters onboard the ship.

We have seen the farms they keep—what cattle they have
here. We have seen King U'Rel's terrible tremors. De'rea haba,
Sam calls it. Dead Man's Hand.

They are cannibals. Eaters of men.

We are living among monsters, not men.

It is the spring, now, so the herds are returning across the
mountain pass. Game is plenty, and the hunters go out into the
tundra daily in order to bring back wildebeests for the game warden.

Does that make us safe?

King U'Rel is gracious, yes. Pleasant, yes.

We are not safe.

Captain Samuel is stowing a refugee away in the bowels of the
ship. Thom, he calls himself. He is young and plump; prime pickings

for the winter months. He knows not how to read or write properly—he is truly more animal than boy.

I have taken it upon myself to educate him. I am hoping a bit of activity will keep her ghost at bay. At least, then, I will be clear-headed enough to focus on what I need to do.

At least, then, I will have a bit of peace.

Eliot

CHAPTER 21

Eisle of Udire

THE FRIGID AIR outside the walls of the fortress is crisp and clean. The snow ceased to fall while Emerala and the crew dined within the thick walls of the Frost Fort. Now, a bleak silver moon sits high in the night sky.

Emerala follows closely in Thom's wake, her foots punching easily through the thick powder that coats the earth. All around her, the crew picks through the aftermath of the storm like wraiths; their shoulders hunched against the chill, their faces obscured by shadow. She studies the creeping forms of the men, searching for a pair of golden eyes in the moonlight, a lanky frame slinking beneath the trees. The Hawk is nowhere to be found.

She wonders if he made it out of the fortress unharmed.

She wonders if he made it out at all.

Glancing up at the wide frame of Thom's shoulders, dark against a sky pocketed with brilliant white stars, she rebukes herself for caring. She shouldn't care. She shouldn't even think of him. All that matters is that she gets back to the ship alive.

She pauses, peering over her shoulder at the empty shadows behind them. The wind barrels into her, howling like a woman in mourning. Just like a woman in mourning, in fact. The cry is high and shrill—almost bestial. A few feet to her left, a member of the crew pauses in the snow, his hand flying to his sword.

The wind dies. The whistling falls silent.

That shrill, bestial cry continues.

"Keep pushing to shore!" cries out a voice from the darkness. "Don't stop! Don't look back!"

Several cutlasses are drawn from their sheaths. The starlight shivers upon the curved blades.

"It's a hunting cry," Emerala hears Thom say, his voice nearly too quiet to be heard.

"What game are they after?" Emerala asks, although she already knows. Her blood turns to ice in her veins. There is a sharp whistle—loud against the static night air. It is followed by a quiet grunt. In the dark, a man drops to his knees, an arrow protruding from his chest. Blood saturates the white powder, seeping out from his corpse in fingers of red.

Emerala turns toward Thom, hovering only inches away from her. His eyes are hard, his face as undisturbed as stone. Still, she can nearly smell the fear rolling off of him. She is reminded, suddenly, of what the Lethal said about the island making beasts out of men.

"Run t'the ship," Thom instructs. "Keep beneath the trees."

The rest of the crew has already heeded similar advice. They scatter beneath the dizzying stars, relegated to little more than passing shadow against the snow. Unused to the terrain, several of them stumble in the snowdrifts.

For a fraction of a moment, Emerala stands frozen—watching.

And then she runs.

Her breathing comes in short, uneven spurts. Grey bursts of air explode on the bitter air before her. She spots a copse of trees and races toward them. The snow is lighter beneath the bent boughs of the towering branches. It is easier for her to run. Ducking beneath a curving branch, she picks up her pace, chest burning. Her boots catch on the slick ice where the snow melted and refroze beneath the feeble daylight. She teeters uneasily, her arms flailing as she fights to maintain her balance.

Another cry echoes out from the battlements. There is a rush of whistling, the sound of weapons finding their mark. A volley of arrows cuts through the night sky, disturbing the starry quiet that yawns above the trees. Emerala cringes, muffling a cry, and yet the arrows do not reach her beneath the thick evergreens.

Turning her attention back toward the tundra, she continues to run, doing her best to keep to the trees. The moon does not reach her. Swallowed by darkness as she is, she has lost all sense of direction. It dawns upon her that she doesn't know which way to go in order to get to the ship. Her already unfamiliar surroundings have become alien to her beneath the heavy snowdrifts.

A strange and horrible sound peals out in the night. Instinctively, she claps her hands to her ears. Someone, somewhere, is blowing into a horn. Deep and resonant, the instrument makes a sound like nothing she has ever heard in her life. She races on, trying to ignore the sudden, feral sound of bellowing that shatters the silver serenity of the evening. She knows well enough to know that the shouts are not the voices of the crew. They are guttural and foreign and far too close.

She hears the shivering sound of swords meeting swords, and she knows that the hunters have reached some of the crew. She wonders why no one thought it necessary to provide her with a weapon.

If she is caught, she will surely be killed.

A gunshot rings out from somewhere behind her, eliciting a muffled cry. The pungent smell of gunpowder stings her nose. Her heart leaps to her throat and she struggles to run faster. She nearly loses her balance entirely as her boots slip upon a patch of ice. Hooves beat against the ground, the cadence muffled by several feet of snow. She curses silently, drawing to a standstill. There is no way she will be able to outrun a horse.

A sharp whinny, just above her head, and she feels a strong hand grasp her waist and pull. Before she can utter a cry of protest, she is wrenched ungracefully from her feet. Her captor ignores her less than savory rejoinder as she lands hard upon the pommel of the leather saddle.

"Keep quiet, Rogue."

The Hawk. The relief that courses through her is instantaneous.

"Oh," she says, trying to ignore the waver in her voice. "It's you."

"You can thank me later," he assures her. He coaxes the horse into an easy gallop, riding out from the cover of the trees and into the snow. Out in the open, a snow squall has picked up with frightening fury. Thin white flurries blow in sideways, clinging to Emerala's eyelashes and obscuring her vision.

"I thought you might have died back there," she says. Her words slur together as they slip past her lips. She feels strangely intoxicated. Behind her, the Hawk doesn't reply. Instead, he coaxes the horse faster.

For a long time, they ride on in silence. Weary from running, Emerala allows herself to lean into his chest. As much as she hates to admit it, she is grateful for the warmth of him. The chill is like needles against her skin, sharp and unrelenting.

She is surprised by how fast his heart beats against her back—surprised by the ragged breath that catches in his throat. His arm snakes around her waist, pulling her into him, squeezing her just a little bit too tight.

They ride onward, the sounds of battle dying off in the distance. Soon, the screaming of the wind and the heavy breathing of the Hawk's stolen horse are the only sounds that reach the pair in the frozen tundra. They have been traveling for too long, Emerala thinks. They should have already reached the ship. She blinks up into the snowy sky, ignoring the pinpricks of ice that sting her cheeks. Through a break in the clouds, she can just make out the muddled outline of the moon. Everything around her is flat and dark—all dark, like an abyss. The wind howls across the piling hills of white, whipping snow as fine as soft powder in its wake. There is no sea before them. There is no sea behind them. They are adrift in darkness, far away from shore—far away from anything at all.

And then, through the dark, she sees it. Several shadowed mountains rise out of the snow, peaking in the sky far above her head.

"The mountain pass," she tries to say, but the words are garbled— tied up in a knot. Her lips are numb from cold. Her vision spins and, for a moment, she is uncertain how many peaks actually paint the horizon before her. Beneath them, the horse slows to a stop—responding to the flick of the reins with a tired whinny. It unleashes a damp, sputtering sound. Wisps of tangled grey breath disperse from its flared nostrils. The Hawk slides effortlessly from the saddle, dragging Emerala to the ground with him.

"Where are we?" Emerala asks, her boots hitting the ground hard. It takes her several seconds to realize that they are standing on ice, not snow. Blue-black fissures snake out from beneath her feet.

She repeats her question. "Where are we?"

"Hold your tongue," the Hawk commands. His grip on Emerala is too tight. It dawns upon her that he expects her to run.

But from what?

Or whom?

Craning her neck, she tries and fails to peer up at him through the swirling squall. All she can see is the shadowed bottom of his chin—the strong line of his jaw locked up tight like a trap.

And then, as suddenly as the snow began, it stops again. The wind dies down with a sigh. Fat white flakes flutter down around them, catching in Emerala's heavy black curls. She tries and fails to wrench herself out of the Hawk's grasp. His fingers only tighten on her arm, drawing her closer still. She collides hard into his chest, the top of her head slamming against his chin.

"Ow," she snaps. "Are you out—"

The Hawk cuts her off, giving her a brusque shake. "Quiet."

"Don't tell me to—"

"Rogue," he hisses, and something in his voice makes her words choke and die in her throat. "*Quiet.*"

Up ahead, a sharp keening echoes out from the darkness. The sound is piercing—as cold and bitter as the storm. Emerala peers into the formless shadows, her eyes narrowed, ice crystals clinging to her lashes. From the howling emptiness emerges a slender figure cloaked all in black. A heavy hood is drawn over the newcomer's face.

To Emerala's surprise, the Hawk drops to a knee on the ice, his head dipping into a bow. His black hair drapes across his face, obscuring his eyes from view as he drags Emerala down to the ground with him.

"Ha'Suri." His voice drips with cautious respect. Emerala starts as she recognizes the name. Ha'Suri, the wind woman of the north. Ha'Suri, the folk's tale.

She was nothing more than an old story—that was what Ha'Rai had told them back in the Frost Forts.

And yet here she stands, resplendent beneath the silvery moon.

"Years, it has been, darling Evander." The voice that trickles out from beneath the midnight cloak is ancient, weighted down by time. "The last time you came to me, you were only a boy, hiding behind your captain. How you've grown."

"Things have changed, Ha'Suri."

"Things are always changing, boy. The tides, the moon, and the earth with them. The world has never stayed still. Even boys with hearts of ice find themselves melting down into something new."

The Hawk stares into the ice, the knees of his breeches darkening. Emerala kneels beside him, the cold seeping into her bones, and glowers at the lanky pirate out of the corner of her eye. Her vision spirals and she sways slightly, his grip the only thing keeping her upright.

"Rise, Evander. Let me look at you."

He obeys, wrenching Emerala onto her feet. She stumbles several steps before regaining her footing, cursing her feet for betraying her. How much did she have to drink back at the forts? She can't remember.

"So handsome," Ha'Suri muses, her voice emanating from everywhere and nowhere all at once. "So changed from what you once were. Is this her? The woman that pierced your frigid soul?"

The Hawk looks up from the ice at that, his sharp gazing finding the woman across the shadows. He unleashes Emerala's arm as though she has suddenly become too hot to touch—as though she has scorched his flesh to the marrow. A sound like a quiet laugh escapes from beneath the woman's hood.

"Love is always a surprising inconvenience, isn't it, Evander?"

The Hawk clears his throat. "You know why I'm here."

"You wish to undo the deed that was done." The woman's voice is an ageless whisper.

"Aye. I do."

"Hmm," the woman breathes. "You've grown into a true man, Evander. Men always want, want, and want. Need, need, need."

"You always knew we would come back for the cipher one day."

The figure of the woman wavers in the dark, her cloak rippling beneath the wind. She looks both impossibly frail and immeasurably powerful. The paradox is unsettling—alarming. "You say 'we'," she says, "but there is only you. That map was bound with the blood of the three, yet I do not see them with you."

"Samuel Mathew and Charles Argot are dead."

"A pity. And Eliot Roberts?"

Emerala bristles at the name of her father, the hairs on the back of her neck rising to stand on end. Her green eyes lock onto the figure of the cloaked woman. A thousand questions rise to the tip of her tongue like bile.

"Roberts is long gone," the Hawk says. "I haven't heard word of the man in near fifteen years."

"Then the map is sealed. I cannot help you."

With a grunt, the Hawk thrusts Emerala out before him. She stumbles, her boots struggling against the heavy snow that blankets the ground. The hooded figure is immediately before her, although Emerala did not see her move. Beneath the cloak the mysterious woman's dark head tilts as she regards Emerala with interest. She hears a quiet intake of air.

"Ah, yes," comes the breathless whisper.

"The son of Cap'n Samuel Mathew has taken the map to Ha'Rai," the Hawk explains. "He's a damned fool for trusting the likes of her, but his blood will be spilt and that's as good as anything."

"Ha'Rai will play her part," the woman whispers. She is only inches away from Emerala. Her quiet breath is colder upon Emerala's face than the wintery air that enshrouds them. Emerala can feel the woman's eyes penetrating her from beneath the heavy fabric. She remains frozen to the ground, panic bubbling within her. She wonders if she ought to run.

You will stay here, daughter of Roberts. The voice in her head echoes against the clamor of her own thoughts, startling her into stillness.

The Hawk tosses something to the woman. Emerala watches as a hand as pallid as the snow itself protrudes from the trumpeted black sleeve and catches an airborne glass vial in its slender fingers. The woman's curved nails are sleek and as silver as ice. They shimmer like mirrors in the moonlight as she raises the vial before her. Ruby red blood fills the prism shaped glass.

"The mapmaker." The woman sighs, and the sound is heavier than the weight of a thousand years. "Pity, Evander, that you spilled it all for such a little taste. You were always so quick to act, to kill."

"His death was necessary."

"No," the woman disagrees. "His blood was necessary."

"Does it matter? You have it. Charles Argot, Samuel Mathew, Eliot Roberts. The blood of the three, or next of kin." The Hawk's voice at Emerala's back is wrought with self-satisfaction. Emerala scowls, trying and failing to piece everything together. Her thoughts move like sludge. Slow. Useless.

The woman reaches out with her free hand and removes the circular glass stopper from the top of the vial. Emerala watches, entranced, as she tips the glass to its side and allows the blood to trickle onto the ice below. The pristine surface is mottled with specks of deepest red. Nothing happens. The wind screams all around them. The woman remains still, her breathing even.

"Give me your hand." The quiet command is directed at her. Emerala hesitates.

Now. The abysmal voice in her head is dangerous. Emerala's arm lifts towards the figure as though it moves of its own accord. Her hand hangs limply from her wrist. Those fingers, pale and cold as death, grasp her own. The woman's colorless skin is as hard as rock and colder than ice. Emerala watches, numb, as the woman draws a dagger from within her cloak. The hilt, adorned with rubies, glitters red in the moonlight. The blade is translucent. Ice. It cuts down on her skin with the slightest pressure, drawing a thick line of blood from the palm of her hand.

Emerala does not cry out. She stares down upon the ground—watching the deep red of her blood plummet towards the ice—and feels as though she is miles away. The droplets merge with the blood from the vial, forming a line of fast freezing red. The color seeps into the ice, staining the fissures that splinter through the glassy surface.

The cloaked woman is whispering now, primeval words falling from her lips in her native tongue. Emerala does not hear her. It is the voice in her head, deep and warm and ancient, that woos her into unconsciousness.

Sleep, daughter of Roberts, it breathes. *And when you wake, remember nothing.*

·•🙾·

The firelight that dances upon the bronze sconces is caught up in a bracket of chilling, source less wind. Here and there, a few of the flames gutter out. Alexander shivers in the chill, his eyes remaining trained upon the map that lies flattened out upon the low table between himself and Ha'Rai.

"It is time. Give me your hand," Ha'Rai says. Her husky voice wavers upon her lips. Her honeyed irises have disappeared behind black pupils. Alexander watches her carefully as he proffers his upturned palm. Ha'Rai draws a curving silver dagger from her sleeve. It catches in the golden light as it hovers over the palm of his hand. Before he can protest, she draws the dagger across his flesh, trailing a thick red line of blood in its wake.

"Ha'Suri, fi'in eae utal," Ha'Rai cries. Her lips move quickly, the dead speech that has been inscribed upon the map tumbles out into the viscous air between them. She flips Alexander's hand over, allowing four plump droplets of blood to fall upon the map. Alexander watches in awe as his blood splinters outward in thinning lines, spreading like ink across the aged map.

"It is done," Ha'Rai says.

She lets his hand drop. His knuckles rap against the surface of the table.

He stares down at the map, marveling at the prominent, blood red words that scrawl out at the bottom of the parchment in the common tongue.

What is sweeter than honey? What is stronger than a lion?

Harvest Cycle 1511
Eisle of Udire

It is done. We have sealed the map—Samuel, Charles and I.

The magic was dark and ancient. My bones still chatter at the very thought of it. My skin crawls.

Surely, I will be condemned to the Dark Below for what I've done.

As I write, the parchment lies unfolded before me, the deep black scrawl of Argot's hand all but faded away from the indecipherable topography. The first leg of the journey is complete. The second begins now.

We sail for the Westerlies.

Eliot

CHAPTER 22

Chancey

NERANI THE ELEGANT darts out from between the shade of an aged grey building, shirking back only slightly as the pale yellow sun washes over her face. She draws her faded brown traveling cloak tighter about her shoulders, ignoring the sticking heat of summer that presses against her skin. There is comfort in the closeness of the itching fabric. She feels shielded from the bustling world all about her as she heads down the cobblestone road, keeping her blue eyes cast downward.

The fabric of her ivory damask gown sweeps dramatically against the street, flaring out like crystalline water bubbling over stone. The dress is handsome—finely made and likely quite expensive. Mamere Lenora lent it to her without question when she informed the matron what it was she planned to do.

They patrol those areas, darling, Mamere warned her, one heavily penciled eyebrow rising upon her head as she took a slow sip of her tea. The cracked rim of the delicate floral china was stained with rouge. *They do. It's likely that you'll be questioned if you go poking your nose around there.*

I'm not worried, she replied. She tried to smile reassuringly, but her lips only twisted into a slow grimace. Her own teacup chattered quietly against the thin, porcelain plate in her palm. *I'm good at being invisible.*

That much was true—so long has she worked to escape notice of those around her that staying unseen has become something of a second nature to her. Keep her head down, keep her face blank, keep moving—it's all she has to do in order to keep those around her from giving her so much as a cursory glance.

She'll need to be invisible to get into the quarters she had shared with Roberts and Emerala. The moment Mamere Lenora had informed her that the properties had not been rented to other potential residents but were sitting abandoned at the outskirts of Chancey she knew she needed to pay the decrepit old home a visit.

It's eerie there—haunted, like. Gives me the shivers just to pass it by. I wouldn't go in there, not if you paid me.

Nerani frowned at the look upon Mamere's face. *Why haven't they been let? Surely the landlords have been losing money on rent since our... disappearance.*

Oh, to be sure, Mamere agreed, setting down her teacup. The sound of china clattering against the dull, secondhand buffet between them set the inside of Nerani's palms to sweating. She mimicked Mamere Lenora's movements, setting down her own tea with practiced delicacy.

It's just, Mamere continued, twisting a gleaming, gaudy ring upon her finger, *folk are frightened of the place. None so much wants to go inside, let alone rent. No, they've been left quite alone.*

She puttered her lips quietly, muttering below her breath as she mopped up a bit of spilled tea with her spoilt handkerchief. *It's only so long before the Guardians take them over, anyhow. General Byron has had his men combing the buildings endlessly.*

Nerani feels something sour twist within her at the memory of the conversation. General Byron's name brings Orianna's ominous divination to the front of her mind. She pushes the unbidden thought away, fighting the sudden urge to peer into the faces of those she passes.

Keep your eyes down, she reminds herself. *Keep walking.*

She left Darianna at Mamere's. The girl would be safe enough there, out of sight in one of the unused boudoirs on the second floor. She had protested well enough, but Nerani would hear none of it. She needed to be alone.

If there were any clues to be found about Emerala's whereabouts, she supposed she might start in their old apartment. They had abandoned the place so quickly—so absolutely—in their migration to the Forbidden City that she had barely had time to gather her belongings.

Take only the most important possessions, Roberts had barked at her, his emerald eyes unusually void of emotion. *And even then, only what you can carry.*

Emerala's things had been left behind. If she had somehow managed to escape the grasp of the Golden Guard, surely she would have made her way back to the apartment. Nerani knows how unlikely it is that she will discover anything among the abandoned artifacts of their old life, and yet she has to check. She needs to check. The thought of Emerala alone and forsaken, unable to find her way to the Forbidden City on her own, has plagued Nerani through too many sleepless nights.

Nerani draws up short, nearly racing directly into a young mother and her swinging toddler. The small boy stops cold, feeling the strange presence looming at his back, and turns to face her. Messy blonde hair sweeps across his forehead as he blinks up into Nerani's eyes. His brown owl's gaze holds her blue stare for a moment too long. Her heart stops. She forces herself to flash him a tiny smile, hoping she looks warmer than she feels. The boy laughs in response, flashing three, white teeth. He waves enthusiastically at her, pulling against his mother's hand. She waves back, keeping the movements of her fingers small and insignificant.

Not noticing Nerani standing so close, the mother leans down and scolds the toddler for pulling at her arm. She continues onward, dragging the boy in her wake as she maneuvers through the busy street. Nerani watches them go, exhaling a small breath of relief. Lost in her thoughts as she was, she had momentarily forgotten to stay unseen.

Her feet are cramped and sweating in the tightly laced leather boots upon her feet. She fans herself gently, lifting her twisted brown locks off of the back of her neck. The obstinate afternoon sun sizzles against the cobblestone underfoot. Something uneasy stirs within her and she feels, suddenly, as though she is being watched. Up ahead, the boy and his mother are long gone. She glances cautiously at her surroundings, feeling naked as she exposes her face to the passing crowd. The mass of Chancians that swells and ebbs around her moves with the practiced ease of habit. No one is looking at her. No one can be bothered to look at her.

And yet she cannot shake the sensation that someone has seen her.

You're being paranoid, she scolds herself silently.

She continues maneuvering through the crowd, now only a few buildings away from the low, stone residence she and her cousins called home. The crowd thins, the conversation growing noticeably quieter as she approaches the row of crumbling grey buildings. Shafts of white light, speckled with silvery dust motes, pour languidly down through the gaps between the buildings. The heat of it tickles Nerani's skin as she moves between sunbeams, keeping her eyes peeled. Gooseflesh prickles across her arms beneath the traveling cloak. She thinks again of Mamere's warning.

Its eerie there—haunted, like. Gives me the shivers just to pass it by.

She stops at the third building on the street, unencumbered by throngs of bustling Chancians. Glancing around, she wishes for the cover of a crowd. It is easiest to go unnoticed, she finds, when she is just another face among many. Here, among the silent, empty buildings, she is out of place. A shiver runs down her spine and she fights the sudden urge to glance over her shoulder.

Was that a footfall she heard upon the stone, or is she imagining things?

She flexes her fingers, chiding herself for being so nervous, and stares up at the building—at her home.

The melancholy quiet makes her uneasy. It feels like she is visiting a tomb.

It's not home anymore, she thinks. *It's a graveyard.*

The door has been left open—no doubt by ransacking guardians. Cool air, dark and undisturbed, spills out from the shadows within. She feels mild annoyance bristling under her skin as she enters, her eyes taking in the negligence of the Golden Guard. The faint smell of wood rot reaches her nose as her damask gown sighs across the crumbling threshold.

It takes her eyes several moments to adjust to the gloom. The staircase, coated with threadbare carpeting, rise up just before her. She starts up the steps, her fingers leaving a trail in the dust that has settled upon the wooden railing. The stairs are old and weathered. They groan beneath her weight as she climbs to the second floor.

She comes to an abrupt stop at the first landing. Behind her, the stairs curve away into obscurity. There was something there—a sound—a slow creaking noise that echoed the cadence of her boots upon the faded velvet rug. She cranes her ears to listen but hears only the distant clip-clop-clip of a horse plodding by somewhere beyond the walls. Another shiver crawls down her spine, lingering in her stomach and putting down roots.

Mamere had told her that the Guardians patrol this area, and yet the building is empty. She is sure of it. No sounds come from above or below—no voices echo out from behind the closed doors of the apartments. She is completely alone. She continues walking, listening for any revealing noises over the sounds of her own footfalls. There are none.

She stops at the third door on the left, breathing a slow sigh of relief at the familiar feel the cool, sticking doorknob beneath the palm of her hand. Ever unlocked, the old wooden door creaks open with a happy groan. She slips inside, letting the door slide closed behind her. For a moment, she stands frozen in the wash of muted light that falls in through the soiled windowpanes. The contents of the apartment are swathed in shadow beyond the reach of the sun. Moving forward into the open expanse, she heads for the old armoire that sits askew at one end of the room.

Prying it open takes some work. In their absence, a leak has formed in the cracked ceiling overhead. The white plaster—browned and bulging with a belly full of rainwater—allows the occasional droplet to plop, plop, plop down onto the unfortunate wooden piece below. The door to the old thing is warped and rotting. She tugs at it for a few strenuous moments, gasping victoriously as the door finally relents with a sigh.

A sickly sweet fragrance wafts out of the opening and she finds herself staring at a stranger. The blue eyes, bright and fierce, are lined with a hostility foreign to Nerani. The pale white face is drawn and thin—the full lips are pressed together in a wary line. So different is this face to the face of the demure young woman that left here only months ago that it takes Nerani a moment to realize she is staring into her own reflection in the dirty, full-length mirror adhered to the inside of the door. She exhales deeply, blowing a stray lock of hair out of her face, and leans down to rustle through the armoire.

Her irritation comes back with a boiling vengeance as she realizes she is not the first person to go through the closet. The shelves have been properly overturned, with the contents strewn carelessly about the bottom. She huffs in annoyance, gathering things within her arms and placing them frantically back where they belong. There is a sharp prick of heat in her finger and she drops the things she is holding with a quiet yelp. Drawing her hand to her lips, she sucks several droplets of blood out of a small cut on the tip of her finger. She glares down into the shadowy interior, anger flaring through her. Several perfume bottles lie shattered across the floor, disgorging that sickly sweet odor into the air. Only one glass vial lies unbroken in the mess, the curves of the rounded flute catching in the sparse sunlight that trickles in between the rusted bronze hinges.

My mother's, she thinks, feeling a wave of sadness wash over her. She bends down, scooping the unbroken bottle delicately into her hand. The glass is cool and familiar within her palm. She pulls out the tiny cork, allowing her eyes to drift closed as she brings the vial beneath her nose. She is met with the soft scent of lavender. A wave of memories come rushing over her, followed closely behind by the salty threat of tears. Nerani swallows and replaces the cork with trembling fingers.

Now is not the time for ghosts, she reminds herself.

She rises slowly, sliding the vial into her cloak. When she straightens, the reflection in the mirror is golden.

Her hand flies unbidden to her throat as she lets out a strangled cry. Her blue eyes stare into the looking glass as she meets the dark gaze of none other than General James Byron. He stands at attention, his shoulders perfectly framed within the crumbling doorway. His jaw is locked as he watches her in silence, unblinking. His lips twist into a contemplative frown.

"You shouldn't be here," the reflection mouths. His voice, low and dangerous, emanates from over her shoulder. She turns slowly upon the heel of her boot, raising her chin in a mild show of defiance as she faces him. Her gaze finds his across the vague shadows of the room and her stomach twists itself into a knot. Unencumbered by the distorted reflection of the rusting mirror, his golden uniform appears ever more imposing against the curling white paint of the distressed doorway. His handsome face is bronzed from the sun, as though he has recently spent a great deal of time out of doors. He studies her in measured silence, taking care to keep his expression guarded.

"This is my home," she says, disappointed to hear her voice wavering. She had meant to sound confident—fearless. Instead, she watches as her words fall flat between them.

The shake of his head is barely discernable in the dusky ambiguity of the afternoon. The muscles in his jaw tighten.

"You shouldn't be here," he repeats.

"Why not?" The insides of her palms are slick with sweat. She wipes them against the ivory of her petticoat and hopes he does not notice.

"It's not safe."

"As if you care for my safety."

The look upon his face causes her stomach to quaver. She tries not to think of their last encounter—tries not to remember the feel of his lips upon hers, of the hunger in his touch. She tries, but she fails. Her palm stings at the memory of how she had slapped him, the sound echoing through the empty street.

She thinks again of Orianna's warning—of her friend's empty eyes and upturned palms, the ridges of her fingers still caked with flour.

You'll love him. It will drown you both.

A wrinkle of embarrassment from crosses the bridge of her nose. The general notices, his expression softening. He takes a careful step into the room, his eyes never leaving her face. His gleaming leather boots creak against the floorboards underfoot. He moves gingerly, walking forward as though she is a frightened doe he is trying desperately not to startle.

"You followed me here," she accuses.

"I didn't mean to frighten you." His voice is apologetic. His gaze is unreadable. "I had a fairly good idea you'd be headed here, and his Majesty has my men and I doing routine sweeps of the apartments. I didn't want to take the chance of you running into another Guardian on your way in."

Nerani's frown deepens. Her cautious gaze transforms into a glare. He stiffens beneath her steel blue eyes, his larynx pulling at his throat as he swallows.

"Why are you talking as though you're any different than them?"

He is visibly affronted by her question. "I'm not certain what you mean."

"You didn't want to take the chance that I would run into a Guardian?" The dust motes swirl about her head in a halo of silver as she takes several steps in his direction. "I *have* run into a Guardian. Perhaps the most dangerous man in all the King's Golden Guard has followed me into my home."

He blinks twice—slowly—and says nothing.

"You're trespassing, by the way," she snaps. "This *is* my home, and I haven't invited you in."

The heat of her temper abates the flutter of nerves beneath her skin. She moves to push past him, her cheeks ablaze. He steps backward into the doorframe, throwing his arm up just before she can storm through the opening. His knuckles are white against the wood. Looking up, she finds herself staring directly into his face. His nose is inches from hers—his gaze earnest.

"Wait." He is so close to her that she can taste his breath upon her tongue.

"Why?" She fights to keep her voice even. His deep, brown eyes flicker back and forth between hers in a way that makes her knees buckle.

"It's not safe out there," he explains. "You shouldn't have left your city."

She scowls. "It's not quite safe in here, either."

His eyes widen at that. "Because of me?" For a moment, he makes a show of studying the splintering cracks in the waterlogged ceiling. When at last he speaks, his tone is plaintive—his words are clipped with frustration.

"I've never given you any reason to fear me."

"Haven't you?"

"You—I—" he stammers, his cheeks coloring with visible ire. "I'm *trying* to keep you safe."

"Like you tried to keep Emerala safe?" Her words are biting. They have the desired effect. His hand falls away from the door as he regards her through a gaze gone cold. She is overcome by a sudden, violent surge of resentment. Resentment for him—resentment for everything he stands for, every facet of his so called justice.

Was it justice, what happened to Emerala?

Will it be justice what happens to her?

He cannot keep me safe, she thinks bitterly. *Not after all that has happened in the name of his damned self-righteousness—in the name of his false king.*

If he claims to want as much then he is nothing but a liar.

"Arrest me," she commands him, the words flying away from her with abandon. Unwanted tears spring to her eyes. He says nothing, only watches her with a trace of dismay knit into his brow. She takes another step towards him, drawing up on the toes of her boots so she is nearly at eye level with him.

"Arrest me," she snaps again, her voice fierce. "You've discovered me here. You know what I am. Take me into custody."

She is close enough to see flecks of gold circling his irises. His shoulders rise and fall beneath his cloak.

"No," he murmurs, frowning down at her. Fury splinters through her and she crooks her elbows, thrusting her wrists hard against his chest—holding them out to be bound. Her nerves are on fire beneath her flesh. Her instincts beg her to hold her tongue.

"I'm no different than Emerala, my crime is the same. You have no reason to let me go," she snaps through clenched teeth, feeling half mad as she glares up at him. His brows furrow still further, a brief flicker of anger passing across his stony gaze. He reaches up and grabs both of her wrists within his fist, drawing her roughly into him. They are nose to nose as they collide, his parted lips only inches from hers. His breathing has grown clipped and shallow—his cheeks are stained with pinpricks of blood.

"Don't be a fool," he orders—his voice caught between a snarl and a whisper. "If they get ahold of you—if you let them take you—they'll break you. Do you understand me?"

"What do you care?"

"How can you ask me that?" His voice is hoarse.

She can hear her heart beating in her ears. Somewhere deep within her, she hears Orianna's voice urging her to be careful—urging her to stay away from General James Byron and all that goes with him.

General Byron's grip on her wrists tightens. The white sunlight of the afternoon grazes the sweeping gold of his cloak. He is studying her through unguarded brown eyes and for a moment she can see stark, naked fear within his gaze.

"They'll kill you," he says. "They'll kill you, and I won't be able to do a thing to stop them. Do you understand?"

"I understand," she whispers, the rage sapping out of her spirit. He nods, feeling her slacken beneath him, and releases her. He takes a slow step back, his footsteps measured and even upon the floor.

"Go back to the Forbidden City," he instructs her. His stilted words are that of a man unaccustomed to asking nicely. "Please."

She says nothing—does nothing—only watches as he backs out into the obscure shadows of the hallway beyond. The musky smell of dust and rot creeps in upon his wake. He is studying her still, his expression curious in the gloom.

Something foreign and unwanted protests deep within her at the sight of his departure. She smothers the unwelcome sensation, batting it down, tucking it away.

Run, Nerani, Orianna had said. *Run as fast as you can. Before the red tide rises.*

She keeps her gaze locked upon his even as her legs threaten to give out beneath her gown. And then he is gone, leaving nothing but a flash of gold and a dull pulsing where his fingers pressed against her wrists.

CHAPTER 23

Chancey

WHAT ARE YOU doing?

James Byron paces the length of the hallway, his hand pressing against his freshly shaven chin. His stomach does an uneasy somersault. The soles of his boots slap stridently against the polished marble floor underfoot. The dimly lit hall is empty, save for himself. Dust motes swirl in the air about his head as he walks, shivering out from between the rusted visors that dot the row of forgotten armor upon the wall to his right.

What are you thinking?

His father was a pragmatic man. A fisherman and a businessman, at that. He may have come from humble beginnings—beginnings which James had thought shameful in the impetuous days of his youth—but he afforded a respectable level of reason to everything he did. In the end, they may have had their differences, but James always looked up to his father's levelheaded ability to rationalize.

It is what he strives for—demands of himself, really—in his line of work. A Guardian does not deviate from reason. A Guardian is the embodiment of pragmatism—of sensibility. It is what allows him to uphold the law, to see that justice is swift and merciless where it need be. It is what allows him, in a manner of speaking, to snuff out his humanity and turn a blind eye to those that meet with Death at the end of Justice's swift sword.

He has always been a man that favored logic over instinct and impulsivity. Always, it would seem, until now.

Where has that man gone?

He was certainly not present in the slums only yesterday afternoon as James followed the blue-eyed gypsy to her dwelling. There had been exceedingly little reasoning that took place there as he pursued her silently up the creaking steps, his troubled gaze locked upon the sweeping ivory hem of her gown. He was the very definition of impulsivity then as he pulled her into him—felt her breath upon his tongue.

Damn it, he growls internally, berating himself. *What were you trying to prove?*

Nothing, he realizes with a start, coming to a sudden stop in the murky quiet of the hallway. He did it simply because he wanted to do it—because he needed to do it. Because, at that moment, fear unlike any he had ever known had grabbed hold of his spirit and refused to let go. Because her very presence before him had filled him with rage as she shouted for him to arrest her—to treat her as he was expected to treat her. She had pointed out the inconsistencies in his heart with flippant anger, her blue eyes blazing like steel. Words were not enough to express what he was feeling, standing uselessly before her and imploring her to understand what he was asking her—to understand what it was he needed from her.

He cannot do his job with her so close. He cannot do what it is he needs to do. Her presence here in the city muddies his ability to think. He is not the type of man to plead, and yet he might as well have dropped his knees down into the rotting undergrowth and begged her to see reason.

Reason.

The word is laughable to him, now. He stares down at his fists, resting at his sides, and lets a derisive laugh escape from between his lips. He has made a terrible tactical error, and that practical voice within his head is quick to remind him just how foolishly he behaved.

What is it to you whether she lives or dies? he thinks to himself. *Let her be caught. She is nothing to you. You don't even know her name, you fool.*

He grimaces and resumes his pacing, feeling utterly disgusted with himself. So consumed is he with his own thoughts that he scarcely notices the polite *hem-hem* of a throat clearing somewhere behind him. He brings himself about, drawing to a squeaking stop upon the marble. The force is so abrupt that his cloak continues on in his wake, momentarily enshrouding his figure in a swatch of gold.

Prince Peterson lingers quietly in the expanse before him, hovering beneath a shaded alcove meant to house a bust or a suit of armor. The shadows that play across his face cause him to appear ashen and lifeless in the dusky hallway—himself emulating one of the countless nameless statues that line the walls of the palace. Two green eyes, as vivid as jewels, blink rapidly in the muted light. James regards the young prince. He thinks of the forgotten statues, all but obsolete, their names and their rich histories all but faded from memory and he notes that Peterson, too, has been forgotten. He is fading away before he has even had the chance to amount to the glory he was born to inherit.

James pities Peterson.

He always has.

"Your Highness." He drops into a respectful bow, keeping his eyes trained upon the shaded figure.

"James." He refers to James by his given name, as he always has. Peterson has known James his entire life. He spent the days of his childhood chasing after Frederick and James as they raced one another up and down the polished floors of the palace. "Get up. You don't have to do that. There's no one around."

James clears his throat, remaining positioned in a bow. "Last time I saw you, you made it quite clear that I was a soldier, and you my prince. I'm only following orders."

James can practically feel Peterson rolling his eyes.

"I was upset. Are you going to hold it against me, or are you going to get up?"

James obeys, straightening his shoulders and studying the boy before him. The perpetual glower on the prince's face suggests that he had not anticipated running into anyone back here in the forlorn hallways of the unkempt western wing. He expects to be scolded—to be sent back to his nursery and his stringent tutors.

"You've chosen a lonely part of the palace to spend your afternoon," James observes.

"As have you."

James adjusts his cloak, saying nothing to address the prince's unasked question.

"It's a lovely day outside," he comments, planting a polite smile upon his face. "Not a cloud in the sky."

"Weather?" Peterson scoffs. "You're really going to comment on the weather?"

"What else would you have me comment on?"

"Anything," Peterson snaps. "Anything else."

"I'm only observing. You should be spending the afternoon out in the fresh air, not holed up in here."

"I would be in the labyrinth, but my father chose to wander it this afternoon. I, of course, am not invited." Peterson's tone is irate, as though Rowland selected his afternoon activity solely to spite his son. James knows that this could not be farther from the case. Rowland thinks as little as his youngest son as possible—a task that he seems to find surprisingly easy. He has never been fond of the boy, a fact which he made resolutely clear by his near decade long negligence.

James thinks of the winding, marble labyrinth that tangles the remnants of Queen Victoria's prized courtyard. In the years leading up to the death of the queen, Victoria had begged the king to allow her to hire a renowned architect to design and build an elaborate maze to showcase her garden. It was to be a gift to her children.

It became a memorial.

She died in childbirth before the maze could be completed—breathing her last, trembling breath as she studied her newborn son through eyes wet with tears. The labor had been long and painful. The entire city had waited with bated breath, whispering about the coming of the prince.

No royal announcement came for the boy. No brass trumpets proclaimed the joyous news. Instead, the funeral bells tolled for days on end.

There was a great scandal, then, in those early days before James took up the duties of his heavy golden cloak. Whispers tore through the streets of Chancey like the shrieking ghouls of the undead, crying aloud of that final, violent shouting match between the ill-fated engineer and the king.

What had been the architect's name? *Roberts*, he thinks—or something to that affect.

No one could quite agree on what was said in that marble court, shut up as it was like a tomb, but they knew it was bad. The architect was never seen again. The maze went unfinished. The child prince was forgotten. And the great bear king slowly began to unravel.

Before James, the forgotten prince, a young man now on the cusp of adulthood, is quiet. Peterson peers into the visor of a skewed suit of armor with a practiced air of boredom.

"So this is what you intend to do all day instead?" James asks. "Wander aimlessly through empty hallways and study the ghosts of your family crest?"

Peterson runs a finger down the welded ridging of an iron chest plate with careful deliberation. "It's better than listening to the constant, droll conversation of my tutors. A little silence every so often is enjoyable."

James mutters a quiet assent and prepares himself to go. He is capable of taking a hint—Peterson would prefer to be alone. He is met with a burning, green gaze. *So unlike his father*, he finds himself marveling, not for the first time.

"Why is my father obsessed with finding the Cairans?" Peterson asks suddenly, his words abrupt. It is clear that he has been working up the nerve to ask.

James opens his mouth to respond and falters. It dawns upon him that he is uncertain how to reply. The words that immediately trickle into the forefront of his mind are treacherous.

His obsession is fueled by greed. He wants the Cairan fortune, if it turns out to be real. It is not his to take, but he will have it regardless.

He clears his throat and pushes the thoughts away. "What do your tutors tell you?" he asks.

"Spoken like a true Guardian," Peterson says.

"How's that?"

"You've gone and answered one question with another. It's entirely unhelpful, and really quite annoying."

"I apologize."

Peterson shrugs, waving him off. "My tutors tell me the same as everyone else. The Cairans have been using old magic, which is forbidden in Chancey."

Untrue, James thinks and catches himself again. Peterson continues talking, saving James from having to formulate a response.

"When I was a boy, before Frederick left us, my father told us that it was a Cairan curse that took away our mother. He said they would have taken me, too, but I was born before the curse could be completed."

James is still before the young man. He's heard this theory before—an enraged Frederick had put his father's bold faced lie on blast one afternoon, pacing the length of his private solar with rage in his inky gaze.

He's putting lies in Peter's head—he's filling him with hate, Frederick had snapped, shattering a vase against the floor. James stood at the door in silence, annoyance flickering within him at the prince's temper.

He's mourning, James said. *Grief manifests itself in different ways.*

He's mad, Frederick shot back, his eyes brimming with angry tears. *He's always been mad—Saints, James, why do you continue to defend him?*

James remembers the day with a tinge of bitterness. He knows better now. Rowland's mind comes and goes, fraught with paranoia and susceptible to bouts of oblivion.

He is a man come undone.

Before James, Peterson continues speaking. "He said that they wanted to kill us all off, one by one, and leave my father without any heirs so that they could take the throne by force. In my last interaction with him, just after Frederick's—just after his disappearance—my father told me that they had finally succeeded in taking him, too."

Peterson swallows and stares down at the polished floor. "He told me that they had succeeded in infiltrating his bloodline with one of their own, and that he would be damned if he would let a Cairan take the throne. It was the last time I have ever been permitted in his presence."

James feels his lips tightening at Peterson's words. He studies the young man before him. The bridge of his nose is narrow, the tip pointed. His lips are thin. His thick black hair, parted to the side, catches the light where his nurse could not quite tame the wild curls. His features are nothing like that of his bear of a father, with his bulbous nose and his fleshy, red laugh. Suddenly the madness of the king becomes all too clear.

Just as King Rowland has concocted the death of his eldest son, so, too, has he turned his youngest into his enemy. He views the boy as a stranger—as something to be feared.

"Do you believe what your father told you?" James asks. Peterson shakes his head slowly, one black curl of hair falling across his forehead.

"I know that Frederick left—I watched him go—and yet my father acts as though he's died. I have never met a Cairan, but I know for certain that my mother died of natural causes." He pauses and appears suddenly hesitant as he fusses absently with one sleeve of his doublet. His green eyes meet James's gaze across the hall.

"I know that you've slaughtered a great deal of Cairans at my father's command. There must be a reason. I've known you my whole life, James, and you've always been a reasonable man. Frederick trusted you more than anyone else in this world, and that means something to me. And so, I ask you again, why is my father *really* obsessed with finding the Cairans?"

The word *slaughter* catches in James's chest and remains rooted there like a knife. He is speechless before the young prince, casting about for an appropriate response. His head is a battlefield of jumbled words as he sways between what he is expected to say and what he feels.

There are footfalls on the marble floor—quick, anxious patters of boots. Someone is coming. James squares his shoulders and watches as a Guardian races around the corner. He draws to a stop when he sees the prince, dropping into a lazy bow.

"Your Highness," he mutters, out of breath. Peterson says nothing, only studies the newcomer in silence.

"What is it?" James asks. There is something frantic in the Guardian's stance. The soldier straightens quickly, one hand pressed firmly against his gut. Dust motes swirl wildly about his head. His breathing comes in deep pulls as though he has been running for a long time.

"His Majesty has us searching everywhere for you," the Guardian says between inhales. "We have a Cairan within our custody."

The knife within James's chest twists violently. He feels his face drop and fights to remain neutral.

"Where is she?" he asks, and his voice is too loud in the dusky stillness. He nearly cringes as the words fly away from his lips. He can feel Peterson's sharp gaze fall upon his face. The Guardian before him is far too excited too have noticed his slip-up. He continues, talking faster than before.

"She's in a holding cell, awaiting her inquisition. They found her at that whorehouse—Mamere Lenora's—over by the edge of the city. One of the harlots turned her in."

For a brief instant, James finds himself desperately hoping that he has been mistaken—that the blue-eyed Cairan listened to his plea and returned to the Forbidden City. There is no need to panic—not yet—Seranai was staying at Mamere Lenora's, and she is exactly the type of woman to try the patience of her licentious housemates.

It could be her, he reasons. *It could be Seranai.*

Something deep within his gut protests loudly—an instinct that is far more visceral than reason whispers that it is exactly who he thinks it is.

"Who is handling her questioning?" he demands.

The Guardian shrugs. "Like I said, the king has had us searching for you for quite a while. He sent Corporal Anderson in your place instead."

At that, James Byron runs.

CHAPTER 24

Chancey

NERANI SQUEEZES HER eyes shut and counts her heartbeats. She breathes. In and out. Slowly. One plump tear presses out from between her lids and makes its slow way down the line of her face. She sits, stalwart and unmoving against the cool stone wall of the cell in which she has now spent an unclear amount of time.

Stupid, she chides herself silently. *So very, very stupid.*

She had not counted on Whinny recognizing her. She had certainly not imagined Whinny turning her in. Whinny, the blonde young prostitute that had spent the greater part of their fractured youth pursuing an unrequited romance with Roberts, who ignored her as best as he knew how.

Whinny had never liked Nerani and Emerala much. The fickle young woman saw them only as obstacles to getting the thing she wanted most. It was as though she believed without the presence of the two sniveling orphan girls; the adolescent Roberts would suddenly reciprocate her continuous advances.

Her dislike was evident, yes, but she had never born them any ill will.

Nerani recalls the empty look in Whinny's dark eyes as she watched her childhood playmate be thrust to her knees before the Guardians. She was silent as they dragged Nerani off—safe in her perch atop the stairs. Just out of reach, obscured beneath the skulking shadow of the eaves overhead. Her lips had been pressed firmly into a smile that tried and failed to retain an air of smug satisfaction.

She missed the mark completely. Nerani remembers thinking she looked half mad as she swayed beneath the dust motes stirred up by the gleaming black boots of the Guardians, her face stained with too much rouge beneath that hollow gaze.

Nerani wanted to call out to her then—to scream with rage at the injustice of it all.

How could you? We were children together.

But she did not. She remained silent.

Her fingers ball into fists and she slams them against the damp wall at her back. Hard.

At least Darianna is safe. The young girl had already melted into the shadowed throng of hungry women by the time the first of the Guardians arrived. Nerani knew she would save only herself. What could the young girl have done for her by then? She hopes fervently that Dari will have the good sense to stay hidden until she can locate a Listener to return her to the Forbidden City. One will drop by Mamere's eventually, she is sure of it. She knows they conduct thorough patrols of the city.

Nerani can only hope that someone will receive word of her capture before it's too late.

And then what? she asks herself. *Orchestrate a rescue?*

She almost laughs aloud at the thought. It is too dangerous. She knows this. Many Cairans have been caught and tried in the past. There is no rescue attempt. There is no struggle against the powers of the king's golden force. There is only execution—swift and painful and public.

She will not pretend to believe she is more important than anyone else.

Her mind wanders idly to Topan and she feels sick. What will he think, she wonders, when he receives word of the news. Will he love her still? Will he mourn her death, or will he view her betrayal as unforgivable?

Her frown deepens at the detachment she feels over this consideration.

There is a sudden, slow exhale from somewhere in the darkness outside her cell. The insides of her eyelids blaze with blanketed orange light. She pries them open and glares up at her visitor.

"What a beautiful little insect I've caught in my web," the Guardian says. His face flickers in and out of shadow. Even in the darkness, the corporal is immediately recognizable. His silver hair catches in the firelight.

"I heard you were discovered at that despicable little whorehouse on the edge of town. Turning a few tricks, were we?" He laughs as though he has said something quite funny. Feeling sick, she forces herself to continue holding his gaze. Somewhere in the darkness she hears a voice. Throaty and half crazed, the words slide out of the darkness in a nearly incoherent babble.

"No!" An earsplitting shriek silences the bubbling words.

The corporal ignores all of this, his gaze lingering on Nerani. "I'd like to talk to you. Shall we go someplace a little bit more comfortable?"

His grin is menacing in the dancing light. Nerani says nothing, She thinks of Emerala. Her cousin would be bursting with hateful retorts. She, however, cannot think of a single thing to say. She presses her lips together and tries to stop herself from trembling. Her eyes swarm with stinging tears. The darkness before her splits into jeweled ember. She hears the rattle of bars as the corporal pries open the door.

"It's polite to respond, gypsy, when being addressed by a superior."

She is silent again, staring into the orange reflection of his boots as his feet click across the floor. She hears him give an audible sniff.

"Oh, good," he remarks cheerfully. "You haven't soiled the floors yet. I'm afraid I wouldn't be in the most pleasant of moods if you had forced me to wade in here through your piss."

He chuckles at this and grips her roughly beneath one arm. She feels a sweeping heat pass over the top of her head as the flames come dangerously close to her scalp. With a grunt, he wrenches her unceremoniously to her feet.

"Come along now. We can do this the easy way or the hard way." He leans in closer to her, his lips brushing against her ear. "I've cleared my entire schedule for the day, so it's really up to you."

She forces herself to walk alongside him. Her feet feel like lead. He leads her through a narrow doorway at the end of the reeking corridor. The room inside is brightly lit. The flames sputter and snap in their sconces, throwing unforgiving golden light upon a long, low table of rusted tools.

The corporal shoves her into a splintering chair at the center of the room.

"Sit," he suggests.

He sets his torch into a nearby sconce and sets to work binding her wrists with rope. She cries out as he twists her wrist too far. His smile widens. He reminds Nerani of a wolf—his fangs bared, his expression hungry.

"Not one for pain, are we? This should go by rather quickly, then."

Something in her expression catches his eye and he pauses before her, one finger caressing her cheek. She jerks her head out of his reach, her skin flaming. In response, he takes her face between his hands and forces her gaze up towards his face.

"I don't want you to worry," he whispers. "This will only be as painful as you make it."

His fingers linger too long upon her skin. She glares into his eyes, trying in vain to look less frightened than she feels. For a frantic moment, she contemplates spitting directly into his face, but thinks better of it. Her gaze travels towards the table of rusted tools and her stomach does an uneasy flip. She knows what's coming. She knows what he will want to know.

His eyes follow hers and he smiles, rising back to his feet.

"What shall we begin with?" he asks her as he studies the tools. His hand runs across a twisted iron bar, its ends caked in flaking bits of brown.

Old blood, she realizes, and another wave of nausea rushes over her.

After a few moments of carefully rehearsed consideration, the corporal makes a small exclamation of pleasure. He lifts from the table a rusted vice with heavy, protruding studs. When he turns back to face her, his gaze is bright—eager.

"I think the pilliwinks will suffice for our purposes, don't you?"

She stares at him in silence and says nothing.

"Let's start with something easy," he says cheerfully. "Have you been hiding out in a place known to your people as the Forbidden City?"

She longs to retreat within herself—to continue to remain silent—but she knows that she cannot. She swallows.

"The Forbidden City is an old legend."

The corporal's mouth twitches slightly. Clearly, he did not expect her to speak so easily. At the edge of her vision she can see his grip on the vice tighten.

"That may be," he assents. "That was not the question."

Her tongue feels like sandpaper in her mouth.

"Will you repeat the question?"

He laughs at that. "Games, is it? Have it your way, gypsy. I'll play along. I asked you if your people are hiding out within the Forbidden City."

"I believe I already gave you that answer."

"Did you?"

"Yes. The Forbidden City is a legend. A myth. It's not real. It's a story told to children at bedtime. It serves at a metaphor for happier times."

His smile is back. "Indeed," he says. He leans down, his hand cupping her chin. Pulling her face up towards his, he sets the vice down hard upon the arm of the chair. The long tip of her middle finger brushes against the cold metal.

"You'd do well to cooperate with me, gypsy," he snaps. The gruffness in his voice does not match the permanent, merciless smile that has taken root upon his face. He thrusts her chin out of his grasp and sets to fiddling with the vice. The coolness of the metal encapsulates the smallest of her fingers and suddenly she knows all too well what is coming. She stares into his face as he winds the vice downward onto her finger. There is a clipped moment of cool, steady pressure before her bones snap beneath the weight.

She had intended to bite down upon her lip and hold the scream within her. She didn't want to give him the satisfaction of hearing her cry out. White light pulsates at the edges of her vision and she gasps. The force of her pain is too powerful to be contained. Her voice spills out across the room in a shrill echo of agony. Tears stream in steady lines of salt down the curvature of her cheeks. He is peering into her face with a grotesque grimace, his gaze inquisitive. She clamps her mouth shut and breathes hotly through her nose. Her vision swarms in and out of focus.

"There." He pats her lightly upon the cheek and she can feel her own blood warm against her face. It drips down his fingers, staining her skin red. "That wasn't so bad, was it?"

She fights to be silent—to suffocate the dull whimper that rises within her throat. Her finger—what is left of it, pulsates in rhythmic, agonizing beats.

"I know the Forbidden City is real. It would be wise to refrain from lying to me in the future."

She stares at the crumbling wall over his golden shoulder. Breathe. In. Out.

Suddenly there is pain in her finger again. He is pressing down on the vice; leaning casually on it as though he doesn't realize her bones are being ground into dust beneath the tightened screws. She screams again, and his smile stretches across his face like a deep, red wound.

"A response would be respectful, gypsy."

Nerani can only gasp in response.

"Tell me," he mutters, leaning down so that his face is level with hers. Her bare feet push back aimlessly against the cool ground underfoot. Her toes curl and uncurl. The pain does not relent. "Tell me you won't lie to me again."

Anything to make the pain stop.

"I won't," she gasps.

"Won't *what*?" He releases some of the pressure.

"I won't lie to you again." The white light is spreading further across her vision. He is right. She is unaccustomed to pain. She wonders what he will do to her if she passes out. Will he revive her and continue? Or will he give up and leave her in her cell to tend to her wounds?

He appears satisfied with her response. He releases his hand from the vice, straightening his spine.

"Splendid," he says gaily and leans back against the table of tools. It shudders beneath his weight, setting some of the rusted equipment to shivering audibly. Her teeth come together with too much force and she tastes blood on her tongue. A low moan escapes from between her lips. Her eyes flutter closed and then open. He crouches before her, studying her with a primeval intensity.

"Where is the Forbidden City?"

She fights back the bile that rises in her throat. She barely comprehends his question over the pulsing pain of her finger. It is all consuming, coursing through her body like a fever.

"Where is the Forbidden City?" he asks again, louder this time.

"I don't know."

He moves away from the table, running his finger along the top of the vice. "You don't know, or you won't tell me? Chose your response carefully, gypsy. I won't have any more lies."

"I won't tell you," she says, and the anger in her voice surprises her.

She gives an involuntary gasp as he shifts the vice upon her fingers and begins twisting again. Cool metal presses lightly against one, unbroken finger.

"Where is the Forbidden City? It's a simple question. Tell me and this can be over. There's no need for you to suffer."

She spits at his feet. Her saliva sits upon her lips, the taste acrid.

"Is that your response?" He appears only mildly displeased.

"Yes," she says, her voice thin.

He smirks, his dark eyes gleaming, and tightens the vice.

"You might be surprised," he says as her bones crunch beneath the unforgiving weight. He raises his voice to be heard over the blood-curdling cry that escapes her lips. "But this saddens me to do. I get no pleasure out of hurting you. I only want your honesty. Lying, you see, is a terrible crime."

She cannot hear him. She cannot see him. The white light has engulfed her vision. Her ears are filled with her thick screams, bubbling with sobs. She fights to gain control of herself—fights to be able to deprive him of the satisfaction he craves.

"Corporal."

The sharp voice that emanates from the doorway is calm, authoritative. The pressure upon her finger stops. She nearly faints as she feels the blood in her hand go rushing back into the broken joints.

The corporal jumps back immediately, allowing the device to clatter to the ground. Somewhere far, far away she can hear the sound of an iron screw rolling across stone. She lets out a long gasp and her vision swarms. The absence of the device brings no relief to her broken fingers. The pain is excruciating.

"General." The grin is gone from the corporal's lips.

Nerani can just make out the figure of General Byron standing in the narrow doorway, almost beyond the reach of the light. He does not look at her. His gaze is trained upon the Guardian before him.

"What do you think you're doing?"

"Interrogating the prisoner, of course, sir."

"I don't recall giving you orders to do so."

At this, the corporal allows himself to smile again. Nerani watches as his lips peel back from his teeth. His eyes are dangerous. "With all due respect, these particular orders came directly from his Majesty."

"He would have given that command to me."

"You were nowhere to be found."

There is a moment of careful hesitation as the two Guardians study each other across the sputtering torchlight.

"I'm here now," General Byron says. "You're dismissed. I'll take it from here."

"General—"

"You're dismissed." There is a sense of finality in his tone. The corporal leers vehemently towards Nerani for a moment before assenting. He gives an angry grunt and heads for the door. As he maneuvers past General Bryon his shoulder slams into his side, forcing him to fall back a step. In a flash, General Byron slams the corporal against the doorframe. They are nose to nose, his fist clutching at the collar of his uniform. The corporal blinks twice in surprise and says nothing.

"You will give me the respect I am due as your superior officer," seethes General Byron. His voice is low and controlled. The only betrayal of anger on his face is the slight flare of his nostrils.

"Duly noted, sir."

"See to it that it is," General Byron snarls. "Touch me again, and watch what happens to you."

Something in his eyes makes the corporal swallow, hard. A slow smile creeps into his lips.

"Yes sir," he says. General Byron releases him, shoving him back into the shadow of the hallway beyond. For a long moment, he stands idle in the dusky quiet, brushing at his shirtfront as though he is wiping away crumbs.

And then he is gone.

General Byron remains frozen in the doorway, his gaze burning. They listen in silence to the sound of the corporal's footfalls receding upon the stone. Nerani forces herself to breathe deep, letting her eyes drop to examine her damaged fingers. She gasps audibly as she takes in the crushed bones, mangled with flesh and marrow. Her stomach heaves violently and she is nearly ill.

Before her, General Byron is staring at the floor with frightening resolve. His gaze is dark and unreadable. His lips are pressed together in a white line.

"I told you to go back to your city," he says at last, and his voice is rife with barely concealed anger. She notes his fingers, trembling only slightly, balling into fists at his side before stretching wide and relaxing. His shoulders rise and fall. He does not meet her gaze. "Saints, I *begged* you to leave."

She opens her mouth to speak, but nothing comes out. The throb of her fingers has overtaken the rest of her body. Every fiber of her being pulsates with the pain. She is weak, she realizes. She is afraid.

She does not know real pain, for this to unravel her so completely. More than ever before, she wishes she could be as strong as Emerala. Tears pool in her lower lids and she tries in vain to blink them away. General Byron is watching her now, his brown eyes studying her face. He moves slowly across the room—cautiously—lowering himself to his knees before her chair and setting to untying the crude rope that binds her good hand to the armrest.

"What was so important?" he asks as he works. She can hear the rage within his words, bubbling just beneath the surface of the question. "What is out here for you that was worth the risk? Because I can't help you now, not anymore."

She begins to cry at this, the tears streaming freely down her cheeks. "I was looking for my cousin."

"Emerala the Rogue?" His brows furrow. "Your people have her."

"No." She shakes her head, ignoring the locks of her hair that suction themselves to her face. Her fingers are sticky with blood. He finishes untying the rope and she watches as it falls to the ground at her feet. His fingers linger on hers just a moment too long. She tries to gather her thoughts through the pain—to remain coherent even as her vision washes with white.

"The last time I saw her she was at the mercy of three Guardians, each with their swords held at her throat. My people believe her to be dead, but I know she's still alive. I know she's somewhere in the city."

The anger in General Bryon's gaze softens. His brows pull together, casting a shadow across the bridge of his nose.

"She's not here," he mutters. His hand rises tentatively to her face. Slowly—cautiously—he pushes several loose strands of hair behind her ears. His thumb wipes a salty droplet from her cheek. She does not have the coherence to question his familiarity, so muddled does she feel from the throbbing pain in her hand.

"Those Guardians—the three you mentioned—they were found slaughtered in the streets, their throats cut."

"Who?" she asks, unable to form a more articulate thought. Her fingers are tingling now—a peculiar sensation. Her teeth chatter.

"We thought it was your people," General Byron says. "The Cairans."

"It wasn't."

"Evidently."

Silence passes between them as he stares contemplatively at her mangled hand. She does not follow his gaze. She cannot bear to look and see the damage that has been done.

When he looks at her again she can see turmoil in his guarded gaze. "You should have listened to me. I serve at the pleasure of his Majesty. Within these walls my hands are tied. To act against him would be treason."

"I don't expect anything from you," she snaps. "I landed myself in this situation. I will get myself out of it."

His expression darkens. "I don't think you understand. This isn't over. The Guardians are going to continue to torture you until you give them what they want."

"I won't tell them anything."

The muscles in his jaw tighten as he grates his teeth together. "They'll expect me to interrogate you."

"I won't tell you anything either," she spits.

His hesitation leaves her aware of the uncomfortable closeness between them.

"Silence is treason, here," he says at last. His voice is tight. "They'll call you a traitor and you'll be hung for your crimes against the crown."

She turns her head away from him, furiously blinking away the flurry of tears that threaten to spill over. She knows that once she begins sobbing— once the tears begin— she will not be able to stop.

"I'm prepared to die," she lies.

"Look at me," he says, surprising her. He takes her face in his hands, guiding her eyes back to him. Anguish cuts through the usually blank veneer of his face—naked anguish, and, deeper still, a desperation that sets her pulse racing.

"You may think you're ready to die, but I'm not prepared to watch. Not when I've just found you again, do you hear me?"

She is silent before him, her breathing hitching in her throat.

I don't love him, she had told Orianna, indignant at the very thought.

But you will.

And it will drown you both.

"I'm going to untie your wrist," he says, his fingers dancing lightly upon the twine that binds her mangled hand. "It's not going to be pleasant. The rope is too tight. All of the blood will go rushing to your fingers."

She nods, steeling herself. She studies the clenched line of his jaw as he works, keeping her gaze away from the constant twitch of her poor, mangled fingers. His own fingers move delicately as he pries at the knot atop her wrist.

And then the rope is falling away. She feels a prickle of surging blood as far back as her elbow. Her fingers tingle for a shivering instant and then there is pain—piercing, pressing pain. It feels as though her fingers are being broken all over again. Fresh blood pushes into the purpling flesh and she wretches.

A flash of white pulls across her retinas and her vision goes dark.

Harvest Cycle 1511

The Hawk suspects that the map does not lead to the Westerlies, but instead to some other location. Somewhere only Charles Argot knows. Somewhere he can collect later, once we have parted ways.

He is a paranoid boy, the Hawk. He believes everyone in this world is duplicitous.

Sam, however, believes everyone can be bought for the right price, duplicitous or not. We paid a hefty sum for Charles Argot's loyalty. The map, when unlocked—if ever unlocked—will bring a ship into the Westerlies.

I will believe that to be the truth. I will trust the mapmaker, if only because we have gone too far to turn back now.

Eliot

CHAPTER 25

The Rebellion

SOMEONE IS SHOUTING.

Emerala wakes in a start. She sits up too fast, drawing in her breath with a frantic pull of air. Her fingers claw at her throat. Her skin is clammy. Cold.

She blinks rapidly, her eyes adjusting to the sunlight that falls across her gown in strips of pale yellow. She is lying in a cot, her shoulders wrapped in an itching wool blanket. Somewhere below she can hear the waves whispering against the hull of the ship. The light pulls, contorting, across the plum cotton of her gown as the galley rises and falls in rhythmic swells.

"Damn it!" curses the voice a second time. The Hawk. "Damn it, this is all wrong."

Emerala paws at her eyes, willing her vision to clear. Her stomach churns. She is back on the ship, that much is clear. But how? How did she get here? Her heartbeat pulses behind her eyes. Her tongue feels like sandpaper in her mouth. She tries to remember leaving the Eisle and realizes she cannot. Her memory is fuzzy, slipping away from her like the remnants of a bad dream.

A second voice joins the fray. This one is calmer than the first, but only just.

"Maybe now is the time to fill me in, mate, don't you think?" Alexander asks.

The Hawk unleashes a laugh like bark. "You want me to fill you in, aye? I've already told you. This map is *wrong*."

"What makes you so sure?"

"Because I know where it's meant to lead, and *this* isn't it."

Emerala pulls the heels of her hands away from her eyes, rolling over in bed to try and get a better view of the room. The chandelier swings languidly overhead. Several bottles of rum clink in the wooden cellarette behind Alexander's desk. At the desk stands Alexander and the Hawk, each of them bent low over an unfurled bit of parchment. Their figures dance on her vision, the lines of them blurring at the edges. She blinks slowly, feeling the room roll. They do not know she is awake—not yet.

She closes her eyes in a futile effort to stop the room from spinning, and listens.

"Are you finally ready to start answering my questions, then?" Alexander asks. His dark voice is heavy with implication.

"I've always been willing to answer your questions, Cap'n." The Hawk sounds weary. Tense.

"Have you? It hasn't felt that way."

"Aye? Maybe you've been asking the wrong questions."

There is a scuffle—the sound of boots rushing across the creaking floor-boards. Someone grunts. Emerala opens one eye. Alexander is nose to nose with the Hawk, a pistol leveled at the bare skin of his heavily inked chest. Emerala notices that Alexander's left hand is bound tightly with gauze, as if he's recently been injured.

"Don't," he snarls. "Do not play games with me. Not today."

"You don't have the guts to kill me. You're not a murderer."

"I've killed before."

"Not like this," the Hawk disagrees. "Not up close. Not looking into the eyes of an old friend."

"You're no friend of mine," spits Alexander.

"Oh, but I am. In fact, I'm your only friend. We want the same thing, you and I. That makes us allies."

The gun remains positioned at the Hawk's chest, but Emerala sees Alexander's finger relax at the trigger. He leans back, a scowl pressed into his lips.

"Allies share information," he says.

"I've shared with you what I know. This map was made to lead to a spot somewhere in the great Westerlies. You've studied it. It's filled with riddles and dead ends. Does that map bring us anywhere near the mainland?"

"No," Alexander admits.

"No," the Hawk repeats. "We've been played, Cap'n. Played for fools. And I knew it. I told your father not to trust the man who made the map—"

Alexander cuts him off. "You knew the mapmaker?"

The Hawk falls silent, his features hardening to stone.

"You *knew* the mapmaker?" Alexander repeats.

"You're asking the wrong questions again, Cap'n," the Hawk warns.

"Right." Alexander scoffs. "You're quite the ally, Evander."

The Hawk smirks and says nothing. The feathered down of Emerala's pillow tickles her nose and she fights back a sneeze, scrunching up her face with all of her might.

"It must be difficult to keep track of all of your lies," Alexander observes. "Perhaps you're finally starting to slip."

"Perhaps."

"Perhaps I *should* kill you now, if you're determined to be useless to me. The map is unbound. Wrong or not, I'm going where it leads."

"You may not like what you find."

Alexander smiles a humorless smile. "You have no—"

Emerala sneezes loudly, launching herself upright upon the cot. Her matted curls fly forward into her face. Wiping her nose, she turns sheepishly toward the desk. The two pirates stare at her, the pistol still leveled at the Hawk's tattooed chest. He laughs, his golden eyes crinkling as Alexander retracts his weapon and holsters it at his waist.

"She lives," the Hawk crows. Emerala scowls up at him.

"We've been waiting for you to wake up," Alexander says. "How are you feeling?"

"Like I've been hit over the head with a rock," Emerala gripes, sniffling. "What happened to me?"

Alexander pulls at the golden scruff on his chin. "We were hoping you could tell us. Thom and the Hawk found you half buried under a snowdrift a few miles inland. You must have been separated from the rest of the group during the race back to the ship."

"I don't—I can't remember."

"We think you might have been poisoned."

She sputters, choking on the word. "Poisoned?"

Alexander nods, a strip of yellow sunlight falling across his face. The light of it sets the golden scruff of his jaw ablaze.

"Are you certain the last thing you can remember is the dining hall?" the Hawk asks. His golden eyes on hers are making her skin crawl. She feels unnaturally cold in the heat.

"Yes," she says, not without a hint of agitation. There is a distinct buzzing noise deep inside her skull—an angry hornet lodged between her ears. She remembers the warm, hazy glow of the dining hall—can hear the discordant hum of dining patrons.

"Think," Alexander urges.

"I *am* thinking," she retorts. Her voice is thick.

"Did you eat or drink anything while we were there?"

"No," she says and hesitates. "I-I don't remember."

"Which is it? No, you didn't, or you don't remember?"

"Well, I certainly didn't eat any of the meat," she snaps, feeling nauseous at the thought of it. "At least, I don't think I did, but I'm having a hard time recalling anything at all."

"You should have stayed with the Hawk," Alexander says. "Going off on your own out there was foolish."

"I—" Emerala starts and stops, a sudden shred of memory coming back to her. She feels the cadence of a gallop beneath her, hears the whinny of a horse, high and clear. And Evander the Hawk's voice in her ear, *keep quiet, Rogue.* She glances up at him, peering at him carefully across the late afternoon sun that sweeps across the floors in dusty shafts of gold. He stares back at her, unruffled, calm.

"I'm sorry," Emerala whispers.

A throat clearing in the background causes all three of them to turn their attention toward the door. Lachlan the Lethal stands perched in the doorway, the yellow light of the sun turned deep red at his back. His small, stocky frame is shrouded in a halo of glistening crimson, pitting the deep grooves of his face into pockets of shadow.

"Sorry to interrupt," he says, not sounding sorry at all. "Thought ye'd like to know there's a stranger onboard the ship."

"Besides yourself?" Alexander asks.

"Aye, well, another, then. He's put up a right stink about being held upon the bowsprit, says as he knows ye."

Now that the door is open, Emerala can hear the sound of raised voices drifting in upon the distant murmur of the waves. Someone curses, his gruff shout lost within the buffeting breeze that snaps at the sails overhead. Over it all, she can hear the guttural screaming of several agitated seagulls.

"Why didn't Thom send for me?" Alexander rises from his seat, the pillow on his lap falling forgotten to the floor.

"Your first mate's been hollering his fool head off since the moment the boarder stepped foot on deck, says we en't like to make exceptions for..." the Lethal pauses, snapping the fingers of his right hand as though eager to recall the exact wording used by the portly quartermaster. "Ah yes," he says at last, and Emerala can see the gold of his teeth catching in the blood orange sunlight. "a poxed, Senadian swab."

The wind outside dies down with a tired sputter. In the sudden quiet the sound of overlapping shouts reaches their ears. Emerala studies Alexander's face, watching to see what he will do. She is surprised to see a look of delight pass over the captain's features. He turns to face her, fighting unsuccessfully to keep his expression blank.

"You," he barks, rather needlessly. There could have been no mistaking to whom he was about to give orders. "Stay put."

"But—"

"Do as I say," he snaps brusquely. He glances up at the Lethal. "Come with me. Put two men on starboard, you take port. Keep your eyes peeled and your hand by your cutlass. There's no telling who else might decide to drop by, this close to the Agran Circle."

"Aye," the Lethal says. His face, as usual, betrays no emotions. The two men abscond from her sight. The door slams shut behind them.

And then she is alone with Evander the Hawk. He meanders toward the door, his swarthy figure melting into the frame. His eyes never leave her face. The sight of him causes an unexpected shiver to run down her spine.

"Cold, are you?" he asks, still smiling. "In this heat?"

"Heat?" The air inside Alexander's quarters is stale but comfortable—silvery dust motes hang suspended in the last remaining trickles of scarlet light that spills in through the soiled windows. "We were in the north only—"

She trails off, uncertain of the date. How long has she been asleep? At the door, the Hawk seems to have read her mind.

"You've been asleep nearly a fortnight. You were on the edge of death when we found you, Rogue. It's a miracle we did."

"Is it?" she asks, her eyes narrowing. "I was with you, wasn't I?"

"You were," the Hawk agrees. "At the Frost Forts. I told you to run, do you remember?"

She blinks, straining to grab hold of something—anything—that will tether her to reality. She remembers his face, spattered in blood, his hair matted to his cheeks. She remembers his voice, hoarse against the sound of steel against steel.

Rogue. Run. Now.

"I suppose—" she begins, stopping again, unable to summon any coherent sort of memory. Glancing up, she meets his golden eyes across the fading light. "Where are we now?"

"We're drawing just north of the Agran Circle." A crooked smile splits his lips. "The Leviathan lives below these waters, here."

"Leviathan?" she repeats, confused.

"I'd reckon you've never heard of anything like it back in Chancey." His piercing gaze unnerves her. Instinctively, she draws the blanket to her chin.

"Can't say that I have. What is it?"

"It's a scaled serpent that lives deep beneath the ocean. They say its breath is so hot that wherever it swims, the water grows warm. Sometimes the heat is enough to make the surface bubble."

Emerala studies his face for any sign of skepticism. "And you believe that?"

"Me? No. But you've spent enough time in the company of pirates by now to know that we're a superstitious lot. Keep watch—you'll see the men crossing themselves whenever they pass too close to port and starboard."

Emerala stares back at him, saying nothing. His golden gaze is unwavering—unapologetic.

Unnerving.

She averts her attention to the empty space above his head, suppressing the sudden chill that tickles the top of her spine.

"Why aren't you up at the front of the ship with the rest?" she asks. "Isn't there some sort of visitor for you to harass?"

The Hawk shrugs, the hair on his chest glinting first gold then red in the fading sunlight. "I've no interest in diplomats. Hang the bloody lot of them."

"He's a diplomat?" she asks, sitting up straighter.

"Aye. A wealthy one, at that."

"We must be close to land, then."

He nods, eying her closely. "We're about a day's sail off the port of Senada."

"Senada? I don't think I've ever heard of it."

"Strange," he says slowly, the wickedness in his grin giving way to amusement. "I should think you would be familiar with its location, given that it shares a strait with the island of Caira."

Caira. The name causes a surge of blood to rush to her head, pressing against the backs of her eyelids. She springs to her feet, ignoring the pins in her fingers and toes. Her legs tremble beneath her weight. She pushes forward, shaking out her fingers as she maneuvers closer to the door. At the sight of her approach, the Hawk pushes himself out of the doorframe and moves to block the opening.

"Where are you going?"

"I think I'd like to meet this diplomat," she says. She moves to push past him but he steps directly in front of her, cutting her off. His breath tickles the tip of her nose. She can smell the sweat off of his skin, brackish and inebriating, like he is leaking rum from his pores. She averts her eyes, trying in vain to gaze over the tops of his shoulders. "I'd thank you to get out of my way."

"Cap'n said you're not to step foot outside of this room, I heard him."

"Since when you do you care what Alexander wants?" she retorts.

"When it comes to you, we generally want the same thing."

"Is that right?" Emerala snaps. "And what, exactly, is that?"

The Hawk pauses for the breath of a second, his tongue darting over his lower lip. Again, that unsettling golden gaze searches her face.

"We want you to follow orders and stay put," he says, a sense of finality in his tone.

"To the Dark Below with him," she mutters, pushing past him with a shove. She turns up her nose and adds, "And you as well."

Slipping through the door, she races across the deck of the ship. Her bare feet drag against the splinters in the wood. She is keenly aware of the Hawk tagging along behind her, never more than a few feet away. She does her level best to ignore him, bunching up her skirts within her fists.

Up ahead, Alexander stands just beneath the bowsprit, his arm outstretched as he shakes the hand of a shadowed man before him. She draws to a stop a few feet away from them just as the stranger—the diplomat—turns toward her. His eyes widen at the sight of her, his mouth falling open as he takes in her bedraggled countenance—her wild hair and her dark, emerald gaze.

She, too, surveys the newcomer in silence. He is handsome—tall—with a polished posture and upturned chin. His jaw is strong and clean-shaven. His deep, dark eyes are as black as the night. His hair, neatly brushed back from the widow's whorl at the middle of his forehead, is as golden as a sunrise. He looks impossibly familiar, and yet she is certain she has never before lain eyes on him. How could she have? She has never left Chancey—has never been to Senada.

And yet the sight of the man before her tugs at her memory, teasing at the corners as the answer—if there is one—dances just out of her reach.

A smile breaks out across the newcomer's face—dimpling his chin—just as the smile upon Alexander's fades to a grimace. He shares a silent look of consternation with the Hawk as the lanky pirate draws to Emerala's side with a shrug.

"Where are my manners?" the diplomat asks. His voice is as deep and as rich as his dark gaze. Emerala is startled by the familiarity of his accent. *He's a Chancian,* she realizes.

He bows, taking Emerala's hand in his own. His lips graze against her knuckles. "Alex, you never told me you had such a lovely woman gracing the holds of your ship. Good evening to you, my lady."

At her side, the Hawk snorts. Emerala ignores him.

"Hello," she says.

"This is Derek," Alexander proffers, still glowering at Emerala. "He's a very old friend."

"You wouldn't know that," Derek says, letting Emerala's hand drop. "Not after all the trouble I had climbing onboard your ship."

"Right, well." Alexander pulls at his scruff. "The crew has been jumpy ever since our visit to the Eisle."

"Understandably so," Derek assents, and gives a theatrical shudder. "Saints, what an awful place. Why you would venture there at this time of year, I'll never know. We can both agree that the map is of great importance, my friend, but could it not have waited until the snow thawed?"

"It couldn't." Alexander's response is too quick—too sharp. "You know it couldn't. The cost of waiting would have been—"

"Astronomical," Derek finishes, flashing Alexander a smile. "You're all too right, my friend, as always. In that case, I'm pleased to see you and your crew made it out unscathed."

"We did."

The sterling moon, as round as a disk, has risen out from behind the undulating black sails that loom overhead. Only a minute tinge of deep red daylight sits upon the edge of the sky. Emerala can barely contain herself any longer—her curiosity has been piqued, and she's never been the patient type.

She turns to Alexander, her eyes bright. "We're going to Caira?" Excitement crowds her words together, rendering them nearly incoherent. Alexander looks as though he has tasted something sour. Reaching up with one hand, he tugs at the rim of his cap. The muted light of the moon cuts across his jaw in strips of silver. A muscle in his jaw twitches, but he says nothing.

"She's a woman with a sense of adventure," Derek marvels, his black eyes glittering. "How extraordinary!"

Emerala smiles at that, liking the genial nature of the well-dressed man in spite of herself. Back on Chancey she would have detested him and everything he stood for—hated his fineries, his mannerisms, the very smile on his face. Here, out on the rolling sea, she takes comfort in his familiarity.

"Are we?" Emerala asks Alexander. "Going to Caira, I mean?"

"I'm going to Caira," he replies, his voice dark. "The Hawk is going to Caira. Derek, here, is going to Caira. You're staying here."

"But—"

"This isn't up for debate, Rogue."

"You may need me," she argues.

"We won't."

"You couldn't have done what you needed to do at the Eisle of Udire without me."

Derek's laugh resonates across the deck, the echo swallowed by the rolling waves. He slaps Alexander on the back, his winning smile bright in the moonlight.

"She's full of fire," Derek barks. "I love it."

"I'm sure you do," Alexander gripes.

"Keeps you on your toes, does she? That's just what you need in a woman, Alex."

Alexander's face catches ablaze, turning crimson from the end of his nose to the tips of his ears. "She's not—"

But Emerala beats him to the punch. "I'm *not* his *woman*."

"No?" Derek asks. "Then under what capacity are you here? You'll excuse me for wondering, but women aren't common sights at sea."

"I'm a member of the crew," Emerala explains.

"She's not that, either." Alexander assures Derek, traces of red lingering beneath his skin. "And she's not coming with us to Caira."

Emerala's arms knot across her chest. "And why not?"

"Because it isn't safe."

"And the Eisle of Udire was—what—a stroll through the park?"

Alexander opens his mouth to retort, but Derek cuts him off, that same, genial smile ever present on his lips.

"Surely it's no less safe for her than it is for us." He winks at her, one black eye disappearing and reappearing.

For the first time in several moments, the Hawk speaks. "Agree to disagree, mate," he says. He moves in close to Emerala, the inked skin of his arm brushing against her shoulder. The stance is protective—possessive. Emerala bristles at his proximity, that same unnatural chill coursing through her. Across the deck, Alexander watches the two of them through unblinking hazel eyes, his jaw locked.

"This is Emerala the Rogue," the Hawk explains. "A Cairan."

Derek's finely manicured brows pull together at the revelation. He scrutinizes her closely, his nose wrinkling.

"Surely not," he reasons. "I thought all Cairans were born with rather distinct blue eyes."

"Aye, that may be so, but this girl's a half blood."

At that, Derek blanches, his face draining of color. "Emerala the Rogue, did you say?"

"I didn't say," she mutters, "but yes."

Derek draws several steps closer to her across the deck of the ship, still studying her face with renewed interest. "Yes," he says, more to himself than to her. "Yes, I see it now. Those are lovely green eyes you have. Like jewels."

She hesitates before responding. "Thank you." Her skin has gone cold.

"Might I ask which parent gave you those eyes? Your mother or your father?"

Emerala is suddenly thrust backwards through her memories, pulled back to that fleeting moment in a narrow alleyway where the Hawk had thrust the ivory dagger into her hands.

Was it your mother or your father that gave you those lovely green eyes?

Now, she feels the pirate tense at her side, the muscles in his arm going rigid.

"My father," she whispers, the chill in her veins turning to ice.

Derek turns to Alexander, forcing a smile. "What have you gotten into, my friend?"

Before Alexander can reply, he continues, "She will accompany us to the island. It won't be safe for her on the ship, not with the anchor being dropped so close to Domio and his spies."

Alexander scowls. "You expect me to believe it will be safer on the island?"

Overhead, the wind picks up, causing the fluttering black banner upon the foremast to snap and sputter upon the post. The simple white skull grins down at them from the curling flag. To Emerala, it feels like an omen. She shudders and thinks of the crew crossing themselves as protection against portents and superstitions.

"Likely not," Derek admits, "But there is little other choice. If we want her to live—and I'm fairly certain that you do—it is imperative that we keep her identity hidden from Domio. I'm afraid it was a poor decision, old friend, to bring Emerala the Rogue to the Agran Circle."

Harvest Cycle 1511

Something is wrong.

Two moons past, I woke in the night to an uproar. Charles Argot is gone. He left without a word, disappeared as a lark with the breaking of the dawn. The map went with him. This does not bode well for us.

The young Hawk is positively crowing with righteous indignation, but the crew will have none of it. He continues to remind me that he never trusted the mapmaker, not for a moment. He has sold my soul for a handsome price, the boy is certain of it.

Captain Samuel listens only in silence. He will not meet my gaze.

In the muted grey of this early morning a second ship appeared on the horizon. She is gaining upon us far too quickly for it to be a coincidence that she is there. The black sails have swallowed the westward winds like a voracious whale. It will not be long before she reaches us.

And what, then?

What, then?

I am not a religious man, but I pray that wherever Charles Argot has gone, his word and his honor were enough to buy his loyalty. I pray that I remain alive long enough to deliver my burden to the shores of the Westerlies.

My faith in my journey must not be shaken. We will keep to the course.

We will hoist the colors.

Eliot

CHAPTER 26

Chancey

SOMETIMES, AGAINST THE pervading darkness of the night, Seranai the Fair finds herself struggling to keep her demons at bay.

She leans back against the warm brick wall of Mamere Lenora's and listens to the barely subdued sounds of lovemaking that filter down through the soiled windows overhead. The night is dark, to be sure. Black as pitch, even. The moon is at the end of its cycle, ready to rebirth in a silvery travail, dragging its empty, white light upon the cobbled stones of Chancey.

She, too, feels as hollow as the moon's empty echo. She tilts her chin upward, her pallid skin glowing in the orange light that flickers out from a second story window. She is a woman in limbo—frozen in time as she awaits her next move. She frowns, the lines around her mouth deepening as the corners of her lips pull downward. Somewhere up above, she hears a faint clattering noise. A light fizzles out, pitting one section of the street before her in increasing shadow. There is a giggle, hushed, then silence. Somewhere off in the darkness, a stray cat yowls.

When will it be time?

She recalls again the Hawk's last, ominous caveat, delivered to her among the peeling wallpaper of the brothel during that first meeting.

There may be blood shed, before the end, he warned her, his golden eyes glittering in the candlelight. *There will be casualties.*

Her fingernails drive themselves hard into the palms of her hands at the memory, and she fights to keep her thoughts from drifting further back— from calling into memory the wet copper reek of pooling blood, from her father's lips opening and closing like a fish as he lay dying on the slab of stone before her.

She thinks, instead, of Nerani the Elegant. Is she the type of casualty the Hawk was thinking of the first day he and Seranai met?

Likely not.

Seranai fiddles with a stray lock of her hair, smiling into the darkness.

Selling out Nerani to the Guardians had been easy enough. Whinny had been clay in her hands, the gullible fool. She swallowed every lie that Seranai fed her as if she was a starving vagrant, clinging desperately onto each and every morsel.

People crave power. They are born that way, whether they get a taste of it or not. Seranai has always noticed that about people—how far they are willing to go to empower themselves—how dark the deeds they are willing and able to do.

Whinny's very existence was powerless. She belonged to the world, to the night—to the men that paid for a space in bed beside her. A woman like that would do anything to take back control. She would do anything to survive.

And so she had.

Yes, selling out Nerani the Elegant had been easy. Laughably simple, really.

It makes Seranai suspicious, the ease with which her plan had fallen into place. She is unsettled, uneasy—waiting for something to go wrong.

Several days ago, she had watched with barely concealed glee as the Guardians threw a hapless Nerani down upon her knees, binding her hands at the small of her back before dragging her off down the cobbled streets. Relief flooded her as they turned out of sight and the sounds of their boots faded to silence. Nerani had not begged. She had not screamed. She had only waited, her sky blue eyes pooling with tears as she was arrested for her crimes.

Seranai should feel magnificent. She should be relishing in her accomplishment, perhaps even breaking into a bottle of Mamere's finest port.

Instead, that niggling unease roots around within her gut like a sniffling rodent, driving her to restlessness. The demons that plague her in the dark follow her now all throughout the day, tugging at her mind and tormenting her senses.

Something is amiss.

Nerani the Elegant should have been burned at the stake.

She should have been hung by the neck until dead.

She should have been, and yet not even a notice of public execution has been distributed among the citizens of Chancey. No herald has streaked through the street upon his horse, trumpeting the announcement of her demise.

What are they waiting for?

She arches her back, ignoring the fabric that adheres itself to her skin in the sticking heat leftover from the unforgiving day. The darkness that settles over Chancey presses against the earth like a blanket, making the stale air hang heavy. It does not bring with it the usual cool relief of night.

She can feel James's presence in the dark street before she sees him. His arrival, as quiet and as sudden as the rain, sends a small shiver down the nape of her neck.

"Hello," she says, opening her eyes at the sound of his footfalls on the cobblestone. He always did have a distinct way of walking, she notes, his footsteps firm and self-assured—a meticulous swagger. His presence on the steps before her is suffocating. She pulls at the high, lace collar of her dress and frowns.

James inclines his head toward her, avoiding meeting her eyes. "Good evening."

"What brings you here?" An uneasy flutter sweeps through her. She recalls the warning he had issued during his previous visit. Is that why he is here, now? The night feels suddenly cold in spite of the heat. There is no wind, but she shivers all the same.

"Come to make good on your threats, have you?" Her voice is constrained. Quiet. James looks startled by her question. His brown eyes momentarily lose their impenetrable exterior. It is then that she notices how unkempt he appears. His is donned in his everyman clothes, his gold standard replaced with grey homespun cloth and black breeches. His face is unshaven. He looks as though he has not slept.

"You look awful," she remarks. Some of her initial fear falls away from her as she studies him. He does not seem to register her remark.

"I need a favor." His brown eyes meet hers. She is shocked to find his usually cold gaze entreating.

"A favor?" she repeats, unable to keep the disgust out of her voice. She is not quite certain she has heard him correctly.

"Yes."

Not likely, she thinks scornfully. And yet her curiosity ebbs at her, willing her to hear him out and see just what it is he wants.

"Just what could the formidable General Byron possibly need from me? A quick fix, perhaps? We are at a whorehouse."

The derision in her voice does not go unnoticed by James. He winces visibly, and for a moment she can see beneath the cracked veneer in his decorum. It hurts him to be standing here before her—hurts him to need anything from her. He closes the space between them, taking the steps two at a time until he reaches the stoop where she stands, partially concealed in shadow. His eyes flicker back and forth as he makes sure they are quite alone.

"This is serious, Seranai."

Hearing her name on his tongue evokes, as always, those sudden, unwanted feelings. She pushes them away, growing angrier with herself.

Quiet, you demons, she thinks.

"I am as serious as I've ever been. The nerve of you, James—coming here on your hands and knees, begging me for help after all of this time."

His shoulders crumple under the weight of her words. She fights the urge to smile. She is stomping relentlessly on his cherished pride, and it brings her more joy than she thought possible. He stares at the floor between them, watching it as though expecting it to open up and swallow him whole. After a few moments of silent consideration he glances back up at her. His dark eyes have once again hardened to steel.

"I'm afraid I won't beg on my hands and knees. But you *will* help me."

"Will I?" A challenge laces her words. She is not afraid of him—not here, when so much as a scream from her will call to the windows all of the inhabitants of the house and her patrons. One scream from her, and the unblemished record of James will be forever sullied. He cannot afford such a mistake. He cannot lay a hand on her here. Her grey eyes narrow into slits in the darkness, matching him in their indifference.

"You will." His echo holds, within it, a sense of finality.

"We will see, I suppose. What is the favor?"

He swallows, leaning in close. "You have contacts of some sort, don't you?" He phrases it as a question, but he does not wait for an answer. "You have a way to get inside the Forbidden City, should you need to?"

"I already told you, the city—"

"Don't," he snaps, cutting her off. His fingers shake at his sides and he closes them into fists. "Don't lie to me. I know it exists."

She purses her lips. Considers.

"I don't know what you could possibly mean by contacts. You more than anyone know that I don't affiliate with my people."

"I also know that you would never enter into any situation without first having an escape plan. If you wanted to get into the city, you could."

She contemplates this. *Clever,* she thinks. But then he always was smart.

"Right?" he demands, after a few moments of uncomfortable silence have elapsed between them. His voice cracks and she starts, surprised at his unraveling conduct. She wonders how long it has been since he last slept.

"Right," she assents. "Let's say that I do have contacts. What is it you need?"

His tongue darts out over his lower lip. "There was a woman arrested here a fortnight past. You may have known her. She is a Cairan, herself."

Seranai feels her blood run cold. Her knees slam together beneath her petticoat. "Yes," she says, and her voice comes out in a squeak. The demons within her are writhing in the pit of her stomach—wailing like banshees deep within her head. She struggles to gather herself. "I know of her. You'll be speaking, I assume, of Nerani the Elegant."

James pauses at the sound of her name, an unusual splash of color rising along the line of his cheekbones. She takes silent note of this and continues.

"What of her?"

James glances around carefully, his brown eyes studying the shadows as though he expects someone to emerge from the darkness at any given moment.

"I need you to arrange for you and Nerani to return to the Forbidden City."

Unable to help herself, Seranai's lips fall open. She gapes at him in silence, incapable of grasping what she has just heard. There is a distinct buzzing in her ears and she fights the urge to shake her head clear.

"But," she begins and falters. She swallows hard, tasting something bitter on her tongue. Her veins run cold beneath her flesh. "She was arrested."

James looks momentarily anguished. His gaze is as dark as the dreaded Dark Below. "I know. I will be bringing her here."

"What? When?"

"Tomorrow night," he states simply, his gaze holding hers.

"You—" Anger surges through her skin, the white-hot heat of it curling in her fingertips. "You can't," she says at last. "You wouldn't. What you're talking about doing—that's treason."

She hisses the last word through clenched teeth, her fists resting upon the wide whalebone netting of her hips. His gaze turns murderous. In a flash, his hands enclose around her throat. She cries out, her skull cracking against the warm brick as he shoves her backwards. Deep red and white spots fan out across her vision. His face is inches away from hers, all traces of decorum gone. In its place she sees only quiet rage.

"You will not mention that word again in my presence, do you understand?" His voice is so low that it is almost inaudible. She lets out a guttural cry, gasping for breath. Her grey eyes widen with realization.

"You're in love with her."

There is a footfall upon the creaking wooden staircase just inside the front door.

"Seranai?"

It is Mamere Lenora. Two hands slide away from her neck, leaving behind a dull throbbing as air rushes down her throat and into her lungs. She can feel him slinking back into the shadows.

"Tell her you're fine," James whispers. He is in control of his voice once again. The words that reach her ears in the darkness are weighted with an unspoken threat: *Or I'll kill you.*

225

She does not doubt that he will. Not anymore.

The front door squeals open and Mamere Lenora pokes her heavily painted face out into the darkness. "Great After, it's hotter out here than it is inside." She tilts her head in Seranai's direction. Her eyes are red and puffy from crying, which, Seranai notes with a heightened level of disgust, she has been doing every day since Nerani's arrest.

"Are you well, darling? I thought I heard a commotion."

Seranai waves her away with an idle hand, acutely aware of her bosoms rising and falling within her tightly laced corset. Her demons claw relentlessly at her insides, raking her gut and tearing at her lungs. "I'm quite alright, Mamere."

"Are you certain? You look as though you've been frightened half to death."

"I had a scare, that's all. A stray cat popped out of the shadows just now."

It is a poor attempt at a lie, but Mamere nods knowingly, as though a wayward cat would be quite enough to strike fear into the heart of anyone. "I understand. We've all been on edge since Nerani's arrest—I can only imagine how *you* must be feeling, poor dear. To see one of your own snatched up like that. Just terrible, it is. Why don't you come on inside? It isn't good to be out here in the open where Guardians might be patrolling."

If you only knew, Seranai thinks scathingly. "I'll be in in just a few moments," she says, trying to smile. "Don't worry yourself about me."

"Of course, dear." Mamere flashes her a warm smile before disappearing back into the house. The door clicks shut behind her and James reappears. His boots are silent on the wooden stoop. His face is as grey and as still as stone. He does not blink.

"I'll bring Nerani to you tomorrow at sunset," he says. "You *will* be waiting here for us. You'll make the arrangements for your safe return back to the Forbidden City."

"And if I refuse?"

"I'll make sure it's you that hangs in her place."

He does not wait for her to respond. He takes his leave in silence, his shoulders squared against the pressing heat of the night. Without the gold of his uniform, it takes him only moments to disappear entirely into the darkness of the crooked alleyways. Seranai stares into the street, feeling revulsion pooling within her stomach like bile.

And then, slowly, the demons within her have settle into silence.

An eerie calm passes over her.

So the fearsome General James Byron has fallen for a Cairan. The great, infallible Guardian finally has a weakness.

A thin smile curls the corners of her lips. She glances up at the new moon and sees only dark, formidable sky.

She will make arrangements to return to the Forbidden City, if that is what he requires of her. Perhaps it is time, after all, to introduce herself to Roberts the Valiant. Returning Nerani to her cousin will certainly sweeten the deal. And there is not much time remaining until the Hawk's promised return.

And then, she thinks, ignoring the sharp throbbing of her head. *And then.*

James Byron has just given her a bit of rope, and she will see to it that when the time comes, it is she who ties the noose.

CHAPTER 27

Chancey

NERANI WAKES TO the throbbing of her hand. The fleeting shreds of her dream dissipate upon the air like smoke. She emits a low, shuddering sob as she stares into the clammy darkness of her cell. For the briefest of moments, she had forgotten where she was. Her brocade gown, chosen so carefully all those weeks ago, pools out around her in filthy folds of fabric. Her lower back aches from lying propped against the dank stonewall. She shivers, feeling hopelessly cold against the relentless blackness of her iron prison. Staring down at her left hand, she stifles a whimper. Although the blood has been washed away and the fingers bound carefully with clean linen gauze, there can be no mistaking the irreversible damage that has been done. Her littlest finger juts outward at an unusual angle, dangling limply from within the folds of fabric. A small brown stain has begun to seep through the layers of gauze. Her stomach revolts at the sight, threatening to upend what little food resides within her stomach.

She is a fool.

All this time, Roberts thought Emerala dead—he swore up and down that Emerala was no longer among the living. And yet General Byron had verified what she had already known to be true.

The Guardians have not killed her.

And yet—

She frowns, ignoring the sharp pains that shoot through her mangled fingers as she shifts her hand upon her lap.

If Emerala is not with the Cairans and not locked away within the prison, where could she be? The pirates had called off their ambush after they were outnumbered by Guardians in the dark streets of Chancey.

Roberts had seen it himself. He had been at Captain Mathew's side as he gave the order to retreat back to the sea.

She heard the shouts of victory spilling through the streets like ink as she and Orianna fled from the square with Emerala at their heels.

Then, they had run away from the battle and not towards it. They had raced inland with silent desperation, never once thinking to turn to the sea and catch the pirates before they departed.

And so she cannot be with them, either.

Where are you?

She wets her lips, feeling the hollow ache of hunger rumbling within her. The Guardians do not bring her food often. When they do, much of it ends up spilled on the ground before it reaches her. The last Guardian to deliver her food was none other than Corporal Anderson.

Here, he had barked, dumping the slop on the ground with a flick of his wrist. His eyes lingered upon her fresh bandages in the darkness. His lip twitched. *Eat it off the ground, animal.*

His hostility was preferable to the cool malice he had displayed in the inquisition room. She shuddered, then, at the memory of her pain—of the perverse pleasure he took in inflicting it upon her.

She shudders again now, quailing briefly against the onslaught of memories that threaten to overtake her. She has been dreaming of drowning—frantic, clutching nightmares that do not seem to abate upon waking.

"Fool," she says aloud. Something squeaks in the shadows, scurrying off into hiding with four scuffling paws scraping against stone. She feels strangely offended by the rat's departure. An oppressive sense of loneliness creeps into her chest.

"Come back," she whispers. She is met with silence.

She does not know when she drifts off to sleep again—she only knows that when she wakes it is because she can hear footfalls upon the stone just outside her cell. She stiffens; prying open her eyes and waiting for the newest Guardian to appear and shove reeking slop into her cell. No swinging orange light accompanies the footfalls. Instead, the visitor walks in total darkness. For a moment, she thinks she must still be dreaming.

She peers out through her bars, struggling to make out a discernible shape in the grey slivers of light that flicker in here and there through the deep stone. She rises slowly to her feet, her stiff knees protesting. In the dim, grey light she can see two fists enclose about the bars.

"Who's there?"

"I am not a coward," comes James Byron's voice, earnest against the darkness. She freezes mid-step and says nothing, clutching her wounded fingers to her chest. She can feel his eyes upon her, pressing into her skin as he studies her. His face is so cast in shadow that all she can make out is the hard line of his jaw.

"I am no coward," he says again, his voice almost a whisper. "And yet I am utterly terrified to stand by and watch as you go to your death."

She opens her mouth to speak, but all that manages to eke out from within her is a hoarse squeak. The thought of her impending death is a paralyzing one. Her heart has risen to her throat. Her stomach twists within her.

"You need to understand, all I've ever done is follow the orders of my superiors. I'm not a man with an opinion. Soldiers aren't *permitted* to have opinions. I am at the mercy of Rowland Stoward. I serve at his pleasure."

"You owe me no explanations," she says, dismissing him. His face is swarming into focus before her—the bridge of his nose and the dip of his brow becoming increasingly more defined as her eyes adjust. The air feels as though it is seeping out of the room, suffocating her.

"But I do." The gold of his uniform catches a trickle of grey light and the regalia of his standard gleams with an unearthly glow. She averts her eyes, staring instead at the dark floor beneath the muddied hem of her gown.

"Look at me," he pleads. The desperation in his voice frightens her. She hesitates, her aching hand pressed tightly against her stomach.

"Nerani," he says, and the sound of her name on his tongue shocks her heart into near stillness. "Look at me."

Her gaze snaps upwards to meet him, and this time she finds his deep brown eyes immediately. Crescents of silver reflect within his irises, cupping the wide black of his pupils.

How does he know my name?

His gaze flickers back and forth between hers, the groove between his eyes deepening as he considers her silently.

"I don't understand how you have managed to unravel me so completely," he says, a hint of bewilderment deluging his words. "Am I a coward?" One hand drops to his side. She watches him wipe it against the leg of his breeches. It closes into a fist. Opens again. Returns to grip the rusted iron bar. "I will be executed if I'm caught letting you go free."

Her heartbeat is in her ears, now, breaking free of its binds and beating faster than Nerani knew it could. She swallows the lump that has been building within her throat. She is at a total loss for words. Somewhere behind her, she can hear the sound of trickling water. She listens to the steady drip-drop-drip of the leak. It is raining outside. She can hear the distant pitter-patter of raindrops against the turrets far overhead. Before her, James Byron is fumbling with a ring of keys at his waist.

"I will have to order a search for you, do you understand?"

"Yes." Her voice sounds strangely distant, as though someone else is speaking.

"As soon as you leave here, you'll head directly to Mamere Lenora's. There is a woman there—she's a half-blood. She has arranged for your safe return to the city. Do not delay. Do not look back."

She hears the clatter of the key in the lock. The rusted bars fall open with a tired groan. There is nothing between them but darkness. She breathes in and out, slowly, the realization of what he is doing washing over her like a wave. He reaches forward, grabbing her good hand roughly in his and pulling her out of the cell. Without a word, he leads her down the narrow passageway of the prison. They move quickly, hastening in and out of dusky pools of light, silver motes swirling up about them as they walk. There is a discernable tremor in his grip, and she realizes that he is shaking. Without entirely meaning to, she grasps his hand tighter.

There is a narrow slot of white light up ahead. He draws to a standstill just beyond its reach, turning to face her. The muscles of his jaw work beneath his skin as he assesses her in the dimness of the passageway. She stares back at him, the bleached light filtering into her deep blue eyes. The rainfall is louder here, the droplets flying sideways against the palace walls.

She opens her mouth to speak, but he beats her to it.

"The door up ahead leads out into the bailey. From there, the portcullis is only two hundred paces away. It is loosely guarded at this time of day— the servants are coming in and out from the marketplace."

He pauses, tilting his head as though he is listening carefully for something.

"The rain has gotten heavier. It will work in your favor. Keep your head down and keep walking. Once you're in the city, stick to the alleyways."

"To Mamere Lenora's," she says, remembering. She feels strangely numb. This reality cannot be her reality. This body—with these broken fingers—belongs to someone else. Somewhere back the way they came, there is the sound of a door slamming. Her stomach does a nauseating somersault. He pulls her to him, his lips grazing the top of her head.

"Run," he commands, his breath tickling her scalp.

And she does.

She flies from the door ungracefully, the heavy fabric of her gown cumbersome. The air is sticky with humidity. She is immediately pelted with fat droplets of lukewarm water. She shivers in spite of the heat, pausing to watch the rain rise back off of the ground in furls of translucent grey. A squealing cart rolls by only a few feet in front of her, a portly man in a baker's cap at it's helm. The cart is piled high with bulging, red apples. The sight of him is so mundane that she nearly laughs aloud. He does not look twice at her in the clamor of the bailey, but merely doffs the tip of his cap and keeps on pushing the cart, whistling a merry little tune as he goes.

She does as James Byron says, keeping her head down and maneuvering with silent determination through the crowd. She sees a basket, hastily abandoned in the onslaught of rain, sitting on its side atop of a barrel. Its contents are covered in a brown, woven blanket. Plucking it gingerly from its resting place, she tucks it under her arm in an attempt to appear as though she belongs there among the milling servants.

Her heart is pounding relentlessly against her ribcage. Up ahead she can just make out the raised portcullis of the outer palace wall. She heads quickly towards it, keeping her head down to keep the rain out of her eyes.

And my blue eyes out of the rain, she thinks darkly. She nearly trips over someone's feet and curses herself silently.

"Watch yourself," snaps a woman's voice.

She apologizes, hoping desperately that the woman does not notice the quaver in her voice. As she draws closer to the barbican she can make out several golden figures, staunch and polished as they idle by the doors. As James Byron promised, they do not appear to be all that alert to the potential presence of danger. One of them stares shamelessly at the backsides of several women as they struggle to take down the wash in the rain. Another polishes the blade of his largely decorative sword, looking bored. A third Guardian scuffs his boot in the direction of six squabbling chickens that fight over seeds beneath the protection of the gatehouse.

She walks towards them, doing her best to appear commonplace.

One of the Guardians glances her way as she hurries past. He gives a sharp whistle in her direction, slapping his companion in the chest with the back of his hand. His fellow Guardian takes a break from harassing the agitated chickens and laughs.

"Keep it together, private," he suggests brightly.

Nerani stares intently at the ground beneath her feet. She keeps walking. The soles of her feet ache within her shoes.

"Good day to you," calls out the first Guardian. She ignores him, picking up her pace. The sound of the rain grows muted as she steps beneath the protection of the portcullis. She hears a soft mewing noise from somewhere on her person and wonders absurdly if perhaps she has been making that noise the entire time.

"I said good day," he calls again, louder this time. The third Guardian has stopped polishing the blade of his ceremonial sword. She hears the metal sing as he sheaths the long weapon in its golden hilt. The brown cloth within her basket shuffles slightly. Another mew, louder this time, emanates out from within it. The chickens are clucking at a more frenzied pace, racing around in distress as the Guardian closes the distance between them.

"You, there." His voice rings out like a bell, rolling down the down the curving stone of the gatehouse. "You look familiar."

The first Guardian snorts. "No surprise there. Been around the serving girls' quarters a few times, have you?" There is a grunt as his companion slaps him in the back of the head. He falls silent.

The third Guardian plants himself directly before her. She stares at the polished gleam in his boots. Her heart beats so fast she is certain he can hear it. She has not blinked in several moments. The lower lids of her eyes prickle in irritation.

"No," he says, and she can feel his breath sliding down the bridge of her nose. He places one gloved hand beneath her chin, wrenching her face upwards. She blinks rapidly, forced to meet his gaze. She feels as though she is going to be ill. "This is no serving girl. I shouldn't think I'd forget a face as lovely as yours," he sneers, leering into her vivid blue eyes. "You're the gypsy we arrested at the stinking whorehouse."

She hears raucous laughter at her back. "Thought you'd orchestrate a jail break, did you?" one of the men hoots. "Thought you'd waltz right on through the king's Golden watch without so much as a hello, there?"

The wind shrieks, forcing the rain in sideways through the rusted teeth of the portcullis. Several droplets splatter across the side of her face. Something purrs in indignation, a soft rumble of sound rising from the depths of her basket. A chicken clucks, sensing the nearby danger. She can smell something pressing upon the air all around them, stinging the insides of her nose.

Gunpowder. The scent is unmistakable. There is a thundering crack of sound and blood, warm and sticking, splatters across her cheek. She tastes metal on her tongue. She lets out a cry of fright as the Guardian holding her chin falls to the ground. Where his right eye was, there is only a gaping, fleshy emptiness. Blood trickles slowly across the earth, saturating the dragging hem of her gown. His arms twitch once. Twice. And fall still. The coverlet of her basket flips over and a small orange cat leaps out—disturbed by the pandemonium. It races toward the chickens in a silent hunter's pose, all of the hair on its shackles standing on end. The already frightened fowl give up their feeding entirely, hopping off the ground with wings outstretched and claws in the air. The stupid animals entangle themselves within the golden cloaks of the Guardians, who—recovering from their initial shock— have begun shouting orders to anyone who will listen, their guns drawn.

"Lower the gate!"

Nerani takes the chance and runs. She drops her basket, stepping carefully over the motionless body of the Guardian. Lifting her skirts within her fists, she races beneath the portcullis just as it begins its halting ascent down towards the earth.

The rain is blinding and the servants, terrified by the wayward gunshot, are everywhere.

"It came from up in the parapet!"

"No," someone disagrees, shouting over the sound of the rain. "I saw someone standing in the battlements!"

"Not from within the palace," someone else yells. "Who—"

But the rest of their words are swallowed by the ceaseless wail of the wind. Nerani keeps running, ignoring the exhaustion in her legs as she pushes through the throng of people. The Guardians will not be far behind her. However much time James thought he would buy for her, that plan was ruined the moment she was discovered.

She takes his advice, ducking her head and turning down a narrow alleyway. Her feet slip out of her clattering shoes and the sound of her footfalls grow silent as her bare feet slap in puddle after puddle. Her waterlogged skirts are dark and heavy, spackled as they are with rainwater. Her chest rises and falls, pushing painfully against the tight binds of her corset.

She turns out of the alleyway and comes to a dead stop before a huddled mass of gold. Their heads are bowed together as they shout at one another above the pummeling sound of the rain. She shirks back into the shadows, her heart pounding in her ears. Mamere Lenora's is just around the corner up ahead. She will never make it without being seen.

"How could she possibly escape?" one of them snaps.

"General Byron went down to retrieve her and found the cell empty."

"But how?"

"It's impossible. She couldn't do it without a key."

"She did, didn't she?"

"It must have been witchcraft."

Another voice is added to the mix, louder than the rest—James. He rounds the corner up ahead, his golden cloak dark and heavy with rainwater.

"Give me one good reason why you're all standing around like useless sods."

The Guardians are appropriately silent before him, eyes downturned.

"His Majesty wants to see an execution, and he's growing impatient. If it gets too late and that gypsy isn't found, it's you lot that we'll see hanging in the gallows."

"Sorry, sir," one of the Guardians apologizes.

"Split up," James barks, ignoring him. "Search the city. Don't rest until she's discovered."

Nerani spins to double back, nearly slipping on stone. One of the Guardians—the private who had whistled at her—meets her gaze through the silver droplets that slice across the air.

"There!" he shouts, pointing a gloved finger in her direction.

Her eyes meet James's. His face is white. His lips are soldered together in a tight line, his shoulders rounded against the rain. He shakes his head, a barely discernible movement in the colorless fog.

"After her," he orders.

She turns on her heels and runs back in the direction she came, distinctly aware that she is heading away from Mamere Lenora's and not towards it. Her heart threatens to break free from her chest. She gasps, the sound of her voice caught somewhere between a scream and a sob. Her fingers are bleeding freely the white gauze on her hand soaked with red. One corner of the bandage has escaped from its binding, trailing down the side of her wrist. She hears the shouts of the Guardians close at her back. Their boots thunder upon the cobbled stones. She struggles to pick up the pace, but her feet become tangled within her gown.

Turning a corner, her shoulder slams against the protruding stone of the building. Something heavy drops to the ground at her back. She can hear a person breathing—can hear the shuffle of feet against stone. She gathers her gown in her fist and tries to run faster. A hand, firm and unrelenting, grasps her by the waist. A second hand slides across her mouth, muffling the scream already poised to fly from her lips. She is dragged backwards, pulled into the shadow of an empty doorway. She struggles, trying in vain to scream through the fingers that are pressed against her lips.

Who will come? asks a small, reasonable voice in her head. *No one is there to hear you but the king's men.*

The door shuts. Slats of white light fall across her face. Outside she can hear the sound of boots as the Guardians race by.

"She went this way!"

"Over here, pick up the pace!"

And then they are gone. The thundering of their steps fades back into silence beneath the sound of the unremitting rainfall.

"Stop struggling," whispers James Byron's voice in her ear. "It's only me."

She can feel his heart beating against her back. His breathing rises and falls as though he, too, has been running as fast as his legs would carry him. He waits until she is still before releasing his hold on her. His fingers slide away from her mouth. She turns to face him, surprised to see panic in his eyes. His face is slick with rainwater. His usually neatly parted hair clings instead to his forehead.

"We'll hide out here," he says. "At least until the turmoil dies down. No point in trying to get you to Mamere's now."

"Will she wait? The Cairan you mentioned?"

"She will." There is no trace of uncertainty in his voice.

She inhales deeply. Exhales. They are in an empty store room. The light falls in through slits in the boarded up windows.

"Where are we?" she asks, trying to quell her nerves. He follows her gaze as she glances around, peering into the musky gloom. Several white blankets cover bulging objects that rest upon crooked wooden tables. The entire room has a mercurial smell, like fish.

"My father's store front." He pauses, catching himself, and clears his throat. "It's my storefront now, I suppose. He passed on years ago."

"Oh. There's nothing in here." It is a painfully obvious observation, but she can think of little else to say. Her mind is a jumble of thoughts, none of them particularly coherent. Her hand throbs relentlessly.

"No," he agrees, a small smile lingering in the corners of his lips. "There isn't. He's a fisherman. Well, was. It was never a trade I had any interest in."

That surprises her. She watches him brazenly, studying the lines of his face. He stares back at her. His pulse flutters in the hollow of his throat as he swallows. She had expected him to be the youngest son of a prominent lord or a wealthy merchant, as many of the other Guardians were.

"Why do you keep it, then, if you have no need for it?"

He shrugs at that, patting a wooden beam on the wall with an idle palm. "I can't bring myself to part with it, I suppose." He blinks, slowly, studying the deepest points of the shadows. She recognizes the look on his face, if only because she, too, often has the same fleeting sensation of staring at ghosts. She shudders, wondering who he sees—what kind of father he remembers—standing beside the covered tables and forgotten tools.

"Why did you do it?"

Her voice startles him to attention, wrenching him back from the torture of memory. She is acutely aware of his proximity to her. Several lines of rainwater run down the sides of his face. His nose is lightly freckled from years of sun exposure. She has a sudden image of him as a young boy, out on the boat with his father as they worked together to haul in nets of squirming silver fish.

"Why did I do what?" He pushes one damp lock of hair out of her face, his fingers moving like a habit, as if this is something he has always done—will always do. The thought terrifies her. She can feel her skin grow hot where his fingers linger behind her ear—hesitate in the place where her neck meets her shoulder.

"Why did you let me go free in the middle of the bailey? There was no way I would have made it through the gate without being halted like I was."

He frowns, pulling his hand away. "I took care of it." His gaze hardens. His fingers tremble visibly. She recalls the smell of gunpowder—recalls the red blood streaking across the ground, tastes it in her mouth. She feels suddenly sick to her stomach. *He has committed treason, killing an armed soldier of the king's Guard.*

"You shouldn't have risked it."

"You would have been executed if I hadn't."

She is quiet at that, watching him.

"What is it about me that sets me apart from any other Cairan?" she asks at last.

"You don't know?" His voice is quiet. His brows pull close together. Something deep within her flutters awake at the wounded look in his eyes. She thinks of the way he had kissed her in the street all those nights ago—the way he had pulled her to him, had used his kiss to say all that he couldn't say there in the treacherous darkness, standing on the cusp of battle. She'd misunderstood him that night. She'd thought him inappropriate—lecherous.

She thinks of how he had followed her to her quarters, panic in his shoulders and desperation in his voice. The look in his eyes, then, had been telling enough.

You'll love him, Nerani.

It will drown you both.

Nervously—hesitantly—she rises up onto her toes and plants a kiss lightly upon his lips. His entire body seems to come alive at her touch. He leans into her, the force of his weight robbing her of her breath. She can feel her lips part beneath his and suddenly the taste of him is dancing upon her tongue. His hands close gingerly around her chin, holding her in place. One stray finger trails against a fluttering vein in her neck, tracing the lines of her. She feels as though her bones are clattering upon the floor at her feet, left to be swept away by the screaming wind that howls just outside.

When he finally moves away from her, his breathing is clipped. His lips linger just inches away from hers. Her good fingers clutch at the golden collar of his uniform. She stares at the damp fabric within her hand, unsure of how it got there.

"Why?" she asks. Her voice emanates from a million miles away.

She does not need to clarify what she means.

"I think I've loved you from the moment I met you." His voice is hoarse—low. His words pummel into her like a wave against the shore. Beneath her petticoat, she feels her knees wobble. She thinks back to that day in the square, when he had insisted on accompanying her to the cathedral. His cordiality towards her had been strange and confusing.

"But you didn't know who I was," she points out. "You thought I was a foreign visitor."

He shakes his head, his gaze earnest. "You told me you were the daughter of a merchant, but I didn't believe you. Your eyes were such a vivid blue. You couldn't have been anything but a Cairan, but didn't matter to me. It hasn't mattered since the moment I saw you."

"And my people?" She draws back from him just a step. Her good hand remains entangled in the gold buttons of his lapel.

"What of them?"

"How can you profess to love me but hate what I am?"

The word *love* tastes strange upon her tongue. She watches as a groove deepens between his eyes. He appears stricken by her question. "I don't know that—" he starts, and stops, considering. His teeth graze his lower lip. "I don't know what I believe. I don't know who I am anymore."

The look in his eyes frightens her. She thinks of Orianna and wishes she hadn't.

Two golden men stand in a red sea.
Two golden men drown in the tide.

Gooseflesh rises upon Nerani's skin in spite of the heat. She pushes all thoughts of Orianna away, glancing instead at the ghostly contents of the storeroom. The shadows are filled with discarded memories of James Byron's childhood.

"I know who you are," she whispers.

"Do you?"

"You're James Byron, a fisherman's son," she says. His eyes widen in surprise. A small smile breaks out across his face. From this proximity, she can see the shallow grooves of dimples on his cheeks. She'd never noticed them before today. She has never seen him smile.

"I suppose I am that," he assents quietly, and kisses her again.

The door crashes open with a resounding bang. There is a hoarse shout and both of them fly apart.

"Get away from her," growls a low voice.

James steps back carefully, raising his arms in compliance. Nerani can see his empty belt at his waist. He is unarmed. She glances up at him. His eyes are hard and cold, his face empty. He stares at the newcomer in calculating silence.

"William Blaine?" he says at last, his words tinted with surprise. Nerani, too, turns to see the man. He looks familiar, and yet she cannot figure out how she knows him.

"What are you doing out here in the city?" James asks.

The man laughs, his dark eyes twinkling as though he has just been delivered the punch line of a terrific jest. Suddenly, Nerani remembers where she knows him. He is a Cairan by the name of Blaine the Eager—one of Roberts's Listeners. She presses her lips together, confused.

"Keep back," Blaine snaps, brandishing a gleaming grey pistol. He holds it steadily, aiming it with unwavering purpose at James's head. "I will be taking the girl with me."

"Take her," James says, and shrugs. Blaine gestures for Nerani to move closer to him. She hesitates, glancing instead over her shoulder. Her heart is in her throat, threatening to choke her. The nod James gives her is nearly imperceptible.

Go.

She takes a slow step in Blaine's direction. Outside, there are footfalls on the street.

"In here!" Blaine shouts. The footsteps quicken, soft flesh against rough stone. Roberts appears in the doorway, flanked by a young woman Nerani has never before seen. Her white blonde hair clings to her face as she peers around the room. Her grey eyes alight on James and she flashes him a wide smile.

"Saynti," Roberts whispers, expelling a relieved sigh as he races towards Nerani. He pulls her roughly into his arms, kissing the top of her forehead.

Her lungs are nearly crushed beneath the weight of his embrace. "Thank you, Saynti," he says again. His voice is gruff. "Damn it, I thought I'd lost you."

It takes a moment for him to take notice of James, still standing with his hands raised in silent submission.

"What's this?" Roberts demands. He takes a step forward, shoving Nerani behind him. His emerald gaze flashes with familiar anger as he glares at the general. "What has he done to you?"

"Nothing."

"Good." The malice in Roberts's voice is frightening. He turns towards Blaine. "Shoot him."

Nerani's heart skips several beats, robbing her of breath.

"No!" She shoves past Roberts and skids to a stop in front of James. She finds herself staring, suddenly, down the unforgiving barrel of a gun.

"Don't shoot him."

"Ani," Roberts starts, slipping in his suprise. His green gaze is riddled with barely contained fury. His words fall out from behind clenched teeth. "What are you doing?"

"You can't kill him," she chokes, unable to meet her cousin's eyes. She is starkly aware of the pistol that sits inches away from her face. "He's—he's unarmed."

The words fall flat upon the ground before them.

"Do you realize who this man is?" Roberts demands, his voice barely concealing his revulsion. "Do you realize what he's done?" He is shouting now, spittle converging at the corners of his lips.

"Yes," Nerani's voice is barely audible, even to her.

A lover, Orianna said. *A traitor.*

"Damn it, Ani, he killed my sister!"

"He didn't!" she shouts back, tears jumping unexpectedly to her eyes. "He didn't kill her, Rob."

"Move out of the way."

"I won't let you shoot him."

"What do you propose, then? If we leave him here alive it won't be long before he sets his dogs on us."

James's voice from behind her startles her into silence. The words that fall from his lips are perfectly controlled. Level. "I won't. You have my word. If any harm befalls you on your way back to the Forbidden City, it will not be at my hand."

"What good is the word of a Guardian to us?" snarls Blaine.

"His word is good," the blonde woman says. "I can attest to that." Nerani meets those pale grey eyes across the dusky room. She is staring past her, her face unreadable—her gaze trained upon James. Nerani refocuses on Roberts, still bristling angrily just before her.

"Please. You're not a murderer. Let it go. Take me home."

There is a terrible stillness in the room. She watches the rise and fall of Roberts's chest beneath his wool jerkin. Finally, his gaze softens. Lines of exhaustion deepen across his face. He holds out his hand.

"Come, Elegant," he says wearily. She takes his hand slowly, feeling her fingers shaking within his. She cannot breathe. Her head is swimming. "My cousin is right. We're not murderers. We need to be smarter than this. Lower your gun, Eager."

Blaine does so, looking hesitant. He turns to go, following out the door behind the blonde haired Cairan woman.

Numb, her heart racing like a hummingbird, Nerani allows herself to be led from the shop. The stale smell of fish clings to her gown, infiltrating her skin. She glances over her shoulders only once, and when she does she sees James standing stalwart in the doorway, his golden figure blurred by the falling rain.

CHAPTER 28

Chancey

IT DOES NOT take long for the summons to arrive.

James Byron stands outside the gleaming wooden doors of the throne room, conscious of his chest rising and falling beneath his golden uniform. His cloak weighs heavily upon his shoulders. The two Guardians that idle before him do not meet his gaze. Their hands are clasped behind their backs. Their eyes are shaded. They stare at the freshly polished checkered floor beneath their feet. He remains frozen in the grandiose hallway, trying to act as though the coldness of his inferior officers does not bother him.

He hears a noise from behind the door—a low coughing sort of sound. The Guardians jerk upright, squaring their shoulders at this strange and wordless cue. They pull open the wide set doors. Light spills across the hallway, momentarily blinding him.

"Enter." Rowland's voice sweeps across the vast emptiness of the throne room, pursued doggedly by its own rippling echo. He takes a measured step into the room. The two doors slam at his back. Five golden shafts of sunbeams split the room into partitions of shadow and light. He can hear the low chuckle of the king, dry and humorless, from somewhere at the far end of the room. He walks forward, his footfalls loud in the silence. Out of the corners of his eyes he can see the looming, noiseless silhouettes of the king's lords and ladies. They move in a shapeless mass of shadow, fans fluttering against the stifling heat of the room.

As he approaches the throne, the figure of the king becomes steadily visible. Rowland Stoward leans forward in his chair, his stomach protruding from beneath his lapel of rich, white fur. He rubs his forefinger and his thumb together absently, his black eyes studying James as he draws to a stop near his feet.

"On your knees," Rowland commands. One corner of his lip curls upward. James drops to the floor, head bowed. On his way down, he catches a glimmer of a silver and gold shadow lingering at the right hand of the king. Corporal Anderson. He fights to keep his face blank, his mood darkening considerably.

"What a mess," he hears Rowland say. "What a dreadful, dreadful mess."

He remains silent, his head angled downward.

"Twice now, is it?"

James swallows hard and says nothing. He is not expected to say anything, not yet. He can feel the polished marble through the fabric of his breeches. It is solid and cold against his kneecaps—the stretched white of his flesh presses hard against bone.

"Twice, yes," Rowland breathes. His tone is that of a disproving father—one who has only recently caught his youngest son stealing bread from the kitchen maid. "Twice I have sent my herald out into the streets of Chancey to declare the execution of a gypsy witch. Twice, I have failed to deliver."

A brief, oppressive silence swallows the inhabitants of the room. It is punctuated by a throaty laugh.

"No," Rowland corrects. "It is not I that failed to deliver, is it, James? It is you."

The time to speak has come. "Yes, your Majesty."

"On your feet," comes the brusque command. James rises slowly, heavily, his golden cloak weighting him to the marble floor like an anchor. He raises his gaze to meet his king. Two round black pits stare back at him.

"She escaped without a key," Rowland says, turning suddenly to glance in the direction of his courtiers. His words have adopted a misplaced tone of cordiality, and yet the faint wisp of menace is still redolent upon his tongue. "And yet she escaped somehow in spite of this, and without any damage at all being done to the cell hold."

The courtiers begin to comment amongst themselves—trained monkeys giving a trained response. The fluttering fans pick up speed as whispers move across the room in a murmuring wave.

"Witchcraft," someone says, too loudly, and a fan snaps shut with an alarming sense of finality.

"Witchcraft, yes, perhaps. It certainly seems to reek of something evil. Perhaps the gypsy summoned the forbidden old magics, as you say, Lord Reynolds." Rowland's black gaze returns to James. "Then again, I find that treason has a similar stench."

James remains quiet. He fights to keep his fingers still at his sides.

Rowland proffers a weary sigh. He leans back into his chair, dragging one heavily ringed hand down the length of his face.

"I am afraid I don't quite understand what happened in the dungeons that afternoon. Perhaps you will enlighten me, James."

"I cannot say, your Grace, I am as in the dark as you."

Rowland leans forward in his chair with frightening immediacy. For a moment James wonders if the great king will topple onto the ground. "You cannot say, or you will not? Which is it?" Splotches of red have begun to prickle his cheeks just above the black line of his beard.

James squares his shoulders, keeping his gaze level with the king. "When I went down to the dungeon to retrieve the Cairan upon your Majesty's orders, I found that she had disappeared."

"And how did you find the cell? What state was it in?"

"It was just as you said, your Majesty. The cell door was closed and locked."

"How?" The echo spirals through the grandiose room—ricocheting off of the vaulted ceiling and landing with a thud at James's feet.

"I don't know."

"You don't know." Rowland leans back, the spine of his throne creaking against the pressure. A twisted smile pulls across his face. He glances down at Corporal Anderson and laughs a great, wheezing laugh. "He doesn't know!" he repeats. "My great and fearsome General, who always has an answer for everything—he doesn't know."

The room is stifling. James swallows, reminding himself of the name that dances upon his tongue. Reminds himself that—if he is perfectly careful about how he proceeds—he holds the key to his own salvation.

Before him, Rowland has managed to pull himself together. He wipes at his eyes with his fingertips, his chuckles subsiding into silence. The only sound that remains is the lingering laughter of several courtiers who, missing their cue, have continued to loudly find humor in the rather humorless situation. Rowland claps his hands together and the sound comes to a choking halt.

"Corporal Anderson explained to me that you intercepted him in the torture chamber and sent him away."

"I did, your Majesty."

"What would compel you do such a thing? He was there upon my orders. Have you no respect for my authority?" The king's voice is low, dangerous.

James delivers the response he had prepared earlier that morning, just after the summons arrived at his quarters. "I felt as though Corporal Anderson was not doing an adequate job at obtaining the necessary information from the Cairan."

"Ah. Then I assume you were able to make the gypsy girl talk."

James keeps his gaze blank. "No, your Grace."

The king cups one large hand around a reddening ear, folding the elastic flesh of his lobe into a makeshift funnel. "Speak up, James, I'm afraid I could not hear you."

"I was unable to gather any information from the Cairan. She was faint from the injuries she had sustained, and her mind was no longer clear. She lost consciousness shortly after I arrived. I'm afraid Corporal Anderson lacks the necessary finesse needed to draw out information slowly."

"What did you do with her, then?" Corporal Anderson asks, his face flushing in irritation.

"I am asking the questions, Corporal." Rowland rebukes before James can reply. He shoots an angry glance at the Guardian out of the corner of his eyes. The figure that hovers besides his throne blanches slightly, bowing his head.

"I apologize, your Majesty, I meant nothing by the intrusion."

Rowland ignores him, turning his gaze instead back to James.

"What did you do with her?"

"I returned her to her cell."

"Why did you not try to revive her?"

"It did not seem important at the time. I had no idea that she would have escaped when I next returned to continue the interrogation."

"Clearly not!" Rowland snaps. The whites of his eyes grow visible behind his irises as he stares down upon James.

"No." Rowland's nostrils flare in an effort to remain calm. "No, it was not dark magic that helped her escape. It was a mortal man. It was a traitor to my throne. It was a man who would shoot one of the my own Golden Guardians dead from within the walls of the palace." His lips curl into a sneer. "I suppose you also have not a clue who might have gained authorized entry to both the armory and the parapets."

"Clearly, your Majesty, it was someone with unfettered access to the palace, otherwise he would have been apprehended long before reaching the battlements."

"Indeed." The sneer widens. The black gaze stares pointedly at him. James expected this—he prepared for this. Why not? After all, it was he who fired the gun. Rowland is not incorrect in his scarcely concealed accusation.

"I'm certain your Majesty is already aware that I've ordered my men to conduct a thorough questioning of the palace staff," James says.

"And you've discovered nothing?"

It's time, James thinks, the insides of his palm growing slick with sweat. *Time to lie to your king.* The word *treason* gnaws at the edges of his mind, and his stomach does an uneasy somersault. He swallows, ignoring the dryness of his mouth, and lets the words rise to his lips.

It doesn't matter what I say, he reminds himself. *Not now. The damage is done. I must protect myself.*

"I have, your Majesty."

At this, the sneer fades slightly from Rowland's face. The dark grooves about his mouth fill in with marked flesh where the skin has lost its elasticity.

"Well?" he barks. "Out with it."

"I have a name. The Cairan was aided by William Blaine, one of the cooks in the kitchen."

He pauses for a moment, letting the announcement settle upon the room. Whispers have kicked up along the shadowed edges of the chamber, the fluttering breath of many tongues swirling the golden motes that hang precariously in shafts of sunlight.

It's not a total lie, he reminds himself. *He was there, in the end. And he has not returned since escaping with Nerani in the city.*

With any luck, he won't return. Not now, after James has ousted him before the court, or else he will surely face immediate death. The crime for killing a Guardian is immeasurably worse than the crimes for which the Cairans have been accused. Murder is a far darker evil than existence, after all.

"I know of no one by that name," Rowland argues, his hands folding slowly upon his lap. He appears perturbed by this unexpected change of course in the conversation.

"I am not surprised, your Majesty. I have come to understand that he began working here quite recently, and under an alias."

"William will not be his real name, then?"

"It is not. He is a Cairan, born and bred. A bastard child, if my sources are correct—born to a Chancian man. His given name is Blaine, as is customary of gypsies."

"A half-blood," the king says, repulsed. "In my palace. How?"

James swallows hard, feeling the lifeless eyes of the angels overhead watching him with pressing scorn. His skin prickles uneasily. "His grandfather, Harold Blaine, has long been a cook in your kitchens, your Majesty. He secured him a job only a few months back."

The black eyes grow hard. "Gypsy scum residing within my walls. Touching my food. Breathing my air." His scowl deepens. "Killing my men. It's treason. Pure treason!" He snaps his fingers and several Guardians jump to attention. "Fetch me Harold Blaine! He will serve the sentence in his grandson's place."

A familiar darkness flashes over Rowland's eyes and he is, for a moment, far away from his great hall and his sniveling courtiers.

"No one will dare call it courage then," he murmurs, his voice dropping to a near whisper. "Not then, when the Cairan's flesh and blood burns in his place while he hides like a coward behind the walls of his city." He glances upwards, his gaze returning to normal and settling upon the hapless herald that idles by the great double doors. "Get the message out—quickly, now. Tell them—tell them that treason and murder do not go unpunished in Chancey. Tell them he will burn at dawn."

Several Guardians abscond from the room, the golden clad herald following at their heels like a dog. James feels his heart sink in his chest. He thinks of the white-haired old cook, idling away among the tomatoes in the gardens, unaware of the turmoil that has progressed.

He will go to his death, James thinks, *and it is I who sent him.*

This is not how it was supposed to happen. Outside, the sun has sailed several inches across the sky, stretching the shafts of golden light into obstinate angles. The shadows that encroach the corners of the great hall threaten to engulf the occupants in pitch-black gloom. Overhead, the immaculate forms of the angels have faded into shadowy obscurity.

James is alone before the king. Abandoned by his father's god.

The Dark Below take me for what I've just done.

Behind him, he can hear the sound of something heavy being dragged across the floor. He does not turn around to see, keeping his eyes instead trained upon Rowland.

"I am disappointed in you, James," Rowland says, looking quite the opposite of disappointed. A delighted sneer has encapsulated the lower portion of his face. He appears otherworldly in the strange throws of afternoon light. James suppresses a shudder as the heavy object at his back is dropped to the floor. The sound echoes through the great hall. The lords and ladies draw back—a rehearsed move of horror reserved for those of weak disposition.

"You were always a shining star, James Byron. I elevated you to the top because I knew you would do great things for the Guardians, even as young as you were. I took you under my wing—cared for you like one of my own sons. Your pitiable father could never have done for you what I've done. I had faith in you, and you've let me down."

His words sting, and yet not for the reason he intended. James thinks suddenly—sharply—of his father, coming home after a long day of work. His skin smelled like the salt of the sea and the sweat of the sun. His bright eyes glistened.

God, we thank you for another bountiful catch, that we may keep the coins in the coffer and the fish in our bellies.

He thinks of what his father would say, were he alive to see the cowardice of his son. He thinks of that and shudders, choosing instead to think of Nerani—of her bright blue eyes taking in the ghosts of his forgotten childhood as she stood shivering before him in his father's storefront.

He thinks of Harold Blaine and of tomatoes.

Something snaps against the marble behind him—the sound of a thinly bound cable sliding against the floor is unmistakable. His skin grows cold. He meets the gaze of the king.

"The men of my Golden Guard cannot see such mediocrity go unpunished. They will come apart at the seams. It is fear, James, that holds a kingdom together. You will understand, of course." The sneer has broken into a full grin. Those two black eyes disappear into the folds of his skin.

The king barks an order that James does not hear. Hands grope at him, pulling his cloak from his back. He shakes them off idly, his gaze going red. If it must be done, he'll do it himself. Squaring his shoulders, he begins to carefully unbutton his waistcoat. The room is impossibly silent as he draws his arms through the sleeves of his undershirt, folding the white cotton carefully before setting it on the floor.

"Thirty lashes, I think, then," Rowland says, the trace of glee in his voice unmistakable. "That will suffice for our purposes, don't you agree, James?"

"Of course, your Majesty." James's voice is even. He turns to the supplementary wooden post that has been dragged to the forefront of the room. As he does so, he catches the gaze of several ladies peeking their heads out from behind quivering fans. He keeps his face blank, inclining his head to the Guardian that grips the whip within his white knuckled hands. The man does not return his gaze.

Somewhere at the far end of the hall, a drum begins to play. The sound is slow—measured—matching his heavy footfalls across the marble. *A superfluous bit of ceremony for the king's benefit*, he thinks wryly. He holds out his wrists to be bound, each fist stretching out on either side of the post. He keeps his gaze trained forward as another Guardian tightens the cords against his skin.

"Sorry, sir," he whispers, the sound all but inaudible.

"On your knees, James," comes the king's derisive echo. James drops, his shoulders erect. The drumming ceases.

The last thing he thinks of before the whip cuts across his skin is Nerani the Elegant.

CHAPTER 29

The Rebellion

"BRING HER ABOUT!"

"Heave to!"

The voices that cut through the viscous heat of the afternoon scarcely register in the slumbering mind of Emerala the Rogue. She smacks her lips once—twice—and sinks farther down into her swinging hammock. She is far away, whisked off by her subconscious and dropped in the merciless tundra of the Eisle of Udire. She dreams of cold, blue ice. She dreams of her blood upon the snow, frozen and glittering like rubies. In fits of gasps and starts, she dreams of circular golden eyes watching her in the darkness— waiting just beyond her reach.

"Loose anchor!"

Somewhere in the waking world there is a sickening lurch. Emerala is thrown out of her cot and onto the damp floor below. Waves collide with the hull of the ship as her spine cracks against the floor. She grunts loudly, the dregs of sleep falling quickly away from her with the impact. Coils of heat press against her skin, slick with sweat. She gasps, inhaling the mildewed scent of saturated wood.

"You often sleep in just your shift in the company of men?"

The voice above her forces another gasp out from her chest. She gathers her coarse blanket to her body, scrambling upright to find a pair of bright golden eyes blinking down at her from the cot directly overhead. The Hawk flashes her a wicked grin and winks, sliding off of the cot in one fluid movement and dropping to the floor.

"I can hardly sleep fully dressed anymore," she sniffs, wary of his proximity in the claustrophobic room. "It was never this hot back in Chancey."

"You'll see a lot of things out here that you've never seen back in Chancey, I reckon."

Seeing him lingering before her in the musky light of the sailor's quarters brings an uneasy sensation swarming into the pit of her stomach. She is suddenly cold in spite of the pressing humidity. His gaze bores into the exposed skin just above the fraying edge of her blanket. Her shoulders prickle and she frowns darkly in his direction.

"Why have we dropped anchor?"

He shrugs at that, his tongue pressing at the inside of his cheek. "We've reached the ports of Caira. If you can call them ports," he adds wryly. "The natives here en't much for seafaring."

Somewhere below, the anchor pulls at reef and rock as the ship is buffeted by a sudden, sweeping wind. Emerala lurches uneasily, nearly falling forward into the Hawk's arms. She steadies herself, grabbing clumsily at a splintering post as she tries in vain to maintain what little cover she has. Up above, several voices are shouting, their words overlapping one another in a jumble of incoherent commands. Above the noise cuts one clear order.

"Bleed the sails!" shouts the Lethal. "Douse the canvas, quickly now!"

Before her, the Hawk's chin is cocked slightly to the left as he listens. His expression has darkened considerably. Only when he notices her studying him does his gaze relax. He tilts his chin back towards her, his eyes gleaming. "Storm's coming."

"How can you tell?"

"I can smell it."

She sniffs twice, but recognizes nothing other than the usual pungent reek of salt and sweat and wood rot.

"Furl the colors!" The Lethal's voice reaches them once again, the husky tenor of his words trickling down amid the bunks with the fragmented shafts of afternoon light. "Put your backs into it."

Emerala wonders where Alexander is and what he is possibly doing that he has entrusted the deck to Lachlan the Lethal for the afternoon. As if reading her mind, the Hawk's grin widens.

"Before I forget, the Cap'n asked that you join him in his quarters." He pauses, reaching up into the hammock where he had been lying and grabbing hold of something startlingly fuchsia. There is an audible rustling of fabric and Emerala finds herself staring suddenly into a monstrous gown of frills and laces. "He wants you to wear this."

"That?" Emerala echoes. She reaches out a hand and fingers the material between her thumb and index finger. Silk. One delicate sleeve of magenta lace, likely nudged forward by a rippling puff of ocean air, gives her a ghostly wave.

"Aye." The Hawk's smirk has broken out into a full grin as he studies her expression. "Derek brought it for you to wear during our trip to the island."

He heaves it into her arms, ignoring her protests as the coarse blanket falls to the floor by her feet. She is starkly aware of her bare skin visible through the sheer tulle of the underskirts. Several tiers of fabric tickle the skin beneath her nose—variations of deep fuchsia and cream petticoat and white lace itch at her arms and her chin. She glares at the Hawk over the top of the fabric.

"But—" she begins in protest. She trails off into silence as she thinks of the already stifling afternoon heat. The Hawk is receding from the room, an amused grin still plastered across his face. That odd feeling of uneasiness continues to linger beneath her skin. She drops the heavy silk fabric down onto the floor at her feet and calls out for him to stop.

He pauses on the steps that lead out into the galley, his silhouette framed in the glimmering motes kicked up in the wake of his boots. His head turns only slightly, the tip of his nose catching fire—pale light blazing down the line of his jaw. She sees his larynx pull at the skin of his throat as he swallows, waiting.

"I've been dreaming about you."

The words escape her too quickly. She cringes at the subsequent look upon his face. One eyebrow arched, he stares back at her in silent amusement across the stifling expanse.

"That's not what I meant to say," she retorts, at the same time that he says, "I know."

She hesitates, uncomfortable. "You know?"

"Aye. You were saying my name in your sleep." He turns toward her, throwing his features into shadow. The wooden belly of the ship unleashes a low groan as the waves roll beneath the hull.

"I was?"

His grin widens impossibly, his wicked eyes crinkling at the corners.

"Oh," she breathes, her cheeks growing hot. She feels that all-too-familiar cold creeping in through her fingers and toes. The palm of her left hand throbs with a dull ache. "It's just—" she begins and falls silent. He is still and dark before her—a perfect, shadowed replica of those golden eyes that haunt her dreams.

"Alexander said you were the one who rescued me in the Eisle of Udire. You and Thom."

The Hawk's nod is nearly imperceptible. "Aye," he says, and waits for her to continue.

"He also said that he thinks I was poisoned."

"Aye," he says again. She wishes she could see his face more clearly. The edges of his features swarm with blue and green pulls of light—tricks of the harsh sunlight that streams in behind him.

"What do you think?" She nudges balefully at the bundle of magenta fabric on the floor, trying to hold his gaze.

He shrugs, scratching at his scalp with one hand. "I found you in the snow and brought you back here. I couldn't say for sure one way or another if you'd been poisoned or not."

Emerala bites down upon her lower lip, considering the piece of information she has withheld from him—from Alexander. "He asked me if I had anything to eat or drink at the Frost Fort," she starts, keeping her eyes trained resolutely upon his face. He is as still as stone as he stares back at her. "I told him I couldn't remember."

"Aye?" He is quiet. His voice has grown dangerous. "And that was a lie, I reckon?"

"You offered me a cup," she says, trying to keep her voice from adopting a tone of accusation. "You practically insisted I have something to drink."

He is silent. She can feel his gaze penetrating her sheer cream slip. One sleeve has fallen from her shoulder, slipping down toward the crease of her elbow. She ignores it, her pulse quickening as she prepares to ask him the question that has plagued her through her endless, breathless nightmares.

"Why?" The lace petticoat crunches softly beneath the layers of silk as she takes a step forward. "Surely you weren't concerned about my comfort. Why did you offer me a drink? Why were you the one who found me lying in the frozen wasteland in the dark—you, out of everyone else on the crew? I'm sure you're the one who found me, even if Thom was there to help bring me back."

Again, he is silent—watchful.

Her throat is dry, but she continues. "Why do I dream of you every night? Most of my flight from the fortress has escaped my memory, but I know for certain that you were there with me in the tundra. You didn't find me by some stroke of luck."

The Hawk is frozen before her, his figure warping slightly against the dwindling light of the afternoon. She is close enough now to see him clearly. She keeps her gaze trained upon his golden eyes as they flicker ceaselessly across her face.

"Evander," she says, using his given name. The words that fall from her lips are slow and concise. "Did you poison me?"

"Poison is a woman's weapon," the Hawk says. His gaze is suddenly disdainful. He turns his eyes up towards the beamed ceiling. "Get dressed, Rogue. The Cap'n is waiting."

He does not wait for her to respond. He turns and stomps up the stairs in silence, his hands shoved deep into his pockets. He stops only at the top, his hesitation so sudden that it startles her.

"And Rogue?" His voice drifts down through the opening, trailed by a muted echo. "Be careful around Derek. Don't trust him. He's not what he seems."

And then he is gone.

Emerala sniffles loudly, annoyed with herself for becoming so emotional. She tries in vain to shake off the cold unease that grips her like a vise, kneeling instead towards the ugly violet gown that lays crumpled at her feet.

His silence was as much of a justification as anything, one small part of her says in derision. Her mind buzzes uselessly—her thoughts are fuzzy with fatigue. She dresses slowly, contemptuously, trying in vain to pull together the frozen fragments of her dreams.

She arrives at Alexander's quarters to find him hunched over his gleaming oak desk, his back to the door. He is muttering softly, his index finger running slowly over an unrolled bit of parchment on the surface.

She squares her shoulders and sighs, glancing quickly at herself in the warped looking glass that hangs askew on the wall by the door. Her hair has been haphazardly pinned to her scalp in a fruitless effort to cool down. Wild black ringlets cascade downward into her face. The magenta gown he insisted she wear constricts tightly against her waist, causing her to breath in short pulls of air. Her bosoms are spilling out over the laced top of the golden brocaded corset, and she stares at these in disdain before clearing her throat.

"I'm here," she announces.

Alexander does not reply, only holds up one finger of his free hand in an abrupt gesture; *wait*. She frowns at his back. He has removed his usual red coat, undressing down to his white, buttoned undershirt. The gathered sleeves have been pushed upward—the cuffs rest just above the crook of his elbows. The cotton is dark with sweat. She feels suddenly quite affronted at having been ordered to shove herself into such an elaborate costume and rush directly to the captain's quarters, only to be ignored.

"The Hawk said you wanted to see me," she says, a little louder.

"A moment, please, Emerala." His response is colored with distraction. He resumes his muttering, stopping only to curse once under his breath. She rolls her eyes, wandering instead towards the ornate windowpanes that run the length of his quarters. The heavy layers of fuchsia silk drag noisily in her wake.

The water outside is a stunning cerulean blue. She stretches her gaze out across the glittering expanse, searching for the sea's end and the sky's beginning. The sun glints white gold off of the peaks of the waves in blinding streaks of rippling light. She leans her forehead against the cool glass and studies the rising and falling crests of sunlight until her eyes begin to water.

"What is sweeter than honey?" Alexander's voice asks from just behind her. She jumps slightly. She had not heard him approach. "What is stronger than a lion?"

She turns her back to the window, surprised to see him standing only inches away from her. The reflection from the ocean dances across his face in fluctuating ripples of light. The hazel in his eyes catches in the dancing glow. He studies her quietly, his gaze thoughtful.

"I'm not sure what you've just asked," she admits.

A small smile curls at one corner of his lips. "It was a riddle."

"Oh, of course," she says dryly. "I'm not very good at riddles."

"No?" He is scarcely listening. His gaze has a faraway look as he drinks in the sight of her clad in her new gown. "You look beautiful."

She scowls at him. "This gown is appalling. There are frills and lace and bows everywhere." She gestures down toward the wide bustle that protrudes from her backside. "Not to mention it weighs several tons."

His expression has twisted into a look of scarcely concealed humor. Something painful flashes across his face and is gone.

"What?"

"It was my mother's gown."

Emerala hesitates, choking on the word. "Mother?" she sputters at last, unable to keep the disbelief out of her voice. She glances down at the bunching layers of ornate fabric, studying the shaded grooves of cerise that cut across the magenta gown.

He nods, his brows furrowing beneath wayward strands of sun kissed brown hair. "Surprised I have a mother, are you, Rogue?" He laughs quietly. "I don't suppose you assumed I just popped out of thin air one day and began pirating."

She shrugs, feeling some of her tension abating. "The Lethal said you were borne upon the waves by merpeople and delivered to the previous Captain of this ship."

Alexander laughs aloud at that, his eyes twinkling. "Merpeople?" he repeats as his laughter subsides. "Lachlan likes to tell a lot of stories, and I've yet to hear one that rings true." He drifts off into momentary silence at the thought, reaching out an idle finger and running it down the length of Emerala's lace sleeve. A trace of melancholy passes across his features like a cloud across the sun.

"As appalling as you may think the gown, it really does suit you. It's quite in fashion in the local seaports." He is smirking, but the sorrow lingers in his gaze.

"When did you get this?" she asks. "I've never seen it before."

"No, you wouldn't have. Derek brought it onboard this morning."

She hesitates, confused. "Derek? But, how—"

He answers the question before she can finish asking. "We've just entered the Agran circle. The island of Senada borders Caira just to the East. They are separated only by a narrow channel."

"Is Senada your birthplace?"

It depends which of the stories you chose to believe, mine or the Lethal's."

"So your mother, she's—" Emerala falters. She fingers the smooth silk of the gown, uncertain how to finish her thought. Alexander catches her meaning, and a pained expression contorts his features.

"Dead? No. But she's unwell. Her mind went years ago, when I was a no more than a boy. She resides in Derek's care at his estate. He's a loyal friend, Derek. And a good man. She's in better hands with him than she ever was with me." He pauses, his eyes glazing over with some distant memory.

"What do you mean by that?" Emerala asks, prompting him only once the silence has become uncomfortable. He looks down at her, startled, as though he has only just remembered she was there.

"When I was young, the only thing that kept us alive was begging." He scoffs. "That, and pickpocketing. My father was a pirate. He came and left with the tide one month. I never knew him, but my mother continued to love him with her whole heart. She never blamed him for our troubles. She never once blamed him. My entire life, I thought him selfish. I didn't understand how he could leave my mother alone and pregnant, without a single copper to call her own."

"She didn't have any family to care for her?"

The look of derision he shoots her is sharp and scathing. "She did, yes, but who would take care of an unmarried woman with a bastard child? No, they cast her out the moment they knew she was with babe. She was ruined to them."

He moves away from her, lost in memory, pressing his forehead against the swirled glass of the window. Outside, several white seagulls snatch at fish with their extended talons. Emerala can hear their screams penetrating the wooden exterior of the ship.

"I hated him—my father. I despised him with every fiber of my being. When I met Derek I was only a few years younger than I am now. He'd been boarded by pirates on his journey—shipwrecked on Senada. I asked him if he knew the name of the ship. He did; it was the Rebellion." He groans slightly, pressing his knuckles hard into the baseboard of the window. "I knew the name immediately. How could I forget? How does one forget the name of a ship when his childhood has been spent standing knee deep in the ocean, watching his mother call out for it to return?"

He pauses, heaving a sigh and allowing his eyes to flutter closed. Emerala takes a slow step towards him, gingerly placing her palm over his enclosed fist. His shoulders relax slightly at her touch, and he continues.

"I left my mother in Derek's care. He is a man of considerable wealth, and he supplied more for her than I ever could. He gave her peace that I could not. The day I left, she no longer recognized me. She cried out at the sight of me, and called me Samuel." His voice trembles. "Saints, I hated him. I came here to kill him. I hunted him down for months."

"And did you?" Emerala asks, her voice a whisper. "Did you kill him?"

He looks at her at that, and she notices that his eyes are filled with tears. He shakes his head, blinking furiously.

"No. I couldn't. Derek and I had made a deal."

"What kind of deal?"

Alexander hesitates, looking suddenly regretful, as if he's said too much. "It's not important. Anyway, he was already dying when I found him." He shrugs. "Consumption."

"And he gave you the ship?"

Alex nods. "Isn't that the beauty of irony?" He gestures around at the captain's quarters around him. "I spent my life hating him and *the Rebellion* for leaving behind my mother, and I've not gone back to her since I set foot onboard. She's mine now—the ship—and his life's mission my own. I couldn't go back to her now, not if I wanted to. I cause her too much pain. It's easier to forget him when she doesn't see my face."

"So why the dress, if it is such a painful memory?" Emerala asks. The lace itches at her skin, and yet she feels a strange solidarity with the constricting fabric as she stands sweating in the stifling heat. She grips his fist tighter, unfazed by her proximity to him.

Alexander clears his throat, shaking his head as though to shake away the cobwebs of the past. "Tomorrow at dawn we sail ashore to Caira," he says. "You cannot be recognized as a Chancian gypsy. They'll order your immediate arrest."

"But I'm one of them, I'm Cairan myself," she protests.

"No," Alexander disagrees, turning fully from the window. "You're not. To them, you're a traitor. Your blood is tainted with the blood of the Chancians. They will burn you alive in an attempt to pacify their gods. It's dangerous to have you as close to the island as we do now, but we don't have many other options."

"I can't stay on the ship?" Emerala feels suddenly anxious. The excitement she had been feeling about their newest adventure quickly subsides.

"You heard Derek, it's too dangerous. Their current leader, Domio, has spies all over the island. I'm taking my best men inland for the trip, and I'm not sure I can trust the rest of the crew to mind their rum long enough to keep you safe."

"So you think this dress will convince them I'm not Cairan?"

"We hope so. You're to masquerade as Derek's fiancée. Domio is fond of Derek. They frequently do business together. He'll be less likely to question a woman traveling in the company of a wealthy diplomat than the company of pirates. Your name is to be Katherine Montclay of Toholay."

"Toholay?" Emerala asks.

"Yes," Alexander quips, appearing suddenly distracted. "A port in the Westerlies. Don't you know your geography? Derek will be by later to go over the finer points of acting like a gentlewoman." He glances at her reproachfully. "And to do something about your hair."

Emerala fingers her wild curls, frowning. "What's wrong with my hair? And my manners?"

But Alexander has turned his back to her. He snaps his fingers in the air, his body suddenly tense with excitement.

"It's not the question," he says. "It's the answer!"

"Excuse me?" Emerala can't help but feel utterly left behind—dragged along without explanation behind the pirates and their endless, self-serving goals.

"What is sweeter than honey? What is stronger than a lion? It's not the riddle. It's the answer. I had it all wrong. Come here, look!" He calls her over, pushing his index finger against the curling parchment that lies upon his desk. She joins him, glancing down to see a sprawling map upon which several words have been penned in slanted red ink. *What is sweeter than honey? What is stronger than a lion?* The sight of the ink sets her hand to throbbing again. A wave of unease passes over her.

"I had it all wrong!" Alexander says, excitement filling his voice. "It's here." She follows his traveling finger until it comes to rest upon several small words scrawled across a scaled creature riding the waves off of the coast of Caira. Smoke billows out from two flared nostrils, penned in ink. The Hawk's fabled leviathan, she supposes, if she had to guess.

She leans in closer, squinting to read the writing.

Only questions will grant you the answer you seek, but careful his answers are scarce for the meek.

Just below that, penned in the same slanted red ink, are several cramped words.

Travel to Caira with the turn of the Tydes, and there you will find the question resides.

She leans back, frowning. "I don't understand."

"Neither did I, at first, but it makes sense now. See this here, the author who penned this spelled tide incorrectly."

Emerala looks again. *Tydes,* spelled with a "y". She had not noticed at first.

"Tyde," he says, excited. "It's not referring to the ocean. It's a man's name. He's a native of Caira. I've crossed paths with him before. He's a master of riddles and puzzles. The question on the map is not a riddle, it's the answer to one."

"Alex," Emerala asks, hesitating. "What exactly are we looking for?"

He laughs at that, his voice ringing out through the quarters. "I haven't a clue," he admits. "But I expect we'll find it with Tyde."

CHAPTER 30

Chancey

PRINCE PETERSON RUSHES through his father's stone garden, the sheer walls of the great marble maze climbing above his head in dizzying shades of grey. Overhead, the night sky is an endless tapestry of dazzling white stars. The moon hangs low on the horizon, barely visible over the high walls of the labyrinth. The path before him is shrouded in a pale wash of white light.

He keeps his head down as he walks, listening to the patter of his shoes upon the shadowed marble underfoot. His stomach is sick. He recalls the sight he came upon only hours earlier, creeping down toward the King's royal chambers in order to once again try to gain audience with his elusive father.

What he had found, upon his arrival before the grand golden doors, had troubled him. There was no armed guard positioned at the opening. In fact, the two doors had been left slightly ajar. He hovered outside the door only a moment, considering his next course of action, when he heard the sound of a whip connecting with flesh. The noise was so stark against the cavernous silence of the hallway that it made him jump with fright. There was a low groan, restrained, but the victim was otherwise silent.

Again, came his father's voice, curling around the doorjamb like tendrils of smoke.

Again the whip snapped against skin. Again there came that same muffled moan. Taking a chance, Peterson had inched forward and placed his eye directly against the narrowing opening between the two doors.

What he saw inside nearly caused him to cry out in alarm. A man, stripped down to his boots and breeches, knelt before a crudely constructed whipping post. His hands were bound tightly around the splintering wood.

265

Across his back were half a dozen angry red lashes. The wounds were bleeding freely; deep red trails traced lines down the curvature of the man's back.

He did not need to see the man's face to know that it was James Byron.

Again, called out his father. He could hear the sneer of pleasure on the king's lips. He did not dare to raise his eyes to see. James kept his chin raised and his eyes forward as the cloaked Guardian behind him brought the lash across his skin.

This time, the groan was louder as the tip of the lash connected with already open wounds. Some of the ladies of the court cried out in alarm. Peterson felt his blood boil with rage. He heard the sound of his father's dry laugh coiling in his ears, but he was already leaving, backing away from the door in horror. He could not stay and watch for a moment longer.

He ran.

He takes a sharp left around one corner of the labyrinth, his breath coming in fast pulls. His skin flushes with anger. He cannot fathom what his father's most trusted guardian could have done to deserve such a punishment. James had been as close as family to the Stowards for many years. He had never done wrong by any of them. To see him punished like that, with his father's smiling face watching from his golden throne…

Peterson shouts suddenly, kicking hard at a shattered bit of marble that lies on the ground by his feet. The fragmented bit of stone clatters down the walkway and skitters to a stop. He breathes deeply, pulling in the crisp night air through widened nostrils. As he looks around at the narrow corridor, it suddenly occurs to him that he is in a part of the labyrinth he has never been in before. Up ahead, he can see the shadows of several overgrown bushes.

There are no trees in my father's stone garden, he thinks darkly.

Yet here they are.

His anger abates slightly, giving way to curiosity as he inches forward down the passageway. As he approaches the greenery, his echoing footfalls are swallowed in the foliage. The air smells sweet here—alive.

I am in the center, he thinks, and his heartbeat begins to race. He picks up his pace, jogging slightly as he turns the next corner. Several trees, overgrown and tangled, dot the passageway. He breaks into a run.

The moonlight catches in the branches of the trees overhead, blocking the light from reaching him. For a moment, he is obscured in total darkness as he races beneath the drooping boughs. Several branches whip across his face, slicing at his cheeks.

He continues to run.

He skids to a stop only once he breaks free of the trees. Glancing around, he lets out an audible gasp. Before him is a flourishing garden. Even in the dark of night he can see the silvery light of the moon tracing the lines of brilliant crimsons, yellows, and jades. He takes a step forward, his breathing uneven. His eyes catch upon an elegant stone figure positioned at the center of the maze. It is the immaculate outline of a woman, her arms outstretched. She stands atop a shallow reflecting pool. The moonlight dances upon the glass surface of the water at the hem of her stone gown, throwing ripples of silver light across her eternal smile.

Mother, he thinks, his lips moving in silent awe. He takes several steps closer to the great stone woman, the brilliant colors of the queen's garden fading into shadow around him. He steps into the reflecting pool, shattering the stillness of the water. The silvery light upon the statue dances spiritedly across her features. She watches the space above his head with emptiness in her eyes. Brown eyes, Frederick had told him once. Why, then, had he been born with eyes of vivid green? So often as a child had he wondered as much, staring into the looking glass in his nursery and making faces at his reflection.

He drops to his knees, a choked sob catching in his throat.

"Mother," he says aloud. His voice sounds hollow as it skips across the shimmering pool. He wants suddenly to touch the folds of her gown, if only to be close to her in a way he had never been able to be as a boy. He runs his hands down the cold, unmoving stone.

"Help me, Mama," he whispers. Tears prickle in his lower lids. He feels momentarily foolish, but he pushes the sentiment away. He is a boy unloved—a forgotten prince. A motherless child.

His hands continue to run across the cool, rippled surface of the gown, stopping in surprise on a rough patch that catches beneath his fingertips.

Something is engraved here, he thinks, his pulse quickening. He crawls forward through the pool, ignoring as the cool water licks at his sides.

There is just enough moonlight that the words inscribed upon the gown are clear.

To my love, I have built you a sanctuary. I have preserved you in stone. We have killed you, he and I. For that, I am sorry.

Peterson runs his fingers over the delicately carved words, his mind racing. Whoever had carved these words had not intended them to be seen. They are small and insignificant, etched cleverly into the fold of the gown. Beneath the words sits a name.

Eliot Roberts.

Peterson sits back, alarmed. The name is not at all familiar to him. He racks his brain, trying in vain to recall such a person. He frowns, sure Frederick would have mentioned someone as important as Eliot Roberts to him during one of his many long-winded stories when they were boys together.

"What are you doing?" The voice that cuts through the silence of the evening is decidedly feminine. Startled, Peterson glances momentarily upwards at the lifeless face of his mother and feels immediately foolish for having done so.

"Hello?" he calls out, rising to his feet. The water shifts with a wet slapping sound, filling in the space where his legs had been. "Who's there?"

He hears the sound of someone dropping from a considerable height. Bare feet slap against packed dirt. A face swarms into focus in the silvery light of the moon and he finds himself staring into two brilliant blue eyes. The girl before him grins pointedly at him, her tiny upturned nose scrunching as she squints at the statue besides them.

"Who are you?" he asks, feeling alarmed at the presence of an intruder in his mother's sanctuary. He sniffs loudly, hoping she cannot tell he has been crying.

"Who are you?" the girl shoots back, pushing her dirty blonde braid behind her shoulder as she leans forward to inspect him.

He stammers slightly, caught off guard. The girl is clad in an ill-fitting gown of dusky rose, her bare shoulders exposed over the plunging neckline. Her feet are muddied and bare beneath the fraying hem. In spite of it all, an unexpected thought occurs to him.

She is the most beautiful girl he has ever seen.

"I'm the prince," he says at last, finally regaining his sense of decorum. He draws himself upright in an effort to appear taller. "This is my father's home, and you're trespassing."

"Oh." The girl appears startled at that. She withdraws her hand from the statue. "I didn't know that. I figured you were a serving boy."

"A *serving boy?*"

She shrugs lightly, stepping into the reflecting pool and kicking up the water with her big toe. "I guess you don't expect to see a lonely prince kneeling in a pool of water in the middle of the night."

She giggles at that, and peers at him closely. Her nose is only inches away from his. He is surprised at how brazen the girl is—not at all like the nervous serving girls that replace the bedpans and tend to the fires in his nursery. He has spent much of his life trying to make conversation with them to no avail. They come and go like ghosts, keeping their chins down and their eyes averted, never talking above a demure whisper.

Yes, your highness.

Of course, your highness.

"Am I supposed to bow, then, if you're the prince?" she asks, an amused lilt in her tone. "Is that proper?"

"You could tell me your name. That would be polite."

She shakes her head playfully, disappearing for a moment behind the statue of his mother. "I can't do that." Those two blue eyes reappear at the other side of the great stone gown, twinkling playfully in the moonlight. "But they call me the Rose."

"Who are they?"

"My people," she replies, as though this is obvious. Something within Peterson's stomach lurches. He stares into her deep blue eyes for a moment too long.

"Are you a Cairan?"

"If I say that I am, will you turn me in to your father?"

"No, I don't suppose I will," he says. "But you shouldn't have come here, it's too dangerous."

She peers at him closely, as though gauging whether or not to trust him. After a moment, she laughs. The sounds peals away from her like bells in the night.

"I'm not afraid of danger."

"You should be," he says. "Don't you know what he'll do to you if he finds you?"

"Who?"

"My father," he responds, certain this was obvious. "He has a rather public history of executing any gypsies he finds."

"I know." She shrugs. "My uncle hung in the gallows two years back. He was accused of a crime he didn't commit. But my mum says we can't live in fear just because there might be death at the end of an adventure."

"Oh," Peterson whispers, robbed of any intelligent response.

The Rose does not seem to notice the weight of his silence. "This is my most thrilling adventure yet," she announces gaily.

She saunters over toward the statue, dragging her feet through the pool of water so that the liquid runs in broken streams of white around her bare ankles. The hem of her saturated gown has turned a deep violet. She drops to her knees, running her fingers over the same part of the gown that Peterson had been tracing only moments before. He takes a step forward, feeling strangely as though his privacy is being in some way invaded, and draws to a stop.

"What is it you were doing down here?" she asks, musing aloud. "Is there some sort of secret hidden in the woman's dress?"

"There's an inscription, yes." He paws behind one ear as he waits for her fingers to find the words. His pulse jumps beneath his skin as her fingers stop, locating them. She leans in, going cross-eyed with the effort of reading in the dark.

"To my love," she begins. "I have built you a sanctuary. I have preserved you in stone. We have killed you, he and I. For that, I am sorry."

The words resonate in Peterson's ears with a foreboding echo. They pitch out aimlessly against the starry night, the secret confession going unanswered by the looming stone effigy of his mother.

"Eliot Roberts," he hears the Rose say. The name weighs prominently upon the air. He wishes he knew who the man was. A strange sort of fervor overtakes him, and he clenches his fingers into fists at his side. The Rose leans back, clapping her hands together. "Oh, how romantic, a secret affair." She turns to look at him. Her wide blue eyes are speckled with stars. "Who do you think the woman is?"

"It's my mother," he murmurs darkly, feeling his cheeks prickling with warmth. He can feel the stone eyes overhead watching the two of them as they linger in the reflecting pool. The moon dances across the agitated surface of the water in a rippling oval of white.

"Your mother," the girl says with awe, blinking up at the statue in new-found reverence. "She was beautiful."

"Thank you. I never knew her."

"So am I right?" she asks, lurching upward so suddenly that he is splashed across the face with the cool, clear water.

"About what?"

"Eliot Roberts. Was he your mother's lover?"

He is stunned by the brashness of the girl's nature. He opens his mouth and closes it again, unsure of how to respond. After a long moment, he shrugs. "I don't know."

"Well, I think he must have been. No one creates such a beautiful memorial like this unless they were in love. It's a magical garden, can't you feel it?"

He nods, frowning slightly at the flora that curls inward against the still night. "I suppose I can. May I ask you a question?"

"Of course," she assents, her nose buried deep within the petals of a rose.

"How did you get in here?"

"I scaled the wall of the maze." She says this as though it should have been entirely obvious to him.

"Right," he says. "Why?"

At that, her blue gaze grows serious. The silver lights of the stars extinguish as her thick black eyelashes drop low. "I came to Chancey with a friend, but she was taken by the Guardians. I think she's here, in the dungeons."

Peterson thinks of the news that had thundered through the palace only a day ago. A Guardian shot beneath the palace gates—an escaped Cairan—a frantic chase through the empty city. He thinks of James on the whipping post, blood trickling from the lashes that intertwined across his back.

Before him, the Rose is perched on the tips of her toes, studying the statue.

"What did you expect to do when you found her?" he asks, annoyance clipping his words. "Charm my father into letting her go? Break her free? You'd just be thrown into the dungeon with her."

"I hadn't really thought it through," she admits. He realizes, looking at her, just how young she is. She cannot have seen more than twelve harvest cycles pass her by.

"Clearly not," he sniffs. "Anyway, she's gone."

"What do you mean, gone?" An air of nervousness seizes the girl.

"She escaped yesterday. No one has been able to find her since. They think she returned to your Forbidden City."

"Oh." Her gaze grows muddled with concern. "I can't get back there without her." She thinks about this for a moment. "I've got nowhere to go."

"Where were you staying before?"

She scowls at that. "A whorehouse on the edge of town. It was rotten. I won't go back. Anyway, it was swarming with Guardians when I left." She thinks about this. "They must have been looking for Nerani," she says quietly, glancing at her toes through the rippling water.

"Where will you go now?" Peterson feels a sudden loneliness tugging at him over the thought of saying goodbye to his new friend. *I've never had a friend*, he thinks.

"I don't know." She twirls absently with the plaited end of her braid. "I'll have to find a place to sleep for the night. I can figure it out in the morning."

Peterson thinks for a moment, his mind suddenly racing. "Would you stay here for the night?"

"Here?" she asks in some alarm, glancing up at the yawning night sky above them.

"Yes," he says. "Just for tonight. I'll come back for you tomorrow."

When she looks back down at him, her eyes are once again filled with stars. She flashes him a toothy grin and he notices a small, dark gap between her two front teeth. "Do you have a plan?" she asks wickedly, as though to have a plan is a most daring undertaking. He thinks of what she said earlier—*we can't live in fear just because there might be death at the end of an adventure.*

He finds himself smiling back at her. "I do," he says. "It will be quite the adventure, if you're brave enough."

Without warning, she thrusts herself noisily across the watery expanse between them. In an instant, her arms are encircling his neck, cutting off his air supply. The front of his shirt is soaked through with water. When she pulls away, her face is glowing.

"You promise you'll be back tomorrow?" she asks. He draws back from her, climbing reluctantly out from the fountain. Something unseen tugs at him as he moves away from the statue of his mother—and from the girl perched just beneath her arms.

"I'll be back," he promises.

She drops into a mock curtsy, still grinning. "Then I should be honored, my prince, to spend my night in the presence of Eliot Roberts and his queen."

He laughs at that, turning away from her and heading off into the shadows of the trees. As the moon disappears behind the black veined leaves overhead, he can just make out the sound of a young girl's quiet voice crooning a soft lullaby.

CHAPTER 31

Caira

THERE IS A muted murmur—the unmistakable thump of something hollow hitting water—and Alexander Mathew finds himself suddenly splashed across the face with spatters of ocean water. He firmly places down his oar—which he had been, until this point, utilizing to keep the small boat from colliding with the ship's hull—and glares upward. Several watchful faces peer unapologetically over the starboard side of his ship.

"Lower the yard tackle!" calls a voice from above. The echo is smudged by the wind, the sound swept off toward the looming shores of Caira. "Easy now!"

Alexander licks his lips, tasting salt, and spits off of the side of the small, four-man wherry in which he sits. The Lethal kneels at the helm, peering forward into the opaque fog that curls on the surface of the water. Just before him perches the Hawk, his knuckles white around the length of his oar. He watches the identical rowboat to their immediate left, his golden eyes narrowed into slits. The wherry's rounded hull is jostled uneasily by the white-capped waves as it touches down lightly upon the water. Alexander follows the line of his gaze, his eyes settling on the terse figure of Emerala. Her deep violet gown is as bright as a beacon through the ghostly grey dawn. Derek sits directly across from her, leaning back as his oars dip downward, breaking the glassy surface of the ocean. She stares resolutely ahead, ignoring him, the curls that cascade down from beneath her hat all but obscuring her face.

She had scarcely spoken to Alexander that morning as they prepared for their trip ashore, and yet it was obvious to him that—in spite of her sour mood—she was eager to set foot on the lands of her ancestors. Her deep green eyes had gleamed with distraction as he attempted to give her last minute instructions. The crisp night air still clung to the deck of the ship as he grabbed her hand and pulled her back to him.

You're not listening to me, he had complained, trying to catch the sweeping emerald stare that had fixated itself on the interminable darkness that lingered just beyond the reach of the ship. He had ordered the men to douse the lanterns just as the sun dipped beneath the ocean that evening—no point in attracting any more attention than was necessary. If not for the silvery stars that danced overhead, Alexander would not have been able to see her at all.

I am, she retorted in distraction.

You're not. This is important.

She cut him off before he could continue, her gaze at last finding his. *Don't you think I know how important this is? I'm about to step foot on the shores of my ancestors. This is my heritage—my blood.*

He shook his head at that, aware that he was still clutching her fingers within his own. *They're not going to welcome you, Emerala. They're going to kill you. You have to be careful.*

Even beneath the cover of darkness, he could sense that she was rolling her eyes at him. He bristled unnecessarily, his fingers tightening. Her knuckles twisted together beneath his grip. *I know,* she admitted reluctantly. Her voice, only a whisper, was nearly swallowed whole by the distant murmuring of the black waves below.

Then tell me your name. Practice it. It can't sound like a question. You have to be confident.

There was a rustle of fabric as she drew herself upright. The silvery light played upon her curls. *I am Lady Katherine Montclay, daughter of Lord Remus Montclay of Toholay.* She paused at that, and he could see a flash of ivory as she gave him a tiny smile. *Pleasure to make your acquaintance.*

He hooks his oar onto the oarlock of the neighboring wherry and pulls the boat astride theirs. Emerala glances up—startled at the sudden movement.

"Sit up straight," he whispers to her.

"I am," she mutters back, her brows dipping in annoyance.

"Sit up straighter, you're a lady."

"Or at least pretending to be one," the Hawk comments, a droll smile appearing on his face. Emerala scowls back at him. From his perch at the front of the rowboat, the Lethal lets out a dry laugh.

"Don't pay any attention to 'em, love. You're not to be blamed, I'd reason these two fools here have spent a great deal of time ruffling the feathers of the noble ladies, but I don't reckon they've had much success with them." He glances over his shoulder and winks, his gaze full of implication. Emerala laughs at that, and sits up just a bit straighter.

Her laugh is punctuated by the shrieking of a bird somewhere nearby. There is the sound of wings slapping against water and a shadow takes off in the mist, sending swirls of fog dancing across their laps.

"They're watching," Derek says, his eyes on Emerala.

"Behave," Alexander whispers to her, and shoves his oar back into water.

They row in silence for a while; the only sound the cadence of their oars breaking the glassy surface of the whispering ocean. Overhead, the dawn is spilling across the sky like champagne. Heat tickles the skin of Alexander's arms. All around them the mist is rising, dissipating off of the surface of the water in curling slivers of silver. Sunlight seeps into the water, illuminating the colorful reefs beneath the surface and casting the depths into shadows of crisp, crystalline blue.

He thinks of the mission before him and his stomach ties itself into knots. He thinks of Tyde, the elusive trickster who was always so fond of puzzles and games. The Cairan used to visit the ports of Senada when Alexander was a boy, traveling across the narrow channel to confound the marketplace with his grandiose stories and his unsolvable riddles. It is no accident that the man's name was written in the riddle upon the map.

Whatever it is that his father so badly wants him to find, it will be hidden with Tyde. He is certain of it. He glances across the still surface of the water, his gaze lingering on Derek. He is leaning forward, his oars momentarily still, as he whispers something to Emerala. She laughs, blushing slightly, and Alexander feels himself cringe internally. His oar plunges into the water with a jarring splash. He stares forward, training his eyes instead upon the ever-nearing beach up ahead.

They are so close, now. He wonders if his old friend will continue to care for his mother after the deal is done. And that was the deal, was it not? He recalls the day he met the wealthy traveler and the conversation that they had. He had heard the newcomer complaining loudly about being shipwrecked by the infamous Captain Samuel Mathew. At the sound of his father's name, Alexander's heart had nearly stopped beating. He had instantly used what little money he had procured that day to buy the man a drink.

Captain Samuel Mathew possesses something of which I am in need, Derek had told him, leaning in over his grog with glittering black eyes. *I want you to get it for me. I will pay you handsomely.*

I don't want your gold, Alexander had responded, his head already thick and swimming with drink.

What is your price, then? Name it, and I am certain I can fulfill your wishes.

My price is his head. If you give me the location of my father, I'll find him and I'll kill him. He could feel himself growing hot with anger, the sparks of the fire fanned into licking flames by the burning grog in his chest. A thick lump formed in his throat. *I'll kill him for what he's done to my mum.*

At that, Derek had leaned back, his fingers interlocking across his chest. He regarded Alexander for a long moment, his black eyes speculative.

She's important to you, your mother? he had asked quietly.

She's all I have in this world.

And you would do anything for her?

Alexander paused at that, wondering what the man's game could possibly be. *I would,* he relinquished at last. *She's not well. She needs me.*

Derek smiled, his gaze friendly—understanding. *What if I could provide for her?*

What do you mean?

I'm sure it has dawned on you by now that I am a gentleman of considerable wealth. I am in the process of purchasing an estate in Senada. It will be equipped with the finest of staff—enough people to attend to your ailing mother's needs day and night.

You would do that? Alexander asked, bewildered. He thought of the dilapidated hovel in which his mother was currently sleeping, waiting for him to come home. She had spent the night before refusing to come out of the ocean. She had seen Samuel's ship, she was sure of it this time, and she was waiting for him. That morning, he had heard her give a watery cough. He could not care for her, not anymore. Not within his means.

Before him, Derek was grinning. His gaze was kind. *She will want for nothing.*

Alexander gestured for the barmaid, waiting as she filled his mug. Only once she had absconded from earshot did he continue speaking. *It must be important to you—this object in my father's possession.*

Immensely so, Derek agreed.

And you can't get it yourself?

I'm afraid not. And I can especially not obtain it if you were to kill your father.

Alexander hesitated, licking his lips as he considered the implications of the deal. He stared at the professionally tailored cuffs of Derek's sleeves—at the polished gleam of his leather boots. If anyone could provide for his ailing mother, it would be this man. What would the murder of his father do for her, after all, besides leave them even more alone than they already were?

We have an agreement, he said, and stuck out his hand for Derek to shake.

A stifled noise from Emerala brings him surfacing back into the present. He glances over at the neighboring boat and sees that Derek has stopped rowing.

"What is it?" Derek asks Emerala, a look of concern spreading across his face. He reaches out and takes her hands. *For show,* Alexander reminds himself. *This is all for show.*

"I—" she stammers and stops, glancing over the side of the rowboat at the glassy surface of the water. "I thought I saw something."

"What did you see?" Alexander calls out to her as Derek, too, glances over the side of the boat. Her oversized hat dips gracefully over her face, the shadow obscuring her eyes. Even still, he can feel her meeting his gaze.

"I don't know, I thought—" she starts and stops again, her face flushing with embarrassment.

"Out with it Rogue, what did you see?" the Hawk snaps, impatient. One hand lingers on the hilt of his dagger.

"Remove your hand from your weapon," Alexander hisses to his companion. "You heard Derek, they're watching."

The Hawk frowns and ignores him, gripping the hilt tighter.

"I must have been imagining it," Emerala says meekly, her cheekbones stained with red. Derek is still peering at the cerulean surface of the water, his brows lowered.

"Well, what did you think you saw?" Alexander prompts.

She opens her mouth to speak, but is interrupted by the Lethal. "A mermaid."

At this, everyone turns to the murderer that crouches at the stern of the boat. He, too, stares darkly at the surface of the water.

"What was that?" Alexander asks, unsure he has heard him correctly.

"The lass thinks she saw a mermaid," the Lethal repeats slowly. The red scar over his eye gleams white in the reflection of the sunlit sea.

"Aye," rasps the Hawk, clearly struggling to hold back laughter. "And how do you figure?"

The Lethal glances back at him with an expression that causes Alexander's blood to run cold. "Because I just saw one, too."

The Hawk throws back his head to laugh, but an undulating movement from just beneath the water suddenly jostles the boat. Alexander glances downward just in time to see a rippling shadow disappearing out of sight among the colorful reefs. He blinks twice, hard, trying to justify what he just saw. Not a mermaid, but something startlingly human regardless.

Derek is the first to be pulled under. There is an outcry of protest and he is gone, his gleaming boots disappearing beneath the surface of the water with scarcely a splash. Emerala is left alone in the swaying rowboat. She gapes at the swelling surface of the water where her companion just disappeared, her lips parted in a silent scream. Two struggling shadows drift together in fragments of dark and light as the water settles back into stillness.

And then there is total pandemonium.

Hands shoot upward from the water, grabbing at the sides of the rowboat and pulling at the wooden edges, rocking, rocking, rocking the boat back and forth. With a hoarse shout, the Hawk drops his oar. Forgetting his dagger completely, he draws his pistol and begins firing at the surface of the water. The air reeks suddenly of crisp, burning gunpowder and salt.

"Stop shooting, damn it," the Lethal demands. Alexander whirls about in time to see glistening fingers enclose about the old murderer's ankles and pull him overboard. He has little time to react. There is a resounding splash and the boat is capsized. The last thing Alexander hears as the roar of the ocean pummels against his eardrums is the sound of Emerala's screams.

He is encased, suddenly, in the pressing blue silence of the sea.

Schools of fish flicker and turn all around him, their scales shimmering silver and blue in the shafts of sunlight that break through the surface of the water overhead. Something is holding his legs, drawing him downward. He kicks aimlessly; shoving his boots toward what he hopes is his captor's face. After a moment, he feels his foot connect with something fleshy. Fingers slide away from his legs and he is free. He kicks for the surface; his eyes trained on the surging circle of yellow that dances against the waves. There is movement to his left and he turns to see Emerala fighting against the heavy folds of her gown. They are dragging her downward; the lavender gossamer and cream lace an anchor preventing her from rising toward the surface. Her eyes meet his in panic and he chances his course of direction. A shadow passes by him—legs kicking fast—and he sees not a mermaid but a man, naked except for a loin-cloth and two long banana tree leaves bound to his feet, spiraling toward Emerala.

As he swims away, Alexander can suddenly make out a glint of silver in his right hand. The man is brandishing a rather imposing looking knife.

Emerala sees him as well. She kicks harder, losing stamina as she fights aimlessly against the saturated material. Her eyelids begin to droop, her cheeks purpling as she fights to keep her breath.

Alexander swims fast, but the man is faster. He reaches Emerala first, using the knife to saw through the heavy fabric of the gown. And then he is rising to the surface, pulling Emerala upwards towards the circular ripple of sunlight. Alexander follows, ignoring his mother's gown as it drifts, ghostly and translucent in the flickering sunlight, toward the ocean floor.

His head breaks through the surface of the water and he gasps, taking in the air in ragged pulls. He barely has time to register his surroundings before he is encased in total blackness. A woven bag, smelling strongly of coconut oil, has been pulled firmly over his head. Fingers circle around his arms and he feels the passing bubbles of paddling feet as his captor pulls him, slowly, through the water.

"Do not struggle," says a heavily accented voice close to his ear. "And we will bring you ashore."

"And if I decide to struggle?" he asks; his challenge muffled by the heavy fabric.

"Then you will be drowned."

CHAPTER 32

The Forbidden City

ROBERTS THE VALIANT paces the length of the great, stone gallery, his head bowed. Tousled black ringlets cascade wildly across his forehead, obscuring the angry glimmer of his emerald eyes. He mutters darkly, the words that fall from his lips scarcely audible to anyone but himself. The only sound in the room is the distinct echo of his bare feet slapping against damp stone.

Across the room, shrouded in shadows and still as the stone walls at her back, sits Nerani. Two watery blue eyes stare out of a pinched, white face. She is flanked on either side by the looming figures of Topan and Orianna, each with similarly stoic expressions frozen across their features. Orianna's fingers are clenched tightly together, the long painted violet of her fingernails scourging her flesh.

"Are you done, Roberts?" Topan's voice rolls softly off of the stone. The flames dance upon their sconces as he takes several unimposing steps forward.

Roberts skids to a halt upon the stone, glancing up at the occupants of the room in some surprise. The flickering golden light that stretches across his pointed features causes the room beyond to fade into black. His dark brows draw close together over his eyes as he stares past Topan and towards the two women lingering just behind him.

"Have you finished shouting?" Topan asks, ignoring Roberts's continued silence. "Because if you have, I'd rather like to give Nerani a chance to speak."

At that, Robert takes a sharp gulp of air, his nostrils stretching as his chest puffs outward beneath his white cotton shirt. He is teetering dangerously on the edge of losing his composure. Again.

"There is nothing for her to say," he says through clenched teeth. "What apology can she offer? She robbed me of the chance to avenge my sister. A life for a life—that would be fair."

"It would be fair if Emerala were dead," comes Nerani's voice from the shadows. She had remained quiet all through the shouting—had let Roberts yell until his voice was hoarse. He resents her for her patience. He wants her to jump to her feet and shout back at him—to give him something visceral at which to point his rage. As it is, his temper is slowly abating. His muscles quake from the prolonged tension in which he has held himself. His knuckles clench and unclench at his sides, skin pulling over bone, discoloring with the strain.

"We've been through this before," he hisses, his voice barely rising above a whisper. He does not finish the thought he started. *Emerala is dead. Gone.*

He sees a small line of color rise in Nerani's cheekbones and feels a perverse satisfaction at having finally, finally elicited some sort of emotional reaction.

"Emerala was not killed," she insists.

"You and Orianna saw her shoved to her knees by three armed Guardians. Surely you remember." He shoves his palm in Orianna's direction, urging her to join the conversation. "Orianna, remind her what you saw."

Orianna's mouth falls open. She shoots a slanted look in Nerani's direction before meeting Roberts's gaze across the dimly lit expanse. "I saw her at the mercy of the three armed Guardians." She swallows. The intonation of her words has adopted a rehearsed cadence—the result of having been repeated time after time. Her voice is thick. "She called out for us to run. And we did."

"We did not *see* her die," Nerani insists, rising to her feet. "Those three Guardians were found dead only moments later, with no trace of Emerala. The Guardians don't have her in their possession and they admitted to never killing her, so she must be—"

"They admitted?" Roberts repeats, his tone a mockery of hers. His eyes fall to Nerani's mangled hand, carefully bound only hours ago by Mame Minera in the infirmary. Already, blood is seeping through the gauze. *She lost the fingers*, the Mame had said. *They were too broken to save.*

"I'm sorry," he says, scowling at her. "I thought it was you who were interrogated, not the other way around."

"Roberts," Topan's voice is dangerous. It slithers across the floor of the room and coils at Robert's feet—a clear warning. Tread carefully.

"No," Roberts says, ignoring him. "I'm curious. Who is it that told you that? James Byron?"

A sharp look of discomfort flickers across Nerani's face and is gone. He remembers the proximity of them in the empty storeroom—remembers the way General Byron had held Nerani's gaze. He would have been a fool not to notice the implications. He feels the anger inside him rising into a full boil.

"Is that why you protected him?" he asks, shouting again. "Are you friends now, you and the king's loyal dog?"

"Why is it so hard to believe that the pirates may have succeeded where we did not?" Nerani is not shouting—not yet—but the tone of her voice quivers with emotion. Her face drains of color and she teeters where she stands. Noticing this, Topan rushes over to her side. His arms enclose about her, steadying her by the shoulders. Roberts watches, seething, as Topan lowers Nerani slowly back into the chair. After she is settled, the deep, indigo eyes of the king turn back to him.

"You're done here, Roberts. Thank you."

Roberts frowns, watching as Topan moves to obscure the figure of his cousin. Over his shoulder, Orianna's gaze is just as imposing.

"Nerani needs to be brought back to the infirmary. Mame Minera will want to change her bandages." A thin line of worry shoots across Orianna's brow as she speaks.

"I'll take her," Roberts says gruffly, his mood softening just slightly at the sight of his cousin's frailty.

"I think you've done enough," snaps Topan. Roberts is startled at the naked disappointment on the face of his friend. "Take a walk. Please."

Roberts grunts an unintelligible reply, turning his back on the group and heading towards the shaded alcove at the far side of the room. Only once he is alone, encased in the total blackness of the narrow stone corridor and out of earshot of any listeners, does he allow himself to breathe again. His knees tremble; buckling at last beneath the weight of his shoulders. He drops to the ground, heedless of the uneven stone that cracks against his bones. His chest heaves in a silent, choked sob. He fights to swallow the surge of emotions that threaten to overcome him as he rocks, alone, in the darkness.

For several quiet moments his lips move in speechless fervor as he fights to calm his raging nerves. When at last a lucid word rises upon his tongue, it dances on his lips in a choked cry.

Eliot.

It is his father that comes to him, there, in the darkness. It is his father's memory—those dark green eyes so similar to his own, watching from beneath the shadow of his hat, wincing at the screams of the child Emerala. He was unaccustomed to children. An eccentric and a self-ascribed loner, he had never been a family man. An artist, their mother had called him. An architect.

Roberts hates him—hates the very fiber of his being. The memories—those he has worked so hard to keep at bay all his life—swarm at the forefront of his mind. They wash over him like a wave, pushing him downward; threatening to drown him. He pushes his knuckles hard into the stone. The snapping of his crackling bones is loud against the silence.

The day his father left, he had knelt before Roberts and gripped him tight by the shoulders. Roberts found himself looking into a mirror image of himself, in spite of their significant difference in years. His father, perpetually young, was handsome to a fault. His slick black hair was impeccably combed—parted down the side just so. His green eyes twinkled out of a pointed, olive face.

That day, those eyes were troubled.

I've got to go away, boy, he said, looking as though he was trying for all the world not to cover his ears with the palms of his hands. Nearby, Emerala was perched on her mother's hip, her little face pinched and red with the strain of screaming. Her hair, wild and black since birth, flew in all directions in curling wisps.

With some amount of effort, Roberts calls into memory the face of his mother—a tall, thin woman with dark brown curls as wild as her children's. Her own skin was fair and smooth, with eyes as blue as the clear sky. She shushed Emerala in distraction, whispering soothing nothings into the child's hair as she attempted to overhear Eliot's conversation with his son.

Look at me, his father had commanded him sharply. His breath was tinged with the pungent stab of cigar smoke. *Things are going to get bad, now, before they get better. But I've been given no other choice.*

Eliot Roberts's eyes had filled with tears, then, and Roberts felt himself starting to sniffle as well. He bit the inside of his cheek, determined not to let his mother see him cry.

They'll kill me if I stay, do you understand? They'll kill us all. He hesitated, pawing clumsily at one eye with the back of his hand. *They'll kill my boy.*

Roberts had the strange sensation that his father was not referring to him. The man suddenly gripped him tighter, pulling him close. *You protect them, do you hear me? You protect your mother and your sister.*

Why can't you stay and keep us safe? Roberts asked, feeling suddenly fearful. He was only a child. What dangers were coming? What could he possibly protect his family from that his father could not?

Don't you understand, boy? His father shook him slightly as he spoke. *That's why I'm leaving. I've no other choice.*

Roberts pries his fists from the cool stone in front of him, straightening his spine as he rests his backside against the heels of his feet. He sighs deeply, his eyes dry. He remembers taking Emerala from his mother—watching as they moved away from the children and into the doorway. By then, Emerala had grown weary with screaming. She smacked her lips contently and gave a stretching yawn.

Sleep, Rob, she had murmured in the saccharine voice of a tired child. She grabbed at his fingers, pulling him willfully. He brushed her away, listening in fear to the rising voices of his parents.

How could you, his mother was shouting. *How could you do this to us?*

I'm protecting you, Alarana.

At that, his mother had slapped his father across the face. He took the slap in silence, scarcely flinching.

How dare you, she cried. *How dare you act as though any of this is for us? It's all for her, isn't it? It's all for her and the boy. I'm not a fool, Eliot. I know the child is yours.*

You'll be safer once I'm gone, Alarana. You and the children.

At the mention of the children, Roberts's parents suddenly noticed that Roberts and Emerala were still in listening distance. They fell silent, turning their gazes to the fearful boy and his drowsing sister.

Rob, darling, take your sister to bed, his mother had ordered. Her eyes were red and swollen. Her face looked drawn, as though she had tasted something sour.

Roberts obeyed, taking one last glance at the dark silhouette of his father as he left the room. Those deep green eyes watched him solemnly, never blinking.

There was no other goodbye.

He breathes deep, letting the air flow in and out—slowly—the measured rising and falling of his own chest the only thing that keeps him afloat against the onslaught of memories—memories that he has spent every waking moment since fighting to repress.

His eyes flutter closed as he relents, at last, to the ghosts of his past.

His mother was slaughtered not a fortnight later, her heart pierced by a gunshot as she struggled against the Golden Guard. Roberts had lain as still as stone beneath the divan in his aunt's tiny foyer, holding his breath and fighting against the sobs that choked in his throat. He remembers her cries as she stood, shivering, beneath the barrel of a pistol.

Please, she said shrilly. *Please, I don't know where he's gone.*

You're a liar, sneered the Guardian. *They're all liars. Shoot them.*

Both of them, sir? asked a second guardian. He stood only a few feet away, his pistol leveled at the back of Anerani's head. Nerani's father, Gerwinge, lay dead on the floor only a few feet away, having been quickly put down after he refused to grant the Guardians permission to enter his home.

Roberts watched as a young, silver haired Guardian stepped gingerly over the corpse, readying his pistol. *Why not?* he asked, as though their lives were so trivial that another death mattered little to him.

Two gunshots rattled the house and they were dead. The Guardians receded, their footsteps staccato as they sidestepped the swelling pools of blood on the floor. The room reeked of gunpowder.

The door shut and Roberts was alone with the corpses of his family.

"I've failed," he whispers into the darkness. "Time and time again, I've failed."

He rocks on his knees, feeling grief wash over him in waves.

"I've let everyone die."

He thinks of the day he received his name, waiting in line with the other Cairan children his age as the Mames made their slow progression across the room. Mame Galyria had peered into the lines of his hand and declared him Roberts the Valiant.

His father had been present that day, looking out of place and uncomfortable at his mother's side, as if he was not quite sure how he had ended up at a Cairan ceremony. And yet, when the Mame announced Roberts's title to the waiting crowd his father had leapt to his feet with pride.

That's my boy, he had called to someone in the crowd, his green eyes gleaming like jewels. *Brave as can be.*

I am not worthy of my namesake, Roberts thinks bitterly. *I've lost everyone, and I nearly lost Nerani, too.*

He thinks of himself hiding behind the divan, crouching in blood—his mother's blood. Useless. Cowardly.

What would he have done if Nerani had died? How could he have continued?

He punches the stone again.

"Are you planning to make a hole in the stone that way?" says a voice from behind him. He jerks to his feet, alarmed. There is the sound of flint against stone and a soft candle dances into light. He watches as the slender figure of a woman, her edges traced in pale flame, leans down and places the candle gingerly upon the ground. Silvery lockets of hair fall around her face, cupping the flickering light in the white curls.

She straightens and he suddenly finds himself looking into a pair of blue eyes so pale that they are almost grey. In the shadows of the corridor, she is as waiflike as a ghost. She appears translucent in the tiny, dancing flame, and for a moment he believes that if he were to stick his hand towards her, it would pass right through her skin and come out the other side.

"I know you," he says, remembering. "You're the woman who approached Blaine and I in the city." He snaps his fingers, trying to recall her name.

"Seranai the Fair," she reminds him, offering her hand in greeting.

"Ah, yes," he assents, and gives her a shaky smile. "Er, how long have you been standing there?"

She proffers a shy smile. "Long enough to hear you talking to yourself."

He gives an abashed laugh, rubbing the palm of his hand aggressively against the back of his neck as he tries to remember what it was he might have said.

"Are you alright?" she asks, inching closer. The light plays across the thin bridge of her upturned nose, alighting in her eyes and causing them to sparkle like silver. In spite of his sour mood, her beauty does not go unnoticed.

"I'm fine," he lies, hoping she does not notice the wild fluttering of his pulse at the base of his throat. The yellow light of the dancing candle burns his retinas, and he wonders how long he idled alone out here in the dark, left at the mercy of his memories. "Why are you out here?" he asks Seranai, diverting the attention instead to her.

Now, it is her turn to look sheepish. "I followed you," she admits. She twists her fingers together in embarrassment, averting her clear grey gaze from his.

"Oh," he says, and feels a slight welling of amusement in his chest. His fury at Nerani almost entirely forgotten, he takes a slow step closer to the young woman before him. He recalls how she had raced toward him in the grey streets of Chancey, the pale red of her gown stark against the bleached afternoon. Then, her grey eyes had been wide with fear.

Roberts the Valiant? she asked. He had started, surprised at her knowledge of his name. *You are one of the Cairan king's Listener's, yes?*

I am, he admitted, exchanging a cautious glance with Blaine.

Come quickly, she breathed, her bosoms heaving with exertion beneath her tightly cinched lace corset. *Nerani the Elegant—he has her.*

Who? Roberts had demanded, his pulse racing at the sound of his cousin's name.

General Byron.

He eyes the woman before him, trying to catch her gaze and bring it back up to meet his own. "You followed me," he repeats, his tone inquisitive.

"I did," she smiles primly at the stone underfoot, watching it flickering between light and dark.

"May I ask you something?" he probes, finally causing her to glance back up at him. She nods, the movement almost imperceptible. Her eyes are as still and as silent as the sea on a misty morning. Serene. Peaceful.

"How did you know my name?" He pauses, continues. "How did you know Nerani's name?"

She smiles wider at that, her plump lower lip curling to cup the smaller upper lip within its corners. Her eyes glimmer knowingly. "It's quite a long story," she says. "Do you know Mamere Lenora?"

"Mamere? Of course I do. The woman was like a mother to me."

Seranai smiles. "She's been like a mother to me these days. She took me in when I had nowhere left to turn."

Roberts feels a genuine smile catching at his lips—the first in a long time. The memory of Lenora is comforting—the connection nostalgic. Seranai the Fair draws nearer to him across the dark.

"Why don't you and I take a walk and I'll tell you everything?"

CHAPTER 33

Caira

ALEXANDER AND HIS captor reach the shore in only a few moments, Alexander's feet touching down on the sticking sand of the beach sooner than he thought. They walk oddly for a ways, a man with flippers leading a man with no vision. At last, he feels the whitecaps of the waves breaking against his ankles as they step out onto dry land. He hears the sound of his captor kicking off the fronds on his feet—heavy leaf brushing against sundried grains of sand.

"Walk," his captor commands. He listens. Somewhere nearby, he can hear the muffled protests of Emerala. He hopes that whatever it is she is saying to her captor, she has managed to remember to act like a frightened lady of considerable wealth and not like her usual, brazen self.

"Unhand my fiancée immediately, if you please," Derek's voice cuts through the cacophony of muffled protests. Several birds scream somewhere overhead, and for a moment the stippled gold light that pierces the stitching of his bag is extinguished by shadow. He hears a voice respond and there is a grunt as someone—likely Derek—is shoved to his knees in the sand. He strains his ears, listening, and realizes that he does not hear the Hawk or the Lethal. He hopes against all hope that their silence indicates that they managed to escape their captors in the water.

From deep within the forest comes the sound of drums. The roll is slow, even, matching in cadence with the steps of someone approaching. Alexander fights the urge to roll his eyes, recalling the Cairan penchant for the dramatic. At last, the drums slow to a stop. The reverberation rolls down the sandy beach and is sopped into silence by the slapping waves.

"Ahh, visitors," breathes a resounding voice—deep and welcoming in spite of the precarious situation in which they have suddenly found themselves. "Pirates, no doubt. I'm sure, friends, we don't have to remind you how we feel about pirates here on Caira."

The speaker claps his hands together and the bag is suddenly wrenched from Alexander's head. He is left blinking madly in the unforgiving white light of the glaring sun. The shadow of the speaker contorts and pulls in front of him, at last settling into the familiar figure of the notorious Cairan ringleader. Domio. He leans casually against a splintering wood sign, chewing a hangnail on his pinky finger. Alexander studies the hand painted words of the sign, the color long-since faded by the merciless sun.

> *Ye who linger here, beware*
> *Pirates will your burdens bear*

Alexander's eyes follow the steep incline of the tree at Domio's back, starkly conscious of the four swinging shadows that hang just above his head. His gaze stops at the first, thickset branch, upon which hang four iron gibbets. From somewhere to his left, he hears Emerala let out a gasp. Three corpses—each in varying stages of decomposition—lie upright within the first three suspended cages. Two of them have been nearly picked clean by the birds; their bones bleached white in the glare of the sun. The third, although lacking his eyes, remains distinguishable as the man he once was. His cloak, unmistakably pirate, bears a familiar insignia—a blood red cross against the faded black of his coat.

Captain Jameson, Alexander thinks, and feels a fluttering of nerves rush through him as he recalls the day he stole his father's map from the mercenary on Chancey.

How did he know to come back here? Alexander thinks, his thoughts churning faster than he can process. *If he was a mercenary, he must have been paid off by someone to take the map. It was only a job. He could not have known where it led.*

He does not have time to puzzle through the mercenary's strange presence just now. Before him, Domio is speaking again, addressing the sodden group of trespassers.

"We'll have to empty out the gibbets," he says, "but it looks like we'll have just enough to accommodate all of you gentlemen. I'm sure their current occupants won't mind." He snickers, and Alexander glances behind him to see the Hawk and the Lethal, similarly restrained. *So much for a daring rescue,* he thinks wryly. The man gripping the Hawk sports a rather bloody nose, his face purpling in color. He glares darkly at Alexander and the captain feels a welling of satisfaction in his chest. At least he managed to do some damage to their captors.

"Domio," calls Derek, still on his knees in the sand. "Is this really necessary?" Emerala, too, has been shoved to her knees besides him. The cream lace of her petticoat spills across the sand like water. She stares at the ground, eyes wide. Even from here, Alexander can tell she is trying and failing to force tears to well in her eyes. She is bursting at the seams with curiosity. He wishes she would play at being a noblewoman just a little bit better. So far, they are not off to a very bright start, and he doesn't need any more complications to arise.

Domio has wandered over to where Derek kneels in the sand, his dark eyebrows raised almost to the top of his gleaming bald head. His deep eyes are as blue as the sea at their backs. He smiles warmly at the sight of Derek, slapping him on the back with one hand and wrenching him to his feet with the other.

"Derek, my boy!" he cries, his eyes twinkling with another kind of mirth. "What are you doing in the company of pirates?" He doesn't wait for Derek to answer. His attention draws to a stop, instead, upon the declined head of Emerala. "And who is this lovely lady?"

Derek reaches down and pulls Emerala gently to her feet. She does her best to appear demure. Alexander prays to whatever gods may be that Domio is convinced by her charade.

"This, old friend, is my fiancée, the Lady Katherine Montclay."

"Montclay," Domio repeats, stroking his chin thoughtfully. "Montclay. That's a name I haven't heard in these parts in ages. A Westerly bride for you, is it, Derek?"

"Yes," Derek says. "Her father is Lord Remus Montclay of the Toholay estates. He escorted her and her dowry to Senada only recently. She's been dying to come and see the beautiful island of Caira, and I must say her experience here has been rather appalling so far." He leans in, lowering his voice. "Was it really necessary to have your men nearly drown us to get us ashore? She's had a terrible fright, thrashing about in the ocean like that."

Alexander is impressed by the quick-witted ease with which Derek lies. He studies Emerala carefully, watching her for any mistakes. She curtsies lightly, offering Domio a trembling hand as she continues to stare at the sand. *Good,* Alexander thinks. There is a flapping of wings as a raven drops down from the sky and lands on Domio's shoulder with a silent plop. It flutters its blue-black wings, eyeballing Emerala with eyes like glass.

Domio smiles kindly at her, a look of apology passing over his features. He ignores the presence of the bird. "I am deeply sorry, milady, for your treatment here today." He leans forward, his lips grazing the back of her hand. "Of course, we would not have responded so immediately had we known it was your fiancé leading the company of pirates."

Alexander feels a small wave of relief wash over him. Domio straightens, letting Emerala's arm drop from his grip. The raven hops idly from one claw to the other, its talons curling deep impressions in Domio's maroon doublet. After a moment, the raven takes off with a guttural shriek. Alexander watches him go, feeling a small shiver run down the length of his spine. He lowers his gaze and finds two blue eyes locked directly upon his. Domio studies the pirates carefully, the curvature of his face pitted with deep shadows, before turning his attention back to Derek.

"Pirates, Derek," he frowns, shaking his head. "What do you possibly mean by bringing pirates to my island?"

At that, Derek smiles. "This is no ordinary pirate, old friend," he says, and gestures toward Alexander with an open palm. "This is Captain Alexander Mathew, son of the late Captain Samuel Mathew."

"Ah," Domio breathes, exhaling loudly through his nose. He turns back to Alexander. "Is that so? I knew your father, I did. Feeding the fishes, is he?"

Alexander bristles. "He is."

"His death was a pity. He did me a grand service, once."

"Is that so?" Alexander tries to keep his voice devoid of emotion—unthreatening—and yet he can feel the distaste for this man curling around his throat like a noose.

Domio takes a few steps closer, studying Alexander with probing eyes. "I am quite eager, in fact, to return such a monumental favor. Friend of Derek—son of Samuel—tell me, what brings you to my shores?"

Alexander swallows, hesitating. He is suddenly thrust back to the Eisle of Udire, to Ha'Rai's throne room, filled with choking smoke and the constant, pressing cold. The map lay translated before them, the island of Caira circled in deep red.

So you will go to Caira, Ha'Rai had said, the ivory teeth of her necklace—spoils of war—gleaming against her exposed clavicle. *You will speak with Domio and you will tell him only truths. Do not lie.*

I won't, he said, his gaze burning as he stared at the cryptic words before him.

What is sweeter than honey? What is stronger than a lion?

But—Ha'Rai said, laying a trembling hand over his own clenched fist. She drew his chin upwards to meet her gaze. *You must not tell him about the map. Do not lie, but do not reveal the map.* She leaned forward, the heat of her breath tickling his ear. Her voice had lowered to a hoarse whisper. *He will take the map, and your life with it.*

Why? He asked. *What is the map to him?*

Everything. It was his past. It is his present. It plagues his future. You must not let him know you possess it. Or you will die.

She had refused to tell him any more.

Before him, Domio is waiting. He straightens his shoulders. "I'm here to see Tyde."

Domio's blue eyes narrow dangerously. "For what purpose?"

Again, Alexander hesitates. *Do not lie*, he hears Ha'Rai say. "I don't know," he admits, feeling foolish.

"Ah, but you must have a reason," Domio smiles, the corners of his lips curling upward in a malevolent coil.

It is the Hawk that speaks next, startling everyone. "We're here on orders from Ha'Rai, regent of the Eisle of Udire." His voice is loud. Confident. Alexander flinches internally.

A lie. That was a lie.

He cannot call it back, not now.

Domio's eyes are locked, still, upon Alexander. "Ha'Rai? Yes, I know her well. She sent you here, to me?"

Alexander swallows, determined to stick as close to the truth as possible in spite of the Hawk's deviation. "We've just sailed here from her island, yes."

Domio's smile widens, but it no longer looks inviting. "How peculiar. She is not one to pass up game at this time of year. Tell me, she gave you no explanation for your visit to Tyde?"

"No, only that we were to come ashore and ask your permission to meet with him, which we've now done. He's a man of riddles, perhaps she thinks he has information we'd like to hear."

Domio nods slowly, considering this. "I wasn't aware that pirate lords were in the business of hiring themselves out as mercenaries," he says. "But I suppose this is a new world, and I'm just an old man. Very well—"

He is cut off by a resounding giggle that echoes out from beneath the shade of the trees. The laugh is punctuated by the dissonant screaming of ravens. Looking up, Alexander feels his blood run cold. Hundreds of the black birds, their glass eyes lifeless, have roosted in the trees. Silent, fluttering shadows of midnight blue, watching, waiting.

"Melena approaches," whispers his captor at his back. The man sounds nervous. His vice-like grip loosens slightly around Alexander's arms.

Sure enough, Alexander can just make out the slender figure of a woman emerging from beneath the trees. Her long, twisting braid of amber nearly drags along the ground at her feet. Her homespun cotton chemise falls from her shoulders, exposing the rounded bosoms that threaten to spill out over her tightly cinched corset, as black and as blue as the sleek feathers of the raven that perches on her shoulder.

"Domio," she sings, and something in her voice causes Alexander to recoil inwardly. "You didn't tell me we had new playthings. I had to hear the news from my darlings."

"Guests, Melena, dear. These are guests." Domio corrects, not turning to look at the newcomer to the beach. He sounds mildly irate at the intrusion.

"Is there a difference?" She titters, the sound rising up into the trees. The ravens echo the noise, clicking their beaks together in an eerie mimic of her laugh. "Anyway, I've come to see the girl. You can keep your nasty, old pirates."

She saunters lazily down the stretch of beach that lies between them, all eyes on her. She draws to a stop just before Emerala, hands on her hips. Emerala continues to stare into the sand with a powerful exertion of will. Her black ringlets have almost completely dried in the pressing heat and the coils gleam as they bounce around her cheekbones.

"Hello, Melena," Derek says, his words clipped and careful. Melena shoots him a playful smile in response, but otherwise says nothing. Directly before Alexander, Domio has resumed chewing at his hangnail.

Melena crouches down, taking Emerala's chin between her fingers and forcing Emerala to look up at her face. Her lips break out in a full grin. She tilts back her head and cackles. Derek's eyes catch Alexander's across the beachfront as the sound of Melena's laugh bounces away from her with maddening force. Derek shakes his head, a nearly imperceptible movement, and returns his gaze to the scene before him.

Melena whispers something to the bird in a language that Alexander does not recognize. With a shriek, the raven takes off upon the air. Alexander watches it soar over the treetops and out of sight.

"Melena," Domio calls, spitting out his hangnail and turning with impatience to the girl. The subtle tone of inquiry in his voice does not go unnoticed by Alexander.

"Domio, come—come and look at her eyes!" Melena squeals in delight, waving to him as though she has only just now noticed that she and Emerala are not the only people on the beach. Domio moves from his position before Alexander, planting himself directly in front of Derek and Emerala.

"Look at me," he commands. Emerala does not move. Heavy silence hangs upon the air. After a moment Derek nudges Emerala with his elbow, his gaze unreadable. He murmurs something to her but Alexander cannot make out his words above the rush of the waves at his back. *The tide is coming in*, he thinks.

Slowly, defiantly, Emerala tilts her chin upwards. Her black curls fall away from her face as the thick sunlight drapes across the deep green of her irises.

Domio clicks his tongue reproachfully. "Derek, it saddens me to know that you have not been truthful with us."

"I'm sorry," Derek says, allowing a small trace of confusion to flicker across his face. "But how exactly have I misled you?"

"The girl—she is not from Toholay is she?"

"She is, I assure you. Katherine comes from the established line of Montclays in the Westerlies." Derek proffers a courteous smile. His voice has not lost an ounce of its initial confidence.

"So you say," Domio replies, his smile equally as courteous. Alexander feels suddenly and thoroughly discomfited by the whole affair. The rushing water of the incoming tide claws at his ankles, receding with the bubbling gurgle of the dying. The sky above his head is strangely empty.

"Domio." Melena's theatrical whisper is too loud as she tugs at Domio's shirtsleeve. Her clear blue eyes glitter in the sunlight. "I must take her to see *him*. How lovely a surprise it will be!"

Domio considers this, nodding. After a moment, he pats her softly on the head. "Of course, my dear," His gaze is still trained upon Derek. His eyes have hardened; their friendly gleam all but disappeared. "Melena will bring your betrothed to visit the Architect." It is not a question. "It has been a long time since you've stopped by to see your old friend. I'm certain he will be pleased to meet the Lady Katherine."

"Who?" Alexander asks.

Domio glances over his shoulder at Alexander, his lips curling into a strange smile. "There is a debtor who resides upon our island. He is somewhat of a pet to our dear Melena, and an old, old friend of Derek's."

Alexander shakes his head, trying to remain polite. "With all due respect, we don't have time to waste. We're here to see Tyde, and then we'll be on our way."

Domio holds up one hand to silence him. "Of course," he agrees. "I would not cross the lady Ha'Rai. You and your men will be taken to see Tyde, and then you will be returned to your ship. Derek and his betrothed will visit the Debtor."

A deep frown embeds itself upon Alexander's face. *Split up?* The idea does not sit well with him. He glances over at Emerala and is surprised to see her gazing nervously back at him, her green eyes as wide and as round as coins. He quickly averts his gaze, hoping Domio did not notice their exchange.

"The girl stays with us," comes a dangerous snarl from somewhere behind Alexander. The Hawk. Alexander cringes internally. Across the beach, a flicker of interest passes across Domio's features.

"Fascinating," he muses. "Surely Lady Katherine is of little use to you lot." He lets his words hang in the air before them, his voice riddled with implication.

"All the same, we'd prefer stay together," Alexander says, mirroring the Hawk's sentiment. Before him, Domio lets out a low chuckle.

"It is of no importance to you, Captain. You and your men will get what you came here for. Melena *will* take the girl to see the Debtor."

Next to Emerala, Derek nods. His gaze is earnest as he again locks eyes with Alexander. He knows what his friend is trying to convey. They have no other option but to do what Domio says.

Alexander disagrees.

A life of piracy has taught him that there are always other options.

"Lachlan," he barks.

"Aye," comes the voice. The Lethal is quiet, calm, soaking in the scene before him in silence.

"Go with them."

Melena lets out a giggle like a hiccup, her shrill voice raising an octave. Alexander squares his shoulders and holds Domio's steel blue gaze.

"You care much for this girl, Captain."

"I've only met Lady Katherine today," Alexander insists, keeping his eyes void of expression.

That same, knowing smile tugs at the corners of Domio's lips. "Indeed."

There is a loud clamor in the direction of the forest. All at once, the ravens begin beating their wings—blue fire catching in their sleek black feathers. With several ear-piercing screeches, they take flight from the tangled branches of the trees. Alexander feels his heart weigh heavy with dread. He watches as they amass together—their beating wings choking out the circular sun—and head inland. Melena hops from one foot to another, fingering her long braid as she giggles in excitement.

"It's time," Domio says. "Tyde is ready to see you now."

Harvest Cycle 1511

The ship is gaining ground behind us; her black sails now visible upon the distant horizon. She is quicker than the *Rebellion*—this strange ship. Larger and sleeker and built for speed. Just yesterday, Captain Samuel was able to make out the silhouettes of her inhabitants through the spyglass. It will not be long now before they reach us.

There is not much we can do but stay the course.

We are a fortnight's sail from the easternmost coast of the Westerlies, heading windward into the bluffs. It is slow going, but we might make it yet. Samuel has confidence.

And I? I am losing faith.

The captain of the ship is a man called Jameson, Samuel tells me. He is known as a pirate for hire—a mercenary willing to do the dirty work of others for the right price. He flies beneath a black banner bearing a blood red cross. I have seen such a sign through the spyglass. There can be no mistaking it for anyone else.

The Hawk says this is proof that we have been sold out by Argot.

But to whom?

We paid the mapmaker a considerable sum for his silence. Who could outbid us? Who out there knows what cargo we carry? Who out there knows about the key and what it opens?

I must remain hopeful.

There is nothing to do but stay the course.

Stay the course or die.

Eliot

CHAPTER 34

Chancey

IT IS DARK when James Byron returns to his apartment. The sun was swallowed beneath the stretching sea hours before, extinguishing with a balmy wink and casting the city of Chancey into blackness. The sky overhead is void of stars and the moon is a muddled circle of blue.

He fumbles with the key to his quarters, struggling to fit the slender brass object into the keyhole. He feels the key catch in the lock and thrusts the door open wide. A muffled grunt forces itself from his chest with the small effort. His body is wracked with pain. His clothes cling to the heavy gauze that encases his shoulders and back like a blanket.

He is met, upon entry, with the shrill whistle of the seaside wind. His heavy curtains slap wildly against the walls of his room, fluttering upwards in the stinging gusts as though they are living things. The room smells of lingering damp and he curses silently. He must have left the window open. He is slipping, he thinks—becoming careless.

He wonders how many days it has been since Nerani's escape. How many days since the summons came and he was sentenced to the whipping post? He leans against the large wooden armoire to his left and allows his eyes to flutter closed. His memory is thick with sludge—the pain in his back splintering his ability to think. Fragments of his time in the palace sick room flash through his mind, offering him fleeting glimpses of the royal surgeon cleaning his wounds—of the loosely stitched fabric of his musty cot. He pictures the small, rectangular window that sat high above his head, and recalls how the light spilled in every morning at daybreak.

Sun up. Sun down. Sun up. He clenches his eyes shut, counting. Three days? Four? His head is spinning. He shoves the door shut behind him, not

303

bothering to bolt the locks. Colors dance in frenzied patterns before his vision as he stumbles forward into the dark room. All he wants is to sleep. His cot feels as though it is miles away.

He groans, falling forward and catching himself on the heavy oak desk that sits just before him. With great difficulty, he straightens, lifting his heavy arms. He pries at the sticking fabric of his shirt, trying in vain to lift it over his head. Blistering pain shoots through his back with the effort of movement. He can feel his blood coursing through every vein of his body. He shuts his eyes and tries to breathe, ignoring the pain that etches across his skin in patchwork patterns of drying blood. The contents of his stomach, although little, threaten to rise in his throat.

Finally succeeding in removing his shirt, he drops uneasily into the wooden chair at his desk. It creaks beneath his weight. Feeling around blindly in the darkness, he gropes for the candle and flint that he keeps at the desk. After a clumsy moment of searching, his fingers enclose around the objects. There is a whispering flutter as a small flame leaps into life before his eyes. A tiny dot of blue quivers on the wick, shivering as it is encased in red and yellow heat. Byron stares into the flame as he presses the candle back into its brass holder. The flame catches in the warped looking glass on the wall, the dual light casting some manner of illumination across James's features. He stares at himself and sees only a stranger in the mirror. His face is drawn and pale. His jaw is coated in thick, untended stubble. Dark shadows cup the lower lids of his eyes.

A gust of wind catches the bare skin of his arms and he shudders involuntarily, suddenly thrust back into a memory.

He was sleeping fitfully upon the cot in the sickroom when a slamming door jolted him awake. For a moment, he wondered if it was the surgeon, come back to change his bandages. The heavy footfalls on the floor, however, were too loud to belong to the contrite old man that tended to the wounded. He made an effort to roll over onto his side, but felt as though a great weight was pressing him deep into the bed. He could not feel the cuts on his back. In fact, he could not feel his back at all—a by-product of the surgeon's salve, no doubt. The overpowering smell of lavender was scarcely enough to cover the stink of camphor that clung to his skin. He gripped the pillow beneath his head, propping himself up as best he could with his elbows. The tight skin on his shoulders stretched, pulling at tender scars.

There was the sound of a chair being dragged across the floor and the visitor dropped into a seat before him. He glanced up, peering into the dim light of the room as the dual figure of Corporal Anderson danced before his eyes. He blinked rapidly, seeing double, and wished his vision would clear.

It's a long fall from your pedestal, is it not, James? The smile on Anderson's face was unmistakable. James cleared his throat. His mouth felt as though it were filled with sand.

Have I fallen? he asked, his voice hoarse. *I don't think I have.*

In fact, Rowland himself had visited him only yesterday—an unprecedented event for a king who was so frightened by the prospect of death. He had sat in the same exact chair and apologized to James, explaining in somber tones that such a public punishment was necessary to maintain a sense of order among his Guardians. It felt like watching his own child be punished, he'd said. But it had to be done.

In front of him, Anderson was grinning from ear to ear.

Maybe not yet, but you're dangerously close to the edge.

He leaned back in his chair, propping his boots onto James's cot. He could see the polished leather in his peripherals as the shoes came close to his face.

Just one more push, Anderson said, and nudged James lightly in the side with the toe of his shoe. In spite of the camphor rubbed into his skin, he felt his back catch fire at the push. He fought to keep his face from showing any trace of pain. His insides contorted viciously.

Anderson dropped his feet to the ground with an audible plop. He scraped the chair once more across the floor, bringing his face close to James's.

When you fall, he sneered, *and you will fall, you can rest assured that I'll be the one who gives you that final shove.*

Is that a threat? James asked, his voice finally lucid against the diminishing light of the room.

Anderson's eyes narrowed. *It's a promise.*

There is a sharp knock at the door—three loud raps in quick succession. James lurches to his feet and immediately wishes he had not done so. The blood courses to his head, causing dizzying spirals of light to dance across his field of vision. For a moment, his reflection in the mirror swarms into obscurity before his eyes. He grips the edge of the desk until his knuckles ache, willing himself to muster through the pain.

Three more knocks, louder this time. Faster.

He maneuvers stiffly toward the door, his fingers wrapped prudently about the pistol at his waist. He draws to a stop at the door, putting his ear to the thick wood. He can hear the rustle of fabric pulling against carpeting—can hear the quiet whisper of a male voice, young.

"It's alright, he'll be here," says the voice. James starts, recognizing the speaker almost immediately. His hand drops from the pistol and he wrenches open the door. In the narrow hallway outside, the young prince of Chancey flinches in alarm.

"H-hello," Peterson says, all traces of formality gone at the brusqueness of James's force. James stares at him pointedly, saying nothing. Peterson is wearing the unadorned traveling clothes of a high class Chancian, his head and shoulders shrouded in a dark brown cloak. At his side is a young girl similarly clad in a pale pink muslin traveling dress, her amber braid tucked inside a matching cloak. The lanterns on the wall throw hazy orange light across their nervous faces, catching in the deep blue eyes of the girl.

A Cairan, James muses, his mind churning at an impossible rate.

"I'm sorry to bother you, General," Peterson says formally. He draws himself up to his full height in a poor effort to appear imposing. "I can see you are not well, but we are in need of your assistance."

James glances down at himself, and realizes he has forgotten to put his shirt back on. He stands before them in his trousers and boots, with his midriff bound tightly in sticking gauze. His shoulders are bare, save for the angry red stripes that peak out from the dressing. When he looks back up at the strange pair on his doorstep, Peterson is speaking again. The words fall from his lips too fast—he is nervous.

"I know it is late, but if we could encroach on your hospitality for just a few hours, we would be very thankful."

James feels one eyebrow inching upwards on his forehead. Again, he says nothing.

Peterson frowns at him, perturbed both at his continued silence and at his compromising appearance. "Actually," he sniffs. "I order you to give us use of your quarters."

The delivery is uncertain, but his emerald green eyes flash with a resolve that makes James grimace. "Fine," he says at last. "Come in, please."

He moves aside, careful not to let the pain show in his face, and watches as the two-cloaked figures hurry into his apartment. Only once he has closed and locked the door behind him does he round on the prince.

"Your Highness," he begins, searching for the proper words. "If I may ask, have you lost your mind?"

Peterson frowns, clearly insulted. "I assure you I haven't, General."

"Ah," James breathes, easing himself into the chair at his desk. The candle at his back flickers wildly, sending the shadows dancing across the room. "Yes, the crown prince sneaks out of the palace unattended to traipse across the city with a Cairan girl. I agree, you're quite in your right mind."

"I am, and I don't appreciate the mockery."

James grimaces. "I apologize, your Highness. It's only that it's dangerous to wander out in the city without an escort."

"Why?" The prince asks, his voice as sharp as a blade. "Because of the Cairans?"

James's gaze slides to the young girl at his side. She is watching him with unabashed curiosity, her wide blue eyes glimmering like sapphires in the flickering light. She looks, to him, like a grazing fawn that has suddenly become aware of a hunter in her midst. Something tightens around his heart and he fidgets restlessly upon his chair.

"You remind me of someone," he says to the girl.

She removes her hood, allowing the warmth of the candle to wash over her tawny hair. When she speaks, her voice is surprisingly self-assured. "I told Peterson you would help us."

That surprises him. "Why would you think that?" he asks, his brows furrowing.

"Because you protected the Elegant," she says, as though it were obvious.

James considers this, keeping his face stony. *How can she possibly know that?*

"Are you in love with her?" the girl asks. The question catches him off guard. He meets the girl's gaze and finds her peering back at him with brazen interest. "I think you are," she says, not waiting for him to continue. Her words are clipped with the dreamy excitement of a child. He frowns at the glaring face of her innocence. "I told Peterson that's why the king had you whipped."

He can feel the young prince ogling the angry lashes that curl across the width of his shoulders. The skin of his stomach itches beneath the tightly wound dressing. He presses the palms of his hands firmly against his knees, steeling himself against the pain that threatens to consume him.

"Let's say for a moment that your assumption is correct, why would I offer you my protection as well?"

The girl's smile falters only slightly. Those doe-eyes remain flooded with determination.

It is Peterson who speaks next, his words tart with pride. "We're not here for your protection," he says curtly. "We need directions."

"Directions?" James repeats, bemused.

"Yes, I'm bringing her back to the Forbidden City."

At that, James lets out a laugh. The force of the sound causes his muscles to contract painfully within him. Peterson's frown deepens, the lines of his mouth pointing downward as he glares at the general from beneath his hood.

"It's hardly funny, James" he retorts darkly, all traces of formality falling away. "You know as well as I what happens to Cairans found in the streets of Chancey. She's only a child."

James's laughter subsides. The muscles in his cheeks ache from lack of use. "She is," he agrees. "But so are you. The palace will be in an uproar by morning when your nurses find out you've gone missing. You've only ventured outside the palace walls a handful of times, and then with an armed escort. If you think you can outrun your father's Golden Guard, you are a fool."

The boy prince stares back at him in silence. He continues.

"What do you think your father will do, Peter, when he finds you in the company of a gypsy? Do you think, for a moment, he'll believe you left of your own free will? Or do you think he'll have the girl condemned to death for bewitching you and stealing you away?" He grimaces, leaning forward. The skin on his back screams in protest as it stretches beneath the gauze. Cold realization is dawning across the boy's face as the bravado of his plan fades away.

"You know as well as I the dark things your father fears the most. He'll make a spectacle of the girl. He'll string her up before the entire island and set her ablaze, and it will be your fault." He clears his throat, glancing toward the open window. The blue moon has cast an eerie radiance across the choppy surface of the ocean below. "Your plan isn't brave, Peter. It's foolish. Its a child's plan, a game for boys, but this—this is not a game we're playing."

"I—" Peterson begins, but James cuts him off, rising to his feet.

"Do you know the danger you've put me in, bringing her here?" James demands. "You could have been followed." He walks to the window, relishing in the cool breeze that wafts across his exposed skin. The familiar smell of salt tickles the inside of his nose. He leans out, scanning the blackness of the narrow street below.

"I wasn't," Peterson argues.

"Do you know that for sure?" A nagging itch prickles the base of James's spine as the night stares back at him in silence.

"No," comes Peterson's reply. The boy's voice is despondent—drained of the guileless swagger that had saturated his words when he first arrived. He is reduced to a whisper, there in the flickering dark of James's quarters.

James feels his shoulders slump slightly; giving way beneath the newest burden he now carries. He sighs, an audible grumble of exhaustion bursting forth from his chest.

"I'll bring her back," he says at last. He turns to face the cloaked pair that idles in the shadows before him. The girl watches him, unblinking. Her face is the picture of composure. "I don't know where the Forbidden City is, but if I bring you safely back to the forest, can you find it on your own?"

She nods slowly, her chin rising and falling as she considers this. "I have the tools to navigate back safely," she explains, patting a small pouch that sits at her waist. "The Elegant left them behind with me when she was arrested."

"Good," James says, his mind spinning. The pain is edging into the corners of his eyes, bidding him to sleep. *Not yet,* he wills himself silently. "I'll return Prince Peterson to the palace immediately."

"I'm coming with you," the prince asserts.

"You're not," James disagrees. "If I'm caught with the girl, I can at least try to use my rank to our advantage." He hesitates. "If you're in our company, we may as well both be sentenced to death."

The stinging wounds on his back serve as a painful reminder.

Do not fail me again.

He thinks of Anderson's sneer hovering at the edge of his cot. This is the push the man needs—this is the one misstep that it will take to bring him down. He cannot afford to make any more mistakes. He pulls the windows closed, the whistling wind curling around the wooden frame and rattling the glass panes. He feels blindly for the brass casement, turning the handle so that the frames click into a locked position. Drawing the curtains, he casts the room into still deeper darkness.

"The girl will wait for me here while I bring you back. I'll tell the Guardians on duty that I found you wandering the streets alone. You will confirm my story, and tell them that you snuck out of your own accord."

"Why would I have done that?"

James shrugs indifferently. "Boredom," he suggests. "Rebellion. A driving need for attention. I'm certain you can think of something."

Peterson shoots him an incredulous look. "My father will have my head," he snaps, his brows drawing together.

"Figuratively, yes," James agrees. "You'll be in quite a good amount of trouble, I'd imagine."

Peterson scowls. "If I snuck out, which I did, I can just as easily sneak back in."

James draws nearer to him, the candlelight catching in the pitted white of his dressing. The open wounds that snake across his skin are angry and red, the dried blood glistening black in the shadows. He recalls, suddenly, something his father told him once when he was a boy.

"Do you want to be brave, Peterson? What you're doing here, sneaking around with a Cairan, it isn't brave. It isn't admirable. Bravery isn't doing something risky and managing to get away with it. That's fool's luck." He chuckles dryly. "No, courage is seeing adversity in your path and choosing to face it head on."

Before him, the young prince is silent.

"So we will go back to your father, and you *will* tell him what you did. You will lie only where necessary, and you will take the full punishment for your actions. Do you understand?"

"Yes," the boy says, meaning it. The light in his green eyes extinguishes. He stares baldly at the angry lines of red that peer out of the top of the gauze and his skin pales. "What of the Rose?" He gestures weakly to the girl at his side. She has withdrawn beyond the reach of the candle's throw, her bare feet scuffing uncomfortably at the cool floor underfoot.

"She'll be safe here," James promises.

"That's not what I mean," Peterson's eyes shoot upwards to meet his, the dark green gaze lined with sudden defiance.

"She'll be protected with me," James says, understanding his meaning. "You have my word. As soon as you're back within the walls of the palace I will see the Rose safely returned to her Forbidden City."

"We can trust him," comes a quiet voice from the girl behind them. She stops scuffling the balls of her feet against the floor, resting instead on the tips of her toes. Her eyes twinkle as she smiles warmly at James. "You'll do it, won't you? Keep your promise to him?" She edges forward, her eyes on his throbbing wounds. "If not for me, for Nerani the Elegant."

"For Nerani," he agrees, and knows that he means it.

As the prince and his Cairan say their goodbyes, James Byron sets to slowly dressing, the pain in his back slowly ebbing as he thinks of seeing Nerani the Elegant again.

A fool's mission, a voice within him says. He pushes it away, ignoring it—extinguishing it as best as he can. Still the voice persists, admonishing him with every beat of his heart, every throb of his pulse.

An act of treason.

A fatal mistake.

A death sentence.

There are no other options. Not for him. Not anymore.

CHAPTER 35

Caira

LIGHT FALLS DOWN around Alexander in broken clusters of gold. He squares his shoulders against the tickling heat that smolders upon his exposed skin. The rustling world around him is saturated with dank olive hues. Moss sprouts up over every rock and rotting stump like a blanket. He steps out of a swath of grass cut by the swinging blade of his cutlass, careful to keep his eyes trained upon the stifling undergrowth. Only a few moments ago he had nearly stepped upon a coiled snake. The reptile was quickly beheaded before it could snap its unhinged jaws shut. Alexander isn't eager for another close call.

He chops away at the undergrowth, relishing in the sharp ringing of the steel blade as it sunders the tangled grass before him. He doesn't need the map to know where he's going. The sun has already begun its dreary descent to the west. He can feel the sweltering glare dancing in shades of orange upon his back. He closes his eyes and pictures the map. *East*, it said. *Go East into the lion's den.* He can see the blood red markings—curling words scrawled painstakingly in the dead language—burned behind his eyelids whenever he blinks. He knows that as long as he keeps the sun behind him he will find the place where Tyde resides, deep within the jungles of Caira.

He lives in the long shadow of the sun. Ha'Rai's voice slithers again through his mind. *He makes his home in a world of riddles and darkness.*

Alexander pauses amid a cluster of ferns that droop toward the forest floor. A bead of sweat makes its slow way down the curvature of his nose. He ignores it, leaning against one of the thin, branchless trees that climb up to the sky. He tilts his head back and lets his eyes travel up, up the trunk, all the way to where the top bursts outward in an explosion of vivid green leaves.

Almost indiscernible among the brittle, topmost branches of the trees are the shuffling black outlines of birds. He swallows, averting his gaze. That creeping feeling of discomfort is back. Of course they are being watched.

In his brief respite, thoughts of Emerala creep into his mind. Unable to push them away, he allows himself a moment to wonder where she is. *Who is the architect?* He frowns at a beetle that lands with a clicking flutter on his sleeve. *And why are they taking her to him?*

He knows that she will be safe in the company of Lachlan—the old pirate is a formidable enemy, and he has no doubt that Melena recognized the infamous murderer the moment she laid eyes on him. Still, he can't help the feeling of unease that creeps within him each time he thinks of the growing distance between them. It is dangerous enough paying a visit to Tyde without having to formulate a potential rescue plan for Emerala and the Lethal as well.

Quiet footfalls rush through underbrush as the Hawk breaks through the tangled grass and emerges into the clearing.

"Took you long enough." Alexander pushes himself upright from the tree. It is all he can do to mask the irritation in his voice. They are so close to the end—closer than they have ever been. As deceptive as the Hawk has been—as much information as he has withheld—Alexander may have need of him yet.

That is the only reason the pirate is still alive.

The sharp golden eyes before him glimmer in the refracted flares of orange sunlight. The Hawk takes a few steps closer, wiping the dripping sweat from his forehead with the back of his sleeve.

"You took off hurtling through the woods. I didn't realize when you said, 'make haste', you really meant throw one's self like a madman into certain death. You've no idea what might be lurking in this jungle."

"We have to be quick. The sun is setting."

"Nothing quick about seeing Tyde."

"You know him." It is not a question.

"No," the Hawk says, shaking his head. "Haven't met him."

The brusqueness of his tone only serves to further irritate Alexander. He plucks at his shirt; the sweat lined cotton growing clammy beneath the breeze, and momentarily sheaths his cutlass.

"You don't know Tyde, perhaps, but you know a great deal that I don't know."

The Hawk purses his lips, his gaze hard. "I've told you everything I know."

"In bits and pieces, yes."

"Aye? What are you suggesting?"

"Nothing," Alexander shrugs. "I'm merely giving you yet another chance to be honest with me. We're in this together, after all. Isn't that what you told me? We're allies?" His words are clipped. Terse—the look on his face is a scarcely subdued warning. The Hawk blinks and turns from him wordlessly, heading off into the shaded jungle.

"Time's wasting, Cap'n," he calls over his shoulder. "Sun is setting."

"Why did you have me bring Emerala?" Alexander asks. The pirate stops, stiffening. His white shirt sticks to the skin between his shoulder blades. He is silent, gripping his cutlass tightly within his fist.

"Back in Chancey, you told me that we needed her," Alexander continues. "You swore to me that she was the key to my father's journey and that we'd be unwise to leave without her."

The hazy afternoon light dyes the Hawk's profile orange. The pointed bridge of his nose turns to copper as he tilts his head in Alexander's direction.

"I know what I said."

"Well, then, why? What use has she been to us? So far, she's done nothing but get herself into dangerous predicaments. Here we are, at the end, and she's been of no use."

A slight smirk curls at the corners of the Hawk's lips. "I wouldn't say that."

The sound barely reaches Alexander's ears over the rustle of the leafy world around them. He feels something malicious coiling in his gut as his skin prickles with sudden, unwanted envy. He thinks of how the Hawk demanded Emerala stay with them back on the beach—how he fought to keep the girl under his watchful eye wherever they went, regardless of the consequences.

Up ahead, the Hawk has resumed walking. His figure is enshrouded in shadow as he glides under the cover of the curling ferns.

"Do you fancy her?" Alexander calls. "Is that why you wanted so badly to bring her onboard?"

The Hawk gives no response, only slinks further into the impenetrable gloom of the jungle.

Alexander stands still for a moment, feeling foolish. His feet press hard into the spongy undergrowth. He groans, unsheathing his cutlass and heading off after the pirate.

He tries to turn his mind back to the map, turning over and over the question inscribed in red.

What is sweeter than honey? What is stronger than a lion?

All around him, the silhouettes of the trees glint with crystalline crimson glares. The day is getting late. They will not be able to find their way back in the dark.

He allows the ambient noises of the jungle to fade into the background as he listens to the shivering ring of his cutlass against the thick blades of grass before him. After a while, the hilt grows sticky in his palm, slick with sweat. He pauses; switching hands, and continues forward. He steps immediately into the outstretched arm of the Hawk. The pirate holds a free finger to his lips, his golden eyes sharp with warning.

Alexander peers past him, staring into the dense undergrowth. From somewhere to his left, its owner concealed by the long-fingered ferns that sprout up in dark green masses, leaks a guttural growl. Primitive and feral, the very sound pierces Alexander through to his core. Goosebumps rise upon his arm in spite of the heat. With a startled cry, a raven takes flight from a fallen tree that lies several yards before them. Its black feathers shimmer from blue to black again as it beats its wings with startling urgency.

"Keep moving," the Hawk suggests, his voice a whisper. Even he cannot keep the unease out of his words. His golden eyes flicker back and forth from the source of the sound to the path before them as the two pirates continue forward.

Alexander resumes slicing through the grass, his shoulders tense. He keeps his ears open, listening for any sort of sound that would indicate they were being followed.

They do not walk for long before the Hawk draws up short, causing Alexander to collide directly into his back. He curses, stumbling back and glancing over the lanky man's shoulder to locate the cause of the delay.

There, upon a mossy rock ledge, paces a restless panther. Its fur, a sleek coat of darkest black, catches in the fading light. Its yellow eyes study them with fearless attention—a hunter surveying his prey. Its midnight haunches swing languidly from side to side as its padded paws press against the muffled rock. A quiet rumble emanates from its chest as it paces—gaze unwavering. Its long, cylindrical tail flicks back and forth with disquieting control.

"Go back," Alexander says, his lips barely moving. He takes a tense step backwards upon the trampled earth as he speaks. As though in response to his action, the panther's jaw drops open to reveal sharp, yellowing fangs. A snarl rises in the back of its throat. It echoes with a bone chattering rumble, the sound pervading the oppressive heat of the afternoon. Alexander freezes where he stands, one still foot suspended in mid air.

He peers at the cat, feeling something strange prickling at the back of his mind. Something is off. The great creature is only feet away from them. They have no place to run—no chance of survival should it choose to leap from its prime position above their heads.

And yet, it continues to pace, the lean musculature of its legs tightening and releasing beneath the weight of its torso. He glances upwards towards the treetops and is surprised when the panther follows his gaze. Above their heads, the birds are still watching. They seem to have grown closer as the jungle thickened, the trees leaning together in the suffocating vegetation. From here, Alexander can make out the lines of their beaks, the curves of their winged backs. They leer at him silently through glossy eyes.

Another deep growl, louder this time, and Alexander's gaze snaps back downward. Besides him, the Hawk has drawn his pistol. He hears the click

as Evander pulls the hammer into place. Something within him is screaming out that this is wrong—all of it. The jungle cat ceases its pacing. Its jaw
drops again as it let out a voluble roar. The sound reverberates against the
trunks of the trees, taking root in the earth and rattling Alexander's bones.

"Don't shoot," he commands. The Hawk gives him a brief sideways
glance before snapping his gaze back to the panther.

"Are you mad?"

"Maybe. Lower your gun," His confidence is growing. Reluctantly, the
Hawk returns his pistol to the holster at his waist. The panther drops down
upon its haunches, its great tail twitching across the moss. Its ancient eyes,
rimmed with streaks of coarse black fur, stare unblinkingly into Alexander's
own.

"Very wise," says a voice to their right. "Very wise, indeed."

From behind a rotting trunk steps a stout, muscular man. His unwashed
hair is pulled into a hasty knot at the back of his head. His face is pocketed
with scars.

"Tyde." Alexander inclines his head. The panther lets out a quiet purr
as Tyde nods.

"I was foretold of your arrival." He jabs a crooked finger at the cluster
of ravens that peer down from the trees. The mass of black feathers have
almost completely blocked out the remaining sun. They are, all of them,
cast in formless grey obscurity. The green leaves close in around them, the
oblong shadows stretching ominously across the pungent foliage underfoot.

"You are the captain of the ship *Rebellion*?" Tyde asks.

"I am."

"And you are here to play one of my games?"

Alexander pauses. "I am."

"Very well." Tyde gestures towards the panther with a flick of his index
finger. "This beast is the guardian of the object you seek."

Alexander pauses for the breadth of a heartbeat, surprised. "You know
what it is I'm looking for?"

"Tsk," Tyde admonishes. "I prefer to speak in riddles, good Captain."

Next to Alexander, the Hawk takes a step forward, opening his mouth to speak. He is silenced immediately by a low snarl. On the rock outcropping, the panther bares its teeth, lips curling back from yellowed fangs.

"He is obedient to my commands," Tyde explains. "He will not kill you so long as you do not advance without my permission. To shoot him would have been certain death for you both."

Alexander peers past the hulking figure of the cat, straining to see into the darkness beyond. Lush green vines stretch down upon the rock wall. He cannot see anything beyond the tangled growth.

Tyde's feet dance across the ground in a swift rat-tat-tat. "The object you are after is of great importance to my people. My instructions have been to refrain anyone from passage at all costs."

His caveat hangs in the air before the pirates.

"So you can't help us?" Alexander asks, frowning.

Tyde waves his finger back and forth, tutting quietly. "No, no, no." He giggles, his voice turning shrill. "I am to send you away. So says the birds, you see?"

The sun has dropped low in the sky beyond the trees. Little light reaches them where they stand. The yellow eyes of the panther glow like circular disks in the fading remnants of day.

"At day she comes without being fetched. At night she is lost without being stolen." Tyde cups his hand over his brow and gazes directly into a narrow burst of sunlight that glistens through the leaves.

"The sun is setting." Another giggle. The panther rumbles again. Its tail flicks languidly across the stone. "Once she is lost beneath the horizon you will be at the mercy of the jungle."

"What do we need in order to gain access to the object?" Alexander asks.

"Nothing. Or perhaps, suffer pain of death. I am not to let anyone through."

Alexander grimaces. "What if I were to make you a deal?" He thinks of Ha'Rai and the instructions written on the map. He thinks of the questions written there in blood. Before him, the smile falls away from Tyde's face.

"What kind of deal?"

"Your riddles are said to be impossible to solve. If I can crack your hardest riddle, Will you call off your animal and allow us to pass through?"

"And permit you to claim the object for your own?"

"Yes. If your riddles are as impossible as you say, there should be no risk on your part."

Tyde's eyes narrow dangerously. His tongue darts out from between his lips and disappears. "What reward is there for me if you guess incorrectly?"

Alexander hesitates, aware of the terrible gamble he is about to take.

He must have confidence in the map. Why else would the answer be written there—the words inscribed in red? Why else would his father go to such trouble to bind the answers in blood?

"If I guess incorrectly, you may set your beast upon us and leave us to die."

The Hawk stammers indignantly. "Us?"

"Both of us," Alexander repeats.

Tyde giggles, a phantom of his echo catching in the sticky evening ether. "You are either a very wise man, or you are a fool who only thinks you are."

One corner of Alexander's mouth twitches. "We'll find out, won't we?" His body feels suddenly cold in spite of the heat. At his side, the Hawk scuffs his boot against the soil, looking restless.

"Very well," Tyde assents at last. "My most impossible riddle." He claps his hands together. The sound is jarring against the inundated murmurs of the jungle. Leaning in close, he gesture for them to listen. His red lips are cracked and peeling. His tongue darts in and out from his mouth, wet and pink and hungry. "Out of the eater, something to eat," he says, his voice low. "Out of the strong, something sweet."

Alexander feels instantly lighter. He fights the urge to smile as the words on the map dance before his vision. He spent hours studying it—obsessing over it—certain that it was a question to which he did not know the answer. Now, he is positive that it must be the other way around. Just as he proclaimed to Emerala that day in his quarters, the question *is* the answer to the riddle.

He pauses, pressing his toes firmly into the front of his shoes. The leather is hot against his feet. He does not want to seem too eager—too confident. It would be infeasible for him to muddle through the riddle and come up with an answer immediately. If Tyde suspects foul play, he will surely loose the panther on them regardless of their deal. He can feel Evander the Hawk's watchful eyes boring a hole into his skin.

Alexander allows his gaze to rove upwards as he pretends to mull over the perplexing riddle. He studies the panther. It has resumed its slow pacing, growing restless. He watches as the pointed bones of the animal's shoulders rise and fall with each step it takes. In the shadows brought on by the sun's descent, Alexander notices the stark rib cage of the animal protruding from its side. Its heavy tongue lolls out across its bottom set of teeth, curling upwards into a pink yawn. Alexander allows a small smile to play across his features as his eyes drop back towards Tyde. The man studies him impassively across the shadowed expanse.

Alexander clears his throat, those blood-inked words dancing in the forefront of his mind.

"What is sweeter than honey?" he asks. "What is stronger than a lion?"

Silence falls upon the jungle. Before them, Tyde's face is unreadable. His lips purse together, causing the scars about his mouth to deepen.

"Impossible," he whispers. "You can't know such an answer."

"Was I correct?"

"You must have cheated."

"I disagree," Alexander says. "How could I have possibly known what you were going to ask?"

Tyde's lower lip trembles. His skin adopts a sickly green pallor beneath the murky dusk. "Was it Argot?" he demands. A thin sheen of gleaming sweat dampens his face.

"Who?" Alexander asks, caught off guard by the question.

"Charles Argot—the mapmaker. It was he that told you, wasn't it? He gave you the answer. He's the only outsider that knew."

"I've never met a man named Charles Argot," Alexander answers honestly. He thinks back to the port of Caros, where they had traveled to find the old mapmaker only to find him dead. He feels a strange foreboding within him as another piece of the endless puzzle clicks into place. He had sought Argot out because he needed someone adept at translating dead speech. He hadn't known that the red writing scrawled across the curling parchment belonged to the corpse they found on Caros.

But the Hawk knew.

Evander the Hawk knew, damn him.

Before them, Tyde's stammering is becoming increasingly unintelligible. He points a crooked finger at Alexander, his gaze accusing. "You've deceived me. No one has ever solved that riddle."

"Except for me."

Tyde gapes at him, his mouth opening and closing like a fish out of water.

"I've answered correctly, and now you'll honor our deal." Alexander takes a steady step forward. With alarming dexterity, Tyde whips a dagger from within his sleeve. He raises it above his arm, the whites of his eyes visible as he stares at Alexander.

"I am not to let anybody pass," he whispers. He is about to loose the weapon from his grasp when a single gunshot fills the air. With a thousand frenzied shrieks, the black birds that roost in the treetops take to the skies. The forest comes alive with the sound of rustling wings as the last of the sunlight is engulfed in shadow.

Tyde lies dead upon the ground. Blood oozes out from his chest, pooling in globules below his chin. Next to Alexander, the Hawk reloads his pistol, his golden eyes already trained upon the panther.

"I was wondering when I was finally going to get to shoot something on this godforsaken island," he grumbles.

Before them, the animal has taken its eyes off of its prey, staring instead at the body of Tyde. Enticed by the smell of blood, it lets out a low, hungry rumble. The slick black hairs upon its haunches rise as its lips curl back in a hungry snarl. Alexander makes silent note of this, gesturing for the Hawk to follow him. They veer to the left, diving into the bushes and out of the panther's sight. It does not notice their departure. Released at last from its bondage and hungry for fresh and easy meat, it pounces down upon the corpse.

Alexander swings himself up onto the ledge from the side, careful to keep his movements as silent as possible. Directly behind him is the Hawk. His pistol remains constantly positioned on the feasting panther below. Alexander moves towards the vines, keeping his hands out in front of him to feel for an opening against the sheer face of the rock. He moves carefully, taking small, quiet steps along the stone. Again and again, his fingers push through tangled leaves and jab against damp rock.

Finally—just as he is about to give up—his fingers fall into a small hollow. He casts around blindly, patting the moss-covered surface until at last he feels the outline of a manmade shape beneath his fingers. He pulls at it, watching as a black rectangular box emerges from the opening. The vines fall back into place as he withdraws his arms from the hollow.

"This is it," he whispers. This is the object for which he has traveled so far and so long. This is the object that stole a father away from a mother and son—the thing that made an old man go nearly mad with searching. Whatever lies inside is the answer to every question he has, he's certain of it. His fingers tremble and, for a moment, he considers ripping the black box open then and there.

Below the rock ledge, the gruesome sound of the panther feasting on flesh rises into the night. Alexander's euphoria begins to abate, replaced instead by a pressing sense of urgency. He casts his gaze around the clearing, his eyes searching for the Hawk in the growing darkness. His companion has already headed away from the rock, his lanky frame slipping in and out of shadow among the pressing trees. Pistol in hand, the Hawk gestures for Alexander to follow him. He does so, hopping off the rock ledge and landing with a dull thud on the forest floor. Stepping carefully, the pair picks their way back into the depths of the jungle.

They do not make it far before a terrible roar rents the dense, dusky air.

Alexander glances over his shoulder to see a pair of hungry, yellow eyes staring back at him in the twilight. Even from where he stands among the ferns, Alexander can see the animal's instinct worming its way in in place of hunger. The scavenged meat before the beast will no longer satisfy. It wants to hunt. The panther crouches low, the sharp blades of its shoulders angling upwards as its haunches stretch above its head. Its black lips curl back over yellow fangs in a silent snarl.

This time, it's Alexander's turn to draw his pistol.

"Run," he mouths to the Hawk. The pirate takes off after him, needing no further instruction. There is another roar—muffled with exertion—and a shiver runs through him. The predator has begun to give chase. They were granted a head start, but little good it will do them, now. The undergrowth is dense and dark, and it will not be long before the surefooted cat catches up to them as they stumble through the putrid fungi underfoot.

He darts to the side, watching as the Hawk follows suit. Taking in his surroundings with a calculating eye, he searches for a tree to climb.

If we can only get high enough, he thinks, cursing the stifling jungle. Surely, then, the panther will be forced to relinquish its chase. Leaning shadows—long and thin—blur together as he passes them by. It is no use. The branchless trees that served as his protection from the hot sun earlier in the day are now condemning them to a slow death upon the jungle floor. He hears the furtive panting of the great beast at his back, and he knows without seeing that the animal is gaining ground.

There is a strangled commotion to his immediate right and the ferns shift as the panther's dark face breaks through the foliage. Alexander lets out a shout in spite of himself, his heart pounding in his chest.

"Here!" he calls to the Hawk, tossing him the gleaming, black box. The golden-eyed pirate catches it, still running. Alexander grips his pistol with both hands, leveling it between the panther's eye.

The beast lunges. Alexander stumbles backwards, losing his footing. The pistol fires aimlessly—reeking powder wasted on the empty night sky—just as he feels claws slicing through the flesh of his leg. He lets out a hoarse shout, feeling the sticking heat of his own blood saturating the leg of his trousers. His spine smashes against something hard—far harder than the mossy undergrowth of the jungle. Somewhere nearby, his pistol clatters against a solid surface. The panther pads slowly towards him, eyes bright. Its footfalls, no longer silent, echo against the ground. The rhythm of its measured pace is hollow. Alexander pulls himself backwards across the earth, grasping uselessly for his pistol.

"Get down!" shouts the Hawk. He hears the clicking of a hammer just as the great cat lunges again. Alexander bellows as the shadow of the beast stretches over him. He is met with a thick, earthy smell and a great weight bears down upon him, cutting off his air supply.

"SHOOT HIM," he screams, his voice hoarse. His fingers claw at the leafy undergrowth as the panther's teeth enclose around his bleeding leg. Sharp pain courses through his limbs, pressing against the back of his eyes and turning his vision red. Somewhere below him there is the sudden sound of splintering wood. The ground beneath them gives away, expunging a black cloud of dust.

And suddenly he is falling. The hazy orange light of dusk is extinguished and he finds himself staring into blackness. There is a harrowing roar as the great weight of the cat falls away from him. He reaches out with his hands, grasping desperately as he free falls—plummeting deeper into a yawning gorge in the jungle floor.

At last, his hands enclose around a crude bit of tangled roots. His body slams against moist soil as he careens to a stop. He is suspended over impenetrable blackness, the palms of his hands sporting fresh abrasions from the coarse root to which he clings.

He lets out a low moan. His throbbing leg is slick with blood. His heart his in his throat. Beneath his dangling feet, there yawns a dark, deep hold. From the depths below comes a desolate purr. Alexander looks up and sees only a violent orange sky, the twilight swallowed here and there by the black treetops.

"Hawk!"

He is met with silence. Beneath him, the panther purrs again. Alexander can hear the pads of its feet against soil as the great cat paces the bottom of the hole.

"HAWK!"

Again, there is no response.

Curse him to the Dark Below, Alexander thinks. He tries in vain to get a foothold in the crumbling dirt. *And curse me. I shouldn't have given him the box.*

He adjusts his grip upon the vine, coughing as clods of dirt tumble into his eyes and nose. He spits, the earth turning to mud in his mouth, and tries to pull himself up. Beneath his weight, a vine snaps. He slips down further into the hole, his stomach slamming hard into the packed earth.

There is a steady shuffling noise from somewhere above him and several more clods of dirt break across his face. He blinks, spitting profusely, and peers up into the fading orange light.

Two golden eyes stare back down at him. Relief courses through him.

"Damned booby traps," the Hawk mutters. "Island must be riddled with them. Give me your hand."

Alexander reaches upward, stretching his arm as far as he can. The Hawk's hand encloses around his forearm and he wrenches him up, ignoring the groan that emits from his captain. Alexander stumbles to his feet and immediately regrets it. The pain in his leg is punishing. He teeters, careening into a nearby tree for support as he shifts all of his weight to his good leg. Glancing down at his lower half, he takes quick stock of the damage. His breeches are torn to shreds. His left leg is too bloody to tell how much deep the injuries he's sustained. His vision swarms in and out of focus as he pats at his head, feeling for his hat.

Across from him, the Hawk studies his injuries in stoic silence.

"Can you walk?"

"I'll have to, won't I? I don't think the hole is that deep. It won't be long before that animal climbs back out."

As if in response to his words, an agitated growl ripples up from the dark opening below them. Alexander studies their surroundings. The trees overhead are startlingly bare of birds. The absence unnerves him. He recalls how quickly they had taken flight at Tyde's death. He knows, beyond a shadow of a doubt, where they were heading—knows that they will already have reported the murder to Domio.

He catches the Hawk's golden gaze in the mounting darkness.

"He'll go after Emerala," the Hawk says.

"Then we'll have to get to her first."

CHAPTER 36

Caira

EMERALA SLAPS AT her skin, brushing away the crumpled black insect that had alighted there only an instant before. Its veined, translucent wings twitch as it falls weightlessly toward the ground. There is a faint buzz as something flutters by her ear, rustling a stray curl, and she slaps at that, too.

She scowls, casting a dark glare at the twirling figure of the shapely woman before her. The woman has long since undone her sand colored braid, allowing her curls to stream out from her body like a rippling brook. The fading gold sunlight of the dwindling afternoon plays upon her hair as she does a pirouette, her hands prying up the russet cloth of her gown from the tangled leaves underfoot.

They have been following Melena deeper and deeper into the jungle for nearly an hour. An hour, and still Emerala has received no answer to the questions that have twisted up like a knot inside her head. She disentangles herself from an upended root, the gnarled bark curling like a beckoning finger, and rushes to keep up with the twirling woman. The sticking heat of the jungle adheres to her skin, brackish with salt left over from her plunge in the ocean. She thinks of the shadow she saw rippling beneath the boat, and of the fear that had gripped her as she drowned.

The Lethal had spent a great deal of his time on deck regaling her with imaginative yarns.

Anything to keep ye from talking on, he had said to her one afternoon after she asked why he continued to oblige her with story after story. *At least I've got something worth saying, whereas ye are like to babble on until I lose me mind.*

Her favorite story was the story of the selkie—a mermaid like creature that could shed its skin and climb aboard a ship. Once shed of its sea skin, the Lethal told her, a selkie was said to take on the form of a most beautiful woman. Often, the beauty of the selkie was enough to seduce a sailor right out of his bed and lure him overboard.

Many a sailor be drowned that way, he said, leering at Emerala over the torn yard mast he mended one afternoon.

Why are you looking at me? she had asked, drawing back from him. His breath smelled, as always, of his private stash of imported cherry tobacco.

I en't lookin' at you any sort of way.

You are.

He grinned, the motioned crinkling the white pinched flesh of his scar, and leaned in closer. *The men are like to whisper, ye know. Horrible gossips, the lot of 'em.*

What do they say?

That you be a selkie, lass, come up from the sea and shed your skins. And one dark night soon ye'll lure the captain overboard and drag 'im back to the bottom of the sea.

Emerala remembers that day, shuddering slightly. She had not thought of the story when she saw the shadows beneath the swelling surface of the sea. Then, she had thought of mermaids.

She recalls the feeling of hands, rubbery with brine, enclosing about her feet and hauling her overboard. The layers of her gown were so heavy that the entire rowboat had capsized with her. And then she was pulled downward, her head immersed in the stinging salt of the crisp, blue sea as two hands dragged her towards the sandy floor beyond the corals.

It was only then, as her lungs began to burn beneath the pressing ocean, that she remembered a single word. *Selkie.*

She glares ahead at Melena, her eyes narrowed against a dazzling array of golden sunlight that has managed to break through the leaves overhead. The woman has taken pause against a rotting stump, its base covered in a dense layer of moss. She watches the trio approaching with gleaming blue eyes.

"Keep moving," she sings, the hint of a smile tugging at her lips. "We don't want to keep him waiting."

She waits only for a moment longer before dancing off into the shadows, the echo of her giggle trailing behind her like a veil.

Emerala shoots a sidelong glance at the Lethal. He lingers at her side, unspeaking, his attention trained on the jungle around them. He is listening, she knows—sorting through the discordant symphony of noises that emanates from all around them.

"Maybe I am a selkie," she whispers to him, her eyes blazing. "If so, I'd like to start by drowning *her*." She gestures towards the distant figure of Melena with a tilt of her chin. The Lethal says nothing. Even so, she can see the faint glimmer of a smile in his gaze. It's all she can hope for, with him. To say the old pirate is not in possession of a sense of humor would be an understatement.

She takes a lurching step forward only to be drawn back by Derek's fist enclosing roughly about her upper arm. He pulls her back, careless of the lace of her chemise as it snags against the snarled roots.

"Careful how we speak of our hostess, Katherine, dear," he hisses in her ear. His eyes wander upwards with implication. "You never know who might be listening."

"I—" Emerala begins, but her words fade to silence upon her tongue beneath an admonishing stare from Derek. A sharp flapping of wings overheard startles her as a raven takes off from the shadows. It glides low over their heads, its wings fluttering against Emerala's wild curls.

There is a dull rustling behind them—the sound of someone pressing through snatching ferns—and the trio whirls about to see Melena studying them through probing blue eyes. The raven alights on her shoulder. Stunned, Emerala glances over her shoulder to where she could have sworn she just saw the woman disappearing into the brush ahead.

"You—" she stammers, pointing. "I—"

The raven gives a guttural cry. Emerala turns back toward Melena, trying to ignore the glassy eyes of the preening creature on the woman's shoulder.

"Walk with me," Melena commands. Her voice is shrill, her smile unsettling. She takes Emerala's arm, prying it easily from Derek's grip. Emerala chances a look at the Lethal as the woman leads her away. He nods once, the decline of his chin almost imperceptible in the speckled shade that dances across his face.

"Men can be *so* dull," Melena titters into her ear. "Don't you think?" Her breath stirs Emerala's hair, causing the thick curls to tickle the side of her face. She feels the hair on the back of her neck stand erect as unease creeps through her.

They walk a ways in front of Derek and the Lethal without saying a word. The occasional shrill screech of the glossy raven is only noise that cuts through the viscous heat of the dying afternoon. Emerala listens intently for the sounds of boots crunching against thick foliage, reassured by the fact that the men are just behind them. She doesn't dare to turn around. She attempts to look prim—a little frightened, even. Surely a lady of such a fine upbringing as Katherine Montclay of Toholay would be frightened in the company of gypsies.

Emerala the Rogue—herself a gypsy—is frightened here, among the alien sights and smells of the jungle, far from home and in the company of a woman who listens to the whisperings of ravens.

"So, which one do you think it is?" Melena asks, drawing Emerala in close as though to share a secret. Her eyes widen to impossible circles and she bites her lip, a giggle barely restrained upon her tongue.

"Sorry, what are we talking about?" Emerala asks, confused. She fights to keep her voice sedate but finds that annoyance with the Cairan woman is winning the battle for her words.

"The two pirates that accompanied you and Derek." Melena titters, flashing a look at Emerala as though it should be obvious. She glances over her shoulder to see if the men at their backs are within listening distance. Her tresses tickle the mossy undergrowth as she does so. When she looks back at Emerala, her gaze is positively wicked. "Which one do you think fancies you?"

Emerala stiffens, stumbling against the untamed roots that snake in and out of the rich soil.

"I don't believe one does." Emerala catches her feet just in time to keep from falling. The raven gives off a lilted screech, cocking its head to one side and glaring at Emerala. Melena clicks her tongue, tut-tut-tutting reproachfully. The raven mimics her, clicking its beak together in an admonishing echo.

"Don't lie to Melena," she sings, touching Emerala lightly on the tip of her nose. "They couldn't bear to let you out of their sight." She leans in, lowering her voice to a whisper. "How terribly dramatic of both of them."

At that she gasps aloud, startling the raven into taking flight. It circles above their heads with an unsettling cry before returning to Melena's shoulder. "Perhaps both of them fancy you—wouldn't that make for the perfect tragedy?"

Emerala clears her throat, feeling her cheeks growing hot. "I'm quite happily engaged to be married, if you'll recall."

"No you're not." Melena's singsong voice lilts upwards towards the treetops. Emerala fights the growing urge to slap the woman across the face. She looks at the curled, black talons of the raven and thinks better of it.

"But we can keep pretending you are, if it suits your fancy," Melena says with a simper. "I adore games, and this one is delightful." Her eyes twinkle with a knowing gleam. She drags Emerala forward through the jungle at a quickening pace, and Emerala finds herself struggling to keep her footing in the dense undergrowth. Behind them, she can no longer hear the footfalls of Derek and the Lethal.

Next to her, Melena sighs. "Pirates are just hopeless romantics at heart, don't you think?"

"I wouldn't know," Emerala says darkly. Up ahead she can just make out a looming, rectangular silhouette pressing through the trees. She stares into the vegetation, trying to fathom what they could possibly be approaching this far out in the jungle.

"It's their fatal flaw." Melena snickers. "Take Lachlan the Lethal, for example."

Emerala hesitates, her eyes drawing away from the oblong structure beyond the tangled, grey tree trunks. Overhead, something hoots in alarm. The sound echoes three times in succession before fading away into silence. There is an audible rustling—the reverberation of something heavy climbing through the branches. Emerala shivers, glancing over her shoulder. Derek and the Lethal are nowhere to be seen.

"How do you know him?" Emerala asks, buying time. Somehow, she can't imagine anyone choosing the phrase *hopeless romantic* to describe the gruff old murderer.

Melena flashes her a knowing grin. "Everyone has heard of him, of course. I'm surprised you haven't, since you're so firmly pretending to be a Westerlies bride."

"Oh." Emerala sniffs, unsure of what to say. Melena leans in closer, and Emerala notices the raven on her shoulder is gone. She feels a shiver of unease go down her spine. She had not heard or seen the bird take off.

All around them, the jungle is oddly void of wildlife. The dissonant sounds of life that buzzed and fluttered incessantly on their journey have faded into silence. The sun is drawing closer to the earth, the crisp gold of the afternoon giving way to an ambiguous halo of red that splinters through the leaves like spilt wine. The world around the women is cast in dangerous hues of olive and violet.

"There is an old story about Lachlan the Lethal—one almost as notorious as the stories of his misdeeds." Melena straightens, her gaze searching. That same smile is still pressed into her lips—a permanent, irritating fixture upon her face. "You do know that your pirate friend is a convicted murderer, I assume."

"So I've heard," Emerala murmurs. She can feel the looming presence of the structure before her and wonders if this is where the man they called the architect resides. A prickle of anticipation sends her pulse fluttering.

At her side, Melena does a little dance, her feet shuffling lightly against the earth.

"His fate, it was set, his rights, they were read, and Lachlan was hung by his neck 'til dead," she sings, stringing two fingers around her neck like a noose. Emerala stares at her and says nothing.

"He wasn't always a killer, you know." Melena's eyes are shining in the dying light. The muddled red sun paints her face the color of blood. "Have you heard of the four wind women of the seas?"

"I have not."

Melena giggles loudly, the sound spilling away from her like water. It saturates the silent space around them, the echo of her laughter rolling down the branchless trunks of the leaning trees and colliding with Emerala's sticking skin.

"Another mistake," she whispers, nearly hopping with excitement. "Mistake after mistake, it isn't good if you're hoping to win our little game."

Emerala scowls. Through the trees she can hear the crunch of a boot against brambles and feels a surge of relief rush through her. Melena moves so close to her, then, that her blue eyes double before Emerala's vision. Her breath is tinged with the crisp scent of mint leaves.

"They say it is only a great fool that falls in love with an immortal woman of the wind," she whispers. "Lachlan the Lethal has been called many things in his first lifetime. A fool was never one of them."

She draws back with a wink, her hair fluttering into her eyes. Emerala glowers at her in silence.

"It's a lovely story," Melena says, "You should ask him to tell it."

She lets out a cackle at that, setting off once again to dancing. Emerala watches with relief as Derek and the Lethal break through the tangled trees and emerge into the clearing. Their faces are slick with sweat. The Lethal's cutlass is drawn. He lowers it at the sight of Emerala, his expression unreadable. The white scar that runs down the length of his face appears fresh and red in the fading light.

"And down came the wind with a wretched old shriek and bade, then, the dead man to rise up and speak," sings Melena as she twirls away from Emerala. In the dusky violet shadows of the trees, Lachlan the Lethal freezes. His gaze darkens as he fingers the blade of his cutlass, studying

the spinning figure of the woman. His lips are pressed together in a tight, white line.

Melena pauses, peering out at them from behind a tree with eyes that glitter like jewels. Her voice croons softly in the twilight. *"The story is old, the whispers, they grow. Where Lachlan is now, the dead men will know."*

Lachlan scowls, ignoring her. "Are ye alright?" he calls out to Emerala. His voice is hoarse.

"Fine," she calls back, unnerved by the expression that flashes across his face. The cutlass in his hand catches the dying sun, throwing fragments of ruddy light across his features.

"We're here," Derek says. He approaches Emerala slowly, watching her through reserved eyes. He pulls her into a hug, letting his lips graze against her ear. "Be careful," he whispers.

"She knows," Emerala whispers back. "She knows we're pretending."

Derek pauses for a long moment. When he speaks, his voice is tense. "It doesn't matter. We're too far now to turn back. There's nothing to do but keep playing along."

He draws back from her, and the dark look in his eyes is frightening. "It's the only way we'll get out of here alive," he says. His voice is nearly inaudible. Emerala swallows hard, feeling inexplicably cold.

The reunited trio follows Melena through the thin copse of trees that stand between them and the shadowed structure. Emerala emerges from beneath a low hanging bush of fanning, green leaves, a gasp falling from her lips. Rising up before them is an immense wall of crumbling stone. Clearly manmade, the structure stretches out on either side of them, the ends—if there is any end—swallowed in the choking vegetation.

"What is this?" Emerala studies the structure in awe, her attention catching on a clear-cut opening in the rock. A short ways beyond the opening is another wall of cobbled stone.

"It's a labyrinth!" Melena squeals, clapping her hands together. She hops up and down on the balls of her feet, her hair spiraling out from her like a web.

"Or a prison." The Lethal sheaths his cutlass, eyeing the stone with suspicion.

"He constructed it himself, the architect," Derek says. His gaze is thick with careful implication as he watches Emerala.

"Why?" Emerala asks, raising her voice to be heard over the incoherent singing coming from Melena's direction. The raven drops out of the sky with a flutter of feathers and begins to vocalize as well, its raspy cries pitting off of the stone.

"He's a hostage here," Derek explains, his brows pulling together. "A rather famous hostage, at that. According to the stories, when he was first taken captive he asked the Cairans for one thing and one thing only—to be permitted to build his own prison. It was an odd request, but Domio obliged him. He's a curious man, Domio, and he wanted to see what kind of prison a man would choose to build for himself. He was not disappointed. The labyrinth is a masterpiece."

"Right," Emerala says, still studying to stone. "But why am I here? I've nothing to do with any of this."

Derek falls silent, a shadow passing over his features. Looking up, he studies the treetops. "You shouldn't ask questions unless you're certain that you want the answers."

"Of course I want answers," Emerala snaps.

Derek looks her in the eye, his black gaze penetrating. "Answers can be dangerous things, Katherine. Deadly things." Something in his voice causes a shiver to creep down Emerala's spine. Derek shoves his hands into his pockets and sighs, turning to survey the entrance to the great stone prison. "You'll go into the labyrinth alone, I expect. You should be safe enough."

"Alone?" Emerala stammers. "But I don't know the way."

She is startled by the sudden presence of fire very near to her face. The heat tickles her cheek as the orange flames cast a red glow across the bridge of her pointed nose. Beyond the throw of light she can just make out Melena's grinning face—her ivory teeth gleaming next to the flickering torch that she holds in her claw-like grasp.

"Follow Marvala," she commands, thrusting the torch into Emerala's hand. "She knows the way." Melena gives her a push, shoving her towards the opening in the stone.

Emerala stands unmoving in the opening, watching the great stone walls yawn over her head.

"I don't know who Marvala is," she says dryly.

As if in response, the raven on Melena's shoulder takes flight, whisking off into the shaded opening and veering to the right. There is a moment of silence and then an impatient squawk echoes out from beyond the stone.

"Of course," Emerala intones. "The raven is Marvala."

"Go now," Melena sings. "And go quickly. The sun is setting and the shadow spirits are getting ready to come out and play. I don't think you'd enjoy the kind of games they like, Katherine Montclay from Toholay."

"The shadow spirits?" Emerala repeats, ogling the settling dusk. But Melena is already dancing away, a song in her throat and laughter in her eyes.

CHAPTER 37

The Forbidden City

NERANI CLIMBS THE rungs leading to her quarters slowly, her bare feet finding the smoothed stone inlets with precision. Her toes linger against the cool slabs as she idles just below the narrow opening leading to the tiny space she shares with Roberts. Her left hand throbs with a dull ache as she rests her wrist against the stone. The tiniest finger of her left hand is gone—removed with careful fastidiousness by Mame Minera's skilled hands. The other two fingers have been set and bound. The dressing is clean and tight and the camphor lotion on her skin does much to numb the pain of healing bones. She stares at the shallow dip in the dressing where her pinky should be and blinks back tears. Swallowing the tickle at the back of her throat, she continues to climb.

She has not seen Roberts in days. Since his shouting match in Topan's quarters he has made himself scarce, staying away from the infirmary where he knew his cousin to be staying. Nerani did not mind the solitude. In fact, she reveled in it. She spent the hazy days of her recovery lost in thought—staring at the shadows of her decisions and contemplating their possible consequences.

She had kissed him—James. Standing before him in the musty old storeroom the day of her escape, she had allowed herself to succumb at last to her emotions. It was a dangerous development—an impossible development. And yet she cannot bring herself to regret what she has done. She thinks of James Byron and of the look upon his face as she was led away from him that afternoon. Something unfamiliar twists within her stomach—a soft fluttering of wings brushing against her insides—and she scowls.

Orianna knew before she knew—Orianna saw it that day in the kitchens as she took Nerani's hand within her own.

It will drown you both, she said, her words caught between a whisper and a chant. The warning had been ominous. Deadly. Nerani cannot bring herself to think about the meaning behind them. She cannot bring herself to think of the future, and what kind of punishment fate has in store for her betrayal.

And it is a betrayal. It is a deep, dark treachery. She is twisted up beyond belief, wrought with despair and strung out to dry. She is jumping at shadows, choking on her guilt, sleeping on a bed of paranoia.

But she loves him.

She does.

If there was any denying it before the stolen kiss in the boarded storeroom, there is no denying it now. The very thought makes her at once both buoyant with joy and weighted with dread. Her stomach roils within her.

Two golden men drown in the red tide.

It's impossible, she thinks, berating herself silently. *What you feel is impossible.* The flesh beneath the bandage aches as she flexes her good fingers, gripping hard at the stone. Her foot snags in the hem of her gown and she nearly slips out of her foot wells. She catches herself ungracefully, a small gasp escaping from between her lips, and continues to climb.

She slips into the dark of her quarters with relief, allowing herself to be enveloped in the cool darkness of the hovel they have come to call home. The tumultuous sounds of the bustling cavern below rise up into the mouth of the room—drifting in with the smell of freshly baked bread. Her stomach grumbles and she realizes with a start that she has not eaten yet today. She takes a step into the cramped expanse and stops short at the sound of a muffled giggle.

"Hello?" she calls into the darkness, squinting at the shadows across the room. There is the sound of pulling fabric and someone whispers something unintelligible. A candle whisks into life. The dancing flame sends spirals of orange light careening across the jagged stone ceiling.

"Nerani," Roberts says, sounding surprised to see her. He is sitting upright in his bed, his tousled curls matted to one side. His green eyes are unusually bright. Next to him, her flaxen locks fanning out over the edge of the cot, lays the young woman that had appeared with him the day of Nerani's rescue. She giggles again as Nerani meets her sharp, grey gaze. Deep scarlet pools in her cheeks and she draws the blanket up to her nose.

"Good morning." Her voice is muffled beneath the thick wool coverlet.

"I didn't expect you back so soon," Roberts explains, looking only mildly sheepish. He eyes the bandage wound tightly about her remaining fingers. Her right hand has closed at her side. She remains silent before them. Unmoving. "Mame Minera said you were a few days away from being fully recovered. She said your finger—" he pauses, falling into silence as he catches a glimpse of the look upon her face.

"Are you alright?"

"I'm quite fine, thank you." The voice that falls out from between Nerani's lips is strangled. "You're clearly occupied. I'll come back later."

At that, the woman sits upright, clutching the blanket to her with hands like white-porcelain.

"I can leave." Her hair falls around her face in waves of silver, framing her plump, cherry lips. Nerani scowls at her.

"No, that's fine," she says, just as Roberts blurts, "No, don't go." His hand closes about the woman's arm, pulling her back into his chest. His lips graze the top of her head and he surveys Nerani in implicative silence.

She shoots him a mangled smile. "I'll go visit Topan," she says, backing towards the door.

"Good. That's good. He's been worried sick about you."

"I know. He's visited me in the infirmary often." She allows the words she did not say to hang in the air between them.

Unlike you.

Roberts does not reply, nor does she wait for him to come up with a response. She is already backing out of the room—lowering herself as quickly as she can down the stone steps. She is scarcely out of the opening when there is another giggle and the candle is extinguished with a sigh.

Her cheeks blaze with heat as she climbs back down towards the main cavern. A smattering of anger ripples through her, though at what—or at whom—she can't be certain. Roberts has done nothing wrong. It is Nerani who has allowed her heart to lead her astray—Nerani who has behaved traitorously.

And yet she doesn't like the silver haired woman. She doesn't trust her cool grey eyes—doesn't trust the whisper of a smile on her painted lips.

The sounds of the cavern below envelop Nerani like a blanket, and she revels in the warm flicker of the firelight against her skin. Her run in with Roberts and his lady friend left her feeling cold. Uneasy. Her bare feet hit the cool floor and she sweeps the deep navy hem of her muslin gown away from the steps.

She heads through the crowds of milling Cairans, their heads bowed low together in conversation or thrown back in contempt as they lose at another hand of cards. Several dark gazes shoot in her direction as she passes and she balks at the stares, confused by the malice she finds there. Keeping her head down, she picks up her pace, heading with purpose towards Topan's quarters at the far side of the cavern.

"Nerani!"

She is pulled back by the sound of Orianna calling her name. She draws to a standstill at the edge of the crowd, reluctant to step back into the throng. Glancing over her shoulder, she spots her friend rushing towards her. Her violet corset is cinched tightly at her waist and her jet-black hair frames the stark blue of her eyes. She frowns as she draws close, scrutinizing Nerani through narrowed eyes.

"The look on your face is enough to curdle milk."

Nerani's scowl deepens. "Thank you."

"I suppose you've met Seranai." Orianna twists the fabric of her tiered gown within her fist, a bad habit she developed when they were young. Blues and blacks and violets cascade out from between her fingers in crumpled ruffles.

"Who?"

Orianna shrugs lightly, the smooth skin of her shoulders rising and falling beneath the sagging white sleeves of her blouse. "You know, that blonde wench that has been hanging on Rob these days. I saw you climbing down from your quarters just now and supposed you had finally met her." She glances over her shoulder, her black hair gleaming violet in the firelight. "They are up there, aren't they?"

"Unfortunately," Nerani says, following her friend's gaze. "Who is she?"

"I don't know," Orianna admits, turning back to face her. Her gaze is sullen—her lips tight with scarcely concealed bitterness. "Isn't she awful? Rob claims she helped rescue you. Apparently she saw General Byron dragging you inside an abandoned storeroom."

Orianna lets her words wane into silence as she studies Nerani for any sort of reaction. Nerani remains taciturn before her, avoiding her friend's probing gaze. Looking down, she picks at a loose thread in her bandage.

"I'm not an accomplished seer, Nerani," Orianna says at last, lowering her voice to a whisper. "Not yet, anyway. But I know what I saw that day in the kitchens. It was as clear as if it were happening right in front of me."

Nerani continues to inspect the unraveling thread. She twists it round and round on the index finger of her good hand, watching as the tip turns first red, then purple. She tries not to think of James. She tries not to think of the feel of his lips against hers—of the smell of his skin, slick with rainwater.

She tries and she fails.

"Nerani," Orianna snaps, dragging her attention back to the present. "People are starting to talk. No one has escaped captivity. No one. How did you get out?"

Nerani swallows. Her throat feels like sandpaper.

"He helped you, didn't he?" Orianna asks.

"Yes." The answer that ekes out from between her lips is nearly inaudible.

Orianna's face twists as if wound by an unseen hand. She reaches out and takes Nerani's wrist within her grasp, forcing her to let go of the thread. Blood rushes back into the tip of her finger with a prickle, and the color of her skin fades slowly back to ivory.

"Nerani, look at me."

Nerani obliges, blinking rapidly in a futile effort to blink away the turmoil that rages just behind her eyes.

"James Byron is the enemy. He's our enemy, Rob's enemy, *Emerala's* enemy. He has sentenced so many of our people to death in the name of the usurper. He's not a good man."

"You don't know that," Nerani whispers. "You don't know what kind of man he is."

"Yes I do. And so do you. Don't be a fool, Nerani. You're playing with fire, and you're going to get burned."

Nerani wrenches her wrist from Orianna's grasp, her mood souring. A headache is blossoming behind her left eye.

"I'm playing with fire, I'm going to drown in a red tide," Nerani intones; her brows drawing low over angry eyes. "You're talking in riddles and metaphor. That's the kind of thing Roberts used to laugh at when we were children, don't you remember? He always told us to believe in fact."

"Do you want facts?" Orianna asks. "Fine. I don't need the Sight in order to understand the look on your face."

"And what look is that?" Nerani's reply comes as quick as a whip.

"Infatuation."

"I'm not infatuated," Nerani argues, turning away from her friend. Her nerves flutter within her. A hard lump builds in her throat. She feels, suddenly, as if she might cry.

Traitor, a small voice within her says. *You're a traitor.*

Orianna grabs her hard by the arm, stopping her short. Her painted fingernails press indentations into Nerani's flesh.

"Wait. Please, Nerani, I don't want to argue. Not with you."

Nerani steels herself, blinking back unwanted tears as she turns back towards her friend. The look in Orianna's eyes is plaintive, apologetic. Her teeth graze her lower lip—another habit from childhood, a nervous one.

"I didn't come looking for you in order to pick a fight."

"Why did you come looking for me, then?" Nerani asks hotly, still feeling bitter.

"I spoke with Topan," Orianna says. She pauses and adds, "You've been avoiding him since your return."

"I haven't been able to avoid him," Nerani counters. "He visited me in the infirmary every day."

"And according to him, you were asleep every time." A smile teases at one corner of Orianna's lips. "Strange, you were never asleep when I stopped in to check up on you, or when Mame Minera came to change your bandages."

Nerani lets out a strangled *harrumph*, embarrassment flickering through her. She crosses her arms over her chest and glowers at the look of quiet amusement that stretches across Orianna's ebony features.

"You can't tell me you haven't at least considered the possibility of his offer."

Nerani shrugs. "I have considered it."

Her slow recovery in the infirmary left her with nothing but time to think. And think. *Obsess* would be the more fitting word to describe what she did, tossing and turning in her cot and replaying the events of the past few days over and over in her head.

When she did sleep, she dreamt of James.

She dreamt of his father's storeroom, wrought with ghosts. She dreamt of the gunshot in the bailey, and of racing through the cobbled streets, slick with rain. She dreamt, too, of the feel of him against her—of the taste of his lips and the touch of his fingers against her skin.

When she awoke, she would find Topan asleep in a chair by her cot. Immediately, the guilt that stalked her during her waking hours would creep back through her. It choked off her air supply and left her clutching at her sheets in a panic.

Traitor, the small voice within her would hiss.

In front of her, Orianna is scrutinizing her warily.

"He'll make wonderful husband," she says.

Nerani winces. "I have no doubt that he will. For anyone but me."

She turns away from Orianna, continuing to press through the throng of Cairans that mill about the cavern. She moves through a cluster of middle-aged women repairing garments with needle and thread, Orianna hot on her heels. The women fall silent, each of them starkly aware of the listening ears and the waiting tongues eager for a bit of gossip to while away the hours. Only once they have moved away from the crowds and beyond the light of the torches does Orianna venture again to speak.

"Why are you so hesitant to move forward with his proposal?"

"You know why," Nerani murmurs. She gathers her skirt within her fist and picks up her pace, unsure where it is she's heading—unsure why she feels the need to get there so quickly.

"Because of General Byron?" Orianna asks, keeping easy stride beside her. "You can't be with him, Nerani. Whatever it is you're feeling, surely you know that. You need to be reasonable."

Nerani stops at that, falling still so suddenly that Orianna continues onward for several steps before she has even realized Nerani is no longer with her. She does a quick about face, her hands pulling her skirts off of the stone.

"There's nothing reasonable about any of this." Nerani's voice is dark. She feels inexplicably cold.

"You would be the queen of the gypsies," Orianna says.

"I don't love him."

Orianna scoffs. "No one said anything about love, Nerani. A seat of power is being handed to you. Real power. All you have to do is reach out and take it."

"Maybe I don't want that kind of power."

"Everyone wants power," Orianna counters.

"Maybe I'm not ready to marry," Nerani snaps, narrowly avoiding a woman cradling a bulging basket of freshly laundered linens.

"Not ready? Most women in our year have already paired off."

Nerani rounds on her, her temper finally snapping. "If you're so keen on the idea, why don't you stop pining after Roberts and marry Topan instead?"

Orianna's mouth snaps shut. She recoils from Nerani, hurt spreading across her face.

Nerani sighs, pushing her hair back behind her ears. The headache behind her eyes is engulfing her entire head, setting her skull to throbbing. A white aura pulses at one corner of her vision.

"I'm sorry, Orianna. I didn't mean that. I don't know what's wrong with me today."

Orianna proffers a sad smile, taking Nerani's good hand within her own. "I meant what I said. I don't want to fight. I'm just trying to protect you."

"From what?"

Orianna hesitates, reluctance twitching her lips.

"Protect me from what?" Nerani repeats.

"From *him*," Orianna relents. She lowers her voice to a murmur and adds, "I won't let you throw your life away for James Byron."

Nerani opens her mouth to speak but is cut short by the sight of a familiar man crossing through the shadows near Topan's quarters. She stares at the figure; her hand still entwined in Orianna's, and tries to recall the man's name.

"Who is that?" Orianna whispers, following Nerani's gaze.

The man heads silently towards the entrance to Topan's public chambers—the cavernous side room where he often holds meetings during the day.

"Blaine," Nerani says, suddenly remembering. "He's a Listener. He was with Roberts the day of my escape." She recalls how the man held James at gunpoint—recalls the unfamiliar terror that had pierced her heart at the thought of losing him.

She watches as the man disappears into the narrow opening in the stone.

"Come on." She pulls Orianna along with her as she heads after Blaine. They veer off as they reach the yawning tunnel of the main entrance, heading instead to the dark side tunnel that branches off to both Topan's personal quarters and his receiving room.

The women pause just outside the open doorway, hovering in the arched stone entrance as they listen for the sound of voices. The din of the cavern outside softens to a murmur as they idle in the shadows. After a moment, they can hear the muffled speech of conversation. Nerani holds a finger up to her lips, bidding Orianna to follow her as she creeps closer.

"They've executed my grandfather," says a man's voice, terse with barely suppressed grief. "He was innocent. He had no idea what I was, or what I was trying to do."

"I cannot express to you how sorry I am, friend," comes the quiet response of Topan. His words resound through the narrow gap of the opening with a profound sense of melancholy.

"The usurper had him publicly executed so that he would have a solution to his problem. He needed closure to keep his so-called peace, and he found it by killing an harmless old man in my place."

"You shouldn't blame yourself, Blaine."

There is a scoff—jarring against the tomblike silence of the impenetrable stone.

"I don't," says Blaine. "I blame Nerani the Elegant."

Topan is silent. Nerani feels her heart seize within her chest and she desperately wishes she were close enough to see his face—to know what he is thinking. Next to her, Orianna squeezes her hand. The expression on her face is grim.

"She had no business being out in the city," snaps Blaine. His voice is laced with contempt.

"You're right," Topan agrees. "She did not."

Nerani can hear the sound of boots against stone as Blaine paces the floor. After a moment, he skids to a stop. There is the soft echo of a rock skipping against the smooth surface of the ground, and then there is silence.

"I did my job, I brought her back safe," he says.

"You did, and I am grateful for—" Topan is cut off by Blaine, his collected cadence suffocated by the spitfire rate of the man's anger.

"I did my job at great cost. I paid the price of my grandfather's life in exchange for correcting a young woman's foolishness. Was his death worth that?"

Topan's voice is low, dangerous. "I made a promise."

"You made a promise to bring down the usurper, not to risk constant exposure rescuing damsels in distress."

"Protecting her family was part of that promise, I would not be doing my job if I let her die at the hands of Rowland Stoward."

"Don't be so transparent. Emerala the Rogue and her brother were the ones that needed protection. The Rogue is gone, and you've got Roberts the Valiant wrapped around your finger. Nerani the Elegant's rescue was personal, nothing more." Blaine pauses, the sound of his breathing loud against the ringing quiet. "You can only ask so much of us, Topan."

A treacherous silence fills the flickering expanse. Nerani holds her breath, waiting.

When at last Topan speaks, his voice is cool and composed. Nerani can picture him perfectly—his shoulders erect against the multitude of burning candles at his back, his jaw locked—his shining black hair pushed back from his piercing blue gaze as he watches the Listener before him in stony calm.

"What exactly are you suggesting, Blaine?"

"You are losing control."

"Am I?" Topan's even voice is so quiet that Nerani can barely hear it.

"Do you not hear the whispers among your people? Their dissention is rising. They can only live like this for so long—hiding under the earth, waiting for deliverance."

"That day will come," comes Topan's response. "With patience."

"And who will deliver them?" Blaine snaps. "You?"

"Not I. Roberts the Valiant, as it was foretold."

Nerani hears Orianna stifle a gasp besides her. There is an audible shuffling of a gown as someone new enters the room from the main entrance. The newcomer gives a watery hiccup as she attempts to hold back a sob.

"Help her to a seat," orders Topan.

A chair is scraped against stone as Blaine obeys the command.

"What's happened?" Topan speaks again, his words soothing.

"I-it's my daughter, your highness," chokes the woman. "She's m-m-missing."

"Your daughter? What is her name?"

"D-d-darianna the Rose," stammers the woman between great heaves of breath.

Nerani feels her blood run cold within her. She steels herself against the cool stone of the wall, listening intently.

"Are you quite sure she's missing?" Topan asks. His words are reassuring. "The Forbidden City is a large place, and still unfamiliar to many of us. Perhaps she's only with a friend."

"N-no," the woman wails, the tears coming easier now. "It's b-b-been days. She would have come back by now." There is a tentative pause as the woman blows her nose into a handkerchief. "I t-think... I think she may have gone into the tunnels."

There is a period of quiet as Topan murmurs discreetly to the frantic woman. His voice reaches Nerani and Orianna in a muffled hum, but his words are unintelligible. After a moment, the chair scrapes again as the woman rises to her feet.

"Take her to see Mame Minera in the infirmary," Topan commands. "Perhaps she can rustle up something to ease the woman's nerves."

"And my d-daughter?" The woman asks, calmer now.

"We'll find her, Moria, I promise you that."

Nerani listens as Blaine leads the woman out of the room. Their departure is followed by complete quiet. Nerani and Orianna exchange glances in the darkness, their eyes wide and uncomprehending. They are jolted out of their silent exchange by the sound of Topan's voice very close to their ears.

"You can come out of there," he says. "I imagine you have a number of questions for me."

Harvest Cycle 1511

Sometimes in the dark of night, I lie awake and sweat out my regrets.

I am a man with many regrets.

If Jameson should catch up to us—if I should be taken and killed—I wonder what sort of legacy I will have left behind on Chancey.

I wonder if Roberts will grow to be a good man. I wonder if he'll be a stronger man, a braver man, than I could ever have hoped to be.

And Emerala, too, that little sprite of a child—that wild, frightful thing—I wonder if she'll be like her mother. Her mother always reminded me of water. She was impossible to hold onto, but Saints when she wanted to be, she was as terrible and as strong as any storm at sea.

And the boy. My boy. He has my eyes, that's what I've heard. My eyes and my will. Saints preserve him, a boy who wears my face will never survive Rowland's uncompromising paranoia.

Tonight I will sleep with my regrets. Tonight I will spend another midnight choking on my cowardice. Perhaps tomorrow will be the day the fates finally catch up to me. Perhaps tomorrow I'll finally be able to rest, even if that rest should be at the bottom of the storming sea.

Eliot

CHAPTER 38

Caira

SHADOW SPIRITS OR not, the labyrinth is an eerie place. Emerala shivers as she idles in the great, stone corridor, her torch flickering dangerously beneath a quiet breeze. Overhead, the settling night has extinguished the sun, leaving behind the sticking humidity of day. Emerala's black curls adhere to her neck and she pries them away with her free hand. Up ahead, she can see the raven waiting for her on a bit of crumbled stone. The bird waits until Emerala reaches her, her feathered head askew.

"Well, Marvala, looks like it's me and you," Emerala says, and feels immediately foolish. The bird clicks its beak together and takes off with a solitary flap, gliding silently between the oppressive stone walls. Emerala follows, feeling her heartbeat quickening.

The maze is small, the corridors narrow. It isn't long before she begins to feel claustrophobic amidst the endless grey shadows. She startles often, wary of the creatures that may be lurking in the darkness. Overhead, the night sky is an endless pit of black. The dancing firelight of her torch swallows whatever stars may be illuminating the creeping jungle.

She follows the raven in silence, feeling her agitation growing with every turn.

Why am I here? she wonders. *Who am I to these people?*

They can't possibly think her to be Cairan. Like Alexander said, they would have killed her immediately. And yet, Melena made it clear that she knows Emerala is lying about hailing from the Westerlies. It was her green eyes that made the woman take notice. It was her green eyes that caught Derek's attention upon the deck of the Rebellion. It was her green eyes, as well, that caused the Hawk to approach her in the marketplace.

Her green eyes were a singularity in Chancey, to be sure, but they were nothing to marvel over. Her eyes are all she has left of her father—her green eyes and Roberts's lasting resentment. She remembers nothing of the man. She has not even a ghost of a memory.

And she is all the better for it, she imagines.

There is a raucous cry from the bird and she stumbles to a stop. The firelight dances precariously upon its sconce, threatening to extinguish and leave her to fend off the dark alone. She lifts the torch above her head, casting light upon her surroundings. She is in a small clearing, no longer entombed within the corridors of crumbling stone. She cannot see Marvala, but a flutter of wings in the dark tells her that the raven is near.

The air feels hotter here—heavier. She peers into the clearing, blinking slowly, her heart in her throat. It takes a few moments for her to realize that she is no longer standing in the dark. The clearing around her is well lit by a series of torches set in sconces. Next to her, mounted on the circular stone, is an empty sconce. She rises to her toes, gingerly planting her torch within the rounded iron bracket. She shakes her hand out, relieved. Her fingers were beginning to burn. She takes a few steps forward into the clearing, keeping her eyes pealed for any sign of movement.

A soft thud lands upon the ground—a sound almost like a footfall. Emerala freezes. A warm gust of wind continues on in her wake, colliding against her damp back. The thin lace of her chemise ripples forward. Her legs appear as though they have been swathed in mottled flesh.

She holds her breath and listens. Her heartbeat pounds in her ears. Is she hearing things? Was it Marvala? Now, there is nothing but silence. Silence, and the soft sound of insects singing somewhere beyond the stone. She inhales softly—slowly. The air tastes stale upon her tongue. Dense and stagnant, it quivers against the pressing dark. She can feel the relentless humidity saturating her skin.

The silence begins to unnerve her. Surely she heard something—she knows someone is here. The architect. The debtor. The prisoner. He has many names, and yet he is still a stranger. And strangers can be dangerous.

She strains her ears. The hair on the back of her neck prickles warily. She feels eyes upon her. Trying her best to appear braver than she feels, she glances idly at her surroundings. The derelict stone rises ominously about her. Shadows encroach the crumbling corners, obscuring...what? The prisoner may be watching from any direction.

There. Another footfall, closer than before. Emerala whirls about, eyes blazing. The expanse before her is empty. Her thin lips snap together. She exhales heavily through her nose. Damp locks of her hair suction against her cheekbones. She pushes them away with an flick of her fingers.

Over the sound of her own breathing she hears boots dragging against the sand. The sound is barely audible, but it is there. Panic begins to bubble in her chest. She gives an involuntary shudder. The dull sound of the boots has stopped, but the echo of heavy breathing clings faintly to the lagging wind. She feels suddenly panicked. Frantic images of a hunched and wild man begin to play through her mind.

Emerala takes an uneasy step forward. Her heart leaps against her ribcage as she prepares to run. From within a small, teetering building at the end of the clearing there comes the sudden sound of laughter. She startles, staring. She had not noticed the dilapidated hut, so obscured had it been by the dancing shadows.

The voice that emanates from the hut is brittle. The sound trails out from the blackened doorway as though it is a wisp of smoke, dissipating upon the sultry evening air. It sends chills down her spine. She glances back over her shoulder. Behind her is only oppressive stone, but the clear night that stretches overhead is a silent void.

The Lethal will hear her if she screams.

"Come in," a voice spills out from the open door. "Please."

Emerala moves slowly, forcing herself to place one foot in front of the other as she steps within the lopsided frame. The one-roomed hut before her is immersed in darkness. Across the small expanse she can see the vague outline of a man seated upon a chair. She cannot make out his features. One shaft of dancing orange light falls in through a hole in the thatched ceiling.

The only other source of illumination comes from the oblong flicker of red that trickles in behind her.

"Step inside." The voice that emanates from the shaded figure is hoarse from lack of use. "You have nothing to fear from the shadow spirits that play among the stones. They will not harm you."

"What are shadow spirits?" Emerala asks.

"They're wild things," says the man. "Lovely, deadly creatures that only come out to play beneath the silver moon."

"And you believe in them?"

"Oh yes," the man says. "Spend a night in the jungle, and so will you."

Emerala hears the shuffling of garments as he shifts his weight upon his chair. The rotting wood creaks beneath him. "They have sent you to me, the Cairans. Why?"

"I don't know."

"No? Let's puzzle it out, then, you and I. What is your name?"

She swallows, thinking, and decides to stick to her lie. She has not been instructed otherwise. In this case, she has not been instructed at all.

"I am Katherine Montclay, sir," she says unconvincingly, her voice shaking. She clears her throat. Continues, "I am engaged to be wed to Derek."

"Montclay? Where were you raised?"

"Toholay," Emerala replies.

"That is a lie," the prisoner says, scarcely missing a beat. "You don't say it correctly. Your accent is wrong—the word is too stiff on your tongue. Tell me again, where are you from?"

Emerala inhales a small gulp of air. "Toholay."

"A *lie*."

Emerala takes a step forward, her burning curiosity getting the best of her. She has questions of her own—thousands of them, each clamoring for a voice.

"Why are you kept here?"

She can feel the prisoner's eyes alighting upon her in the darkness.

"Kept?" he repeats, speaking as if he doesn't know the meaning of the word. "I am not kept. I simply can't return home. Domio has provided me with a safe haven. He's a good man, Domio—he operates on a system of service. I did him a favor, once, many years ago. Unintentionally, of course, but a favor is a favor, and Domio is a gracious host."

"Melena said you're a prisoner here. She calls you the debtor."

The man's voice is weighted with grief. "The debt is my own. This prison was fashioned by my hands alone."

"But I don't understand," Emerala presses, feeling more and more confused with each passing moment. "Why would you imprison yourself?"

"You are far too inquisitive for a lady of Toholay," comes the sharp response. "It isn't proper."

Emerala quails at his words. He's right, of course. Lady Katherine Montclay would not be asking questions of a stranger. She would be demure, quiet—perhaps even a little bit frightened.

But then, the man before her does not believe her anyway.

"I have answered your questions honestly," he says. "Perhaps you will pay me the same respect. I will ask you again—where are you from?"

Emerala chews her lip, unsure whether to stick to her lie or to be honest. She knows what Alexander would say, were he here with her. But Alexander is gone, far off on the other side of the island. Their hastily laid plan fell to pieces the moment their boats were capsized offshore. Emerala swallows hard and decides upon the truth.

"I sailed here from Chancey."

The man heaves a great sigh. Beneath the shadows, she sees him slump forward in his seat.

"Of course," he whispers. His voice sounds as though it is coming from miles away. "They suspect. They are no fools, they know Saynti's prophecy as well as I."

"Prophecy?" Emerala repeats, perplexed. The man looks up at her, straightening upon his chair. In his new position, she can just make out the black tangles that cascade over his shoulders. He looks wild—unpredictable. His frame is slender but strong. His gnarled hands clasp between his knees. His voice shakes when he speaks.

"Step into the light," he commands. Emerala opens her mouth to protest, but he cuts her off before she can speak. "I beg you."

Uncomfortable, Emerala obliges. She steps carefully into the flickering firelight that falls down upon the damp floor. She feels the blood-orange aura tickling her features. It spills into her eyes, blinding her to her surroundings. The shaded figure of the man blinks into obscurity.

In the dark, she hears him let out a gasp. A strange choking sound fills the cramped hut. It takes her a few moments to realize that the man before her is weeping. The sound spills away from him in great, heaving sobs. His shoulders rise and fall in the darkness.

"It can't be," he says. His voice cracks, laden with grief. "How is it you have come to be here?"

Emerala's mouth works silently as she fumbles for an answer. She does not know how she can continue to lie to the sobbing figure before her.

"I sailed here onboard the pirate ship *Rebellion*."

"Impossible," he whispers. "It's impossible. You sailed here with Samuel? Samuel Mathew?"

"No," Emerala says. "He has a son—Alexander."

Another muffled sob, choked into silence.

"I'm sorry," Emerala admits. "But I'm not quite sure what is going on."

"They'll string you up." The man's voice is muted. She realizes his face is in his hands. "I struck a deal. I struck it to keep you safe. You were so young—so innocent. All of you." His fist swings out and makes contact with the stone wall of the hut, causing Emerala to jump. Dust falls down into her eyes as bits of thatch dislodge from the roof.

"He swore that if I left, no harm would ever come to you. It was all for you. I had nothing left. He promised me your safety, and his promises mean nothing to me if you are here."

He is babbling now, his words stringing together with a strange incoherence.

Emerala opens her mouth to speak and is cut off by the hoarse screaming of ravens. The flickering throw of the flames overhead extinguishes with a wink. She races to the door, glancing upwards to see hundreds of the glossy black birds wheeling and diving over the clearing. The fluttering of wings sets the flames to sputtering in their sconces. The entire clearing looks as though it is ablaze.

"They're here," comes the prisoner's voice from behind her. He is staring up at the opening, listening as the ravens settle upon the roof of his hut. A few of them alight on the crumbling stones scattered here and there throughout the clearing. Their shivering wings gleam blood-red in the leaping firelight. They ogle Emerala through inky eyes. Emerala drops back into the shadow of the doorway. Not for the first time, she wishes someone had thought to provide her with a weapon. Behind her, the prisoner has fallen into useless silence.

A triumphant caw, and one raven drops down through the gap in the ceiling. Its fluttering wings kick up the dust that lines the ground, causing Emerala to choke on the air. The bird's head wrenches in her direction. It gleams with an unnerving iridescence in the obstructed firelight. With another shriek, the bird flies towards her, its claws extended. Talons rip across her cheek, tearing at flesh. She waves her arms in a frantic attempt at defense as the raven flies at her again and again, black feet tearing through the skin of her arms and hands. She drops onto the floor, rolling away from the bird. Her eyes glance frantically around the room as she searches for something heavy.

"Here!" the debtor calls. He does not rise from his chair, but she can see him lob something in her direction. She catches it, realizing it to be nothing more than a broken leg from an old wooden chair. It will have to do. The bird claws at her head, loosing that throaty cry as its feet tangle in the mess of her hair. She wrenches her curls away and rolls onto her back. The bird circles around, a blood curdling screech emanating from its open beak, and drops towards her face. She swings the leg, elation surging through her as the wood connects with the creature's body. It flies across the room, striking the stone before sliding limply to the floor.

Emerala stands and dusts herself off. She wonders if the Lethal is still watching for her outside the maze. She can make a run for it. She wonders how far she will get before the birds begin to pursue her.

Her thoughts are interrupted by a gunshot. A horrible, high-pitched shriek tears through the air and is silenced. The shot came from far off, beyond the bending stone corridors of the labyrinth. It takes Emerala a few seconds to realize the voice had been human, so bird-like had it sounded.

More gunshots buffet the air in response to the scream. The sounds volley off of one another, the echoes rattling Emerala's bones as she stands frozen in the dark hut. Her stomach pools with dread.

She hears uneven footsteps racing across the clearing, the sound growing ever louder. Someone is approaching the hut. Emerala grips the leg in her hands and positions it to be swung again.

"Rogue!"

The voice, hoarse from running, belongs to Alexander. A raven screeches, taking flight from the roof. It's talons hyperextend before it as it surges forward with a flap of its wings. There is a gunshot and the bird crumples lifelessly to the ground. Another gunshot sounds—closer this time—and Emerala hears the agitated cries of many as a cluster of ravens take to the air. She races out of the doorway right as Alexander slows to a walk. He is limping—even in the darkness she can see as much. Blood has dried against his pants, adhering the tattered fabric to his skin.

"We have to get out of here," he calls. Pain is etched across his face. He glances over Emerala's shoulder at the man in the hut. Emerala follows his gaze. In the shadow of the room she can just make out the form of the rising prisoner. He stands with difficulty, his figure weighted down by fatigue.

"Samuel?" he asks in some surprise. "Well sink me, if you don't look a day older."

Alexander's arm moves around Emerala's waist, drawing her closer to him. His gun remains trained upon the ravens that leer menacingly down from the rooftop.

"I'm not Samuel."

The prisoner seems not to have heard. "You finally came for me, you old bastard. Took you long enough." His laugh is loud. The sound catches in his throat and he wheezes.

"I'm not Samuel," Alexander repeats. "That was my father." He glances down at Emerala. "Melena is dead. We have to go."

The prisoner takes a step forward, shaking his wild hair out of his eyes. The shadows dance upon the lines of his face. His eyes swim with moonlight. "You shouldn't have brought her here, Sam. Not her. Not my girl. They'll take her. You know that's what they'll do."

Alexander's eyes narrow as confusion flits across his features. He says nothing, only remains tight-lipped in the door, his grip on Emerala steady.

Emerala feels something twist within her.

My girl?

She frowns at the shaded man before them, wishing he would step into the light.

My girl.

"Wait," she says. The screaming of ravens swallows her voice whole. The night sky is alive with the fluttering of wings. The air around them reeks of gunpowder. She can feel Alexander's sense of urgency pressing against her through his fingertips.

"Rogue," Alexander says. His voice is low. Urgent. "We have to go."

"Just a minute," she snaps, turning toward the debtor. "Who are you?"

"A dead man," says the shadowed figure. The shrieking of birds grows louder. "A memory. You should run, little Emerala. Run now. Run fast."

"What's your name?" Emerala asks, but the man is turning away—returning to his hut.

"Domio is heading this way," he says over his shoulder. "I can buy you some time, Sam, but only a little. Get her back to the ship. Take her home. She doesn't belong here. Promise me, Sam, will you?"

"What's your name?" Emerala repeats, shouting now to be heard over the shrieking birds. The man disappears through the doorway of his hut, fading back into shadow and dust. Alexander's hand encloses about Emerala's fingers, wrenching her several steps in the opposite direction. She rails against his grasp, trying and failing to pull away—to head back to the hut.

My girl, the debtor said.

My girl.

"Damn it, Rogue!" Alexander pulls her again, firing his pistol into the air as talons descend upon them. Emerala ducks as a curved beak comes inches away from her eye. Turning on her heels, she races after Alexander as he sprints out of the clearing and back into the crumbling stone of the labyrinth. She keeps easy pace with Alexander as she runs, her heart in her throat and her head burning with unasked questions. Beside her, Alexander runs with a considerable limp, his face contorted in pain. His skin, slick with sweat, has taken on a ghostly pallor.

"What happened to you?" Emerala pants as they round yet another corner. The pressing corridor is narrow and she rams hard into his shoulder. The motion nearly sends him toppling face first into the dirt. He groans, stumbling several steps before regaining his footing.

"Ask me that later."

"You might be dead later," Emerala points out.

He shoots her a murderous look across the darkness.

"What? I'd hate to miss out on a good story."

He laughs, the smile cutting across his lips in a grimace. "You won't get rid of me that easy, Rogue. Now keep quiet and run."

Up ahead, Emerala can just make out the decaying entrance of the labyrinth. The moss that carpets the crumbling stone has been painted red with fast drying blood. Emerala tries not to look—tries not to search the undergrowth for the corpse of Melena, left out, she is sure, as carrion for her birds.

She and Alexander emerge into the dark jungle to silence. She slows to a stop, a cramp rooting in her side like a dagger. Gasping for breath, she places her hands upon her head and turns her face up toward the clear night sky. Overhead, the shivering starlight casts a silvery blanket of light over the leaves.

"Where is everyone?"

The voice that answers her belongs not to Alexander, but to the Hawk.

"They went back to the ship," he says. His slender figure slips out of the shadows of the trees. Moonlight spills into his sharp golden eyes. "The Lethal can't afford to stick around after taking Melena's head clean off, can he?"

The image makes Emerala's stomach churn. She swallows, her throat and lungs burning. Next to her, Alexander's posture has grown tense as he glowers at the Hawk.

"You should be at the ship with them," he snaps. "Those were your orders."

"That was an order? I thought it was more of a suggestion."

Another grimace passes across Alexander's lips. "Don't be glib."

"I'm not. I've already saved your life once today. The way I see it, you should be grateful I'm here. That thing is still lurking in the jungle, and you're not in any shape to fend it off."

Alexander gives a derisive snort. "You're insulting my intelligence, Hawk. Let's not pretend it's me you're here for."

Emerala blanches at the insinuation in his voice, suddenly unable to meet the pair of golden eyes that watch her from the trees.

"We should keep moving," she suggests.

"I agree," the Hawk says. He studies Alexander. "Can you run?"

"I'll be fine," Alexander snaps.

"Aye? You look like you're about to keel over."

Emerala glances up at Alexander at that. He is leaning against a nearby tree, his face glistening with beads of sweat beneath the moonlight. His chest rises and falls erratically. His sallow skin is caked with streaks of drying blood. His lips are tinged with blue. Looking down at his leg, she realizes that she can see torn bits of flesh through the gaping tears in his breeches.

"I'm fine," he repeats. He moves to stand and stumbles, nearly collapsing into a heap. Emerala rushes to him, grabbing hold of his left arm and throwing it over her shoulder. He leans into her without protest, his skin aflame.

"I'm fine."

"Hawk," Emerala calls, glowering at the lanky pirate that hovers still in the trees, his gaze watchful. "Help him."

"He says he's fine."

"Don't be such a child," Emerala snaps. When the Hawk continues to idle in the shadows, Emerala glowers at him, meeting his gaze head on for the first time in minutes.

"Evander," she barks. "*Help him.*"

The muscles in his jaw work as he turns a scathing comeback over on his tongue. Finally, he emerges from the dark overhang of trees and moves beside the pair. Leaning down, he grabs Alexander's free arm and thrusts it over his shoulder.

"Do you still have it?" Alexander asks him, his face pinched in pain.

"Aye, right here." The Hawk pats a bulge in his jacket pocket and grins. He and Emerala pull Alexander slowly through the jungle, picking through tangled roots and thorned bramble.

"Is that it?" Emerala asks, eyeing the Hawk's jacket. "Is that what we came here for?"

"Aye, it is."

Alexander chews at his cheek, biting back a cry of pain as he limps between them. Glancing toward Emerala out of the corner of his eye, he catches her attention.

"Reach into the holster at my waist," he says. "Take my pistol."

"I—" Emerala begins, a protest already at her lips.

"Do it," he orders. "Now."

Emerala obeys, marveling at the cold weight of the gun in her hands.

"Listen to me," Alexander barks, his voice laced with agony. "If you see anything coming towards us, I want you to shoot at it. It doesn't matter who—or what—it is. Do you understand?"

She hesitates for a moment, dumbfounded. From somewhere beyond the greenery comes a low, guttural growl. She startles, nearly dropping the pistol. Alexander's weight against her feels suddenly suffocating.

"What is that?" she asks. She struggles to keep up as the Hawk picks up the pace, nearly dragging Alexander across the jungle floor.

"Run now," Alexander grunts. "Questions later."

Another growl, closer this time. Emerala points the gun toward the shadows. The jungle breathes at her. A twig snaps and her heart flies to her throat. Somewhere far overhead, she can hear the distant shrieking of thousands of birds in flight. The oppressive evening heat clings to her body like a blanket, but she shivers all the same.

"Keep moving, Rogue," barks the Hawk. "One false move, and none of us make it out of this jungle alive."

Harvest Cycle 1511

There are drums in the dark.

 Jameson is here. They have come for me.

 But who hired Jameson? Who bought Argot?

 By the time I know the answers to my questions, I fear it will be too late.

I am a dead man.

 A memory.

 This will be my last entry.

Eliot

CHAPTER 39

The Rebellion

LACHLAN THE LETHAL is waiting for Evander the Hawk when he returns to his cot.

Evander draws to a stop before the sloping hammock, watching the old pirate evenly through his piercing golden eyes. The floor beneath him lurches uneasily as the ship is buffeted by a wave. Somewhere beyond the groaning belly of the sloop comes the menacing rumble of distant thunder.

"Didn't think you lot'd make it back alive," the murderer says. "That was quite a mess we left back there on Caira."

"We're a resilient crew." Evander leans back against a splintering post, keeping the Lethal always within eyeshot. He crosses his arms protectively over his chest. "What do you want?"

The Lethal purses his lips, withdrawing Eliot Roberts's weathered old journal from within his jacket pocket. He flips over the cover and stares at an entry. The white of his scar pinches as he begins to read in the thickening darkness. He licks his thumb, flipping forward several pages. Evander watches in silence as the murderer's eyes flicker back and forth across the hastily scribed words.

"Eliot Roberts," the Lethal muses, still reading.

"Aye, what about him?"

"This is his journal. His name is on every page."

Evander's response is wry. "What a profound observation."

The Lethal murmurs under his breath, ignoring Evander as he continues to read. One blackened fingernail traces the line of words across the page. Evander can feel himself prickling with impatience. His bones tremble with exhaustion and his head aches from a day in the jungles of Caira without water or food. All he wants is to sleep.

His eyelids flutter, nearly closing, and he groans. "Are you going to make me try and guess what game you're playing at, or are you going to let me in on it?"

At that, the Lethal peers up at him. He looks far older than his years in the purpling shadows of the oncoming storm—ancient. The deep grooves of his face are pitted with black. He jabs a finger at the page before him.

"You're mentioned in this book quite a bit, boy," he says.

"Am I?"

"Ye are, and ye know it, so let's not pretend like we haven't both read this thing through and through."

Evander shrugs. Uncrossing his arms, he slips his hands into the pockets of his breeches. "Fine," he agrees. "I've read the journal. And read it, and read it. And it hasn't told me a thing I don't already know."

"Why's it so important to ye, then?"

"Who said it was?"

The Lethal does not respond. A small smile curls in one corner of his mouth as he thumbs through another page. He reads on in silence for a moment, his lips fumbling over the words. Evander watches him carefully, studying his fingers as they tap at the cover.

"Here," he says. *"And Emerala, too, that little sprite of a child—that wild, frightful thing—I wonder if she'll be like her mother."* The Lethal looks up from the page, his eyes glittering.

"Curious thing, en't it?"

"What's that?"

"Why didn't ye tell the Rogue that it were her father being held prisoner by the Cairans?"

Evander hesitates, his chest tightening. The ship lurches precariously to the side and he staggers, fighting to hold his balance against the tipping floor. There is the low rumble of creaking wood and a splintering crash as a barrel topples to the floor. The ship falls back upon the swell of the sea as the wave ebbs, sending the cask barreling noisily across the wood. Evander glares up at the Lethal, watching as the old man continues to read in silence.

"What makes you think the debtor had any relation to her?" he asks.

The Lethal looks up at that, his eyes gleaming. "I've read the journal. It en't much of a leap to reach such a conclusion. That man on the island—the debtor—he's her father. Eliot Roberts. There's no doubt in my mind. What I'm not sure about is why ye didn't tell her so."

Evander shrugs. "It makes no difference to me."

"Ah, quite the opposite," says the Lethal with a dry laugh. "Quite the opposite."

He looks back down at the journal, chuckling aloud as he spits on his thumb and flips the page. Evander is silent before the murderer as he considers his options. He fingers the hilt of his cutlass. It will be a silent death— quick and easy—if he can move fast enough. His pulse quickens beneath his skin as he thinks of the blood seeping through his cot.

He's read the journal. He knows too much, he reasons silently. *He is putting the pieces together too quickly.*

"I wouldn't try and kill me," says the Lethal, not bothering to look up from his reading.

"Give me one reason why not," Evander hisses.

"Don't be a fool, boy. Ye know who I am. Ye know what I am." His demeanor is eerily placid against the crisp reek of the incoming storm. "Ye'd be dead sooner than ye can draw your weapon."

"I'm handier with a blade than you seem to think."

"Aye? Are ye willing to stake your life on that?"

"I am." Evander's fingers close around the hilt. He draws the blade partially out of the scabbard, letting the bowed steel sing against the punctured leather at his belt. The Lethal continues to read, his eyes scanning the page at a leisurely pace as he takes in the text.

"And Emerala the Rogue? Are ye willing to bet her life?"

Evander pauses in the dimly lit expanse, his breath slowing. His fingers loosen about the hilt of his cutlass. The Lethal sets the journal down upon the cot and looks up, meeting Evander's eyes across the dark.

"Hit a nerve, have I, boy?"

Evander swallows hard and says nothing.

"Interesting development, I should think," the old man comments. "I'd suppose, then, you haven't told the Rogue about her father because ye somehow believe you're protecting her from the truth." He gives a callous laugh, his eyes catching in the grey light as he holds Evander in his gaze. "A hopeless romantic, Melena called ye. Maybe she was right."

Wrong, Evander thinks. He watches the pirate through stoic eyes, careful not to reveal his final card. Let him think the Rogue is nothing but an infatuation if it suits his feeble, old fancy. *She has a part to play yet, murderer.*

"Put away your weapon and play a game with me," the Lethal says.

"What's the game?"

"It's an easy one," the Lethal says. "Ye answer my questions with the truth, or I slit the Rogue's throat."

Evander pauses for the space of a heartbeat. "You're bluffing."

The Lethal smiles, his scar wrinkling as grooves split his cheeks. "Ye can call my bluff. Or ye can play along."

Evander bites down hard against his tongue, his golden eyes blazing as hard as steel.

"Good," the Lethal says. He looks back down at the journal and continues thumbing through the pages, muttering beneath his breath. Evander catches fragments of familiar words and phrases as he listens closely. His blood boils beneath his skin and he fights to keep his temper in check.

After a moment of disjointed mumbling, the Lethal pauses, his finger stopping on a line of text.

"There. *He flies under a black banner bearing a blood red cross.*" His gaze rises from the page to meet Evander's. "That's that old mercenary bastard Randall Jameson, what he mentions there."

"I know who he's mentioning," Evander snaps, irate.

"Aye, that's right. Ye were there when Jameson took Eliot Roberts, were ye not? Drums in the dark, he said. I imagine ye heard them, too. I imagine ye even tried to save the poor bastard. Ye and the old Cap'n."

Evander frowns, thrust suddenly into an unwanted memory.

He was a boy, then. No older than a teen. The night Jameson came for Eliot Roberts was the first time he had ever killed a man. He had been sleeping in the crow's nest when they came—had fallen asleep on duty. The moon that night was black. Even the stars were sleeping. Jameson and his men crept aboard under the cover of darkness, robbing Eliot Roberts from his cot.

Shortly after midnight, Evander had awoken to the sound of drums. He sidled down the yardarm in a panic, his cutlass drawn, but Jameson was already gone. So, too, was Eliot Roberts. The alarm had been sounded and there was a skirmish upon the deck. All around him was the coppery reek of blood and the metallic singing of blades upon the rippling night air. It was a wordless pandemonium—a perfectly orchestrated descant of carnage.

There is a bitter taste upon his tongue as he remembers the ease with which his cutlass had slid through the pirate's throat. The boy—and he was no older than a boy, a runaway perhaps, like him—had sunk to his knees with a quiet gurgle. It chilled him through the bone—to see those lifeless eyes accusing him in the darkness. He kicked the boy over with the toe of his boot, rifling in his pocket for something—anything—to cover that unblinking gaze.

All that he had was a handful of copper coins.

Before him, the Lethal is watching him with a knowing twinkle in his eyes. The night air sticks to Evander's skin, itching at his neck beneath his collar.

"Harboring regrets, are ye, boy?"

Evander ignores him. "What are you playing at?"

"I'm only tryin' to connect the pieces. Surely ye can't begrudge a curious old man for that." The Lethal returns his gaze to the page before him, scouring the text for a moment more.

"Randall Jameson's body was rotting in one of them gibbets back on the shore of Caira," the Lethal comments. "I recognized the insignia on his jacket right away. But ye knew that, didn't ye, boy?"

Evander is silent.

"Ye didn't look at all surprised to see him there," the Lethal continues. "Alexander told me he stole that map of his from Jameson back on Chancey. Ye knew Jameson took that map the day he took Eliot Roberts. Ye knew he'd go back to the start, didn't ye? When a job goes wrong, ye always go back to the boss."

"You're more observant than the Cap'n," Evander says, relinquishing a bitter smile. "I didn't know who hired Jameson—not until Cap'n unlocked the map in the Eisle. But aye, when a job goes wrong, you go back to the start. It's code."

The Lethal studies him through narrowed eyes. Evander can nearly hear the cogs turning behind his skull—can picture the pieces falling slowly into place. "Eliot Roberts spent the final entries of his journal wondering who paid off Jameson and Argot. The journal ends before he found out. But he did find out eventually, didn't he?"

"Seems that way," Evander agrees. "I never saw him again."

"Domio hired a mercenary to abduct Eliot Roberts fourteen harvest cycles past. Why?"

"Don't know," Evander says.

"Careful boy," the Lethal warns. "Don't lie to me, now. If Domio hired Jameson, why'd he kill him and set the birds on him once he returned to Caira?"

"Because he failed," Evander says. "Eliot Roberts was never the intended target. He's a mule—a vessel. Nothing more. Domio wanted the cargo Roberts carried. He wanted the map to stay out of the wrong hands. Once unlocked, the map would lead its owner directly to Caira, and to the object Domio worked so hard to steal."

"What object is that?" the Lethal asks.

Evander's lip twitches and he ignores the question. "Jameson never should have let Alexander Mathew get his hands on the map. An inexperienced pirate like him should have been easy pickings for an old mercenary like Jameson."

"But he wasn't, because ye helped him get the map in Chancey."

Evander shakes his head. "I didn't do a thing. Jameson was a sodding drunk. A child could have stolen the map. He failed at his job. He deserved what he got."

The Lethal peers at Evander through slitted eyes as he turns over what he has just heard. Evander stares back at him, waiting.

"What I en't able to figure is how Charles Argot ended up exiled on Caros?"

Evander sniffs. "You work it out, old man. You seem clever enough."

The Lethal clucks his tongue reproachfully against the roof of his mouth. "Don't get smart on me. That's not how we play, boy. Ye answer my questions with the truth."

"These questions are getting a bit too invasive for my liking," Evander retorts.

"Perhaps ye forgot the stakes, then." The Lethal snaps the book shut and hops down from the cot. His boots hit the ground with a thud that reverberates through the empty crew's quarters. "I don't know why, but I know that the Rogue is worth more to ye alive than dead. Whatever it is you're doing, ye need that pretty little throat of hers to stay intact."

Outside, Evander can hear the shouting of the crew as they fight to secure the lines against the oncoming storm. He stares back at the old pirate and says nothing.

"Aye, well if you're going to make me work for it," the Lethal growls. "I know that Argot took a hefty payout from Cap'n Samuel to make the map, but he took a bigger payout from Domio to deliver Jameson the map and Eliot's location when it were done."

"Obvious." Evander smirks. "Much of that was written in the journal."

"So what happened to Argot after he delivered the map to Domio?"

Evander shrugs. "I don't have a clue. Cap'n Sam and I found him three sheets to the wind in a Westerly port six harvests later. He'd gambled away all his earnings and was failing to win them back at a game of blackjack."

"Argot told me, once, that he ended up in Caros over a bad game of cards." The Lethal scrunches his nose, recalling old conversations with men long since dead.

At this, Evander allows a full smile to break out across his face.

370

"Aye," he says. "He did. He was betting money, then, but I upped the ante with my hand. I made him bet his freedom. He was so drunk he didn't even recognize me until the game was over. By then he'd already lost."

"So it was you that left Argot marooned on Caros," the Lethal concludes.

"I did," Evander admits. "I left him there until I needed him again."

"Needed him?" The Lethal frowns. "Ye went back eight harvests later and put a blade through his heart."

Evander locks his jaw and says nothing.

"Ye needed him dead?"

"Maybe I did," Evander assents, studying the man before him.

"Maybe ye did," the Lethal repeats. The gold caps of his teeth catch upon the dwindling light. The patch of sky visible through the doorway capitulates to the skeletal clouds that spiral in from the west. An eerie green clings to the ship like a wet blanket. The air is electric.

"Or maybe," the Lethal muses, "maybe ye murdered Argot to keep Cap'n Mathew from findin' out the truth."

"I'm on the Cap'n's side," Evander opposes. "We're after the same thing."

The Lethal nods. "Aye, for now. But not forever."

"What are you, his protector?" Evander snaps. "You'll do well to remember that Alexander wanted you dead from the very start. *I'm* his right hand man."

"A right hand man who almost left his captain for dead in a triggered booby trap," the Lethal reminds him. "Or so I've been told."

"I'm still better than you," Evander snarls. "You're nothing. You're an incompetent old man with a long list of sins. If it weren't for me talking the Cap'n into trusting you, you'd have been left for dead at the Frost Forts."

"Appearances can be deceiving, as they say," the Lethal says, eyes gleaming. He drops the book to the ground with a clatter just as a strip of lightning snaps across the purpling sky. For a moment, all Evander can see are the whites of his eyes and the glimmer of his blade as the room is captured in a white frame of light.

And then they are cast again in the crisp darkness of the storm. The ship rocks to the side, barreling upon the waves as thunder rents apart the air. Evander freezes, a blade at his throat and a voice in his ear.

371

"You're a man with a plan, Hawk, and I en't like to miss it. Ye can play your game, but mind ye don't take any missteps. I like the Cap'n. He's a good man with an unsullied heart—rare in these parts of the world. Ye so much as make a move that I don't like, I'll slit yer throat."

Evander swallows, his larynx pulling against the sliver of steel against his skin.

"And the Rogue?" Evander asks.

The blade slides away from him as the Lethal chuckles.

"A bluff, for now," the murderer whispers in the darkness. "But it's good to know ye have a weakness should I need it."

Another flash of lightning streaks across the sky. The air crackles with electricity, causing the hair on Evander's neck to stand upright. The light contorts into blackness and the Lethal is gone, leaving Evander alone to his thoughts among the rolling cots.

CHAPTER 40

The Rebellion

EMERALA STANDS IN the dusty silver light that falls into the ship's hold, listening to the rain that trickles intermittently through the open hatch above her head. The ship rises and falls against the swollen sea and she stumbles, nearly losing her balance. Her slender fingers cling onto a barrel for support. She cannot shake the creeping feeling of disappointment that has taken root within her. After all this time, she was certain that the trip to Caira would provide her with the answers she so desperately sought. She frowns, kicking at the ground with her bare toe. She knows less now than she did before.

My girl, the prisoner had called her. *My girl.*

It's impossible that the man at the center of the maze knew her. Surely she would have remembered him—surely she would have recognized something, anything, about him. A single deep groove forms between her eyebrows as her mouth drops into a sullen pout. The ravings of a madman, that's all it was.

"Blood of the three, queen you'll be." The nasal croak of the silver parrot to her right startles her. He has been watching her through silent black eyes as she paces back and forth, hopping to and fro on the wooden beam in his masterfully woven menagerie. All around him, six other identical silver parrots are napping, their heads tucked down beneath their wings. At the sound of his voice, the closest parrot startles awake, glaring out from beneath his wing.

"Quiet," he snaps in irritation. He flutters his feathers, his grey stomach puffing outward, and shuffles away from the other parrot. His black talons move one over the other in sluggish steps.

Emerala frowns at the bird. He watches her silently, his black eyes full of watery understanding. She has been trying all morning to get him to mimic

373

her, with no results. The parrot has been content to stare at her, his head cocked in confusion.

"Sure, *now* you talk," Emerala remarks in exasperation.

"Ahoy there." The parrot flutters his wings. "Ahoy."

"Yes, hello to you," Emerala replies tersely.

"Emerala the Rogue," the bird sings. "Blood red ice for diamond wars." He flaps his wings again. Emerala feels a chill go through her at his words. The dreams that have plagued her of late come rushing to the forefront of her memory. Overhead, there is a low rumble of thunder. Her hands drop to her sides as a chill grips her. She stares at the bird, remembering the sight of her blood spilled across the snow. She blinks and sees the Hawk, his golden eyes intent as they watch her through the dark.

Ghosts, she thinks. *Or nightmares of ghosts.* Whatever they are, she shakes them away, shivering in the musty hold.

Someone drops down the hatch, startling her. The newcomer lands with a dull thud at the foot of the ladder, his figure shrouded in thin, grey light.

"I thought I'd find ye down here," growls the Lethal. His scalp glistens with flecks of rain. "Sulking with the birds are ye?"

"I'm not sulking," she replies, crossing her arms over her chest.

"Aye, that ye be."

"What are you doing down here?" Emerala asks.

The Lethal pats a barrel in response to her question. "Fetching some rum for the Cap'n. Mate's got it bad, he does."

Emerala grimaces at the memory of Alexander's leg, shredded nearly to the bone in places. The last time she'd seen him, Derek had been barking orders over his limp form. His matted hair was plastered to his ashen skin. His eyes were hollow pits upon his face. She has not been to see him—not once. The sight of him makes her uneasy. Strange, she's never been the type to feel squeamish around blood.

"How is he doing?" she asks.

The Lethal shrugs. "Well enough. Damned cat nearly tore his leg off. Lucky for us that that the diplomat remains on board. The boy has been able to keep the wound cleaner than a whistle, at least."

He studies Emerala across the musty hold, his expression unreadable.

"Ye know," he says. "I've been thinking—a girl like ye, stuck at sea in the company of such black hearted men—ye ought to know how to fight."

Emerala's reply is instantaneous. "I can fight."

"Nay, ye can't," the Lethal disagrees. "You're quick on your feet, there's no question there, but ye know shite about swordsmanship. You've ended up on the wrong end of a blade several times now, haven't ye?"

Emerala sniffs. "I haven't been keeping count."

"Aye, well I have. Catch." He pulls his sword from the scabbard at his waist and flips the blade in one fluid movement. The shivering knife-edge dances on his calloused palm as he holds the hilt out for Emerala to take. She does so grudgingly, surprised at the weight of it in her hands. The moment the Lethal lets go, the blade dips toward the ground.

"Keep your blade up," the murderer snaps. "Parry."

"Parry?" Emerala repeats, as the Lethal kicks a broom into the air and snaps it over his knee. He lunges effortlessly, knocking her blade out of her hand and catching her upside the head with the broken end of the sweeper. Emerala cries out in pain, rubbing at her scalp as she leans down to pick up the sword. The wooden broom comes down hard across her knuckles.

"Parry," the Lethal says, "means block. That'll be your second lesson."

"And what's my first?" Emerala asks, scowling at him as she clutches her throbbing knuckles to her chest.

"Don't drop your sword. If there was a blade in my hand, ye'd be dead already."

"Sweet as honey, strong as a lion," the parrot sings, interrupting them both. It makes a strange, guttural noise. For a moment, Emerala wonders in a panic if the creature is choking. Only after it settles back into watchful silence does Emerala realize that the bird had been trying to roar. The wooden broom catches her upside the head, sending stars spiraling across her vision.

"Ye'd do well to leave those damned birds alone," the Lethal says. "Now parry."

Emerala looks up just in time to see the broom swinging towards her face. She ducks, thrusting the blade of her sword hard against the incoming blow.

"Why?"

The Lethal swipes again. She deflects the assault, but only just. "They en't pets. Try as ye might to get them to talk, they won't say what you want them to. They'll only do their job."

"They have jobs?" Emerala asks, chancing a look at the birds. The sleeping forms look thoroughly useless behind the curving wires of their cage. The broom swipes the backs of her knees, knocking her flat on her backside. She groans, nearly losing her sword a second time.

"Aye," the Lethal says, holding out a hand to help her up. "They be messenger birds for the seven pirate lords."

"Pirate lords?" Emerala rubs at a fast forming bruise on her elbow, feeling forlorn. The Lethal grimaces at her, jabbing a blackened fingernail at the cage.

"Who's the parrot, Rogue, ye or those feathered rats? Stop repeating everything I say."

"Sorry," Emerala mutters darkly, not feeling sorry at all.

"Ah, don't be." The Lethal waves her apology away with a swipe of his hand. "How would ye know? Ye en't a girl of the sea, ye landlubber." He flashes her a toothy grin. "The pirate lords are the seven appointed men assigned to keep control of the oceans."

Emerala hesitates. "Is this one of your stories?"

"Nay, lass, this be the truth, strange as it may seem. It's an old legend, yes, but the core of it is real as you or I. Now try and hit me."

"Excuse me?" Emerala asks.

The Lethal paws his chest, holding out his arms in welcome. "Try and hit me."

"I'm holding a sword," Emerala reminds him. "Not a wooden broom."

"Try anyway."

Emerala shrugs and swings, bringing the blade singing clumsily through the air. The Lethal moves like water, dancing out of harm's way and into the shadows of the hold.

"Again," he commands. "And I'll tell ye about the pirate lords."

Emerala thrusts her blade forward a second time, again missing her mark. The Lethal moves in and out of darkness, thrusting and parrying, thrusting and parrying. Emerala never comes close to touching him. As they duel, he speaks.

"A long time ago, this world was at war, ye see. Parry. Men of the land fought one another upon the endless oceans for control of the water. He who had control, see, would be undefeatable. Faster, Rogue. Keep up. Anyhow, it turns out that man was not meant to hold the ocean in his hands. It en't possible."

He pauses and holds out his hand, catching a shaft of grey light that falls through the hatch overhead. The beams plummet through the slits of his fingers in dusty shafts of silver. "Falls right through, ye see?"

"So what happened?" Emerala asks. Captivated, she draws to a stand-still and lets the blade of the sword drop towards the ground. The Lethal flashes her a dark look.

"Well, I'm tellin' ye, if ye'd just stay quiet."

"Sorry."

"En't got to be sorry, just bite your tongue and raise your sword."

"Sorry," she repeats.

The Lethal brings down the broom hard atop her head. "Faster next time. As the legend goes, the spirits of the old world grew tired of drowned men polluting the brine. They wanted the spoils of war to remain on land, where they belonged. So they intervened."

"Sorry," Emerala interjects. "But did you say spirits?"

"Aye, spirits, Rogue. Ancient ones."

"I thought you said this was a true story, not one of your fables."

"It is a true story," the Lethal snaps. "Ye think because ye've seen some of the world that ye know all there is to know about it? There's things out there what you can't ever begin to understand. Dark things. Ancient things—swimming around in the dark just underneath this ship."

The boat lurches as it is buffeted by an incoming swell and Emerala feels the hair stand up on her arms. The Lethal lunges at her from beneath the shadows, bringing the broom sailing through the air. She sees it just in time, watching the arc of it as it sails towards her shin. She pirouettes, bringing the blade hard against the sweeper—hard enough to send a sliver of wood skittering across the floor at their feet.

"Not bad," the Lethal relents. "Not good, but not bad."

"Tell me about the spirits," Emerala says, thrusting the blade clumsily forward.

"The four oldest spirits of the earth selected seven of the most fearsome sailors on the seas, one for each great ocean upon the map. They called these men the seven pirate lords and gifted them with the tools needed to prevent another widespread war upon the seas."

"Ha'Suri knows the way!" screams the parrot. The name startles Emerala into stillness. She blinks rapidly, feeling the familiar unease—the cold caress of disquiet—creeping into her. There is a fluttering sigh from the sleeping birds and then quiet.

"Who is Ha'Suri?" she asks.

The Lethal drops his broom down at his side and studies the parrot. He does not look at Emerala. He gives no indication of having heard her speak.

"It's just," she continues, "I heard you mention the name on Caros, and the bird keeps saying it to me." She clenches her hand into a fist and subsequently loosens her fingers, shaking out the ache that resides within the palm of her hand. The air around them is thick with humidity. She shivers all the same.

"Ha'Suri is the wind woman of the north," the Lethal says simply.

"Right," Emerala says. "Is a wind woman the same as a spirit?"

"Aye. The very same. In fact, Ha'Suri of the north was the first to suggest the peace treaty.

"I've been dreaming of her, I think."

"Indeed?" A flicker of interest passes across the Lethal's face and is gone, his mask of apathy slipping back into place as quickly as it had disappeared. "What do you see?"

Emerala scrunches her nose in an effort to remember. The images slip in and out of her grasp in fleeting bursts of color. "There is a woman all in white. Her skin is as cold—like death. In her hand she wields a dagger of ice." She pauses, shivering as the memories give way to the image of the Hawk—of his sharp golden eyes watching her through the heavy snow.

The Lethal's voice wrenches her back to the present. Her ears ring with the faint memory of howling wind.

"Ye saw Ilispin, did ye?"

Emerala rubs furiously at the gooseflesh that has risen upon her forearms. She frowns at the Lethal. "Ilispin?"

"Aye. Ha'Suri bound the seven pirate lords together by bloodspell. As the story goes, she united them with Ilispin, a blade of ice forged by shadowmen in deepest winter."

"Shadowmen?" Emerala repeats. Her fingers are numb at her sides. The palm of her hand pulsates with a slow, deep ache. A sudden image of bloodsoaked snow flits through her thoughts.

The Lethal shrugs. "Another story, for another time."

"Why does the parrot keep calling out her name?"

"No clue. They be messenger birds, as I said. Perhaps the winged rat is trying to convey a message."

"Were they a gift from the wind women as well, the birds?"

"Aye, they came from the eastern wind—a spirit so old so as not to be named in human tongues. According to the legend, she breathed the gift of speech into the birds and sorted them into groups by color. Each pirate lord received seven birds. Should they be let free, they act as a summons to the other pirate lords, bidding them come to the aid of the one who set them to the skies."

"It's a call to arms," Emerala marvels, studying the sleeping birds. Their feathered chests rise and fall in unison. The largest parrot remains awake, studying her through black eyes like beads.

"Aye, so they say, but I en't sure about that," the Lethal says, glaring at the cage. "I've been on plenty of other ships where the birds stay stocked away below deck. Feathered rats, I say. The lot of 'em. En't nothing but a mess of feathers and feces everywhere, each of them louder than the rest."

"What were the other two gifts?" Emerala asks.

"Well, let's see," the Lethal muses. "Airaida of the south wind gifted the men the hot breath of the leviathan in their sails. It's said that the seven pirate lords and their ships can outrun even the finest fleet in any navy, should they need to."

"And the western wind?" Emerala asks. "What did she give?"

Something shifts in the Lethal's countenance and Emerala watches as a sadness befalls the old murderer. He appears suddenly older than his considerable years—tired. Overhead, the rain has picked up. It patters at the deck of the ship in a relentless rat-tat-tat.

"Nolane, they called her," the Lethal says. "She gave the pirate lords their ships." He picks up the broom and spins it in his hand twice before tapping it against the wooden floorboards beneath his feet. "This ship, in fact, is one of 'em. Said to be unsinkable—fashioned from the last remaining trees of the old world in the Westerlies."

He pauses, clearing his throat. His good eye finds her across the dark. The look on his face is stark, intense. Emerala thinks of Melena, and how she had mocked Lachlan the Lethal as they trudged through the jungle.

They say it is only a great fool that falls in love with an immortal woman of the wind, she had giggled, dancing away from Emerala with a wicked gleam in her eyes.

Emerala opens her mouth to speak, but the Lethal cuts her off.

"Talk as much as ye do, and your enemies are like to cut out your tongue," he snaps. "Stay on your toes, now. Parry."

Emerala sulks, narrowly dodging a blow from the broom. "We haven't finished the lesson?"

As if in answer to her question, the wooden broom comes down hard upon her knuckles. "*Parry,*" the Lethal barks.

"So," Emerala begins, dancing out of reach of the broom and thrusting her blade forward into the empty air. She groans, frustrated, and thrusts again—lunging at shadows. "Are you trying to—ouch—to tell me that *the Rebellion* is one of the original ships of the seven pirate lords?"

"Aye," the Lethal says. The broom cuffs her just below the chin. "Although it—pay attention, girl—it did not always have such a name. Its original name be of the dead speech. En't around any longer."

"Is Alexander a pirate lord, then?"

"Aye, that he be. Faster, now. You'd be dead if ye moved that slow."

"Does he know?"

"Know he's a pirate lord? I'd reckon his old man told him, aye. He's bound by blood and the death of his ancestors. It en't a fate that gets passed down lightly."

Emerala falls still, disengaging from the duel in order to nurse her steadily growing wounds. Bruises fan like purpling stains beneath her skin.

"I don't believe a word of it," she insists. "That kind of magic doesn't exist."

The Lethal spins the broom deftly, bringing it inches from Emerala's eye. He smirks as she recoils from the proximity, drawing back against the wall. "Aye, ye are correct in that, Rogue. The women of the wind have long drawn back from the eyes of men. Nolane of the western wind commanded it, years ago."

Emerala thinks again of Melena's words, and of the stricken look upon the Lethal's face when he came upon her singing in the jungle.

"You speak as though you knew her."

"Aye. I knew her as well as ye can know anyone. But that were a lifetime ago."

"You were in love with her," Emerala says. It is not a question.

"Once, ages ago when I was still a boy. A fool boy." He flashes Emerala an unexpected grin. "Ruined me, she did. Left me an old man, hardened and broken."

Emerala shudders in the sudden chill that envelops them. Outside, the rain is slowing, sapping away with it the lingering heat of the pressing day. She watches as tendrils of grey moisture rise in curls off of the floor.

"Blood red ice for diamond wars," the parrot sings again. He hops back and forth upon his wooden ledge, startling the other birds awake. They squawk unintelligibly as they flutter around their cage.

"Dinner! Dinner," one of them shouts, sending the rest of them into a cacophony of unpleasant noises. Only the first of the seven parrots remains quiet, his black eyes regarding Emerala closely. The Lethal groans, lowering his makeshift weapon.

"Messenger birds me arse," he snarls, heading over to a burlap sack that overflows with grains. "I tell ye, the only damn thing this lot is good for is eatin' all the stores."

He thrusts a cup into the sack and draws it out, trailing yellow grains in his path as he heads over to the menagerie. He barely manages to pry the door open before the largest silver parrot bursts into movement. He flutters to the forefront of the cage in a wild frenzy of flapping wings, screaming into the Lethal's face as the pirate upends the cup of grains onto the bottom of the cage. The rest of the parrots dive upon the food as the Lethal shoves the door shut.

"Saints," he snaps, flailing his arms in a harried attempt to catch the parrot. The bird circles above his head in self-satisfaction.

"Emerala the Rogue," the parrot screams. He drops down, landing on Emerala's shoulder. "Daughter of Roberts!"

Emerala freezes. The bird flutters to a standstill upon her arm. Her gaze locks upon the Lethal. He idles before her, a thoughtful frown upon his face as he studies the creature on her shoulder. Emerala's heart flutters beneath her chest as she feels the talons tighten against her skin.

"How does he know who I am?"

The Lethal shrugs, pawing at the back of his head with his free hand. "En't a clue."

"Pretty, pretty green eyes," the parrot sings. He plucks at a bit of Emerala's hair with his black beak.

Emerala frowns and attempts to wave the bird off of her shoulder. He squawks in alarm, taking flight only briefly before settling back down on her shoulder on the other side. The Lethal lets out a low chuckle at the sight of Emerala's annoyance. The parrot opens its beak and gives a satisfied squawk, hopping back and forth upon his black talons.

"Parry!" the bird shouts. "Awk, parry the blow!"

"Smart little beast," the Lethal says. In an instant, Emerala sees the broom sailing through the shadows towards her face. She pulls the sword up just in time, nearly splitting the wood in half with the force of her thrust. The bird takes off from her shoulder with an indignant screech, settling among the rafters. The Lethal laughs, shoving her back so hard that she stumbles into the wall. The blade dips low and she feels the Lethal wrench the blade from her hands. Before she can utter a protest, the blade is pressed against her throat.

"What was the first lesson, lass?"

Emerala fumes. "Don't drop the sword."

A shadow drops down from the hatch overhead, landing on the ground at the Lethal's back with a quiet thud and startling the birds into another frenzy.

"Murderer," screeches the bird from his perch in the rafters. "Copper! Copper eyes!"

The blade falls away from Emerala's throat as the Lethal is wrenched back into shadow. Emerala hears a grunt, the sound of a body colliding into the groaning wood. She peers into the shadow, her eyes struggling to adjust to the darkness. There, in the light that falls down into the hold in broken, dusky shafts of grey, stands Evander the Hawk. His cutlass is at the Lethal's throat. The old murderer peers up at him through a crinkled smile, his blind eye shut.

"What are you doing down here?" the Hawk snarls. His dark hair hangs down into his eyes, dripping rivulets of rainwater down his cheeks. The sinews of his arms are tense, his posture coiled like a snake ready to spring.

"What is wrong with you?" Emerala snaps. "He's been teaching me to fight."

The Hawk ignores her, pressing his cutlass harder against the Lethal's skin. The murderer makes no attempt to fight back—no attempt to defend himself. His good eye creases in amusement.

"I told you to stay away from her."

"Worried for her pretty little neck, are ye?"

The Hawk scoffs. "Not as worried as you should be about yours. I know what your life is worth, murderer. I know the reward for spilling your blood."

"Strange to hear ye calling it a reward. Most men would think it a curse."

The Hawk sneers. "I'm not most men."

"Nay, most men are smarter than ye, boy. I told ye what would happen if ye tried to kill me. Are ye here to call my bluff?"

The Hawk's expression darkens. His shoulders fall and he pulls back from the old man, sheathing his sword. His golden eyes are riddled with contempt. "Not yet," he mutters darkly. "But I want you to leave."

At the far side of the room, Emerala's temper finally snaps.

"Hawk," she calls. He ignores her. "Are you mad? You have *no* right—"

The Hawk cuts her off, his eyes still on the murderer before him. "Get out," he snarls. "Now." His fingers dance across the weapons holstered at his waist.

"Gladly," the Lethal says. "Before you do something you regret."

He slips out from between the wall and the Hawk, heading lithely towards the forgotten barrel of rum. He tips it over with ease, laughing to himself all the while. The liquid within sloshes against its wooden container as the cask falls back to the ground with a thud.

Evander the Hawk stands like a statue in the dwindling light, staring at the shadows where the Lethal had stood. Wetting his lower lip, he begins to whistle. The sound rolls off of the curved walls of the musty hold, reverberating in the grey silence of the expanse. The tune is familiar, and Emerala struggles to place it. At the foot of the ladder, the Lethal pauses. His face is split between the light and the dark.

"Think you've got me pegged, do ye?" he asks. The Hawk continues to whistle, angling his jaw upwards as he stares through the grates overhead. The failing light of day fills his eyes as he begins to sing.

"His fate it was set, his rights they were read, and Lethal was hung by his neck 'til dead."

The Lethal sucks in his cheeks, his good eye gaging the lanky pirate. For a moment, all of the air seems to leave the room.

And then he smiles.

"Your arrogance will ruin ye, boy."

He turns to go, heading with ease up the ladder. Emerala listens to the sound of the barrel rumbling across the deck overhead. The rain is quieter—the sounds of the rollicking waves have faded away to near silence.

Emerala rounds upon the Hawk, her skin already burning beneath the lace of her blouse.

"You—"

"Saved your life," the Hawk finishes for her.

"My life wasn't in any danger."

"No? Seems there was a sword at your throat when I arrived."

"I've already told you, he was teaching me to fight."

The Hawk's lips twitch downward. "You have no idea what he was doing."

"No idea? I'm not entirely certain how dense you think I am, but—"

"He was taunting me." The words fly out of the Hawk's lips like a reflex— unguarded, reactive. His golden eyes burn with an unfamiliar intensity.

Emerala gapes at him, incredulous. "Taunting—" she starts and stops, not comprehending. "Saynti, not everything is about you, Evander."

She moves to storm away from him, unable to stand the sight of him for one moment longer. He grabs hold of her as she passes him by, drawing her within inches of him. They are eye to eye in the grey light of the hold, each brimming with ire. His chest rises and falls beneath the loose homespun of his undershirt. The sleeves, slick with rainwater, adhere to the curvature of his arms.

"Go ahead, storm away. Hate me. But I'm keeping you safe."

"Is that what you call it?" She wrenches her wrist free of his grasp. "You're protecting me? Who from? From where I stand, everyone you've warned me about has turned out to be a better man than you."

He drops his fist, his expression contorting into something unfathomable. His golden eyes remain trained on her as she turns away from him, bristling with annoyance. Overhead, the parrot lets out a bloodcurdling shriek, dropping down from the rafters and landing with surprising grace upon Emerala's shoulder.

"Murderer!" he screams, flapping his wings against his sides.

Emerala leaves the Hawk alone in the dwindling grey of the ship's belly, her thoughts turning instead to old things—ancient things. Overhead, the stinging wind howls as it sidles against the edge of sloop. She thinks of the Lethal's story—of the four wind women of the sea. She thinks of the look upon his face at the memory of Nolane. Whether legend or otherwise, the Lethal's love for the woman had been real.

She thinks of Ha'Suri, with her hands like ice, and of Evander the Hawk, always watching, his golden eyes hovering constantly at the edge of her dreams.

I do hate him, she thinks, her mood turning petulant as the anger saps away. *I hate every piece of him.*

Somewhere within her, some soft, unspoken thing urges her to turn around. She squashes it down, bunching up her skirts within her fists and slamming her boots against the ladder with purpose as she stalks up onto the deck and into the rain.

CHAPTER 41

The Forbidden City

"WALK WITH ME. I have something I want to show you."

Nerani places her hand into Topan's outstretched palm, slow apprehension building within her as she takes in the gleam of excitement in his eyes. Behind her, she can feel Orianna drawing back.

"I'll need to head to the infirmary," she lies. "Mame Minera will start to wonder where I am if I'm away for too long."

Topan nods once, distracted. He scarcely seems to have heard Orianna at all. Nerani listens to the receding footfalls against the stone, wishing it were appropriate to call her friend back—to implore her to stay. She does not wish to be left alone with him, not now. Not when she knows the question that dances behind those pale blue eyes.

She flinches, finding herself unable to look anywhere but back at the Cairan king. He, on the other hand, watches her with an intensity that unnerves her. The light from the torches flickers across his face, casting him in soft illumination.

In spite of the damp chill of the subterranean cavern, Nerani finds herself burning. She is on fire, ablaze with questions that have no answers. The conversation she heard between Topan and Blaine replays on a loop in her mind. Her stomach is ill.

Topan turns away from her as he leads her across the narrow receiving hall. His hand tightens around her fingers, enclosing her good hand firmly within his own. His hand is strong—his palm warm. Her fingers tremble all the same.

At the far side of the room sits a dark alcove. Topan heads in that direction, drawing a torch from its sconce upon the wall. The flames drip down around them like rainwater—soft nips of orange heat extinguishing against the cool stone underfoot. Topan ducks his head beneath the low hanging doorway, ascending silently down a steep set of manmade steps.

"Watch your footing," he says over his shoulder. "The stairs are quite slick."

She can hear the slow, staccato sound of water dripping onto stone. She listens to the steady cadence, pressing her feet firmly against the damp steps under her gown. The deep navy hem drags audibly beneath her feet and she is forced to remove her good hand from Topan's grasp in order to pry the material off of the ground.

The staircase is short, and it isn't long before the pair emerges into a cavernous room. The air is colder, here. Tighter. The quivering echo of her breath slides down the clammy stone. She finds herself thinking of a tomb—cold and black—and shudders.

There is a quiet *whoosh* of air as another torch catches ablaze. Topan stands a few feet away from her, lighting the sconces on the walls. As the fire spreads, the room around them begins to glow, the firelight bringing the contents of the space to life. Nerani lets out an involuntary gasp, sitting down hard on the bottom step.

The stone walls, cramped with dripping rock formations, have been painted gold. The color catches in the flickering light, throwing gilded pools of brilliance upon the ground. Nerani sits, frozen amid the dazzling expanse, and blinks away the golden glare that blurs the edges of her vision. She cannot believe something so breathtaking could have been hidden away under the earth all this time.

"Where are we?"

Topan watches her from across the room, his silhouette cast in a dazzling gilded frame. He smiles at the sight of her bewilderment, following her gaze across the golden walls. The firelight quivers in the brass sconces. "This is the first room of the Forbidden City. It was erected during the reign of King Lionus."

Adorning the golden walls are the most masterfully woven tapestries Nerani has ever seen. Rising to her feet, she studies the intricate details of the artist's handiwork. On the tapestry closest to her she can see the familiar outline of the island of Chancey. The city is pictured from a bird's eye view. The buildings appear to glitter in the sunlight.

The sheer amount of detail steals Nerani's breath away. She moves closer to the tapestry, allowing her fingers to trace over the cresting waves upon the beach. The glossy green of the sun kissed water looks so realistic that she is surprised to feel the rough hew of woven fabric beneath her fingertips.

"Who made these?" The question falls away from her in a reverent whisper. She has the lingering sense that she is in the presence of something immortal—not to be disturbed. When she receives no immediate response, she turns to find Topan. He stands behind her, his hands clasped in the small of his back. He does not marvel over the tapestries alongside her, but instead watches Nerani's reaction. Her eyes meet his and he smiles, one cheek dimpling.

"They were made by Queen Saynti," he explains. "She wove these during her reign as queen."

"They're marvelous. I never knew she had such a profound skill."

"She did. She was known for it, in fact." He peers over her head at the woven representation of Chancey.

They stand together in quiet contemplation, each studying the tapestries that hang upon the walls. Nerani is acutely aware of his proximity to her in the firelight. She stands frozen among the artifacts of royalty and tries not to think of James. Not here. Not now, in the presence of her ancestry. Beside her, Topan clears his throat. He extends his fingers, shaking out his palms. A nervous tic, Nerani knows—she has seen him do it many a time when he thinks no one is watching.

"The tapestries are beautiful, yes," he says, a nervous edge creeping into his voice. "But I brought you down here for a reason."

She glances up at him and is at once unnerved by the intensity of his gaze.

"You and Orianna were eavesdropping, weren't you?"

Heat flushes her cheeks. "We were. I'm s—"

He cuts her off, his nerves making him jumpy. "You must have questions after what you heard."

"I do," she admits. "Although I don't think I have any right to ask them. It was wrong of me to listen in on your conversation."

"No," he disagrees. "I've keep you in the dark long enough. I've kept all of you in the dark." He pauses, scanning the tapestries that line the walls. "This room is where you'll find the answers you seek."

Nerani follows his gaze, her mind turning over what she had heard, idling in the darkened corridor outside Topan's quarters.

"You told Blaine you swore to protect my family," she says and pauses. She remembers the naked anger that had twisted Blaine's words. *Nerani the Elegant was personal.* "You swore to protect Rob and Emerala."

"I did." Topan's voice is tight. He gestures for her to follow him, heading off into the shadows of the room without a word. He pauses to lift a small, brass candelabrum from a rickety table at the center of the expanse. Holding it to a flaming sconce, he allows each candle to catch fire in turn. Firelight catches in the hollows of his cheeks, casting his features into shadow.

Holding the candelabrum before him, he heads wordlessly across the room. Nerani follows. As they reach the furthest corner of the expanse Nerani can just make out the shaded corners of another tapestry resting in the darkness. Hanging from ceiling to floor, the weaving is by far the largest of them all. As they draw nearer, their movements stir the corners of the great weaving. A musty stench—the stink of age, the reek of decay—tickles Nerani's nose.

Topan draws to a stop directly before the darkened rug, placing the candelabrum upon the ground. The tapestry is cast, suddenly, in flickering gold. The weaving that stands before Nerani is devoid of the same intricate images that made up the others. And yet, in its simplicity, it seems all the more stunning.

The colors, gold and black, are richer than any weaving she has ever seen. She stands staring at it for a long time, her gaze locked upon the rimmed yellow eyes that stare back at her without blinking. There is something noble about the stillness of the great, black face before her. Her hair rises upon her arms as she peers at the width of the jaw and the curve of the yellowed fangs.

"What is it?" Her words are whispered into the dark, as though any sort of noise might disturb the creature before her.

"That is a panther," Topan replies. His voice feels too loud in the reverent silence of the dimly lit space.

A panther. When Nerani was a child, she had heard Mame Noveli regaling the Chancians with countless stories of wildebeests that stalked the wild jungles of faraway lands. There are no panthers on the island of Chancey. The only truly wild animal she has ever seen is the occasional hunched, red fox that creeps past the city walls at dusk. Even the wild boars of the tangled forest stick to the shadows, ever eluding the sharp edge of a hunter's knife. All her life she has only ever been able to imagine what a jungle cat from Mame Noveli's stories would look like. Staring into the tapestry, she realizes that her imagination has not done the animal justice. The majestic creature woven into the tapestry before her is regal beyond words.

"He's beautiful," she whispers, running a finger down the bridge of his nose.

"He is," Topan agrees. "Wild cats are abundant upon the island of Caira. No doubt Queen Saynti would have missed the sight of them during her life in Chancey."

Nerani feels a sudden, unwanted pang in the middle of her chest. She thinks of Emerala, and how excited her cousin would have been to stumble upon this room of woven art. Her eyes flutter closed and she imagines the way Emerala's face would spill over with wonder at the sight of the panther, as black and as formidable as deepest night.

She opens her eyes, aware of the tears prickling at her lower lids. She can feel Topan's attention upon her as he studies her closely across the light of the candelabrum.

"Why are you crying?" he asks, drawing closer to her in the quiet. His hand sweeps tentatively across her face, catching a tear like dew upon his finger.

"I was thinking of Emerala," she admits. "She would have loved this room."

"Ah." Topan sighs, his gaze falling. "You asked me what I meant when I told Blaine I was sworn to protect your family."

"Yes."

He draws his hand away from her face, staring at the shivering bead of moisture that lingers upon the tip of his finger. "You are familiar, I assume, with the legend of Saynti's treasure."

"Of course. The gypsy fortune—everyone has heard the stories."

"A refresher, then," Topan says. "When King Lionus Wolham discovered the malcontent brewing among the lords at the sight of a Cairan queen upon the throne, he ordered this city built. It was to be used as a safe haven in case the tides turned against the Cairans and they were cast out from Chancey."

Nerani glances upward at the dripping ceiling of stone overhead. Somewhere in the darkness, she can hear the soft plunk of droplets hitting a surface of water. "And here we are," she whispers. "He wasn't wrong."

"No he was not," Topan assents, following her gaze. "When he built the city, he ordered a secret room built within the royal chambers—Saynti's chambers. In it he buried away the immeasurable treasure brought overseas by the Cairans when they first arrived to the Chancian shores."

Nerani nods—she knows the story. "There was a prophecy, wasn't there? A seer told King Lionus that a usurper would come along and take the throne from his lineage."

Topan's face brightens. "You know your history."

"My mother used to tell me this story when I was a child."

Topan's gaze lingers upon her face, studying the sadness he finds there as she draws her mother into to forefront of her memory. She recalls, not without difficulty, the soft tickle of her mother's breath upon her hair—of the serene sensation of being rocked to sleep within her lap. She would sing Nerani the old songs of the Cairans—ballads meant to immortalize the deeds of those who had come before them.

Fragments of a song trickle into the forefront of her mind and her eyes prickle with fresh tears.

Her voice, it falls down like the rain from the gods,
Dear, the sacred queen Saynti is urging me on
'Back to the sea where you can do no wrong,'
She says, 'back to the sea where you know you belong'.

"It was Lord Stoward that finally usurped the throne," Topan says, his voice gentle as he presses on through the ghosts that threaten to consume her. His eyes, warm and empathetic, catch upon hers in the hazy golden glow of the room. "I'm sure you know the rest of the story. After all, Rowland Stoward still sits upon the throne today."

"I do," she says. "But that was centuries ago. The world is much changed, and many of those lines have died out."

"Many of them have," he agrees. "But there was a second part to the prophecy. A part that doesn't live on in the stories told by the Mames."

Nerani hesitates, frowning. "Why would they leave anything out?"

"They were asked to do so by King Lionus." Topan holds out his hand for her to take, drawing her over to another tapestry on a nearby wall.

"There," he says, pointing. Nerani peers through the darkness to see the woven tapestry that flutters against the stone in the wake of their movements. This tapestry is simple—not at all like the intricate patterns woven painstakingly into the other rugs. The colors are plain and the stitching is rushed. It depicts a woman, tall and thin, her blue eyes staring lifelessly out from a pinched, olive face. At her back stand three men, two young and one old. The older man glares out from eyes of deepest green, his mustache curling over a sour expression. His hands are pressed against her bulging stomach.

Nerani feels unease prickling at her skin as she studies the tapestry. "This doesn't look like the tapestries done by Saynti," she says.

"That's because Saynti did not do this one. It was done by one of the Mames—rather hastily, I might add. The queen was going into labor when it was made."

Nerani studies the bulging belly again, her eyes traveling upward to stare at the vivid blue eyes of the woman in the tapestry. "This is her?" she asks, astounded. "This is Queen Saynti?"

"The very same," Topan says.

Nerani squints, leaning in closer to inspect the painting. "Who are the men in the background?"

"The older man is King Lionus, her husband. The two boys are her sons, and the rightful heirs to the Chancey throne. I'm certain you'll recall that Lord Stoward and his companions tragically slaughtered the two young princes during the famed treason that cast King Lionus and his line off of the throne."

"Yes, but I also remember that there were *only* the two sons. Queen Saynti and King Lionus didn't have a third boy."

Topan exhales sharply, the sound almost a laugh. "You are correct. They had a daughter."

"A daughter?" Nerani repeats, baffled. "But how—"

"It was foretold that a daughter would survive the sacking of the palace long before the queen was even with child. King Lionus kept his wife's pregnancy a secret. He hid her away within the farthest wings of the palace. The day of the Stoward betrayal, Queen Saynti gave birth to a daughter as her sons were slain before the throne. They sacrificed their lives to buy their mother more time."

"What happened to her?" Nerani asks, enthralled. She stares up into those endless blue eyes and feels as though the sadness in the queen's expression is enough to swallow her whole.

Topan grimaces. "You know what happened to her."

Nerani does. The story goes that the Queen was stripped of her gowns and jewels and dragged out to the square to be executed before a bloodthirsty mob of Chancians. A witch, she was called. A sorceress of the darkest order. They say Lord Stoward set her ablaze himself, and laughed while he watched her burn.

Nerani shudders at the thought. "What happened to the daughter?"

"She was stolen away under cover of night, brought to safety by the Mame that delivered her. She was raised as a commoner and married off to a Chancian man who was none the wiser. And she has been watched, all this time. All these years."

His voice is filled with implication. Nerani's eyes slide away from the stricken face of the queen, moving instead to the dark glare of the king. His green eyes are wide with fury as he holds the bulging stomach of his pregnant wife. His black curls are wild beneath his crown.

It can't be, Nerani thinks, her heart quickening within her chest. *It's impossible.* She turns to Topan. He is watching her in silence, his expression patient as he waits for her to connect the pieces that lay before her.

"What was the second part of the prophecy?" she whispers. The candles dance wildly upon an unseen breeze.

"It was foretold that King Lionus's line would be restored by the ancestors of his daughter, but only when her blood was crossed with Cairan blood and royal blood once more."

Nerani swallows. Her throat is dry. "Who is the Chancian man that the daughter married?" She asks. "What was his name?"

One corner of Topan's lips tug upward in a smile. "Edwin Roberts," he says. He pauses a moment before adding, "the great, great, great grandfather of your uncle Eliot."

"No." Nerani's knees feel weak. "It can't be possible. Does—does he know?"

"Roberts?" Topan shakes his head. "No, he hasn't any idea. But he's important—immensely so. The moment he was born, the Mames alerted the Cairan king, my predecessor. He was charged instantly with keeping your cousin alive."

Nerani's mind is spinning. She feels her vision blur in and out of focus as she struggles to process this new information. *It can't be true,* she thinks. *It can't be.*

In her efforts to put together a coherent thought, only one question rises to the surface of her mind.

"What does all of this have to do with the Cairan fortune?"

Topan's smile widens. "An excellent question," he says. He takes her hand and leads her back over to the panther that adorns the nearby wall. When he speaks, his words fall away from him in harried excitement.

"The problem with the prophecy was that it was delivered in the company of much of King Lionus's court," he says, tugging at a thick golden tassel caressing the side of the heavy tapestry.

"So Lord Stoward got wind of it," she muses. She stares as Topan pulls hard at the tassel, allowing the tapestry to curl upward in a procession of bunching fabric. She finds herself suddenly staring at a strange, oblong stone structure fitted within the wall of stone. It has been painted a violent red hue—so deep that for a moment she is convinced she is staring at dried blood. At the right of the structure sits a small hole, pitted with black. She peers at the structure, surprised to see something carved there. Snatching the candelabrum off of the floor, she maneuvers closer to the wall.

"May I?" she asks, glancing over her shoulder at Topan. He gestures for her to go ahead, his expression eager.

Leaning forward, she studies the intricate words carved into the stone.

The footsteps of the ancients lead to find
The blood-wealth of the blessed Saynti's kind.
Yet if ye seek what lies beyond the blood red stone
A treasure beyond measure that is not your own
You'll find those ancient footsteps are erased,
For dead men's footsteps in the sand cannot be traced.

Nerani leans back with a shiver, gooseflesh rising upon her arms.

"This is where it is," she says.

Topan makes a quiet grumble of assent, moving to stand close at her side. His finger brushes hers in the darkness. "Guarded always by the black panther of Caira," he says. He turns to face her, his eyes glittering like jewels in the darkness. "It was hidden here when the prophecy was made. Only one key exists to open the door."

There is an edge in his voice that causes her to hesitate. She places the candelabrum back upon the floor. "Where is the key?"

"Gone," he says simply. "When Roberts was born the Mames began to worry that King Stoward would get wind of his existence. One half of the prophecy had been fulfilled, after all. Saynti's line had borne another Cairan. Rowland's ancestors never knew where the daughter of Saynti had gone, and yet they were always watching—always prepared. They, too, have passed the prophecy down between them over the years. You remember my predecessor, Ubeldo?"

Nerani nods, feeling uneasy. The old king had killed himself—that's what her mother had told her. She remembers the day so clearly—perhaps because it had happened the day before her mother and father were slaughtered by Guardians. Her stomach twists at the recollection and she swallows hard. She has worked hard all her life to keep the ghosts at bay. She will not allow them to come rushing back—not now. Not here, beneath the shadows of kings.

"He viewed his death as his duty," Topan says solemnly. "He died in order to take the Cairans' darkest secret with him to his grave."

"And what secret was that? The existence of my cousins?"

"No. The location of the key." Topan pauses, studying her. "I told you the prophecy would be fulfilled when Saynti's bloodline joined together Cairan and royal blood once more. Your cousins are Cairan, that is for certain, but I think you will agree that they are not royal."

Nerani nods, eying the red stone to her right.

"For a long time, my predecessors watched for a marriage between bloodlines. Even I assumed for a time that perhaps Emerala would wed one of the Stoward princes. But they were wrong. I was wrong. It wasn't a marriage that would restore the throne to Saynti's line. It was a brotherhood."

"Brotherhood?" Nerani asks, confused.

"How well did you know your uncle, Eliot Roberts?"

"Very little," Nerani admits.

"I'd imagine so. He disappeared shortly after your name day, if I'm not mistaken."

Nerani nods, remembering the bitter cold that crept around the front door the day her aunt had moved in with Roberts and Emerala in tow.

He's gone for good this time, her aunt told her sister. *I won't waste another tear.*

"Your uncle has another son," Topan says, startling Nerani out of her reverie. She exhales sharply, the pain of her mother's memory always like reopening a wound.

"Eliot?" Her voice has grown hoarse.

"Yes," Topan says, gripping her arms firmly—steadying her. She is grateful for his support. She didn't realize how faint she has grown beneath the pressing dark of the flickering room. "Prince Peterson Stoward."

Nerani's eyes flutter closed for a moment as she considers this. "No," she breathes. "Impossible."

She recalls a fight she had heard, once, between her mother and her aunt. The women had been up late arguing long after they thought the children had gone on to bed. Nerani had lain awake, sandwiched between the snoring Roberts and the mumbling Emerala, fighting back tears and listening to the rising voices outside the bedroom.

Are you sure it's his, the boy? demanded her mother.

I'm not a fool, her aunt snapped. *You wait until he's old enough. If Rob and Emerala are any indication, the boy will look just like the man.*

"How?" Nerani asks.

"The story goes that Eliot Roberts and the late Queen Victoria carried out a sordid affair while he was drafted to oversee the construction of King Rowland's labyrinth," Topan explains. "Queen Victoria died in labor delivering the son of Eliot Roberts."

"And the Roberts line—the line of Saynti's heirs—was crossed with Cairan blood and royal blood," Nerani whispers.

Topan nods. "Knowing that it wouldn't be long before King Stoward made the connection himself, Ubeldo entrusted the key to the Cairan fortune to the one man that would be desperate enough to take it far away."

"Eliot Roberts?"

"None other," Topan says. "I, in turn, was left with the rather rigorous task of keeping the remaining Roberts children alive."

He pauses, pawing at the back of his neck. "It's been a challenging task. Emerala the Rogue has not made it easy."

Nerani feels suddenly dizzy. The floor spins beneath her feet and she wishes there were somewhere to sit down. It's all too much to take in—too much to process.

"You'll go to war for them," she says.

The expression on Topan's face is grim. "If it comes to that, then yes. One way or another, a Roberts must take the throne."

A thought occurs to her then, as she stands before him in the dark.

"What about me?" Her voice is quiet. "I'm not a Roberts."

Topan purses his lips, a nervous energy rippling through him. "No," he says carefully. "You're not."

"Why keep me safe?"

A frown tugs at his lips. "Is it really that big of a mystery to you, Nerani?" He steps closer to her beneath the shadows, setting the firelight to dancing. "You were listening in on my conversation. I'm certain you heard every word Blaine said. I believe he called me transparent. Rescuing you—keeping you safe—that's personal. I've been called to keep Emerala and Roberts alive, and to return the line of Saynti to the throne. That you happened to be there along the way has been both the best possible outcome and the worst possible distraction."

Nerani swallows, saying nothing. Before her, Topan is reaching into the inner pocket of his jacket. She watches as he fumbles with the material. Her blood runs cold within her veins. The room around her seems to fall away, leaving only the two of them among the pressing dark.

"There are some treasures that never made it into the collection that lies beyond the door," he says. From within his coat he draws a glittering diamond necklace. Nerani stifles a gasp as it catches the light from the candelabrum, sending fragmented shards of brilliance dancing across the dark stone. The necklace is made up of a string of tiny, dazzling rhombuses that drop down into a graceful diamond droplet. Cut to perfection, the stone is more magnificent than any piece of jewelry Nerani has ever seen. She gapes in silence, hardly caring that her mouth has fall fallen open.

Topan is tense as he stands before her in the wavering light. "This belonged to Queen Saynti. It was recovered by one of my Listeners while scourging the palace."

Nerani blinks several times in succession, her lips snapping shut. Her nerves pulse beneath her skin—flutter in her stomach. "It's stunning."

"It is," he agrees. Hesitance dances behind his eyes and he says, "It would be even more so if you were to wear it." He moves forward, holding it out as though to fasten it about her neck. The diamonds dance before her in the candlelight and she feels her knees go weak.

"You must know by now that I have asked Roberts for your hand in marriage, and he has given me his blessing," he says, stumbling slightly over his words. The diamond falls against her collarbone. He brushes her hair aside, moving to fasten the clasp at the back of her neck. Her skin bristles at his touch. The jewel is weighted against her throat. She fights the sudden urge to draw back from him—to pull away. Her eyes catch upon the gaze of Queen Saynti, her eyes stitched with thread of deepest blue. The pinched, dour face stares lifelessly at her across the shadows.

She thinks suddenly, impractically, of James Byron. His face flashes into her mind like a candle coming alive. His voice sears across her thoughts and she clutches to it, her memory unrelenting.

I think I've loved you from the moment I met you.

A sob rises unbidden to her throat and she swallows it, her face burning. She thinks of Orianna's warning, of the dire premonition she'd made in the kitchens all those days ago. *She'll find nothing but death in the arms of a Guardian.* What kind of fool is she, to have carried on as she has?

They are on the brink of war. They are teetering on the edge of something big—bigger than her, bigger than James, bigger than stolen moments in an old storeroom.

A seat of power is being handed to you, Orianna said. *All you have to do is reach out and take it.*

Nerani thinks of Emerala. What would her cousin say, she wonders, if she were here? What would she think of what was happening?

It's too much, she thinks wildly. *It's too much for me.*

Topan is standing directly before her, now, his hands entwined around her fingers. Nerani feels as though the air has been cut off from her lungs. She presses her lips together and waits.

"Nerani, I have failed you in so many ways," the Cairan king says, his gaze subdued. "I've lost Emerala, and for that I am sorry. It was my job to protect her—to keep her safe. I would be honored if you would allow me to protect you from this day forward, not as your king, but as your husband."

Nerani's lips part, allowing a shaky breath to escape from between them. The darkness claws at her skin, threatening to consume her. She can feel the eyes of the king and the queen looming in the shadows, their faces beseeching. What can she say, beneath the gaze of the kings? How can she turn her back on her ancestry?

She has no future with James Byron. She cannot.

But with Topan—

Her fingers shake and she watches as Topan draws them to his chest, his eyes imploring as he searches her face.

"Nerani the Elegant," he whispers. "Would you give me the honor of being my bride?"

Nerani's heart is breaking into pieces, shattering under the weight of her grief. The significance of the evening does not escape her. Topan has shared with her his greatest secret. The fate of the Cairans is bigger than all of them, now. This decision is greater than all of them. She cannot go back. She cannot dwell on fleeting moments in the rain with General James Byron.

The prophecy will be fulfilled, she thinks. *And I will be left behind.*

"I will," she says. "I would be honored to be your queen."

CHAPTER 42

Chancey

ROWLAND STOWARD LOBS a half empty glass of claret at the gilded wall before him, watching as the corrugated crystal shatters to the floor with a sigh. The spilt wine slithers down the wall in rivulets of crimson. Overhead, the deep hazel eyes of his late wife regard him in wordless antipathy. She stares down from her canvas portrait, hands folded primly in the rich violet satin of her lap, and refuses to acknowledge his despair.

"Why?" he shouts, his voice hoarse. The saturated wool of his undershirt clings to his chest, itching at his skin. "Why have you forsaken me?"

He chokes back a sob, swallowing his grief in a throaty hiccup. He is not drunk—not yet—but he is well on his way to becoming so.

And he is well within his rights, if he dares to say so himself. All his life, he knew this day would come. He suspected. His father before him had borne the weight of the prophecy—the curse of the Stowards. So, too, had his father's father. The cursed divination—that which foretold the fall of the Stoward line—had hounded his ancestors for a near century. And yet each king came and went from this world with nary a threat made toward their seat upon the Chancian throne.

He was only a young boy when he was told what was to come. Even then, he had known it would be him. The paranoia took root within his spirit, gripping his spine like a vise and twisting, hard—a little bit each year—until his mind was ground to mush and crawling with maggoty fear.

It would be him; he knew it would be him.

And yet he could not have fathomed that the betrayal would come at so great a cost.

Eliot Roberts.

402

The name flicks across his mind like a flame, licking at the back of his eyes and setting his vision to stinging.

Eliot Roberts had impressed him, initially. The young man showed great promise, even at his age. He was a mastermind—an artist. There was no question that he should be hired to design and build Rowland's great, stone labyrinth.

And yet it would be Eliot Roberts that would bring his empire crashing down around him. Curse him to the Dark Below for being so blind. Rowland had thrown open the doors and invited the snake into his halls. He had welcomed him at his table, had entertained him beneath the glittering halls.

He glares up into the unblinking eyes of Queen Victoria and feels the putrefaction of his heart decay still more. His throat tightens with rage, his hands tightening into fists at his sides.

He had not seen it—not at first. How was he to suspect that his wife's disloyalty was in fact only the fulfillment of an ancient prophecy? He was too blinded by heartbreak to see what her betrayal had set into motion.

It was not until the girl was delivered unto him—not until Emerala the Rogue had been dragged before him at her execution—that he realized the significance of the Queen's infidelity. He had taken one look at her face—at those green eyes so like the eyes so like Eliot Roberts's—and his heart had broken still further.

The line will be restored when the blood of Saynti is crossed with Cairan blood and royal blood.

He shudders at the recollection of the prophecy—of the words repeated to him by his father time and time again when he was a boy. The Stowards took every possible measure to maintain the purity of their line. The sons of kings married only the daughters of presiding lords within the court. Often marrying close cousins, the Stoward men had done their due diligence to guarantee that tainted blood—Saynti's blood—did not infiltrate their inheritance.

And yet Emerala the Rogue had brought the confidence of the Stoward line shattering down around Rowland's ears. His search for the missing Eliot Roberts had become something of an obsession following the death of his wife. The man had disappeared upon the wind, leaving no trace of his ever having existed. Rowland knew his face better than any—had etched the memory of him into his mind.

There could be no question that Emerala the Rogue was the man's daughter. The resemblance was uncanny.

Rowland slides down upon the floor, his back resting against the wrought iron posts at the foot of his great bed. His right hand falls into a sticking pool of wine, but he makes no effort to remove it. He stares at the slippers on his feet, his breathing laborious.

The boy is the child of Eliot, too. Of that there can be no question. He knew the moment the boy began to walk and talk that the small, dark haired creature was not his. The resemblance to his father—his real father—was too great.

It came from the depth of the Dark Below, he thinks, picturing the eyes like emeralds peeking out from those wild, black curls. *And here it remains to taunt me. To remind me of my failures.*

And so it is brother and sister, he muses—not for the first time, *and not husband and wife.*

He should have killed the boy, should have arranged for a horrible accident to suddenly befall the babe when it was asleep in its crib. He should have, and yet he did not. He could not bring himself to destroy his last possible connection to her—to Victoria. His greatest love, even still.

"You have undone me," he says, pointing a wine stained finger at the portrait upon the wall. Her gaze follows him wordlessly to his slouched position upon the floor. "I hope you're happy."

Heat curls suddenly beneath the collar of his undershirt. He feels the flesh of his skin grow thick with sweat as his cheeks redden. *It's not over,* a voice deep within him snarls. *Not yet.* He can right his wrongs—he can hold the throne. The prophecy does not have to come true. What good are the words of a wretched old gypsy woman? They are nothing. They see nothing. Their powers are dark and evil, and the gods have never sided with those that elicit the old magics.

Only I am worthy of the throne, he thinks.

He will find the Forbidden City. If he controls the fabled wealth of the wretched Cairan queen, he will hold the city within his hands.

And then—then...

His thoughts trail off into silence. He thinks of his son—of Frederick Stoward, his rightful heir. His thoughts jumble into one another as he scrambles to call the memory of his eldest—his only—son into his mind.

Cold and hard and dead, he thinks. *Dead at the bottom of the sea, my son is.* A face of flaking marble passes through his vision in fleeting shades of white. He feels suddenly nauseous. He squashes the protestations that rise from a small, buried voice in the recesses of his mind.

Dead. Frederick is dead.

He does not like to think of such things. Crossing himself, he thinks, instead, of the path that lies ahead. He will waste no more time looking back, mulling over the ghosts of his greatest mistakes.

Forward, he commands himself. *Ever forward.*

Months have gone by, and not a single result has come from his endless hunt for the Forbidden City. Something will need to change.

It's there, he thinks. *It has to be there.* He rubs vigorously at his temple, pushing at the skin by his brow with his thumbs. He massages in a slow, circular motion, his mind spinning.

There is a knock at the door, and he nearly jumps out of his skin.

"Who is it?" His thumbs drop away from his temples as he pushes himself back onto his feet. His slippers whisper against the marble floor underfoot. He watches as one of the double doors falls away from the strike plate with a subdued click. The faces of two nameless Guardians—each the same golden hue as the other—come into view.

"Your Majesty," says one, inclining his head.

"Speak," Rowland snaps, irritated at the intrusion.

"You have visitors, your Grace."

"Visitors?"

The Guardian nods, keeping his eyes averted towards the floor below. "General Byron is here, your Majesty. He brings with him your youngest son, Peterson."

Rowland feels himself bristle with annoyance at the mention of the boy's name. He glowers darkly at the Guardians for a moment before responding.

"Send General Byron in," he barks.

The Guardians hesitate, eyeing one another across the shadow of the entryway. "And the prince?" asks the second Guardian, returning his gaze to somewhere just above Rowland's naval.

Rowland harrumphs loudly, waving his hand in a show of dismissal. "The boy can wait in the hallway."

The two Guardians disappear without a further word, dipping into low bows as they back out of the opening. An identical flicker of gold replaces them as General James Byron sweeps into the room through the opening. He, too, drops into a bow, straightening quicker than the inferior soldiers that came before him.

"Your Majesty." General Byron's expression is serene. Respectful. "I'm sorry to have disturbed you."

"Not at all, not at all."

"I've come to speak with you about your son."

Rowland feels that familiar heat prickling at the nape of his neck. He scowls.

"My son is dead."

General Byron pauses, his mouth hanging slightly open. Something indiscernible passes across his gaze. At his back, the door to the hallway remains ajar. The creeping shadows that spill in through the opening make Rowland's skin crawl.

"I meant to speak with you about your youngest son, your Majesty," General Byron reminds him. His voice is patient. Rowland feels his scowl deepening, stretching the flesh around his mouth.

"What trouble has the cretin gotten into now?"

"Your son—" General Byron begins again, and the words rip into Rowland's chest like a knife. He holds up a hand for silence. He can feel the anger coursing through his veins, setting his nerves to trembling.

"Dear James," he says, his voice seeping out through clenched teeth. "The boy outside those doors is not, and will never be my son. I appreciate if you refrain from referring to him as such."

The shadows leech out of the floor as the heavy door falls shut. From behind the great gilded frame comes the muffled patter of footfalls receding quickly upon the marble floor of the hallway.

Before him, General Byron's face is dark. His brows draw low over stony eyes.

"You were saying?"

"Nothing, your Grace," General Byron says. He clasps his hands at the small of his back, the golden fabric of his uniform creasing at the elbows.

"You mentioned you had news of the boy," Rowland reminds him, feeling agitated.

"I must have misspoken," he smiles. "I simply came by to tell you that I will be conducting a mounted sweep of the farms during my shift tomorrow evening. Perhaps one of the field workers has some clue as to the whereabouts of the Forbidden City. Since my task will take me outside of the city walls for a considerable amount of time, I'll be leaving the city patrol in Corporal Anderson's capable hands."

"Ah." A smile breaks out across his face for the first time all night. "I admire your initiative, James. I fear the rest of my men are slipping. They have failed to be properly motivated to find the Cairans."

General Byron nods, his face unreadable. "I am certainly motivated, your Majesty."

Rowland thinks of the whipping General Byron had received upon the polished floor of the great hall. He had remained stoic and silent beneath the cracking whip—a shining, gold paradigm of strength.

His silence was—to Rowland—treacherous.

"Excellent, excellent. Perhaps you can rouse the rest of your men into a similar frenzy. We must be like dogs on the hunt, dear James. All we need is a whiff and we've got them. One whiff, and we can flush them out of their fox holes like the creeping beasts they are."

"Of course, your Grace."

A heavy silence fills the room. If it were any thicker, Rowland would choke upon it. General Byron's shoulders are stiff. Discomfort flickers through his eyes, leaving as quickly as it came. The sight is unsettling to Rowland. Disquieting. The soldier—his loyal protégé—clears his throat.

"If I may take my leave of you, now, I'd prefer to head to the stables and make my arrangements sooner rather than later."

"But of course," Rowland says. "You are dismissed."

He peers at Guardian as he dips into a bow, scrutinizing the golden figure for cracks—fissures in that stony countenance he wears like armor.

He is hiding something, Rowland thinks. He waits, brooding silently, until he hears the sound of General Byron's footsteps fade away upon the echoing marble.

"Guard!" he shouts, his voice hoarse. The door opens and a blinking, indiscernible face appears in the shadowed space.

"Yes, your Majesty?"

"What is your name?"

"My name?"

"Yes, soldier—your name. You do *know* your name, do you not?"

"It's—it's Private Masters, your Grace. Joseph Masters."

"Private Masters, it would appear that General Byron is embarking on a journey tomorrow evening." Rowland plucks idly at a hangnail on his left thumb. He feels the lifeless eyes of his wife studying him from her permanent place upon the wall. He ignores her, his skin itching.

"Oh," Private Masters says, stumbling slightly as he fishes for something to say in response. "Where is he going?"

Rowland sneers. "An excellent question, that."

He thinks of the Forbidden City, and of the treasures just outside his reach. He thinks of his wife, and the vow she made him before his court— he recoils from her ghost as he remembers how quickly that vow was broken.

The infidelity of his wife—the illegitimacy of his false heir—it is enough to bring him to his knees.

He thinks, at last, of the intensity that had blazed in General Byron's eyes as he succumbed to the lashes upon his back.

It is possible, Rowland thinks, *for loyalties to change.*

"I want you to follow him," he says.

CHAPTER 43

The Rebellion

"WHERE?"

Alexander sputters, choking on his drink as the word flies unbidden from his lips. The rum scorches his throat as it slides down his windpipe and he coughs loudly, pounding his chest with his fist. Before him, Derek studies him beneath drooping brows. His gaze, normally carefree, is serious.

"You heard me." He clasps his hands behind his back and waits as the coughing subsides to a whistling wheeze.

Alexander clears his throat, the taste of rum still stinging the back of his tongue.

"Yes, I heard you quite well, in fact. You want the *Rebellion* to point her sails east."

Derek juts out his lower lip and nods amicably, clearing feeling as though such a request is perfectly reasonable. Alexander takes another sip of rum as he considers the diplomat's suggestion. He takes care to swallow slowly, wiping the lingering alcohol from his upper lip with the back of his sleeve. At the far side of his desk, Derek remains silent and watchful.

Outside his quarters, the rain patters relentlessly at the deck of the ship. Beyond the soiled panes of the windows the brute wind drives the watery torrents sideways against the resolute wooden hull. The effect of the sound, coupled with the churning of the white, frothy waves below, makes Alexander feel as though he is trapped within a drum. Hollow—that's how he feels. The numbness of his chest reverberates against the echoes of the rolling thunder, and he feels his leg pulsate with the dull ache of his injury.

"There is nothing to the east but Chancey," he says, staring past Derek and out into the endless, grey ocean.

409

"Chancey is exactly where we need to set sail."

At that, Alexander lets out a laugh. The sound is snatched too quickly into silence as his hand curls into a fist on the desk between them. "I don't intend to return to Chancey."

"Why not?"

"There's nothing there for me." He leans back against the knobbed wood of his polished oak chair, listening to the creaking of joints beneath his weight. His leg protests as he stretches it out across the floor.

His eyes follow Derek as he glances down at the dark, wooden container upon the desk between them. The box is closed, but Alexander can feel the looming presence of the object beneath the lid. He thinks of the words inscribed on the folded parchment within, and a chill creeps down his spine.

"You know as well as I do that the answer to this newest riddle lies in Chancey, Alex," Derek says. His voice is quiet. Alexander drains the dregs of his mug, relishing in the slow burn of alcohol that takes root in his chest. His skin prickles with the curling warmth of drink. He sets the mug down hard upon the desk, letting the spherical bottom obscure the small outline of Chancey upon the map below.

"Perhaps I didn't make it clear to you what happened the last time I visited Chancey," he says. He thinks, unexpectedly, of the lifeless head that the mounted Guardian—the notorious Corporal Anderson, if he remembers correctly—had held aloft the night of the ambush.

There is no leniency for piracy in Chancey, he thinks.

Across the desk, a knowing smile teases at one corner of Derek's mouth. "You've regaled me with the story of your escapades, true enough."

Alexander clicks his tongue, rapping his knuckles across the splintering grain of his desk. "Then you'll remember that there's bound to be a price on my head. There's nothing there for me but a trip to the gallows."

"If you're lucky," Derek says, his face splitting into a grin. Alexander scowls back at him. "I've never known you to shy away from danger."

"Maybe not," Alexander relents. "But I'll be damned if I lead my crew to the gallows with me. They're getting tired of following me to the ends of the earth without anything to show for it. If I keep this up, they'll mutiny." He lifts up his arms to interlock his fingers behind his head. His leg aches in protest at the movement and he frowns down at his trousers. He can feel Derek scrutinizing him through narrowed eyes, and he does his level best to ignore him.

"It's not them," Derek says.

"Sorry?"

"This has nothing to do with your crew. You know as well as I that the answer lies in Chancey—it would take a fool to think otherwise. It's her. You don't want to take Emerala the Rogue back to Rowland Stoward."

Alexander bristles slightly, wincing at the pain in his leg. "This has nothing to do with the Rogue."

"On the contrary, friend," Derek disagrees. "It has everything to do with her. You may be tried and hung as a pirate, but the girl has a far worse fate in store for evading the clutches of the king, does she not?"

Alexander is silent. At the far side of the room, the door to the quarters swings open with a groan. The sound of the rain increases to a thundering volume as the figure in the doorway steps inside. The heady scent of rainwater tickles his nose. The air that wafts in through the opening quivers with electricity.

At the sight of the visitor, Alexander jumps to his feet. His leg immediately gives an angry throb in retaliation. He favors the injured limb, leaning instead upon his good leg as he flashes a smile at Emerala the Rogue. She stands framed in the door, her gown mottled with rainwater. Her dripping curls cling to her face. She pushes them away absently as she sashays further into the room. The door sweeps shut behind her with another low groan. Upon her shoulder perches a silver parrot.

"Cold," he squawks in irritation. "Wet."

"No one forced you to come," Emerala grumbles angrily at the bird.

Amusement floods Alexander at the sight of the creature clinging to the saturated fabric of her gown. "What are you doing with my parrot?"

"I can't get rid of him," Emerala snaps.

"Emerala the Rogue," sings the parrot. "Pretty, pretty girl."

"Rogue," Derek says politely, inclining his head in Emerala's direction. She blinks at him through owl eyes, but otherwise remains silent. "I'm afraid that Captain Mathew and I were in the middle of a conversation when you walked in."

Emerala gives a light shrug. The parrot shakes his feathers, his beak clattering audibly. "You can continue," she says, drawing closer and dropping carelessly onto the edge of Alexander's desk. He can smell the sharp sting of salt on her skin from this proximity and he studies the profile of her pointed face as her eyes fall upon the dark box on his desk. Her fingers tense visibly, her nails rustling one corner of the map.

Derek sniffs, visibly perturbed by the gypsy's appearance. "You'll understand, of course, that we were discussing matters that don't concern you."

At Derek's words, Emerala meets his gaze head on, staring at him from the top of her upturned nose. "I think they do, actually. I heard my name mentioned more than once before I came through the door."

Derek's smile curdles slightly. "Eavesdropping, were we?"

Alexander cuts into the conversation before Emerala can speak again, knowing that her sharp tongue will only further incite the temper that broils beneath the gentleman's collar.

"She's welcome to stay, Derek. I sent for her, earlier."

He cringes inwardly at the look of impertinence that Emerala flashes in Derek's direction.

"Old bones, new bones, no bones," the parrot sings. He watches Derek sideways through watery black eyes. Derek ignores the bird, running his long fingers through his golden hair. The skin of his nose, normally fair, has grown red and peeled from exposure to the sun.

"I'll take my leave of you, then," Derek relents at last, eyeing Alexander over the top of Emerala's head. "I would prefer to continue our conversation at another time. Emerala." He inclines his head in her direction by way of farewell. She watches him through eyes like jewels and says nothing.

"Alex." He nods to Alexander, his gaze thick with implication. He turns to go, pulling open the groaning door and allowing the silver rain momentary reprieve from its thundering upon the wood. He pauses before exiting, turning back to face them. His grey coat is already stippled with rainwater.

"This storm will blow over, friend. When the sails are hoisted once again, you'll need to choose a direction. I trust you will make the right decision when the time comes. It would be foolish to come this far only to allow emotion to cloud your judgment at the close."

"Thank you, Derek," Alexander says, punctuating his words with a tone of finality. Derek smiles at that, shooting a wink over his shoulder at Emerala. And then he is gone, the door groaning shut behind him as thunder tumbles across the sky.

"I've chanced my mind," Emerala says when he is gone. "I don't think I like him."

Alexander lowers himself back into his chair with a muffled grunt. "He's a good friend, Emerala." Leaning down, he massages his leg. He is aware of Emerala's eyes upon him, but she makes no comment.

"Well, he doesn't like me."

"He just doesn't know what to make of you," Alexander says, and immediately wishes he had not. The look Emerala shoots him is chilling.

"What does that mean?"

Alexander chews his lip, choosing his next words carefully. "You're not like many of the women a man of Derek's stature has come to know in his lifetime."

"You mean I'm not Katherine Montclay?" she asks wryly. On her shoulder, the parrot tugs at a dripping ringlet of hair. She does her best to ignore him.

Alexander laughs. "You most certainly are not. Although if you were, I'm certain you'd be a good deal more pleasurable to be around, and not as much work for me. I've had to save you from the clutches of death three times now."

Emerala glares at him, but there is the hint of a smile in her emerald eyes. "Have you?" She leans forward over his desk and he is suddenly granted an alarming view of the slope of her bosoms peeking out from her laced corset. He clears his throat, averting his eyes. "I believe two of those times I was only put in such dangerous situations because you and the Hawk were playing roulette with my life. Anyway, you've needed me more than once. So, really, I'm an invaluable asset."

"Is that so?"

"It is." She grins wickedly, her eyes glittering. "I'd like to see Katherine Montclay outrun those thugs at the Frost Forts."

"Old bones, new bones, no bones," the parrot screams into her ear. Alexander stifles a laugh as she winces, swatting at the bird with both hands.

"Go away for a moment," she snaps, looking surprised when the bird obeys. The silver parrot flaps across the room, setting the papers on Alexander's desk to fluttering in his wake. He settles awkwardly on the brass knob atop a dusty, old globe in the corner.

"He's taken a liking to you, I see."

"Unfortunately," Emerala huffs, staring darkly at the silver parrot.

"Avast, Salty!" The parrot's scream is piercing. He flaps his wings, watching them with alarming intensity.

"It's strange," Alexander says, considering. "We all thought he would die after my father passed on. The damned bird used to follow my father everywhere he went. When the old man died, the parrot lay still for days at the bottom of the cage. He refused to eat. He never warmed up to me, like he was meant to. He's supposed to be a familiar of some sort, I've been told."

Emerala's face screws into confusion. "A familiar?"

He nods. "In the old magics, those who possessed abilities were also often gifted a spirited animal of some sort to attend to them. You saw a familiar on Caira, in fact."

Emerala's eyes brighten in realization. "Marvala, the raven," she says, and frowns. Her brows draw together in recollection. "It attacked me in the maze."

"At Melena's orders, no doubt."

Doubt crosses Emerala's face. "I never took you for the kind of man to believe in the old magics."

Alexander shrugs. "When you've been at sea as long as I have, it becomes impossible not to accept that there are things in this world we will never fully understand. There are darker powers at work than you and I can possibly comprehend."

Emerala shoots a dubious look at the silver parrot. "And that *thing* is part of those darker, ancient powers?"

"So I've been told," Alexander muses, following her gaze. "Although it was me he was meant to form a connection with, not you. The largest of the flock on each ship is supposed to bond with each new captain."

"But he doesn't like you," Emerala notes, watching as the parrot glares at Alexander from his perch.

"He most certainly does not. He's done quite a bit of damage with that beak. I gave up trying to make friends with him a long time ago."

"Avast, Salty!" the bird screams again, puffing out his chest.

"He keeps repeating that," Emerala says, disgusted. Alexander is surprised by the sudden, sharp memory of his father that comes swarming to the forefront of his mind. He inhales deeply, pushing his chair back from the desk. The wooden legs scrape against the ground.

"That would be my father's doing," he explains. "My father used to call him Old Salt. Salty—to be exact. So he has a name, if you were wondering."

"Captain Salty," shouts the bird, shooting an admonishing gaze in their direction.

Alexander smirks at the animal and raises a finger to the brim of his cap. "Apologies."

"Old bones, new bones, no bones," sings the parrot again.

Alexander frowns. The words evoke a strange sense of worry within his gut. He thinks of the bones of Captain Jameson rotting in the gibbet back on the island of Caira and gives an involuntary shudder.

Before him, Emerala is openly ogling the box upon his desk. He can see the intensity of the unasked questions that lie just behind her eyes. Her hair is drying quickly in the sticking heat of his quarters. Moisture rises in visible tendrils of grey from her glistening shoulders as her black curls bounce back to their usual weightless ringlets. Outside, the rain still patters tirelessly against the deck but the thunder has grown distant. It is nothing but a rumbling whisper, now—the silvery flashes of lightening only a dull speck of white upon the grey horizon.

"You're wondering what's inside the box," he says, studying the slope of her pointed nose.

"Yes," she admits. She does not look at him. The index finger of her right hand gives an instinctive twitch.

"Open it."

Her gaze flickers towards him at that, her green eyes wide. "Are you sure?"

He flashes her a smile, thinking of Derek. *We must set sail to Chancey, Alexander. There are no other options. Surely, you can see that.*

"Of course," he says. "I need your help. There's a riddle inside, it seems. I'm not enough of a historian to be certain of its meaning."

Her lips twist with doubt at that, her brows drawing together as she studies him closely. "If you don't know what it means, then I don't know how you expect me to know. You might not be a historian, but you're far more well-traveled than I."

"Maybe so." He twists his fingers together in his lap, ignoring the nagging ache of his leg. "Open it and see."

She does so, removing the heavy lid of the box with careful fingers. The musty smell of damp velvet spills out across the desk. She moves cautiously, reaching inside and pulling out the small, rolled bit of parchment that rests near the top of the container. Fingering it within her hands, she looks at him quizzically.

"Go ahead," he prompts her, his nerves buzzing with anticipation. He is no historian—that much is true. Neither is Derek. But Emerala—if Chancey is the answer to the riddle, she will certainly know.

When the sails are hoisted once again, you will need to choose a direction, that's what Derek told him. His companion is certain the direction is east—certain that they must return to Chancey. If he is correct, the welcome that will await the *Rebellion* upon the Chancian shores will certainly be fatal. The Hawk left several elite officers of the Golden Guard dead following the ambush—General Byron and his soldiers will not have forgotten.

Emerala unrolls the parchment gingerly and grasps the crumbling edges between the thumb and forefinger of each hand. He watches as her eyes slide back and forth across the neat, curling words upon the page. Her breathing fades into silence. Her bosoms cease to rise and fall beneath her bodice.

"Read it aloud," he instructs, watching her.

She does so, the words like molasses at her lips. "The footsteps of the ancients lead to find the blood wealth of the blessed Saynti's kind. Yet if ye seek what lies beyond the blood red stone, a treasure beyond measure that is not your own you'll find those ancient footsteps are erased," she pauses, glancing up from the page. Her face has drained of color. Her eyes find his across the desk and she holds his gaze. "...for dead men's footsteps in the sand cannot be traced."

He allows the silence to settle between them as Emerala returns to staring at the parchment. Her lips move silently as she rereads the carefully inscribed words upon the page.

"Is that it?" she asks at last, the volume of her voice startling him slightly. Salty flutters his wings in agitation.

"No bones on a dead man," he screams.

Emerala ignores the bird and jabs a finger at the parchment. "What is this?" she asks hotly. "What does it mean?" Her green eyes blaze in his direction.

"I was hoping you could tell me that," Alexander says.

"I've never seen it before, obviously."

"Is it Chancian?" he asks her, leaning forward and bringing his elbows to rest upon the desk. His leg groans in time with the creaking chair beneath him. "Derek mentioned that the name Saynti is Chancian."

"The name Saynti is Cairan," Emerala snaps. She rolls the parchment quickly and thrusts it in Alexander's direction. "She was the only Cairan to ever sit on the Chancian throne. That was nearly a hundred years ago."

"I've never heard of her," Alexander says honestly, taking the parchment and laying it aside. "At least, not until I opened this box."

Emerala shrugs, her gaze dark. "I'm not surprised. Her existence was kept quiet by the false king that took her throne. The usurper thought it an embarrassment that tainted blood had been in the palace."

She spits out the last sentence like poison, clearly offended.

After a moment, she continues. "Is that all that's in the box? Another riddle?" She folds her arms across her chest, disappointment blazing across her features.

"No, it's not," Alexander says, leaning still forward to peer into the box. "Lift up the velvet flap and see for yourself."

She does so, moving with alacrity. Her fingers are hungry for answers. She pries open the black velvet interior and gasps. Nestled into the rich fabric is a golden key. The bow of the key, intricately woven with thin webs of gold, is adorned with tiny, glittering emeralds.

As green as Emerala's eyes, Alexander thinks, just as he had the first time he opened the box. Emerala stares at the key in silence, her fingers gripping tightly at the wooden edge. He reaches within and removes the key from its position, careful not to drop it. The cool gold is heavy within the palm of his hand, the shank smooth against his fingers. Emerala follows the glittering emeralds as they move closer to his chest. She leans forward, almost instinctively, her drying curls tickling his cheek as she attempts to get a closer look.

"It's beautiful," she breathes. He can feel her breath against his nose.

"It is," he agrees.

"What does it open?"

He sighs. "Therein lies the next riddle, doesn't it?" he asks, not expecting her to give an answer. She does anyway, her gaze meeting his.

"You want to go to Chancey to find out."

He shakes his head, aware of how close her face is to his. The tip of her nose brushes against his as she sits back upon the desk. He glances quickly back at the key, his pulse quickening. He can feel her frowning down upon him. His gut aches unexpectedly.

"I don't want to take you back there," he says. "It's not safe."

"Since when do you care for my safety?" she asks, her voice flippant. "You've nearly let me die loads of times."

"I care," Alexander counters. The response is clumsy, ineloquent.

Emerala purses her lips, studying the key in Alexander's hand. "Derek thinks we should go," she points out. "Doesn't he?"

He looks at her sharply at that. "Derek has his agenda. I have mine. You're one of us now, and we take care of our own. I'm not about to deliver you into the clutches of the Golden Guard."

And neither is the Hawk, he thinks, feeling something sharp and bitter flare up within him at the quiet realization. Evander the Hawk would put the ship at the bottom of the sea before he let Emerala go, Alexander is certain of it. The thought doesn't bring him comfort.

Emerala eyes the parchment, two of her fingers dancing over the surface of the unfurled map. "Why did you have me read that, if you don't plan to sail to Chancey? It's clear that's what it means."

Alexander shrugs, feeling as though he is being pulled in several different directions. He considers his crew, hungry and tired and waiting for their next payday. He thinks of his mother, surrounded by strangers in a world of oblivious finery and perpetual solitude.

He thinks of Emerala. Their eyes lock across the desk and he recalls the day he met her in the square—recalls the way the sun had filled her eyes, how it made him think of the sea before a storm.

"I suppose I just wanted to be certain that we were headed in the right direction."

"Did I convince you?" she asks.

Alexander grimaces. "If Saynti was queen upon the island of Chancey, there can be no other choice. The sails must be hoisted one way or another. I'll tell the crew we sail eastward in the morning. If there are more answers to these endless riddles, I expect we will find them in your homeland."

A visible shiver of excitement runs through Emerala and she smiles a feral, catlike grin.

"That doesn't frighten you?" he asks. "Returning home?"

"A pirate isn't afraid of a little danger, Alexander," she sings, her eyes twinkling.

"Old bones, new bones, no bones," Salty screams.

Alexander swallows the instincts that churn within him, batting away the misgiving in his gut. They'll sail back east, gallows be damned. Alexander has slipped the noose before. He can do it again. His eyes meet Emerala's storming gaze and he winks.

"To Chancey, then, Emerala the Rogue?"

Emerala laughs gaily, her face crinkling in delight. "Tell your crew to hoist the colors. We sail east when the storm breaks."

CHAPTER 44

The Rebellion

THE ONSLAUGHT OF rain has stopped. Only a faint spattering of silver trickles down from the sky. Evander the Hawk leans back in the fighting top of the foremast, letting his spine unfold against the rounded cabin. The roll of the waves below is much more pronounced at this height and he steadies himself as he feels the ship rise and fall upon the swell of the sea. He tilts his face up towards the sky, shutting his eyes and allowing rivulets of rainwater to roll across his cheeks. The stinging salt air is cool and refreshing after the blistering heat of Caira.

He pictures the black box in Captain Mathew's possession and a small smile tugs at his lips. The sight of the box, after so many years, had been like discovering an old friend. It was a relief, a loosening of the constant pressure upon his shoulders. The weight he bore for years had grown heavy, and finding the key was, at last, a step in the right direction.

I've come so far, he thinks. *And righted so many wrongs.*

He must play his cards carefully, now, this close to the end of the game. All of his wagers are on the table. One wrong hand, and he could lose everything.

There is a shout from below, the sound snatched away by the buffeting wind. The temperature has dropped considerably since the storm's end. He shifts his weight upon the floor and crosses his arms against the sudden chill. His chest glistens with rain in the naked light of the silver moon that peeks out from behind the dissipating storm clouds. He thinks, suddenly, of the stripped, white bones of Captain Jameson rotting in the gibbet upon Caira, and his smile widens.

I got you, you old bastard, he thinks. *I finally got you.*

His last conversation with the old drunkard had taken place on Chancey, just after the mercenary was arrested following his altercation with Captain Mathew. Evander had not seen the sailor in years—not since the disappearance of Eliot Roberts—and even then, justice was as sweet and as ripe as an apricot.

Evander came upon Jameson at dusk as he stood, nearly asleep, in the marketplace pillory.

Wake up, you old fool, Evander barked, snapping his fingers together in the old man's ear. With a hiccough and a snort, Captain Jameson opened one swollen eye. The rotting innards of a tomato had dried to the side of his cheek. Clumps of seeds clung to his hair. Evander sniffed in disgust, garnering a faint whiff of excrement somewhere on his person. Captain Jameson hiccoughed again, a scowl of recognition passing across his features.

Hawk, he growled. *I en't seen you since you were a snot-nosed little brat, parading around at Sam's heels.*

Evander smiled at that. *I've grown up a bit since then.*

Aye, I should have known you were behind this. You wanted that map more than anyone I knew, you did.

Evander chewed at a hangnail as he studied the mercenary. *Must be uncomfortable in those stocks—a man of your age, and all.*

Jameson gave a hoarse laugh. *Uncomfortable, aye, but just for a day or two. They don't keep you long for the ale. Just long enough to take the piss out of you. As soon as I'm out, I'll get that map back, boy. Mark my words.*

I don't think you will. It's mine now.

The tone of Evander's voice caused both of Jameson's eyes to pop open. The lids were purpled and swollen, the whites of his eyes tangled with thick red veins. He had clearly taken quite a few hits before being left in the pillory. No surprise there—the Guardians were hardly likely to show favor to a drunkard.

That map's worthless to you, boy, and you know it, Jameson hissed. *Not a damn fool on this side of the ocean can make sense of the dead speech Argot coded on that parchment.*

Evander scoffed. *I take it from your tone that you've tried. You can always trust a mercenary to be only as loyal as his payout. Does your employer know you're hoping to get the key for yourself? After all he paid you to bring it to him?*

I didn't know what it was, then, Jameson spat. *I didn't know how valuable it was.*

I'm sure if you'd known, you would have asked for a larger sum, aye?

Jameson ignored him. He twisted his fists within the circular wooden openings. Even in the settling darkness, Evander could see that his wrists were raw and bloody from hours of rubbing against the splintering grain.

You'll never decipher the damn thing, boy, it's impossible. The men that bound it are gone, all of them. Dead, or scattered to the winds. Argot is halfway on the other side of the world by now.

Ah, Evander breathed, patting Jameson upon the head. He drew his palm away quickly, wiping the sticking remnants of rotting vegetables upon his trousers. *That's where you're wrong, old friend. Argot is exactly where I left him. I'll collect him when I'm ready.*

And Captain Samuel Mathew? I heard tell the man is feeding the fish at the bottom of the sea. En't much use to you dead.

Evander chuckled. *I've got better than the old fool. I've got his son. The pirate that stole the map from you this morning? That was Alexander Mathew, newest captain of the Rebellion. His blood is bound to be the same as his father's, I'd reckon.*

For the first time, Evander saw a flicker of fear pass through Jameson's bloodshot eyes. Evander straightened, arching his back and stretching his arms wide as though waking from a deep slumber. He gave a deep sigh and smiled, holding the mercenary in his piercing golden gaze.

Looks uncomfortable in there, mate, Evander said again. *Wish I could help, but I've got work to do. You understand.*

He turned his back to the old mercenary, relishing in the total darkness left behind by the extinguished sun. The night was cool and deep. Silver pinpricks danced in the sky above his head.

Wait, Jameson called. Evander hesitated upon the cobblestone, smiling.

What about Eliot Roberts? Panic was beginning to bubble beneath Jameson's words. *What about him? En't a chance in the Dark Below you'd ever get within a mile of the man. Not where my employer's got him.*

Evander turned slightly, letting the starlight encapsulate his features in the dark. He could just see the outline of the old man hunched in the wooden stocks, breathless, waiting.

I'm glad you asked, Evander said. *Your little trip to Chancey led us right to Eliot Robert's birthplace. He's got a daughter on the island. Lovely girl. Beautiful, really. She's got eyes just like her father's. I'm thinking about taking her with me when I go.*

Evander was met with silence. The rusted locks of the pillory rattled as the old mercenary began to shake.

Give up, Jameson, Evander sneered. *You've failed.*

Evander is snapped out of his reverie by the sound of Emerala's laugh. It rings out across the night like a bell, the echo of it subduing the whispering waves below. He shifts his weight, drawing up to his knees to peer over the side of the fighting top. The night is late, and the deck below is void of any crew members.

He finds Emerala quickly enough. The light of the moon spills across the deck like water, bathing the ship in muted grey light. She hovers in the doorway of the captain's quarters; peering up into Captain Mathew's face. He leans into her, his lips grazing her ear as he speaks. She laughs again, quieter this time, and presses her curls back from her face with her fingers.

Something within Evander jolts at the sight, and he frowns down upon the figures. His fingers tighten against the wooden edge of the lookout. There is the jarring screech of a bird and he sees Emerala and the captain break apart as the insufferable silver parrot comes into view. The parrot lands with a triumphant *harrumph* on Emerala's shoulder, his black talons curling into her skin. Evander feels a small flicker of satisfaction in his gut at the bird's untimely interruption. Below, Emerala makes a quiet comment, proffering a small shrug as her words are carried off by the wind.

"No matter," Evander hears Captain Mathew say. He hesitates for a fraction of a second before leaning down and kissing her lightly upon the cheek. Even from his seat high above the deck, Evander can see the deep crimson hue of Emerala's cheeks. Captain Mathew absconds from sight, disappearing back into his quarters. For a moment, Emerala lingers before the closed door, one hand pressed against her cheek.

"Emerala the Rogue," calls the parrot's voice. "Pretty, pretty girl."

Emerala jumps, turning redder still at the parrot's screams. She rushes away from the door, prying up her gown in her fists. The deep violet fabric billows out behind her, caught upon the wind that rushes across the deck.

Now, a voice within Evander snaps. *Do it now.*

He kicks into motion, swinging his legs over the side of the lookout and grabbing hold of the shrouds. He climbs down nimbly; his hands moving one over the other as he sidles down the net of knotted rope. Emerala is just below him when he at last allows himself to plunge silently from the cords.

She gasps as he drops to the deck before her, startled at the sudden appearance of a shadow in the darkness. With an agitated squawk, the parrot takes off from her shoulder. He alights upon a barrel a few feet away, glaring in annoyance at Evander.

"Hello," Evander says, grinning.

"You scared me half to death," Emerala snaps, pushing her wild, black curls from her eyes.

"Sorry." He is starkly aware of Emerala's gaze lingering on the moonlit gleam of his chest, and his lips split into a bawdy grin. His eyes catch hers and and her scowl deepens. Gathering her gown once more within her fists, she pushes past him.

"Where are you going?" he asks, following her.

"Into the hold." Her voice trails behind her as she walks. She whistles and the parrot glides over toward her, alighting once more upon her shoulder. "I want to put this bird back where it belongs."

The parrot tugs at a lock of her hair, grumbling a wordless protest. Ignoring him, Emerala pries open the grated door of the hold, grunting with the weight of it.

"Here, let me," Evander says, leaning over her and taking the hatch from her grasp. He lifts it with ease, gesturing for her to climb down the ladder. The look she gives him over her shoulder is scathing, but she obliges, dropping down into the shadowed opening. Evander follows her, repressing a smile.

The hold is encapsulated in darkness. The only light that cuts through the shadows falls through the slits of the hatch overhead. Evander idles on the ladder, watching Emerala as she coaxes the parrot back into the cage with quiet, soothing murmurs.

"Pretty, pretty girl," the parrot says sadly, nuzzling her chin.

"I'll take you out tomorrow," Emerala promises, placing him back upon his roost. She locks the door gingerly, careful not to rouse any of the six other parrots that doze within. When she is done, she turns to face Evander. She is silent in the darkness, breathing deeply in the narrow moonlight that falls in slats of silver across her figure.

"If you have something to say to me, say it," she says at last.

Evander frowns. "Are you still sore at me?"

"Do you really have to ask?" She makes to move past him but he stops her, thrusting his palm hard against the wall beside her face. She pulls back from his outstretched arm, huffing loudly, her arms crossing over her chest.

"Why him?" he asks.

One eyebrow arches upward upon her forehead. "Who?"

"Why Alexander?"

Emerala sniffs. "I'm certain that I don't know what you mean."

"Aye, you do," Evander contests. "How can it be him? All he's done is tell you lie after lie. All I've done is protect you."

Emerala's eyes narrow dangerously. Even so, he does not miss the flicker of confusion that passes across her features like a whisper.

"Ever since the day I met you in the marketplace, I've done nothing but keep you safe," Evander continues. "Alex has used you again and again for his own purposes, and you can't see it. You're blinded by his affections."

"His *affections*?" Emerala repeats, her face crinkling in the gloom. Her loveliness is not lost upon him. It never has been—not since the beginning. Beneath the moonlight, she looks almost ethereal.

He chides himself internally, feeling annoyance bristling under his skin. *Stick to the plan,* the voice within him says. *Don't be weak.*

"Evander," Emerala says, and, as always, he feels something unwanted move within him at the sound of his given name upon her tongue. Fourteen harvests at sea, and he still cannot shake the intimacy of his culture's tradition. Before him, Emerala is scowling as she takes another step back from him in the dark. "I have *no* idea what you're talking about."

"You must," he implores, willing his features to twist into something resembling frustration. He closes the space between them, matching her step for step.

"I don't." She stops, inhaling too sharply as her back collides against the wall. Her wild curls press into the musty wood of the curved hull.

"How?" he asks, his voice growing gruff. "How can you not see him for what he is?"

He is so close to her that he can taste her breath upon his tongue. The lace of her bodice rests against his chest, and he feels the steady rise and fall of her breathing. His own breath hitches in his throat. He'd be lying to himself if he said he hadn't thought of this moment a thousand times before—lying if he hadn't lain awake at night with her name swimming on his tongue, the thought of her taunting him into remaining awake.

But this is bigger than Emerala the Rogue.

This—this is the endgame.

This is his bid for the Chancian throne.

That's been the goal all along. With the Cairan fortune—with Emerala the Rogue—he could have it all. He could take what always should have been his, from the very beginning.

Play your hand, fool, he tells himself. *Keep your head in the game.*

"He's lied to you, Rogue," he says. "From the start, Alexander has done nothing but lie. He came to Chancey to find you. You didn't meet him by accident."

Emerala draws away from him to get a better look at his face, her green eyes wild in the pressing dark.

"How would you know that?" she asks, her voice hoarse.

"Because I found you at the marketplace at his orders." He looks down at his boots, hoping he looks properly ashamed. "I didn't know what I was doing," he lies. "I had no idea why he needed you."

When he looks up, Emerala is studying the white flesh of the scar upon her palm. She balls her hand once more into a fist when she notices him staring. Tears gather in her eyes, collecting in her lower lids like jewels.

"Why did he need me?" she whispers. "Do you know now?"

"He needed your blood." At the look of bewilderment that blossoms across her face, he adds, "He needed to spill your blood to interpret his map."

Emerala laughs. The sound is dry and humorless. "Do you hear yourself? You sound like a madman."

"Maybe I do," Evander says. "But it's the truth."

Emerala shakes her head, turning her back to him. Her silhouette disappears and reappears within the strips of pale moonlight as she crosses the hold. Drawing to a standstill at the bottom rung of the ladder, she turns back toward him. The light of the moon swathes her figure in a silver aura. Her black ringlets spill over her shoulders like ink.

"It makes no sense."

"Which part?" Evander asks.

"All of it."

"Rogue—" he starts and stops, taking note of the fury that simmers beneath her gaze. Sighing, he says, "The map was spelled with your blood, and it can only be undone by your blood. Alexander needed you in order to unlock the location of that key. Think about it—why else would he have agreed to waste his time and his resources rescuing you from the Guardians?"

Emerala considers this, fidgeting beneath the moonlight. Defiance etches itself upon her face. "My blood was never used to spell a map," she insists. "I think I'd know."

In the cage, the parrot is awake.

"Blood red ice for emeralds!" he screams.

Evander closes the space between them, drawing tentatively nearer to her in the gloom. "Aye," he says softly. "It was bound by your family's blood. The blood of Eliot Roberts, to be exact."

He is silent as he allows that to sink in. He studies the lines of her, wait-ing—watching as cold realization creeps into her face like the first frost of winter, hardening her features and turning her eyes to ice.

"Rogue," he begins, reaching for her. She cuts him off, sidestepping his outstretched arm. Her eyes, silvered with tears, lock onto his.

"The man on the island—the prisoner in the maze. Who was he?"

"Emerala—"

He reaches for her a second time, but she slaps his hand away.

"Who was he?" She spits each word out like poison.

He swallows, hesitating just long enough to appear reluctant. "Eliot Roberts."

Before him, Emerala's eyes widen into perfect circles. The color drains from her skin, leaving her unusually pale against the deep violet of her gown. When at last she speaks, her voice scarcely rises above a whisper.

"That was my father?"

"Aye, it was."

Anger flares in her eyes like a flame, burning hot and fast.

"That was my father, and we left him there to rot!" she cries, her voice shrill. Raising her arm, she brings her fist down hard against Evander's chest. He takes the blow in stride, steeling himself as she hits him again. And again. A sob chokes out from her throat in a strangled cry.

"You knew—Saynti, you knew." She raises her fist to strike him a fourth time, but he catches her wrist in his grasp, steadying her. She tries and fails to wrench her arm out of his clutch, gasping as his grip tightens. Lifting her free arm, she balls her hand into a fist and prepares to strike. Evander grabs her wrist in mid-swing, drawing her into him with ease. She is surprisingly light, her slender frame like a wraith beneath his shadow.

"All this time, you knew," she says hatefully, glaring up him.

"Cap'n told me not to tell you. He wanted to get the key and get off the island."

She tries again to wrench her wrists free from his grasp and he relents, watching as she stumbles several steps back from him in the gloom.

"And you listened to him?"

"Well, aye, he's my cap'n," Evander argues. "To disobey a direct order would be to mutiny."

Emerala paws at one eye with the back of her hand, trying and failing to collect herself. "Why did he leave my father behind? We were right there—we were right in front of him in the maze. We could have brought him with us."

"He said Eliot Roberts would do everything in his power to stop him from completing his mission. He couldn't risk it—not after coming so far."

"What mission?" Emerala demands hotly, pacing the floor. "Alex has no idea what the key opens."

Evander shakes his head. "That's another lie. He's always known what it opens. And so do you."

"I don't," Emerala insists darkly.

"Did you read the inscription on the parchment?" Evander asks.

Emerala hesitates, her face scrunching slightly in remembrance. "Yes."

"That same inscription is engraved upon the locked door of Saynti's Treasure."

"Saynti's—" Emerala begins and falters, falling into silence. "That's only a legend."

Evander clicks his tongue. "It's not. It's in the Forbidden City—immeasurable wealth, just buried away behind a locked door with no key."

"I don't believe it," she says, her voice barely audible. "Why wouldn't Alexander tell me?"

"Because he's going to steal it."

Emerala blinks. Then blinks again. For a moment, Evander wonders if she hasn't quite heard him. Her pointed features, which he can usually read like a book, are curiously devoid of emotion.

"He's going to steal Saynti's Treasure?"

"Yes," Evander says, wetting his lower lip as he studies Emerala through the gloom. "I'm sorry, Emerala. I didn't know. I had no idea he was going to use you the way he has—the way he will. If I'd known, I would have left you in Chancey. I never would have stopped you that day in the square—never would have given you that dagger."

Emerala gapes at him and says nothing. Behind her red-rimmed eyes, he can almost see her mind churning as she struggles to sift through all of the lies—all of the deception.

"He won't be able to get inside the Forbidden City," she says. "Even if he can find it, the Listeners will never grant him entry."

"They will," Evander disagrees. "With you as Alexander's bargaining chip."

Emerala shakes her head. "I'm not that valuable. The Cairan king would sooner let me die than allow pirates to pillage the city."

Evander lets out a whistle, long and low. A smile teases at one corner of his lips.

"Saints," he breathes. "You have no idea how important you are, do you?"

Emerala freezes beneath a trickle of moonlight. Her tear stained cheeks look as though they've been speckled with stardust. She looks inhuman—otherworldly—like some ancient, wild thing. He could love her for it if things were different—if he was a man with the luxury of romance.

"What are you talking about?" she asks him. She is desperate for information—starved for answers. True or not, she'll eat whatever crumbs she's given. It's the benefit, he thinks, of having a captain as utterly clueless as Alexander Mathew.

He draws nearer to her, taking her hand within his. Easing open her palm, he runs an index finger over the pale, white scar that mars her olive skin.

"The Roberts line has Saynti blood running through their veins," he explains. His forehead brushes hers in the dark. He can feel her tensing beneath him. He raises his eyes to meet her emerald gaze.

"You're royalty, Emerala the Rogue."

She pulls her hand out of his, balling her fingers protectively over her scar. "I'm no such thing," she snaps.

"Aye, you are. I can explain everything to you—and I will. Just promise me that when we get within sight of Chancey, you'll leave with me. Don't stay and allow yourself to be a pawn in Alexander's plan."

She stares at him a long time in silence, her brows furrowed in contemplation as her eyes search his face for any sign of deceit.

"No," she says at last,

He bristles ever so slightly, his patience waning. "No?"

"You heard me."

"You won't leave the *Rebellion*?"

She turns from him, prying her skirts from the ground as she begins to ascend the ladder. "I'll leave," she says over her shoulder, "just not with you."

Evander bites back a curse, the muscles in his jaw working. "And why not?" he demands. She pauses on the second rung and glances down at him, disdain twitching her pointed nose.

"Because I hate you," she says curtly.

He is at the ladder before she can ascend to the next step, grabbing her by the waist and pulling her down toward him. She protests loudly, kicking her feet as she falls into him, nearly knocking her forehead against his chin. All thoughts of the throne—the prophecy, the treasure—fall away. He is left seeing red, his breathing hitching in his chest.

"You hate me?" he repeats, his voice gruff.

"I do."

"You're lying."

"I can assure you I'm—"

He silences her with a kiss, his lips finding hers beneath the moonlight. The embrace is short lived. She pulls away from him, her eyes blazing as her palm finds his cheek. His skin stings with the echo of her slap and he presses his hand against his jaw, a laugh escaping him like a cough. For several seconds, they face off in silence, each of them hovering in the shadows just outside a thin trickle of moonlight. Even beneath the darkness, Evander can see Emerala's crimson cheeks—the erratic rise and fall of her chest beneath her corset.

"You're not a good man," she says.

"No," he agrees. "I'm not."

"I don't trust you. You're untrustworthy."

"I am."

"You've killed people. You're a murderer. You're a thief, a liar, a—"

"Pirate," he finishes. He flashes her a broad grin, his cheeks dimpling. She is through the moonlight before he can say another word, crossing into the shadow of the hold and colliding hard into his chest. He braces her against him, his hands twisting in her wild curls, his fingers dancing at the small of her back. Her mouth finds his—her lips part beneath his kiss and he tastes the briny sweetness of her on his tongue. There is a hunger to his movements—an ache, a need.

And under it, a single thought.

In his arms he holds a future queen.

CHAPTER 45

The Forbidden City

NERANI FINDS ORIANNA in the infirmary, tending to an older man sporting a rather gruesome looking black eye.

"Oh," she remarks, drawing up short at the sight of them. "That looks painful."

Orianna throws a glance over her shoulder but otherwise says nothing, resuming her delicate task of cleaning the man's wounds with a damp cloth. Her patient gives a throaty laugh, and the sharp sting of ale tickles the inside of Nerani's nose.

"It's nothing, it's nothing." The man shrugs, brushing away Nerani's concern with an air of feigned nonchalance. He shoots her a smile, and she notices that he seems to have split his lip directly down the middle.

"It's hardly nothing," Orianna snaps, continuing to tend to the man. "Fighting in the dining hall, Mieran? Is that really going to solve anything?"

Mieran shrugs at that, wincing at the movement. "It made me feel better," he says, the words muffled as Orianna presses a foul smelling poultice against the cut in his lip.

"Looks as though," gripes another voice. Nerani turns to see Mame Minera bustling through the doorway. The scowl on her face is enough to confirm exactly how she feels about Mieran's antics in the great hall.

"Hello, dear," she says, nodding curtly to Nerani as she joins Orianna at the cot. She shoves a steaming mug of something particularly ripe beneath Mieran's nose. He sniffles at it, his face turning a light shade of green.

"Drink," she commands.

"What is it?" he asks suspiciously, eyeing the liquid within.

Mame Minera appears thoroughly unenthused by his question. "A mixture of huckleberries. Easy on the stomach."

"Is that so?" He sniffs the contents, looking unconvinced. "What are the huckleberries mixed with, then?"

There is a fearsome pause as Mame Minera glares down at him. "You'll do well to drink and stop asking so many questions. You've taken several hits to the head. If you think you're in pain now, just wait until later on this evening. Drink." She presses the mug into his hands and rushes off the way she came, muttering darkly beneath her breath.

"You'd better drink that," Orianna warns. She wraps up the remaining gauze and replaces it on a narrow table by the cot. "She'll come back soon and check to see if you've followed her directions. I wouldn't want to be the fool that doesn't finish every drop of that tea."

She wipes her hands on her apron, frowning down at Mieran as he takes a hesitant sip from the mug. He grimaces, recoiling from the contents within the cup. His eyes lock onto Orianna's stoic glare and he gulps, feigning a smile. His lip splits further and he groans, huckleberry stained blood trickling down his chin.

"It's delicious," he lies.

Orianna smiles. "That's what I like to hear. Now finish it. It's even worse when it's cold."

Mieran groans a second time, steeling himself before taking another sip of the tea. Orianna watches him for a moment more before joining Nerani at the far side of the room.

"What happened to him?" Nerani asks, getting the question out before Orianna can ask her why she came. She's not certain she can put into words what she is feeling—what has transpired. She's not even certain she understands the full extent of her experiences in the room of tapestries. Her chest feels tight, her stomach ill. She clutches her fingers in her lap and waits for Orianna to finish folding a pile of freshly laundered linens. Orianna gives her a sideways glance, thrusting half of the fabric into Nerani's hands.

"Fold," she instructs. Nerani obliges, her injured hand leaving the linens lumpy and askew—a stark contrast to the neatly creased squares in

Orianna's pile. Next to her, Orianna studies Mieran as he struggles to finish his tea.

"He got in a fight out in the dining hall," she explains.

"Over what?" Nerani asks, studying the man as she attempts to refold a linen for the fourth consecutive time. Mieran is making faces into his tea, his lip continually getting larger as the blood rushes to the injury.

"Over nothing," Orianna says. "That's just the issue." She snatches the linen out of Nerani's hands, making quick work of the cotton fabric and plopping it deftly onto her growing pile. Nerani doesn't protest.

"It's been happening more and more," Orianna says. "People are getting restless—anxious. We're running low on supplies."

"What do you mean?" Nerani asks. "How is that possible?"

"Rob hasn't told you?"

Nerani looks sheepish at that. "I—I haven't really spoken to Roberts," she admits. "Not since our falling out."

Orianna's gaze falls. "I'm not surprised. He hasn't had much to do with anyone since that little blonde harlot showed up."

Her dark blue eyes flare with barely concealed contempt and she scowls, snapping one of the linens too hard against her lap. She clears her throat, brushing her raven hair out of her eyes.

"Anyway, Rowland Stoward has ordered his Guardians to increase their sweeps of the city. They've extended their search to the farmland and the forests beyond the city walls. They're looking for the Forbidden City, and they've been relentless on their quest. It's getting harder and harder for the Listeners to procure large amounts of supplies without attracting attention."

Nerani thinks of the mounted Guardians that had nearly stumbled upon her and Darianna in the tangled forests just outside the entrance. It had been a close call. Too close. What would they have done if the Guardians had found them at the mouth of the caverns? How would they have explained the caves?

Nerani thinks of Darianna, still hiding out at Mamere Lenora's, stowing away among the women of the night. She thinks of the young girl's mother, and how she had cried to Topan about her missing daughter. Nerani had left

Darianna with concise instructions just before she was arrested, but who's to know if the impetuous young girl bothered to listen.

Wait for a Listener patrol, she'd told the girl. *They come through often enough. Mamere will let them know you've taken shelter with her. They'll get you home safely.*

If what Orianna is saying is true, then the Listeners are pulling back from their excursions. They're playing it safe, staying closer to home. How long will it be until someone makes contact with Mamere? How long will it be before the girl is delivered?

At some point, Nerani will have to come forward with the truth.

It's because of me she's out there, alone.

Before her, Orianna is studying her through speculative eyes.

"That's a stunning bit of jewelry you're wearing," she observes. Nerani starts, her fingers flying instinctively to the teardrop diamond that rests against her clavicle.

"I—" she starts, and stops. The words catch in her throat.

"A gift from Topan?" Orianna asks.

"Yes." Nerani's voice is tight.

"I'm surprised you accepted," Orianna notes, leaning down to inspect the jewels at a closer proximity. "After how fervently you claimed to have no love for the man, I'd have thought you would toss the diamonds directly back in his face."

Nerani is aghast. "I would never," she stammers. "I'm not Emerala, I—"

Orianna silences her, laying a hand on her wrist. "I was teasing," she says, and frowns. "Saynti, you're white as a ghost. Are you alright?"

"He did it." To say the words aloud makes her tremble. "He asked for my hand in marriage."

Orianna's eyes widen, her fingers clasping tighter about Nerani's wrist, cutting off her circulation. "He did? What did you say?"

"What else could I say but yes?"

"I'd have thought you would say no," Orianna says, and shrugs. "You made it fairly clear that your feelings lay elsewhere." Her dark gaze is thick with implication, and Nerani does not need to ask for clarification to know what she means.

"You were right, Orianna," she admits. "I can't expect to have a future with—" she pauses, unable to bring his name to her lips, unable to give a voice to the grief that grips her.

"Him," she finishes, her voice cracking. Something heavy presses against her chest and she feels, suddenly, as though the diamond at her throat weighs a thousand pounds.

Orianna reaches out and takes her hand within her own, her fingers warm, her grasp reassuring.

"I know this is difficult, Nerani. I know your heart is breaking, but this is for the best." Her words only cause Nerani's mood to sour further. She opens her mouth to reply, but is cut off by the sound of shouting from the doorway.

"I'm fine!" shouts a girl, her tone distressed. "Let off me, I'm fine!"

Nerani starts in recognition, rushing past Orianna and back into the main foyer of the infirmary. Mieran is unconscious on his cot, one leg still hanging off the edge and onto the floor—the product of whatever smelled so strongly in his tea, no doubt.

In the doorway, Mame Minera and a familiar looking woman struggle to get ahold of a dirty young girl. The girl pulls away from them, wiping her forearm across her face in an attempt to clear away some of the grime. Her blue eyes gleam with agitation as she stares at them from beneath a tangle of dirty blonde hair.

"I already told you," she snaps. "I'm fine."

"Darianna," Nerani says under her breath. Cool relief floods her at the sight of the girl. She hangs back in the shadow of the doorway, not wanting to involve herself in the unfolding scene at the front of the room. It isn't her place—isn't her business. As far as anyone knows, she and Darianna the Rose have never met.

At Nerani's side, Orianna watches the bedlam through guarded blue eyes. "Is that the girl that went missing?"

"I think so," Nerani says.

"We've got to get you bathed, girl," barks the woman—Darianna's mother, no doubt. "You look a sight awful covered in all that dirt." She struggles to get ahold of her daughter for a moment more, surrendering as the girl twists just out of reach.

"Thank goodness you're back, dear," she pants, beginning to look faintly battle worn. "Where in Saynti's name have you been?"

Darianna pauses at that, doing her best to look apologetic. Her blue eyes are crisp, cool pools of water upon her dirt stained face. "I went wandering in the tunnels," she lies. "I couldn't find my way back, not for days."

Darianna chews her lip, relenting at last to the warm washcloth brandished by the tenacious Mame Minera. Her face scrunches as the Mame scrubs at her cheeks; pink and raw skin emerging from beneath the grime.

"It was frightening," Darianna adds, sounding thoroughly unconvincing.

"Oh," gasps her mother, swallowing a sob. She clasps her hands tightly over her chest, looking as though she might faint.

"Here," Orianna says, finally jumping into motion. She drags a chair forward for the girl's mother, gesturing for her to sit. "Rest a while, you must be exhausted."

"Thank you, dear," the woman splutters. Her eyes never leave her daughter's face as she drops into the seat, fanning herself with the palm of her hand.

"You're fortunate, girl," Mame Minera grumbles darkly, still scrubbing Darianna's face. She ignores the plaintive protests that rise to the girl's lips, working at the grime until the skin is red and raw and new. "Many a child has died in those endless tunnels. Frankly, I don't see how you made it out. You must have had a guide."

The girl's flinch does not go unnoticed by Nerani. Darianna's blue eyes meet hers across the expanse and she gives the scarcest of nods, her lips pressed in a tight line.

"Foolish, is what it was," snaps her mother.

"Quite foolish," agrees the Mame.

"Reckless," her mother adds. "Mad." Mame Minera is quiet as she paws at the girl's face. Leaning toward her basin, she tosses aside another filthy rag. Her eyes scrutinize Darianna from head to toe.

"I've got to go and get more clean washcloths to tackle this mess," she says. She glances over her shoulder, her gaze settling on Orianna. "Check the girl for any injuries."

"I'm fine," Darianna protests.

The look Mame Minera gives her is scathing. "All the same," she barks, and bustles out from the room.

Nerani follows Orianna across the expanse, studying Darianna as the girl plops herself down on one of the cots.

"Are you alright?" Nerani whispers to her as soon as she draws near. She pulls a dirt caked washcloth out from the basin and wrings it out, listening to the water droplets plunging through the cool surface of the basin.

"Yes," Darianna says, a grin splitting her face. "Never better."

Orianna's eyes meet Nerani's over Darianna's shoulder as she inspects the girl for any clear sign of injury. The familiarity between them has not gone unnoticed by her friend.

"Does anything hurt?" Orianna asks, bending her left arm at the elbow.

"Not a bit," Darianna sings. She wrenches her arm from Orianna's grasp, leaning forward towards Nerani. She grabs her wrist, stopping Nerani before she can begin sponging more of the dirt off of her face. The water droplets pool in the ruffled fabric of Nerani's lap.

"He's here," Darianna whispers, her voice low. She mouths the next two words, no sound coming from her lips as she enunciates, "General Byron."

Nerani feels her blood run cold. The washcloth falls from her hands, dropping to the floor with a wet squelch.

"What do you mean, here?" she hisses back.

"He's in the tunnels, not far from where you and I first met."

Nerani fights to keep from looking at Orianna. She can feel the heat of her friend's stare scorching her skin. The diamond necklace at her throat threatens to choke off her air supply.

"Why?" she asks, barely able to breathe. "How?"

"He escorted me back," Darianna explains. Her eyes are bright. "It's quite a long story, and an exciting one. I've had a lot of adventures in your absence."

Nerani takes a step backwards, barely registering Darianna's voice over the sudden hammering of her heart in her ears. Her throat feels as dry as sandpaper. Her blood is sludge in her veins.

"Nerani—" Orianna's voice is low, cautionary.

Nerani cuts her off, unable to meet her eyes. "I've got to go."

She turns and flees the room, her mind racing faster than her feet.

She reaches the tunnels quickly, her chest burning with exertion. Glancing around to make sure no one is watching her, she grabs a lantern from the wall and slips into the shadows of the tunnels.

The firelight engulfs her in a pale halo of orange, keeping the clawing darkness at bay. Shadows encroach upon the edge of the light, leaching out from behind the jagged stones and dripping rock formations. She steps gingerly upon the damp stone, careful to mind her footing. A shiver of anticipation runs through her as she bunches up her pale peach petticoat within her free hand. Her brown brocade corset feels as though it has been laced too tight, so strangled is her breathing.

"Hello?" she calls, moving further into the darkness. The residual light from the cavern beyond is extinguished as she turns a corner. Last time, the darkness was foreboding. Now, it is freeing.

"James?" Her voice is scarcely louder than a whisper in the dark.

There is the sound of rustling up ahead and she jumps, startled by the proximity of the noise. She can see a shape moving in the shadows. The silhouette of a man comes into view as he moves closer to the light. She holds the lantern higher, casting orange radiance into the face of James Byron.

Her heart rises to her throat and she nearly drops the lantern upon the ground. He is dressed in the clothes of a civilian, his white undershirt sullied from his journey through the tunnels. The buttons have fallen open to reveal the top of his chest, and in the dim throw of light she can just see the puckered, red lines of newly healed scars snaking across his shoulders and over his collarbone.

"James," she says again, his name falling from her lips like a sigh.

He closes the space between them in several steps, pulling her into his embrace. His lips find hers in the darkness and he kisses her roughly, desperately. His movements are laced with a sense of urgency as his fingers trace the lines of her face, as his hands entangle within the hair at the nape of her neck. A deep longing takes root within her gut, aching in a place she never knew existed. A place, she imagines, that has always been meant for him. She leans into his chest, surprised by the sudden impossible desire to wrap herself up in him and disappear.

When at last they break apart, her breathing has grown shallow. She takes a reluctant step back from him, setting the lantern down upon a rock. Lit from below, his features are cupped in flickering firelight. He looks tired, she realizes. Tired and troubled.

"You shouldn't be here," she whispers. The space he occupied is cold in his absence and she draws nearer to him, shivering slightly in the chill. She feels the instinctive desire to touch him and gives in, allowing her fingers to trace the line of his jaw—to linger in the itching stubble that has grown in upon his face. It feels strange to be so familiar with him—strange and wonderful.

"I brought Darianna back," he explains, as if such a reason is the most obvious in the world. Nerani is momentarily surprised by his use of her given name. It is personal, warm—the familiarity is unexpected.

"She told me. I don't understand how the two of you found one another."

"It's a long story."

"That's just what she said."

"It's the truth," he says. "And I don't want to waste another minute talking about it. Not now, when you and I are on borrowed time."

Again, Nerani's eyes travel to the puckered scars that snake over his shoulders. James grimaces, fidgeting beneath her scrutiny, and adjusts his shirt so that the marks are covered. His attention falls to her injured hand, which she has been instinctively cradling within her good fingers. Feeling suddenly self-conscious, she lets her hand fall like a dead weight, swinging her wrist behind her back.

"Don't," he says.

He reaches down and pries her arm out from behind her, taking her dressing wrapped hand within his own. She stiffens, achingly conscious of her missing finger as a pang of grief surges through her. He studies her maimed hand through stony eyes. Pain flickers across his brow as he lifts her hand, inspecting the hollow bandage where her appendage once sat.

"I'm sorry," he murmurs, his lips grazing the empty space. His breath, cool and slow, passes through the bandage and curls in the hollows of her finger. His expression is one of anguish. "I'm sorry for the part I played in this."

"You didn't do this," Nerani insists.

"I did," he disagrees. His jaw locks and he swallows thickly. "I've done a lot of things. Things I'm not proud of. Hurting you was the worst of them."

"You didn't do this to me," Nerani repeats. James is silent, his brows furrowed over eyes that have turned cold. Nerani sighs, placing her own hand over his—squeezing his fingers. Beneath his grasp, her mutilated hand aches.

"What are you really doing here, James?"

"I had to see you," he admits. "I needed to make sure you were safe."

She gives a wry laugh. "I'm perfectly safe. It's you we need to worry about. It was a bad idea, coming here. You know what they'll do to you if they find you."

"I don't care," he says. "I'm not afraid."

"You should be. Fear is healthy. Fear is what keeps you alive."

He smiles at that, but the smile doesn't reach his eyes. "I suppose I'm a dead man, then."

"Don't joke."

"I wasn't."

Her eyes fall back to his shoulders—to the twisting scars concealed by his shirt. She takes the collar between her fingers, holding her breath as she moves to peel back the cotton from his skin. He stops her, his hand encircling her wrist. His brown eyes are plaintive, his shoulders tense. She can see the wounded pride on his face, creeping in beneath his reserve.

"You don't need to see that," he says.

He was whipped, she realizes, and feels the slow slink of horror in her stomach.

His hand reaches out, suddenly, to brush against her clavicle as he runs his finger across her diamond necklace. She starts at his touch, panic gripping her. She had almost forgotten the necklace was there.

"It's lovely," he observes, studying the glimmer of the diamond draped against her throat. "A gift?"

She draws back from him, pressing her palm protectively over her throat. "It's nothing." Her voice is curt. Defensive. She flushes, embarrassed.

"It doesn't look like nothing," he says. "It looks important. Regal."

Reality grips her, hard and cold and unremitting. She looks around at the dripping stalagmites, at the creeping shadows of the cavern. *He can't be here,* she thinks. *We can't be here.*

"It's a family heirloom," she lies. "James, I—" she hesitates, the dread within her making it difficult to speak, difficult to think. "This is all wrong. You can't be here."

"Why not?" he challenges.

"Are you completely mad? You know why not. They'll kill you. This is reckless, what you're doing. *Stupid.*"

"Look at me." He takes her face within his hands, his touch gentle as he guides her gaze to his. "There's no way this ends well for either of us," he says, his voice even. "I've known that from the beginning. I've made my peace with it. However much time I have until fate catches up with me, it's better spent with you than without."

Tears swim in Nerani's eyes and her vision blurs, his features warping into shadow. She blinks rapidly, calling him back into focus.

"I love you," she says, without thinking—without planning.

Saying the words aloud feels like opening a door. She can't close it, not now, not anymore, even if she wanted to. The thought both elates and terrifies her.

It will drown you both.

Before her, James has frozen where he stands, his palms still pressed against her cheeks. Her tears gather between his fingers, running in rivulets across his knuckles. The look in his eyes is unreadable as he lets out a long, slow breath.

"Say that again," he commands.

Swallowing hard, she forces her eyes to meet his. "I can't."

She can see his pulse fluttering in the hollow of his throat just above his collar. His gaze is earnest. "Did you mean that?" he asks. "What you said?"

"Yes." Her voice trembles.

A small smile dances on his lips and she feels her heart leap at the sight of it.

"Yes?" His hands drop away from her face and he steps toward her, tilting his head so that his forehead meets hers in the dark. She can feel the heat radiating off of him. The firelight dances in the wake of his movement, pitting their shadows together on the wall.

"Then say it again," he says.

She swallows, choking down the trepidation that builds within her.

"I'm in love with you," she whispers.

He lets out a sigh like a laugh, his eyes growing bright. The firelight plays across his features, and for a moment it seems as though the years of burden, of turmoil, have fallen away. For a moment, he looks like a boy again. He places a finger beneath her chin, gently drawing her face towards his. This time, when he kisses her, it is soft and slow. His lips linger upon hers as though the moment might last forever—as though there is only them, only this endless dark. Her knees go weak and she feels as though she might melt into the floor.

Glass shatters against stone and they leap apart as though they've been scorched. In one fluid movement, James thrusts her behind him and snatches the lantern from the rock. Holding it aloft, he peers out into the darkness of the tunnel.

Standing in the shadows, her face partially shrouded in the grey smoke that twists upward from a broken lantern, is Orianna.

"I knew it." Her dark blue eyes scrutinize James in contempt.

Nerani steps in front of him, her fingers trembling as she holds them out to her friend in an empty gesture of goodwill. "Raven," she begins, and her voice shakes. "It's not what you think."

"It's exactly what I think," Orianna snaps. "Saynti, how could you?"

"You can't say anything—not to anyone."

"Are you *mad*?" Orianna demands. Her voice reverberates off of the oppressive stone, rolling down the dripping rock formations.

"Please," Nerani whispers. "They'll kill him."

Orianna blinks at Nerani in disbelief, her brows furrowed, her mouth agape. Groaning, she paces several steps into the darkness before rounding on Nerani.

"I told you how this would end, Nerani. I told you what I saw."

"It doesn't have to end that way," Nerani insists. The proclamation sounds weak—timid—in the face of Orianna's rage.

"It does," Orianna disagrees. "It will."

She is drawing back into the shadows, her face lined with fury.

"Raven, wait!" Nerani calls, but the only reply is the mocking echo of the endless stone.

Orianna is gone.

CHAPTER 46

The Rebellion

EMERALA TOSSES AND turns within her hanging cot, her mind churning. All around her, the dimly lit quarters are filled with the sleepy rumblings of the crew. She stares without seeing at the bottom of the cot above her, watching as dusty grey light spills in through the cracks in the ceiling.

It is easy, in the obscurity of the dawn, to settle into impassivity. It is easy to be numb—to become a blank slate, floating—peaceful—upon the cerulean waves of the sea. That's what she needs. It's what she craves above all—serenity.

It won't be granted to her, here, in the stifling gloom of the ship's belly. Not today.

Too much has happened. Her stomach does an uneasy flip as she tries again to swallow all that she has learned Time and time again the captain had insisted that he was just as in the dark as she—that he was blindly following the dying orders of his father, nothing more.

Emerala should have been more suspicious of him from the very start.

A memory creeps into the forefront of her mind, and she is suddenly back in the musty gloom of the cathedral, staring up at Alexander's crooked grin.

Why are you trying to help me? she had asked him, drawn by the promise of adventure in his hazel eyes.

The look he gave her, then, was wicked. *Do I need a reason?*

Yes.

Boredom. The response was so immediate—so believable—at least to someone as prone to boredom as she. Then, she was happy merely to be given the opportunity to escape Chancey. She ignored Rob when he insisted the captain was bound to have some darker, ulterior motive. She brushed away his worries with a flick of her palm. She didn't care. She had no cares.

Heat seeps into her cheeks as she recalls how easy it had been to fool her. She is nothing more than a naïve child, she thinks, to have fallen for empty words and a smile. Everything the Hawk told her made perfect sense. His confession answered every question she had—quelled every whispering doubt at the back of her mind.

According to the Hawk, her father had left the island of Chancey to keep the Cairan treasure safe. He left with the key in tow, desperate to protect his legacy—to keep the young Prince Peterson from being discovered as his illegitimate son.

He left because, in short, he was blackmailed into doing so by the Cairan king.

The thoughts that swim to and fro in Emerala's head are too large for her to comprehend. That she is part of a prophecy is inconceivable to her— that she could be a queen is beyond her wildest imagination. Something deep within her urges her to be more suspicious—to give credence to her nagging doubts.

He could be lying, a voice within her says. *Evander the Hawk is an excellent liar.*

Whatever she might feel for him, whatever has transpired between them, she knows better than to trust him completely. And yet, for the time being, he is the only one giving her answers that make sense.

Her thoughts trail off into silence as she sees a shadow slip out from the cot nearest her. The long-limbed silhouette of Evander the Hawk moves like a wraith through the rows of sleeping crew, heading lithely towards the stairs that lead up onto the deck. She shuts her eyes, her heart skipping a beat as he passes by her cot, his boots scraping against the wood underfoot.

Where is he going? Tonight isn't his night for the watch, she's certain of it. She lies still, her chest rising and falling as she listens for his footfalls to recede upon on the creaking steps. Opening one eye, she glances towards the door. It swings open on the breeze, letting the rising dawn flood the staircase.

Emerala remains in her cot for the space of several heartbeats, trying and failing to will herself to fall back asleep. Curiosity needles her into remaining awake. Holding her breath, she swings her feet over the edge of her cot and slips out onto the splintering wood. The ship rises and falls beneath her and she steadies herself, taking care not to make any noise. In the cot to her left, a hulking shadow snorts loudly, rolling over with an incoherent grumble.

She hurries out from the sleeping quarters, glad for the feel of the breeze upon her skin. Outside, the deck is empty. Quiet. The sails have been doused for the night and the canvas hangs limp against the yardarms. The grey dawn gives way to morning as color leeches back into the world, staining the murky sea and painting the sky a clear, clean blue. Beyond the bow of the ship, the brilliant orange sun rises up over the eastern horizon. Emerala makes her way to the forecastle deck, shielding her eyes against the glare. There, in the distance, she can just make out a sliver of black at the space where the sea meets the sky.

Chancey.

The sight of her birthplace causes something to well within her. Grief? Homesickness? Apprehension? She cannot put a finger on her emotions— cannot pin down her thoughts long enough to understand what it is she feels. Life at sea has done that to her, she is finding. The ocean has chewed her up and spit her back out—has left her a dizzy, shambling shadow of herself. The Emerala who is returning home is not the Emerala that left, all those months ago. She expected the world to be endless—unconquerable. Her foray into piracy has taught her quite the opposite. The world, as it is, is impossibly small.

She stares at the strip of land until her eyes water, pressing her wind-blown ringlets out of her face and steeling herself against the wind. She wonders if Nerani and Rob mourn her, wonders if they believe her to be dead. What will they think, when they see her again?

She hears footfalls upon the deck behind her. She turns, his name already at her lips.

"Evander, you—"

But it is Alexander that idles on the deck before her, his knee-length jacket caught up in a gust of wind off of the sea. His cap is pulled low over his eyes, casting his features in shadow. He leans onto his good leg, keeping his weight off of his injury as best as he can as he surveys her through eyes that have grown ruddy with drink. At the sound of Evander's name, a bitter smile cuts across his face.

"Sorry to disappoint," he slurs.

Emerala sniffs, feeling herself bristling with fast rising anger. Without another word, she charges past him, the rising sun scorching her back as she heads across the deck.

"Emerala."

He grabs her arm, wrenching her backwards. They are face to face, her wild curls sweeping against the golden scruff of his jaw. She can taste the putrid ale rolling off of his tongue, can smell the rum that leaks from his pores like sweat.

"You've been avoiding me," he accuses.

"You're fairly observant for a drunk." Emerala pries her arm from his grasp. Hurt passes across his face and he teeters where he stands.

"What have I done?" he demands, the long fuse of his temper finally, finally running out. "What have I said to make you so angry with me?"

"Nothing at all," Emerala says. "That's the problem."

She brushes past him, her shoulder slamming hard into his as she walks away. He curses, the sound of his voice carried off by the snapping wind. Overhead, a lone seagull shrieks a plaintive cry.

"Saints, you can be insufferable at times, do you know that?"

Emerala draws to a stop, trying and failing to steady her temper. The cotton of her gown ripples past her, caught in the wind as it wraps around her legs. She glances over her shoulder, squinting into the sunlight. Alexander's silhouette is black against the rising sun. For all of his bravado, he balks beneath the look upon her face.

"The man on the island," she says, a snarl curling in her throat. "The debtor. He was my father."

Alexander's mouth opens, but no sound comes out. His lips snap shut. Open again. The stinging wind dies down with a sigh, leaving behind the murmur of waves against the hull and the thick, brackish smell of the sea.

"He was my father," Emerala repeats, her voice high and clear in the quiet. "And you left him there to die."

She turns and walks away from him, her feet slapping against the deck. This time, he does nothing to stop her from leaving. Her stomach feels hollow. So, too, does her head. She is empty, all of her, void of that which has always driven her, betrayed by the life at sea she spent a lifetime coveting.

She climbs the short steps to the gun deck, feeling hopelessly disillusioned. The sound of voices reaches her across the upper deck, causing her to draw up short. Glancing toward the quarterdeck, she can just make out the figures of Derek and Evander as they lean against the starboard side of the ship, each of them shrouded in a dissipating cloud of smoke.

Emerala draws as close to the upper deck as she dares, ducking down between two barrels that sit at the base of the stairs.

"You can ask me as many times as you like," Evander is saying, staring out to sea as he takes a drag from his pipe. "I'm not telling you."

Derek smiles gallantly, his manner forced—rehearsed. "And why's that?"

"Because," Evander says, expunging stinging smoke into the air before him. "I don't like nobility. I don't trust nobility."

Derek's smile wanes. "I'm a diplomat, not a nobleman."

Evander laughs, spitting another cloud of smoke from his lips. It is snatched away by the stinging wind.

"Let's not waste time lying to one another, your Highness." The title is delivered like an insult, the inflection scathing—scornful. Beside Evander, Derek blanches. He recovers quickly, the smile returning to his face, dimpling his cheeks.

"That's an interesting attitude to have," he observes, "coming from someone who spent his childhood living off of the generosity of nobility."

Evander tenses, his shoulders hunching beneath the scorching sun. When he speaks, his voice is low—dangerous. "You have no idea what you're talking about."

"Don't I?" Derek asks. "I thought I recognized the name Evander the first time I met you. It's quite a badge of shame, isn't it, to carry the mark of a bastard?"

Evander slams his pipe down hard against the wood, rounding on Derek and grabbing him by the cuff of the collar.

"You like your tongue, don't you, Stoward?" he snarls.

"I am rather fond of it, yes."

"Keep it in your mouth and maybe I won't cut it off."

Derek grimaces, unruffled by the pirate's temper. "How charming. I'm sure I don't have to tell you how unwise it is to threaten a prince."

"Why not?" Evander challenges. "Everyone already thinks you're dead."

"And I take it you'd delight in the opportunity to finish the job," Derek observes. Evander relinquishes his hold on him, shoving him aside with a grunt. He glowers as Derek adjusts his lapel, running his palms down the front of his jacket.

"What I'd like is for you to mind your own affairs," Evander says. "And I'll mind mine."

"Out of curiosity," Derek begins, "whose affairs will Emerala the Rogue be minding?"

Emerala stiffens at the sound of her name, her skin turning crimson as she realizes Derek is staring directly at the barrels behind which she crouches. Evander turns toward the gun deck, his golden eyes finding her immediately as she rises sheepishly from her hiding place.

"I was—I didn't—"

Derek holds up a hand to silence her. "Don't bother coming up with an excuse," he says. "I was just leaving."

He saunters easily down the steps toward the gun deck, breezing past Emerala without so much as a glance in her direction. Emerala is left standing alone before Evander, twisting her fingers together and waiting for him to say something—anything—to fill the silence. He watches her with amusement splayed across his features, his golden eyes catching the sunlight.

"How much of that did you hear?"

Emerala shrugs. "Enough to know that Derek doesn't like you."

Evander closes the space between them, taking the steps two at a time and drawing Emerala into him with the crook of his arm.

"Aye, well, that makes two of you," he says, his gaze riddled with implication as he kisses her once, twice. "Three if you count the cap'n." He kisses her a third time. "Four if you count the sorry sod I beat in cards last night."

Emerala presses her fingers to his lips to prevent the fourth kiss from landing.

"I don't—"

"Hate me?" Evander finishes, his voice muffled by her hand. "I believe that was your exact wording."

Emerala scowls, feeling suddenly defensive. "I don't know what I'm feeling," she admits. "I'm all turned around."

"I can remind you," he says, reaching up and prying her hand away from his mouth. He presses his lips against the underside of her wrist, where her pulse is visible beneath her olive skin. His golden eyes, wicked and sharp, never leave hers. She can feel his lips stretching into a smile against her skin and she pulls her arm out of his grasp, her heart skipping several beats.

"Don't gloat."

"I'm not gloating," he assures her. "I'm relishing."

"Well don't relish," she orders. "I have questions."

"Aye, I don't doubt that you do." He leans forward, pressing her hair behind her ear and letting his lips graze her neck just below her ear.

"Ask away," he whispers into her skin, his breath warm. His wild, black hair tickles the underside of her chin. She struggles to maintain her focus, her gut stirring at his touch.

"You called Derek a Stoward," she says.

"Aye." His lips are at the hollow of her throat, lingering just above her fluttering pulse. "That's not a question, love."

"Is he?" she asks. "A Stoward?"

Evander pulls away from her, a smile teasing at his lips. "What do you think?"

"I think he's Frederick Stoward, Rowland's eldest son, but that can't be right."

Mirth flickers through Evander's golden gaze. "And why's that?"

"Because he's dead," Emerala says. "I attended the funeral procession Rowland held in his honor."

Evander examines her quietly, the muscles in his jaw tightening. "Rowland Stoward is far too prideful of a man to admit that his only legitimate heir refused the crown."

"What kind of man would refuse to be king?" Emerala muses. "Everyone wants to be handed a seat of power."

"Aye," Evander agrees. "They do. Frederick Stoward is no different. He wants the throne as badly as anyone—more, still. He'll go after it, too, if Alexander manages to get his hands on Saynti's Treasure."

Emerala shakes her head, confused. "Why would he need to go after the crown if he turned it down in the first place?"

Evander smirks, his fingers dancing distractedly over the laces of her corset. "A kingship requires a man to take a queen. Rumor has it our good friend Derek had irreconcilable differences with his father over that particular account."

Emerala considers this, staring out at the dark mass of land on the eastern horizon.

"Does Alexander know?"

"Know what?" Evander asks, shading his eyes against the sun as he follows the line of Emerala's eyes. "That his good friend Derek is actually the long lost heir to the Stoward throne? Aye, I'm certain that he does."

Emerala scowls, her mood souring. *Another lie. Another secret.* The *Rebellion* feels suddenly too small, too oppressive. She stares out at the sea, the surface ever changing beneath the wind, and wishes—for the first time in her life—to be back in Chancey.

To be home.

She leans against the starboard siding of the boat, letting the wind whip her curls against her skin—reveling in the salty spray of the sea upon her face. She feels Evander behind her, feels the warmth of him as his arms encircle her waist.

"I have something for you," he says. "Hold out your hand."

"Why?"

"Don't be so suspicious, Rogue, just hold out your hand."

She does so, reluctantly unfurling her palm. She sees a flash of iridescence as something cold and smooth is placed in her grasp. She gasps quietly, weighting the familiar blade within her hand as her fingers close around the hilt.

"My dagger," she marvels. "But—how?"

She had abandoned it at the site of her arrest, leaving it near the prisoner's carriage during her narrow escape. There hadn't been time to retrieve it, not with the Golden Guard so hot on her trail.

Evander is silent for a long time, his chin resting on the top of her head as he stares out to sea.

"I came to find you," he says at last. "Cap'n ordered us back to the ship when the ambush failed, but I came looking for you. I found the dagger sticking out of some poor sod's shoulder. Your work, I'm sure."

She nods, remembering the feel of it—remembering the way the Guardian had crumpled beneath her. In her hand, the fragile blade is timorous beneath the dawn.

"I gave it to you the day we met," he reminds her—as if she needed reminding. That day had changed her life. "It was a gift. Rude of you, I think, to leave it behind."

"I won't lose it again," she promises, tucking it away within her corset. Her gaze travels back to the horizon—back to the looming mass of land, her land, in the distance. How long will it take, she wonders, until she returns at last to the cobbled streets of her childhood?

"Just a day more," Evander whispers, reading her mind. "I've already prepared a rowboat. We'll leave before the rest of the crew wakes."

"And then what?"

His breath is warm in her ear, and she catches a faint whiff of tobacco on his breath. "Then we go back to Chancey," he says. "I'm taking you home."

CHAPTER 47

The Rebellion

ALEXANDER AWAKES TO a bloodcurdling scream.

He leaps out of his bed in a single bound and immediately wishes he hadn't. His injured leg screams in agony and he nearly crumples back upon the cot. His vision swims, an aura pulling at the edges of his eyes as a nasty hangover roots about within his skull. Bracing himself, he limps across the uneven floor of his quarters and wrenches open the door. Warm morning light sweeps across him in a blinding swath of gold and he blinks furiously, his heart and his head pounding in time with one another. He hears the fluttering of wings as something swoops low over his head, rustling his disheveled hair.

Spinning on his heels, he sees Salty flapping wildly about his quarters, black talons extended.

"Emerala the Rogue," screams Salty. "Gone to die! Awk, gone to die!"

Something cold grabs hold of his insides as he watches the parrot.

"She's gone," comes a low growl behind him. Alexander glances over his shoulder to see the Lethal framed in the open doorway. The old pirate is grim and grey against the dazzling light behind him.

"Bloody bird has been screaming all morning."

"What do you mean, gone?" Alexander demands. He recalls the last time they had spoken, and the ardent hatred that had riddled her emerald gaze. He isn't surprised, he realizes, only disappointed. He snatches a pair of trousers off of the end of his cot and begins sliding his legs into them one at a time, hopping slightly to stay upright. His injured leg objects to the movement with a sharp ache.

"Lass left before sunrise," the Lethal says, looking sour. He adds, "with the Hawk."

At that, Alexander draws up short, one leg of his trousers still crumpled around his knee. He studies the Lethal's face. There is, as usual, no trace of humor in the murderer's expression. Disappointment gives way to something darker and angrier. His skin broils.

"Damn him," he curses. "Damn him to the Dark Below."

"What do ye need from me?" the Lethal asks, his face unreadable.

Alexander finishes dressing, his thoughts jumbling into one another. "How close are we to Chancey? Are we close enough to take the rowboats in?"

"Aye, we are."

"Then we'll follow them to shore," he says. "Fetch Thom, let him know where we're going. He'll be in charge while I'm gone."

"And the ship?" the Lethal asks. "We're getting mighty close to port. En't good to be spotted at a time like this."

"No, it's not." Alexander chews his cheek, considering his options. "Tell Thom to have the men bring the ship in quietly—dock her in one of the coves offshore. She'll be out of sight, then, at least."

"Ye want me to accompany you, then?" The Lethal's fingers dance at the hilt of his dagger.

"Yes," Alexander says without hesitation. "If it comes down to a fight, I need you on my side."

The Lethal draws his dagger from the scabbard at his waist. He flips the weapon easily, catching the hilt in his hand. "It will have to be a quick kill. I've got sleight of hand when it comes to fighting, aye, but the Hawk—well, the boy's merciless."

Alexander shoots him a grim look as he buttons the top of his undershirt. "Do whatever you need to do when the time comes."

The look that the Lethal gives him is frightening. "Aye, Cap'n."

The waves are calm as they paddle ashore. The wind has settled into an indulgent breeze, and the warmth of it tickles the back of Alexander's neck as he draws the oars towards him. The rhythmic splashing of the paddles that shatter the glassy surface of the sea is as low and as a slow as a drumbeat.

Drums of war, he thinks, giving way to the anger that simmers just within him. It is close to boiling, now, to bubbling over and scalding everything within reach. All this time, he knew that the Hawk had some ulterior motive. He knew that the golden-eyed pirate had some deeper, independent plan. He knew, and yet he had let Evander the Hawk continue on unbridled—unchecked.

I thought that if I gave him enough rope, he would hang himself, he muses. He sees, now, that he was wrong.

He should have been more protective of Emerala—he should have been more guarded. The moment they brought her onboard, the Hawk had made himself her shadow. He had followed her everywhere, coveting her, cornering her. Jealous, Alexander had chalked it up to nothing more than an infatuation.

Jealousy, he thinks, chiding himself silently. *Jealousy is a child's vice, not a man's.*

His feelings for Emerala have made him blind. He assumed that the Hawk's behavior was due to feeling similarly—not due to his constant, calculating planning.

"I'm a fool," he says aloud, unthinking.

Before him, the Lethal is quiet as he fingers the blade of his dagger. The parrot rests upon his shoulder, his beady black eyes catching in the sun.

"Are ye?" the Lethal asks, one eyebrow rising upon his forehead. The dull coloration of his partially blind eye is pronounced in the sunlight.

"I am. I should have seen the Hawk for what he was." Alexander shakes his head, frowning as the paddles hit sand. The tide is low—the pale beach stretches out before them, interspersed with formless blue shadows cast by the looming cliff wall.

"And what is he?" the Lethal asks.

"A liar. A traitor. A thief."

"Murderer," squawks Salty.

The Lethal gives a wry laugh. "So he's a pirate, then, aye?"

Alexander scowls at him as he leaps from the rowboat. His boots squelch into the damp sand underfoot. He grabs hold of the wherry, watching as the Lethal does the same. The water is up to his knees. A dark line of saturation plies at his trousers. Together, they drag the boat ashore and upend it on the sand. Alexander peers out across the rippling ocean, shielding his eyes against the dazzling sunlight that plays off of the white-capped waves. The tide is still leeching from the sand, dragging the breakers farther from the cliff. They have several hours before they need to worry about the rowboat being carried off.

Squaring his shoulders, he scours the beach. His fingers linger at the ready just above his cutlass. The beach is empty—there are no flashes of gold, no Guardians in sight.

Not yet, anyway, he thinks.

A quarter mile or so ahead he can see a slender figure making her way down the long stretch of beach. Her features are obscured by the blue shade of the cliffs, but the curves of her are unmistakable.

Emerala. He is unsure whether to feel anger or relief.

The Hawk is nowhere is sight.

He curses under his breath, his eyes scanning the shadows. "Where is he?"

"Likely saw us coming," the Lethal snarls. "Tread carefully, now."

They pick their way cautiously down the beach, keeping their weapons in their scabbards. They are silent as they study the shadows beneath the crumbling stone outcroppings of the cliffs. The sun is rising higher in the sky, dragging a sheet of glistening gold across the fast drying sand.

Several uneventful moments pass them by. Up ahead, the figure of Emerala is growing smaller. Silently, Alexander gestures for the Lethal to follow her. The old pirate nods in a show of understanding, taking off down the beach. He sticks close to the lapping waves, his eyes trained upon the cliffs.

Alexander draws closer to the crumbling rocks, his head cocked as he listens for any sort of sound. All he can hear is the whisper of the wind and the murmur of the sea. A soft breeze tickles the tall, yellow grass that rises between the rocks upon the sand. The movement pulls his attention and he draws closer, his cutlass sliding out from the scabbard at his waist with a shivering sigh. A thin sheen of sweat rises to Alexander's skin beneath the itching collar of his undershirt. He flicks his hat upwards upon his head to paw at his forehead, freezing in mid-movement as he feels something cold and hard press against his skull.

"Hello, Hawk," he says coldly. He curses himself inwardly for not hearing the pirate slinking up behind him in the sand.

"Cap'n." He can hear the sneer in the Hawk's voice. The pistol presses harder against the back of his head. "Drop your sword."

Alexander obliges, listening to the ringing of steel as his cutlass falls against the sand.

"Are you planning to kill me, then?"

"Not just yet," the Hawk replies. The pistol moves away from his head as the pirate swings around on the sand so that they are face to face upon the beach. The sun is rising higher, still, above the cliffs, throwing golden light upon the breakers. Beneath the cliff, he and the Hawk are still blanketed in cobalt shadow.

Alexander stares into those gold, unblinking eyes and says nothing.

"Shouldn't have followed me, Cap'n."

"You shouldn't have taken Emerala."

The Hawk throws his head back and crows in laughter. "Taken? You think I *took* her? The Rogue wanted to leave. It was her choice."

Alexander frowns. "I'm sure you had a hand in convincing her."

The Hawk shakes his head, still grinning. "I'm innocent," he says. "My only crime, as it has been from the very beginning, is wanting her."

The bravado in his words is off-putting. Alexander scowls at him, trying to read the lines of his face—to see whether or not this is another bluff. He is always playing a hand—always upping the ante. Alexander is growing tired of the game.

Before him, the Hawk presses the barrel of the pistol firmly between Alexander's eyes. "You asked me why I wanted her on the ship, aye? You asked me what *purpose* she served."

Alexander is silent, waiting beneath the cold lip of steel at his brow. The Hawk winks at him, his gaze thick with implication. A lewd grin splits his face in two.

"She served a fine purpose for me."

Alexander can feel the heat of rage curling within him. Fury rises into his cheeks. His scalp grows hot beneath his hat. His fingers tighten into a fist; the flesh of his knuckles pull against bone, fade to white.

A bawdy laugh escapes the Hawk, the skin around his eyes crinkling. "Hit a nerve, have I, Cap'n? Did you think she was yours all this time? Did you think it was you she wanted?"

He takes a slow step forward, the pistol lowering ever so slightly. Alexander notes this in silence, the white-hot anger still simmering beneath his skin—the sour ache of a hangover still taking up residence in his skull.

"I can let you know what you've missed out on," the Hawk says, still grinning. He leans in, lowering his voice to a whisper. "I can tell you what she tastes like."

Alexander shouts, his voice spilling from him in a wordless cry as he surges forward in a rage. In one sweeping movement, he knocks the pistol from the pirate's hand as his fist makes contact with the side of his jaw.

The Hawk curses, stumbling back several steps as he searches the sand for the pistol. His temper still boiling, Alexander swings his fist a second time. Gratification ripples through him as his knuckles make contact with the Hawk's lip. Blood trickles down his chin, dripping onto the sand in glistening globules of red. The Hawk stumbles into an outcropping at his back, bracing himself against the rock. He spits blood upon the sand, wiping at his mouth with the back of his hand. His fist comes away bloody and he growls, charging Alexander like a bull.

He slams hard into Alexander's midsection. The pair hits the beach with a painful collision of bone against bone, sand flying up around them in sprays of gold. Alexander flinches as the Hawk's bloodied fist comes into contact with his nose. Red shoots across his field of vision and he shouts in pain, thrusting the Hawk off of him. He rises to his feet, spitting blood and sand out of his mouth.

His nose throbs with the steady blood flow that trickles down into his lips. The pain is sharp, pronounced. Nauseating. It's definitely broken. He presses his boots into the sand and looks around for the Hawk, his fists at the ready.

Before him, the Hawk is equally worse for the wear, a dagger at his throat. The Lethal stands astride him, his gaze cold as he glowers at Alexander.

"Fighting like boys," he says, and scoffs. "Both of ye."

"Where's Emerala?" Alexander demands. The taste of blood is metallic on his tongue.

"Halfway down the beach, by now, I'd reckon," snarls the Lethal. "Couldn't get her, what with ye two carrying on to kill one another out here in the open. Is it the attention of the Golden Guard ye want, boys? Because that's what you'll get if ye don't keep quiet."

Alexander takes several steps closer to them, aware of the rising sun burning the side of his face. The Lethal is right—the Guardians will begin patrolling the beach with the dawning morning. They won't be safe here, not for long. He lifts his cutlass from the sand, leering at the oozing cut that splits the Hawk's lip down the middle. The pirate stares back at him, his gaze jovial in spite of the sliver of steel pressed beneath his larynx.

"You're too easy, Cap'n," he says.

"Shut your trap, boy," snaps the Lethal, pressing the dagger harder into his flesh.

Alexander's grip tightens upon the hilt of his cutlass. His injured leg throbs beneath him and he quails, his vision spinning. His fury keeps him upright—keeps him rooted to the ground underfoot.

"You're right," Alexander says to the Lethal, his gaze still trained upon the Hawk. "The Guardians will be here soon. So I'd say we have to act fast."

"Aye," agrees the Lethal. "Let's move on from here, all of us."

"No." Alexander shakes his head. He jabs a bloody finger at the sand. "This is where Evander the Hawk dies. This is how he dies. Right here, beneath the blade in my hand." He angles his cutlass, tilting the blade until it tips just beneath the Hawk's chin.

"Think about what you're aiming to do, Alexander," the Lethal cautions.

"I have thought about it," snaps Alexander. The blood coursing to his nose is making him dizzy. "He's done nothing but lie and cheat since the moment this whole thing began. His usefulness has run out."

The Lethal frowns, his good eye scrutinizing Alexander beneath the scorching sun. "Is murder what ye really want?"

"Interesting choice of words," the Hawk muses, " coming from a murderer."

"Shut up," Alexander snaps. The coppery taste of blood on his tongue is nauseating. "Not another word out of you."

The Hawk laughs. "Or what? You'll kill me? Seems like you've already made that decision, Cap'n."

"Think this through," the Lethal says, lowering his dagger as Alexander presses the blade of his cutlass against the Hawk's throat. Blood drips from his nose, landing against the quivering blade with an audible plop.

"You're supposed to be on my side," growls Alexander.

The Lethal's expression is grim. "I am. I am on your side. But ye need to listen to me. The Hawk knows things—things we don't know. He knew Emerala's father was the man in the maze. He knew how that map of yours was spelled."

He pauses, wetting his lower lip, and adds, "He killed Charles Argot on Caros."

Alexander's headache explodes behind his eyes, setting his skull to throbbing. He glowers at the Hawk, his fury burning hotter still.

"You bastard," he curses. "You treacherous, lying—"

"Argot was worth more to you dead than alive," the Hawk says, pawing at the fast-drying blood on his chin.

"Is that right?" Alexander snarls. "Turns out, so are you."

"So kill me already," the Hawk challenges. "If the tables were turned and I had a blade to your throat, you'd already be carrion for the birds."

"There won't be enough of you left for the birds when I'm finished, traitor."

The Lethal steps between them, placing his palm firmly against Alexander's chest and shoving him back a step upon the sand. He forces

Alexander to look at him, grabbing him by the cuff of the shirt and shaking him hard.

"There are other ways to make a man talk. Effective ways. Painful ways. Don't be rash, boy. We can find out what ye need to know."

There is a low grunt and the Lethal's eyes widen into circles. Blood pools within his lower lip, staining his teeth red. Horrified, Alexander glances down to see the silvery point of a knife sticking out of the front of his chest—directly through his heart. Deep red seeps through the fabric of the murderer's undershirt, staining the moth-eaten brown of his jacket. Over his shoulder, the Hawk crows triumphantly. The Lethal gives one last gurgling gasp and sinks down onto to his knees in the sand.

"This is going to cost me," Evander says. "But Saints, I've wanted to do that for a long time." Lifting his boot, he kicks the old pirate to the ground with the heel of his boot.

CHAPTER 48

Chancey

EMERALA RUSHES DOWN the beach, her bare feet slipping upon the sun cooked granules of sand. The damp hem of her violet gown whispers against her bare ankles, and she bunches the skirt within her fists to keep from tripping.

Her heart pounds in her chest, rising to her throat and forcing her to swallow, hard. She is so close—so close to seeing her family again. She does not know how to feel. She does not know what to feel.

She only knows that she needs to keep running.

Her hair falls down around her face in bouncing ringlets, the strands pulled loose from where she has bound the bulk of it into a loose bun. She allows the rippling wind that rolls down from the cliffs to sweep the tendrils of black from her eyes, picking up her pace as a salty squall caresses the small of her back.

Evander told her to run.

They had seen Alexander and the Lethal approaching in the rowboat long before the pair made it to shore. Something uneasy had twitched within her at the sight of them. Some deeper, wordless instinct implored her to see reason, assured her that this—what she was doing—was wrong. Everything was backwards. Everything was ruined. She stared into the dazzling sun as it played upon the cresting waves, squinting at the distant outline of the rowboat drifting to shore.

Run, Evander instructed. *Hide. I'll deal with them.*

What will you do? she asked. Then, before he could answer—*Don't hurt them.*

I won't, he promised. *I'll just slow them down.*

And so she ran.

She gasps as something passes by her face with a flutter and a scream. Alexander's silver parrot circles around her, wings flapping furiously. His black eyes are murderous as he drops down to her shoulder. His talons scrape against her skin and she winces.

"Emerala the Rogue," he squawks. "Pretty, pretty girl."

He plucks contentedly at a ringlet with his beak.

"Copper, copper eyes," he sings. He bends down low, extending his neck and ruffling his feathers. "Awk! Murderer!"

Emerala hears a hoarse shout at her back. The sound is barely audible over the waves, but it is there. She whirls about, the talons tightening upon her shoulder. Scanning the beachfront, her eyes land upon two figures in the blue shadows of the cliffs. It is Evander the Hawk and Alexander, of that there can be no doubt. She hears a grunt as Alexander's fist connects with Evander's jaw. He stumbles several steps backwards upon the sand, quickly regaining his balance. Alexander takes another swing, again making contact with Evander's face. He groans, his fingers flying to his mouth.

Emerala is running, again, this time in the direction of the pirates. Anger courses through her like wildfire. She sees Evander lunge in Alexander's direction and the two men topple downward, falling out of sight behind a grey outcropping of fallen rocks. For a long time there is silence. Emerala wavers upon the sand, her heartbeat threatening to crack her ribcage as she gasps for breath. She stares into the undulating grass that snaps and sputters in the wind, waiting for some sort of sound.

Any sort of sound.

The wind carries with it the low, angry murmur of men's voices. She cannot hear what they are saying, not from here. She begins to inch slowly closer—moving as cautiously as she dares—when she hears another angry cry. Again, the sound has come from Alexander. With a snarl and a curse, the singing of steel starts up in the morning sun. Her heart seizes within her chest as she hears the rhythmic thrusting of one blade meeting another. The shivering song of swordplay echoes across the beach.

The wind that tickles the back of her neck picks up, suddenly, urgently—swallowing the sound of steel upon steel as invisible fingers wrench at the hem of her dress. The unexpected gale snaps at the top of the rolling breakers, making the waves lap at the beach with rabid fervor. Skeletal clouds clutch at the westward sky overhead, their grey tendrils creeping toward the sun. Emerala shivers in the chill, caught between the buffeting wind to the west and the golden sunbursts to the east.

She races around the edge of the stone, stopping short at the sight before her. Alexander and Evander are head to head, one bloodied face glowering into the other as their swords meet between them. With a grunt, Evander shoves Alexander back, sweeping his blade again in his direction. There is another ringing clash as Alexander parries his blow, his face scrunching in exertion as blood trickles from his nose and into his mouth.

"Stop!" Emerala screams, her voice shrill against the sound of the whistling wind. Salty echoes her cry, his voice guttural. She stamps her foot in irritation, kicking up granules of sand. The men before her continue to fight, heedless of her commands. She runs forward, her cheeks red and angry.

"Stop this instant! Both of you!"

Her order falls on deaf ears. The men continue to parry and advance, their weapons playing off of the other in an equal show of swordsmanship.

At last, Alexander uses his blade to thrust Evander backwards, the force of his weight overpowering the lanky pirate. Evander falls back hard against a rock, keeping his sword held out before him. Seeing her chance, Emerala rushes between the two men. Squawking in indignation, Salty takes off and finds somewhere safer to nestle.

"Stop!" She extends a palm towards each of the men. They stand on either side of her, their chests heaving with exertion. Alexander's sword lowers obediently, the point dropping down toward the sand. His hazel eyes are lined with defeat.

"Are you two *trying* to kill each other?" The wind whips at her hair, tugging stray tendrils into her mouth.

"That's the idea," Evander mutters from behind her. She turns around to glare at him pointedly, furious. He is dabbing at a shallow cut that runs the length of his cheek, his golden eyes flashing with annoyance as he surveys the blood that comes away on his fingers. His black hair falls into his eyes, pushed forward by the wind at his back. Behind his head, the ominous grey clouds creep ever forward, bleeding through the clear blue sky at an alarming rate.

"Drop your swords, both of you," she commands. The two pirates stare at her in silence, unmoving.

"Do it." She jabs a finger at the sand. "Unless you want to fight through me, and I don't think either of you plans on killing me today."

Alexander is the first to follow her directions, reluctantly returning his cutlass to the scabbard at his waist. She continues to glare at Evander, waiting for him to do the same. At last, he obliges, the glimmer of sunlight on the blade extinguishing as it slides into the leather hold.

"You said you wouldn't kill them," she seethes. "You promised."

He wipes one bloodied hand upon his trousers. "Did I?"

Emerala says nothing, only scowls at him across the gathering dark.

"He lied to you, Emerala," Alexander says. "I don't know what he's told you, but I promise you it was a lie. All of it."

Emerala turns to face Alexander, surprised by the sincerity in his voice. He regards her through plaintive eyes, his face crusted with blood.

"I don't know what to believe anymore," she says.

"Believe me," Alexander insists, pressing four bloodied fingers firmly into his chest. "*Believe me.* I had no idea your father was involved in any of this. If I knew he was being held prisoner—if I knew—"

His voice trails off into silence and he swallows, hard, his gaze beseeching. Behind her, she hears Evander let loose a bitter laugh. Something dark and hostile twists within her.

"Why should I trust you?" she snaps, scowling up at Alexander. The wind whips at her back, nudging her forward several steps across the sand.

"You shouldn't," Evander says. Emerala rounds upon him, her eyes blazing with fury. The crooked grin saps out of his lips at the sight of her.

"Why should I trust *either* of you?"

467

"Emerala," Alexander says slowly, and something within his voice makes her turn. His words are desolate—heavy. "Emerala, look. Look what he's done."

He gestures toward the cliff and she follows the line of his finger, her eyes dropping to a figure upon the sand a few feet away. Her heart seizes within her chest as she recognizes the dark silhouette to be none other than Lachlan the Lethal. The brutish wind tugs at the hem of his jacket, lifting up the bloodied flap of leather just over his heart.

"No," she whispers. Tears prickle in her lower lids, obscuring her vision. The dark figure on the beach blurs in and out of focus.

"No." Her voice is swallowed by the howling wind. The sound mimics a plaintive cry as it whistles across the beachfront. The entire form of the Lethal's corpse seems to dance upon the breeze and she gasps, stifling a sob. The sun is swallowed by the coiling clouds overhead. The golden light extinguishes against Emerala's skin and she is left shivering beneath the oncoming storm.

She spins on her heels, kicking up sand as she charges several steps toward Evander. Her blood courses through her veins, red and hot and sticking.

"You did this."

His face is impassive. "Aye."

"How? How could you do this?" Her voice rises to a shout, the sound muffled by a sudden rumble of thunder out at sea. Her fingers close instinctively around the dagger hidden within her corset.

Evander shrugs, smirking. "It had to be done."

"You're a monster." The wind shrieks atop the waves, driving the white-caps hard against the shore. Lightning snaps across the sky. The air hums with electricity. Her wild curls whip in and out of her eyes, cracking against her skin like a whip.

"It had to be done," Evander repeats. His voice is devoid of emotion. "He was about to ruin everything."

At her back, Emerala can hear Alexander beseeching her to stay calm—to back away. She ignores him, blood pounding within her ears. She draws the iridescent hilt from within her gown, rushing at Evander with the blade outstretched. He snatches her easily in his arms, the ghost of a smile on his lips.

"Easy now, love," he chides. "You wouldn't kill me with my own weapon, would you?"

"I trusted you." She tries and fails to rip free of his grasp.

"Didn't your father ever tell you not to trust pirates?"

He draws her into him, his nose inches from hers. The proximity of him is familiar—too familiar, now—and she hates herself for it at once.

"Bad men, the lot of us," he says, smiling. "Good men gone rotten inside, or so your father used to tell me. We're not very trustworthy at all, it would seem."

Emerala pulls back from him, her eyes locking on his. "You knew him? You knew my father?"

Evander's only response is laughter, the sound stolen away by the rising winds.

"Emerala, get away from him," Alexander orders. His voice is calm, level. This time, when she tugs at Evander's grasp, he lets her go. She backs away from him, her heart sinking, breaking.

"I never thought you were a good man," she whispers. Her voice is lost beneath the storm. "But I let myself believe in you anyway."

"That was your first mistake," Evander says. His piercing eyes linger too long upon hers and—for an instant—Emerala thinks she sees a flicker of regret pass across his features. His fingers open and close and his side.

"That's all you have to say to me?" Emerala asks. "That I made a *mistake*?"

His jaw locks and he swallows, saying nothing.

A laugh, high and clear, leaks out across the beach, drawing their attention toward the cliffs.

"Emerala the Rogue," calls a disembodied voice, shouting to be heard over the wind. "Back from the dead, I see."

Two cutlasses shiver beneath the wind as they are drawn, once more, from their scabbards. Emerala sees Evander lock eyes with Alexander, his expression grim. They draw back to back, searching the length of the beach for the owner of the voice. Emerala scowls up at them, frustration coursing through her.

Bloody pirates, she thinks bitterly.

"Noble," says the voice. "But we mean her no harm."

"Who are you?" demands Alexander.

"I am nobody you want to trifle with."

"Show yourself," Evander calls.

"Sheath your weapons first."

Evander sneers, his golden eyes scanning the shadows. "Not a chance in the Dark Below."

There is a moment of silence before the voice responds. "Then you will be regarded as enemies, and the Rogue your captive."

"I'm not a captive," Emerala calls out over their shoulders, ignoring the reproachful look she receives from both of them. She rises onto her toes in order to get a better look at the stone. She can see the shadow of a man lingering behind an outcropping up ahead. Raising her voice, she adds, "I'm here of my own free will."

Slowly, cautiously, the shadow emerges from the rock wall. Surprise courses through her as she recognizes the newcomer at once.

Topan. He is the picture of serenity as he approaches the group, his indigo eyes bright. His dark tunic and breeches lend him a regal appearance. One gold earring hangs from his right earlobe and he fingers this as he smiles cordially at the pirates.

"Just one Cairan, aye?" Evander scoffs. "We can take him, easy."

Emerala opens her mouth to protest, but Alexander beats her to it. "No, we can't." He studies the Cairan king, recognition flickering across his features. "I know who you are. You wouldn't come alone. We're surrounded, aren't we?"

Topan's smile widens. "A wise man, your captain. I won't disclose how many men I've brought with me today, but trust that there is a Listener waiting in every direction you might turn."

"How did you find us?" Alexander asks.

The wind tugs at Topan's sleek, black hair, sending loose strands flying into his eyes as he draws closer to the trio. "The better question may be how we found you before the Golden Guard. Your arrival drew quite a bit of attention. This is a small island, Captain Mathew. Someone is always listening. Someone is always watching. Now if you would please put away your weapons, I'd be hugely grateful."

Alexander frowns, sheathing his weapon. Evander mutters crossly, but follows his lead. Reaching behind him, he takes hold of Emerala's arm, repositioning her out of sight. The maneuver is impulsive—instinctive. She pries her arm out of his reach, recoiling from his touch.

"Keep your hands off of me," she hisses up at him.

"That's not what you said several nights ago." The words leak out from the corner of his mouth, his voice just loud enough to be heard over the rising storm. Quick as a flash, Alexander rounds on him, his pistol leveled at the space between Evander's eyes.

"Say that again," Alexander challenges.

Emerala flinches, humiliation coursing through her. "Alex—"

He ignores her. The hammer clicks into place. "Go ahead. Say it. I'll bury a bullet in your skull."

Evander scoffs. "You keep threatening to kill me and then you don't deliver. It's becoming disappointing."

Before them, Topan interlocks his fingers, his expression stoic. He barks a command, but the sound of his voice is snatched away before Emerala can hear him. Several Listeners emerge from the shadows, closing in noiselessly across the beach. Emerala catches the dwindling light shivering on the blades of several dozen daggers.

"Put away the gun, Captain," Topan orders. "Hands in the air, both of you."

"You heard the man," Evander says, his lopsided grin wicked. His hands raise obediently, palms outward, as he stares at Alexander down the barrel of the gun.

"This isn't over," Alexander snarls. He replaces the gun into his holster, raising his palms over his head. Before them, Topan is scrutinizing the trio in unreadable silence.

"Clearly I've interrupted something," he says. "Unfortunately, we don't have the time to work through whatever personal problems you're having.

We need to move quickly. A platoon of Guardians is heading toward the ports as we speak. Your—antics, if we will—have not gone unnoticed. You'll understand if I'm not all too eager to let Emerala the Rogue fall into the usurper's hands a second time."

"What do you want from us?" Evander demands.

Topan appears startled by that. "From you? Nothing. We're here to take the Rogue home."

"And what about us?" Alexander asks. "Will you kill us?"

"Kill you? Saynti, no." Topan glances towards the corpse of Lachlan, prostrate upon the sand. "We're not in the habit of murder. I find it distasteful."

"So you'll let us go?"

"No." Topan's indigo gaze returns to Alexander, his brows dipping low over a troubled visage. "You'll come with us."

He nods to someone in the circle of men and there is a sudden flurry of movement. In an instant, both Evander and Alexander have been shoved to their knees in the sand. Blindfolds are placed over their eyes as their hands are bound at their backs. Evander unleashes a torrent of curses, thrashing as best as he can beneath the hold of several men. Next to him, Alexander is silent.

"What is this?" Emerala snaps, irate. "What are you doing?"

"The location of the Forbidden City is quite a valuable secret these days," Topan explains. "I'm not willing to divulge that kind of information to our guests just yet."

"Are they your guests?" she asks. "Or are they prisoners?"

Topan studies her shrewdly, peering at her through the sticking green ether of the storm. "Your time away hasn't made you any less persistent, I see."

Emerala ignores him. "Are they your prisoners?" she repeats.

"They're pirates," Topan says. "Outsiders. There are no outsiders permitted within the walls of the Forbidden City."

Topan snaps his fingers and the pirates are dragged to their feet. Emerala watches as they are led off down the beach, Topan trailing in their wake.

Emerala hurries to keep up with him, her movements slowed by the sheer force of the driving wind.

Falling into step beside Topan, she says, "You still haven't answered my question."

Topan purses his lips, staring up into the storm. "No," he relents. "They're not prisoners. Not yet."

He stalks off in silence, ending the conversation. For a moment, Emerala hangs back, her attention turning to the lifeless shadow on the beach—to the body of Lachlan the Lethal. She feels a sudden stab of anxiety at leaving him there, but there is no other option. There is nothing she can do. The Guardians will be upon them soon, like vultures drawn to carrion. She cannot risk her life for the dead; she learned that lesson once already.

Up ahead, the Listeners and their captives are growing smaller as they head down the stretch of beach. Topan stands at attention, his indigo eyes guarded as he waits for Emerala to catch up to him. When at last she does, dragging her heels through the inundated sand, he sighs.

"There's a war coming, Emerala the Rogue," he says, leaning in to be heard over the wind. "Like it or not, you and your pirate friends have a part to play."

CHAPTER 49

The Forbidden City

NERANI FINDS ORIANNA pacing restlessly in her quarters, her youngest brother resting on her hip. Drawing to a stop in the opening, Nerani watches as her oldest friend murmurs softly into the tousled hair of the toddler, her gaze troubled. The boy blinks up at her, his wet, blue eyes gleaming in the throw of the lantern that hangs upon the wall. His thumb moves in and out of his mouth, the finger pruned from suckling. His red cheeks are stained with tears.

"You'll be alright, Eram," Orianna reassures the boy. "It was just a little spill."

Orianna catches sight of Nerani, still lingering in the open doorway of the cramped quarters. The frown upon her face deepens. Eram mutters sleepily, his words thick and unintelligible as they catch upon his thumb. Orianna turns her back to Nerani, placing the small boy down upon the cot and drawing a coarse blanket over his shoulders. Eram makes a quiet sound of protestation but otherwise allows for his sister to tuck the covers around his curling figure. He is asleep within seconds, the soft rising and falling of his breathing visible beneath the pilled cotton.

When Orianna at last turns back to face her, she is brimming with barely controlled rage.

"Orianna—" Nerani begins. Orianna holds out one shaking palm to quiet her.

"I don't know who you are anymore."

Nerani recoils, drawing back upon the stone.

"How can you say that?"

Orianna shakes her head, running her fingers through her sleek, black hair. "I never thought you would be the kind of person to run towards danger. That was always Emerala—she was the impulsive one. She made the poor decisions. But you—you've never been one to misstep."

Nerani feels shame coursing through her like wildfire. She recalls the look upon Topan's face as he asked for her hand in marriage—recalls the way he had gripped her hand to his chest when she at last obliged. She made him a promise. She promised him her heart, but it was never hers to give. How costly her mistakes will be, she cannot presume to know. And still, something stronger than guilt—something deeper than shame—prickles within her.

"I love him," she says, defiance lacing her words.

The look in Orianna's eyes is sad. "I know that. Saynti, I know that. But it's an impossible love, Nerani, and James Byron serves a far stronger master."

Nerani feels the first sting of unwanted tears gathering in her lower lids. She blinks them away furiously. Before her, Orianna continues to study her sadly, regretfully.

"You can't expect to have a life with him. I've already told you how it ends—I told you what I saw. If you continue to carry on as you are it will end in death. For both of you."

"Don't you think I know that?" Nerani asks, her voice snapping like a whip. Her fingers tremble. "What do you want from me? Do you want me to never see him again? I will—I'll do it. Only—" she pauses, inhaling shakily. "Please help me to get him out of here."

"Nerani—"

"*Please*," Nerani repeats, her voice a shadow of a whisper. "Do this for me."

Orianna heaves a great sigh, her features desolate. Her glossy, black hair is cobalt beneath the firelight. She twists it round and round upon her index finger, tugging at her scalp as her eyes flicker back and forth across Nerani's face.

"He can't be allowed to leave the city," Orianna says. Her words are careful—cautious. "He can't be trusted, not now that he knows where we are. Rowland Stoward has more than enough incentive to make him talk."

Nerani can feel the desperation rising within her, choking her. She resents the sympathy in Orianna's eyes—hates the even keel of Orianna's temper.

"He won't say anything," she insists. She thinks of the angry, red lash marks that disfigured his skin, of the Guardian lying dead at her feet in the palace courtyard.

Orianna studies her for a long moment before replying, "You can't know that for certain."

"He would never sell me out to the usurper."

"Maybe not you," Orianna agrees, "But what about your people? He's a man, Nerani, and men are weak. He would sell the rest of us out in an instant. His love for you means nothing to me." She looks over her shoulder at Eram, sleeping soundly in the cot.

"I have to protect my family."

"He won't give us away," Nerani repeats, but the mettle has leaked out of her words. Her hand passes absently over the space where her fingers once were and she feels suddenly hollow—helpless.

Orianna reaches out and takes Nerani's hand within her own. "The hate in the usurper's heart is far stronger than General Byron's love for you, and you know that. Don't be naïve."

Heavy silence settles between them. They stand facing one another, listening as the muffled sounds of the main cavern drift into the opening.

"This story is not about you and James Byron," Orianna begins. "Not anymore. It's about all of us. It's about Rob. It's about my brothers. It's about everyone out there in the dining hall. You're hiding the enemy in our midst, Nerani. He can't be allowed to leave—not knowing what he knows."

Nerani swallows, grief sticking in her throat. "What will you do? If I can't convince you otherwise, will you go to Topan?"

"I already have," Orianna says. Nerani freezes at that, her body going cold. Her lips open and close as she searches for something to say, but no words rise to her lips.

476

Before her, Orianna looks tired. "He wasn't there. He's left the city."

Nerani pauses at that, feeling a small rush of relief wash over her. She has time then, for whatever it's worth. "Where is he?"

"I don't know." Orianna frowns down at her feet, her gaze dark. "Rob was there, in Topan's gallery. He told me that Topan had business to tend to in Chancey."

Nerani feels a second surge of relief, larger this time. Orianna did not tell Roberts that James was hiding out in the tunnels. For that, at least, she is grateful. Where Topan would have handled the news with his usual amount of calm rationale, the impulsive Roberts would have only reacted.

She does not want to imagine what her reckless cousin might have done. The very thought makes her stomach sick.

"He wouldn't tell you what the business was?" she asks Orianna.

"I don't think he knew."

There is the sudden, reverberating sound of a pistol being fired somewhere outside. The echo of the blast collides into Nerani's chest as though she herself has been shot. With a wail of alarm, Eram awakes. He reaches for his sister, his eyes rounded with fright. Orianna collects him within her arms, shushing him. Her eyes meet Nerani's over the top of his head.

There is a flurry of movement in the doorway and Nerani spins upon her heels to get a better look at the newcomer. Another of Orianna's brothers—Petram—skids to a stop against the stone, his blue eyes fearful. At his back, Nerani can see a crowd of Cairans surging across the flickering cavern. They swell and break like a wave, their voices overlapping in climbing terror.

"What is it?" Orianna demands of her brother. "What's happened?"

"A Guardian—" Petram gasps, fear cutting across his face. "There's a Guardian in the city."

Nerani does not dare to look at Orianna. She can feel her friend's eyes boring a hole in her skin. Her stomach is weighted with dread. Her blood is ice within her veins. Petram surges into the room, taking refuge in the shadows. Outside, the shouting has risen to a roar. Feet stamp against the stone. The very foundation of the city seems to shake.

"Where is he?" Nerani demands.

"In the dining hall. He's been shot."

Nerani races from the room before Petram has finished speaking. Blood pounds in her ears, turning her vision red. She sees Orianna thrusting Eram into Petram's arms, bidding him to watch his younger brother. And then her friend is at her side—silent, unreadable. Together, they shove through the throng of clustered Cairans, ducking beneath flailing arms and pushing past whispering kitchen maids.

They break through the crowd after several moments of struggling, emerging through a barrier of Listeners and stepping into a circular clearing. The torchlight that flickers upon the wall is ominous as it dances across the pressing faces of onlookers. Before them looms the impenetrable darkness of the tunnels. Nerani takes a step forward and finds herself stopped short by an arm flying across her chest.

"Stay back," orders a Listener. Nerani scowls at the floor, drawing away from him.

"There," Orianna says. Her fingers claw at Nerani's wrist as she points with her free hand. Nerani follows her gesture, her eyes finding Roberts at the center of the circle. Head bowed and hands in his pockets, he stands watch over a figure that lies prostrate upon the cool stone. Nerani races forward, this time ignoring the shouts of protest from the Listeners that hold back the crowd. At her side, Orianna matches her step for step, her skirts billowing.

Roberts looks up at the sound of their approach, his surprise quickly giving way to annoyance.

"Nerani. Orianna. You were ordered to stay away, I'm sure."

Nerani ignores him, pushing past her cousin and falling to her knees besides the man at Roberts's feet. Fingers of blood saturate the cotton of her pale petticoat. She looks down at the figure and gasps.

The man before her, clad in the golden regalia of King Rowland's Golden Guard, is a stranger. He looks at her through bitter, brown eyes, his chest rising and falling erratically as he struggles to breathe. His face is stark and white in contrast to the blood that coagulates upon his lip, burbling in time with the stressed cadence of his last few breaths.

"He's a traitor," he whispers, his voice gurgling.

Nerani clutches at her chest as horror and relief fight for control of her heartbeat. She backs away from the Guardian, her skirts dragging through blood. Nails nearly puncture her skin as Orianna's hands lock around her upper arm, prying her upright.

"It's not him. It's not him, come away."

"Nerani," barks Roberts. "Nerani, get up."

She ignores him, her knees weak—her heart faltering. Out of the corner of her eye, Nerani can see the blurred flicker of approaching torches. Several Listeners trickle out from the dark pitch of the tunnels. The sound of Roberts's shout causes her to jump, her hand flying to her throat. Her fingers leave streaks of blood upon her pallid skin.

"Did you find anyone?"

"No," someone replies. "There's no one there. We went as far out as we dared."

Roberts curses. "And we're certain the shot came from inside the tunnels?"

Nerani looks up at that, turning her attention toward the Listeners at the tunnel.

"He was shot inside—of that I have no doubt," says a man, regarding Roberts through dark blue eyes. His curling brown hair is pulled back from his neck by a fraying, black ribbon. "Several witnesses saw him stumble out from the tunnels just after the shot was fired."

"We found a trail of his blood inside one of the passages," another Listener calls.

"Go back in there," Roberts orders. "Look again. Someone had to fire the shot. They can't get far—not without getting lost in the caverns."

The Guardian before Nerani is whispering, repeating something over and over as if he's reciting a prayer. Nerani leans toward him, tilting her ear closer in order to hear him over the chaos.

"James Byron," he gurgles. "James—J—James Byron."

Panic flares within Nerani and she draws away from him, grateful for the volume of the pressing crowd. She is stopped short as the Guardian's hand closes about her arm, wrenching her towards him. She is surprised at the force of his grip.

"I follow—I followed him." His dark eyes lock onto hers. His voice is accusatory as he gasps for breath. "I saw you together. *I saw you.*"

Nerani is starkly aware of Orianna and Roberts waiting just a few feet away. Her cousin has fallen into silence—his gaze bores into Nerani's back.

"You're nothing but a filthy, gypsy witch," the Guardian wheezes. "You—you bewitched him."

Nerani scowls down at the Guardian, wrenching her wrist from his grasp. His fist drops to the ground, his knuckles rapping audibly against the stone. She rises to her feet, allowing the blood soaked hem of her gown to sweep against the floor like a whisper. His dark gaze follows her. His eyes are riddled with hate.

"You'll burn in the Dark Below for this, witch," the Guardian calls as Nerani turns away from him. Her eyes meet Roberts's across the clearing. "You'll both burn."

There is a final, choking wheeze and the Guardian falls silent. The sharp smell of death is redolent upon the smoky air. Nerani returns her cousin's stare, her head held high.

"What have you done?" Roberts asks.

Nerani is saved from having to answer by the shrill sound of shouting from the far side of the cavern.

"Get your damned hands off of me!"

Before Nerani, Roberts's entire countenance changes. The hard lines of worry melt away from his face. The tension leaks out of his shoulders. His golden eyes, sharp and clear, widen into perfect circles.

"Emerala," he mouths.

"Make way," barks a voice, struggling to be heard over the turmoil. "Clear a path!"

The crowd parts like a wave, pressed aside by Listeners. Nerani spots Topan among them instantly. His black hair, heavy with rainwater, clings to his face. He locks eyes with Nerani, his expression triumphant as he slips lithely through the crowd of onlookers, trailed closely by two Listeners.

Suspended between the Listeners, her face bronzed by the sun, is Emerala. She writhes uselessly beneath her captors, her bare feet lifting off of the stone. There is another shrill scream and Nerani turns her gaze toward the stalagmites that hang from the ceiling. Circling the jutting stone structures is a bird. He shouts obscenities at the men, lunging with his talons extended and swiping at the tops of their heads.

Nerani gathers her bloodstained skirts to her and surges through the crowd ahead of Roberts, anger flushing her cheeks.

"What is the meaning of this?" she demands, drawing to a stop just before Topan. Orianna is only steps behind her, her eyes glittering with tears as she chokes back a sob of relief.

"Why is she being treated as a captive?" Nerani notices a purpling bruise darkening the cheek of a nearby Listener. The man scowls back at her, looking morose.

Topan turns up his palms in a gesture of goodwill, unperturbed by Nerani's anger. "I'm sure my men would be happy to put her down when she's calm."

Emerala swings upward with surprising strength, angling a well-aimed kick at the man to her right. He narrowly dodges her heel as it flies toward the air between them and she curses, dropping back to the stone.

"I'll calm down when you tell me where you've taken them," she snaps.

"You needn't be so hostile. I've already assured you that no harm will come to your friends. Please have a little bit more faith in me, Emerala."

Emerala snorts—a wholly unladylike sound. "Trust works both ways."

"Not in this case, it doesn't," Topan contests.

"What's going on?" Nerani asks. "What friends are you talking about?"

"My crewmates," Emerala grunts, tugging her arm to no avail. Her captor's grip is unrelenting. Her wild hair dances about her cheeks. The silver parrot drops down to her shoulder with a contented squawk.

"Awk, bloody pirates!"

Whispers surge across the crowd like a wave. The word *pirate* is repeated from tongue to tongue, passing through the cavern with a rippling echo.

"Where are they?" Emerala demands again.

"Nowhere as offensive as you seem to think. They've been brought to the infirmary in order to have their injuries tended to." Topan's voice is tinged with derision. "I imagine they might need some attention after their skirmish on the beach."

There is a moment of silence as Topan stares into the faces of the whispering crowd, his features speculative. His eyes at last fall upon the body—now a corpse, the gurgling breath having finally stilled—at Roberts's feet. His mouth dips into a frown, his skin turning ashen.

Behind Topan, Emerala also takes note of the body. She lets out a low whistle and falls still, her green eyes opening impossibly wide.

"I'm calm," she says. "May I have my arms back?"

Distracted, Topan gestures for his Listeners to loosen their hold. Emerala wrenches her wrists free and steps forward upon the stone, surveying the cavern around her.

"Quite the welcome home," she murmurs, peering at the throng of watchful Cairans. Her gaze at last comes to rest upon Nerani. Her lips twist into a thoughtful frown as she examines her cousin from head to toe.

"Do you know," she begins, "that you're covered in blood?"

Nerani cannot wait a moment longer. She surges forward, colliding into Emerala and throwing her arms around her neck. The silver parrot takes to the air with an agitated squawk. Another figure slams into Nerani and she gasps as Orianna joins the tangle of arms, hiccupping from the effort of stifling her cries.

"Roberts," Nerani hears Topan say. "I'm curious to know what has transpired in my absence that led to a dead Guardian on the floor of our city?"

He is met with silence. Nerani glances over her shoulder, surprised to see that Roberts has moved several steps closer toward the trio. His tousled curls are a mess upon his head. His emerald eyes are wide and wet with disbelief.

"Emerala."

Emerala pries herself out of the arms of her cousin and her friend, turning to face her brother.

"I thought you were dead." His voice is hoarse.

Emerala shrugs. "I've almost died," she says. "Several times, if that helps."

"Saynti." The word ekes out from between Roberts's lips in a sigh. He pushes past Orianna and Nerani, pulling his sister into an embrace. "You're alive." He laughs, pulling her in so close that her feet rise up off of the stone.

"You're alive."

From the edge of the crowd, Seranai the Fair watches in fear.

TURN THE PAGE FOR A SNEAK PEEK INTO THE WINDING MAZE
due out in SUMMER 2018!

CHANCEY

Harvest Cycle 1525

ROWLAND STOWARD DRAWS to a stop before the entrance, scarcely pausing to catch his breath before barreling into the heavy door. It flies open with a clatter, the gilded knob slamming hard into the stone and mortar wall. The chambermaid lets out a scream, dropping her bucket of ash into the fireplace. A cloud of soot distends across the room, coating the furniture in a thin filament of black. The maid falls back against the wall, her hand at her throat—her lips open in a strangled cry.

"Where is the boy?" Rowland snarls.

The sniveling maid stammers uselessly, her brown eyes fearful. It dawns upon her slowly—far too slowly—that she is staring into the face of the king. She drops to her knees with a gasp, pressing her forehead into the soot-covered floor.

"He's in the solar, your Grace." Her voice is shrill. Her nose is flat against the ornate carpet beneath her.

Rowland storms past her, nearly stepping on her fingers as he charges towards the narrow, arched doorway at the far side of the room. It wrenches open before he can break it in and he stops short, recoiling from the boy that appears like a wraith before him. At his back, a pair of Guardians has assumed their position in the open door. A meager wail quavers in the chambermaid's throat. Rowland stares down at the boy in the opening, feeling something bitter and bilious rise in his gut. Two haunting, green eyes stare back at him from a pointed olive face.

"They're here for you, aren't they?" the boy asks. "The black ships?"

Rowland ignores him, trying in vain to catch his breath. His words fall out from his lips between sputtering wheezes. "Your father was a common man. A lecherous man. He was *nothing*. Do you hear me? NOTHING!"

Before him, the boy remains as still as stone in the opening. His fingers clutch like talons at the door. The ache in Rowland's heart is as sharp as a dagger. He presses his hand to his chest and takes a rattling breath.

"You will not be king," he bellows. "You will *never* be king. The throne belongs to the Stoward line."

"Not anymore," the boy before him whispers.

The feeble wailing of the chambermaid falls silent. Rowland's breathing cuts off in his throat. He sputters angrily, his face purpling as his cheeks catch fire.

"What did you say to me?"

"I said," the boy repeats, raising his voice, *"Not anymore."*

Acknowledgements

Fifteen years ago two little girls were stuck inside on a rainy Saturday. They crept up to the attic and spent an afternoon dreaming up an entire world apart from their own. The story took root and the characters of Emerala and Nerani were born. In a weird sort of way, the story of Emerala is like my own personal diary (although I've never been a pirate, or even anything remotely close to one). It's a strangely terrifying experience to have such a personal part of me out there in the world, but I'm so grateful for the opportunity to have gotten to this point.

This rerelease of the series as three standalone books has been a dream, and I'm so thrilled to have this chance to refresh and revamp the series in a way that fits the independent publishing industry. This has been a wild ride already, and I'm so excited to see where the story goes next.

Rogue Elegance has been a special sort of journey for me, and one that I could never have undertaken without the help, encouragement, and boundless patience of the people around me. I can barely remember a time when I haven't been working on Emerala and Nerani's story in one way or another, and most people in my life today never even knew me in the pre-Rogue Elegance era. For that, I owe a great many people a tremendous thank you. To my friends—thank you for putting up with my constant weirdness, occasional sullenness, and my nerdy tendency to talk about my characters as if they really exist.

To my beta-readers, writing classmates, and editors—thank you for always being honest and for telling me what I need to hear. I'm learning the importance of surrounding yourself with a community of writers, and it's been so wonderful building up a network of people who are walking the same path as I am.

To my parents—thank you for being part of this journey every step of the way, and for always being willing to listen to me talk out inane plot points, even when they don't make sense to anyone but me. I was a lucky kid to have had not one, but two parents willing to tolerate my requests for total silence during car rides (a girl needs her creative head space!).

To my husband, thank you for putting up with the late nights, sleepless nights, writer's block, deadline stress, and all around weirdness that comes with being married to a writer. I know that it's been even more challenging than usual these days with a baby in the house, and to say that you've been my literal champion would be an understatement. You've gone above and beyond as a father, husband, and friend and I'm endlessly fortunate to have someone so supportive of my passions.

And to YOU, the reader: if you're reading this, it means you've stuck with Emerala and Nerani through not one, but two of their stories. Thank you for your support, and thank you for reading. It means so much to me to know that this story is finally being read and enjoyed the way I meant for it to be experienced. If you loved it, liked it, or even if you hated every word of it, I'd love to hear from you! Amazon reviews and Goodreads reviews are amazing for an indie author, and I'd appreciate any feedback I can get.

Thank you all, and be sure to check out www.kadowling.com to see what else I've been working on!

Kelly

About the Author

KA Dowling is an award-winning writer living just outside of Boston, Massachusetts. She has been writing stories as long as she can remember, and has been daydreaming about fantastical worlds and imaginary heroines for even longer than that.

Dowling lives with her husband, their infant, and their smelly Boston Terrier, King Henry. Her favorite animal is the Tyrannosaurus Rex and she has wanted to be a sea-faring pirate for much of her adult life. This story is her way of living vicariously through her fictional characters.

She's thrilled that you've picked up her book, and she hopes you enjoyed every last word. To read more of what Dowling has written, check out her website at www.kadowling.com. You can also follow her day-to-day antics on Instagram (@bittercresswriter) and Twitter (@KayAyDowling).

Made in the USA
San Bernardino, CA
11 April 2018